VAMPIRE HUNTER

RAMMEL HAWKING 1
KNIGHTS OF BLACK SWAN

BY

VICTORIA DANANN

Thank you for choosing to begin Elora's journey with this book. I invite you to keep up with this and other series by subscribing to my mail list. I'll make you aware of free stuff, news, and announcements and never share your addy. Unsubscribe whenever you like.

Also browse more from my library at the end of this book.

Victoria Danann

SUBSCRIBE TO MY MAIL LIST

Website

Black Swan Fan Page

Facebook Author Page

Twitter

Pinterest

AUTHOR FAN GROUP

New York Times and USA Today Bestselling Romance Author

Winner BEST PARANORMAL ROMANCE SERIES
–Knights of Black Swan
TWO YEARS IN A ROW!

Most people would say their lives began
the day they were born.
My life was just beginnin'
at the end of this book.

–*Rammel Hawking*

PRESENT DAY

Ram

"LAN!"

I jerked up to a sittin' position, looked around the darkness and jerked again when I felt a hand on my back. That was followed by the warmth of a heavenly body embracin' me, encirclin' me from behind. That touch never failed to bring me away from the nightmare and fully back to the present.

I covered the hand on my chest with my own and sat relivin' the images of the dream, but my breathing calmed and became even as I soaked up the feel of light kisses brushed across my back in strategic places accompanied by the sound of reassurin' feminine murmurs. I scrubbed a hand down my face, and realized my hair was damp with sweat.

Pattin' the arm that hugged me, I pulled away. "Go back to sleep, love. Sorry to wake you." *Again.* "Goin' for a shower." *And a drink.* But I did no' add that last part. Drinkin' in the middle of the night is no' normal, even for Irish.

Do no' get me wrong. 'Tis no' a nightly occurrence.

1

But now and again, something will trigger the nightmare, and relivin' Lans' death, even in a bad dream, leaves me shaken to the core.

The nightmares went away durin' the Great Vampire Inversion, when we foolishly thought the whole thing was over. But as soon as I was back in rotation, on the streets huntin' leeches, the night terrors came back as if they were rested and refreshed from vacation.

There's only one thing in life that could be worse than losin' a partner to vampire. And that's losin' a mate. The first did happen to me. The second almost did. That fear will be a close and unwelcome companion so long as we're still huntin'. Or maybe so long as there are still vampire walkin' the earth.

'Tis lookin' like I will no' be escapin' bad dreams any time soon. So I poured a shot of Irish whiskey and tried to picture summer days in Northern Ireland when the sun shines more than half the day. One thing about bein' a vampire hunter. You learn to love sunlight.

CHAPTER 1

Liam O'Torvall

I REMEMBER 'TWAS a few days after I was elected mayor of Black-On-Tarry, for the first time that is. A hunter, Gordy Darnell if memory serves, stopped by my stoop with news that he had seen a child near the huntin' cottage deep in the old growth part of the Forest where the wild things live.

He claimed he'd called out to the lad and tried to chase him down, but 'twas to no avail. If his eyes had no' played tricks on him, then the boy simply vanished like in stories of the ancients livin' in mounds under the earth.

That the child could evade Gordy was remarkable in itself because Gordy's huntin' skills were nothin' to scoff at. He could singlehandedly feed the village in dead of winter, if circumstances called for it, and we all knew we were lucky to count him one of us. Unlike most of us who were born in the Preserve, Gordy had once lived on the outside. A stockbroker, I believe he said. He swore off the modern world and camped outside the wall for near two years before we gained permission to let him in. Married O'Malley's second daughter after a time and settled right in as if he'd always been here.

I know that's no' what you're wantin' to know. Forgive the meanderin', but I am Irish and what you'd call old school at that.

So I had a mind to take a ride out to the cottage to see what was to be seen. At that time I was still young enough to cut a fine figure on horseback. So I knew it would no' take too long.

Sure enough, there was a small funnel of smoke risin' from the chimney of the cottage. I hobbled the horse by the stream where he could drink and graze like he'd died and gone to heaven, and walked up, no' exactly stalkin', but no' makin' a herald of it either.

There was nary a soul inside, but every indication that someone had been there recently.

I stepped out into the overcast day and yelled, "Hello!"

I waited for a response, but the only sound was the trickle of the stream and the soft pull and grind of grass between the horse's teeth as he watched to see what I would do next. Horses are wary of us, with good reason.

I took in a deep breath and yelled loud, "I have chicken and cheese!" All remained quiet. "Right there in my saddlebag."

A small and curly towhead popped up from the brush just inside the trees on the other side of the brook, lookin' more than anything like one of the wild things that belonged in that corner of the world. My first thought was that, strange as 'twas, he seemed to belong there.

"I'll no' harm ye, elflin'. Would just like to introduce myself to my new neighbor."

The lad stood and came forward a little way, stoppin' on the other side of the water.

"If ye have something with which to wash down my lunch, I'll gladly share with ye."

Then forthright as if he was a grown man, the boy said, "I have ale. I'll share it for some chicken and cheese."

I laughed on the inside, but kept my face serious as I said, "Very well. You have my agreement."

He looked me over as he passed by to enter the little house first. If he was afraid, he did no' show it, but rather seemed fearless as could be.

"Come on in," he said.

"Thank ye kindly," I replied.

The horse watched me with suspicion as I approached to retrieve lunch from the sack that hung from the saddle and was clearly relieved to see me take something and go.

I strode back through the doorway and straight to the table where I pulled out a chair. The young resident had already brought a lidded pitcher of ale to the table. Goodness knows where he'd got it.

"I'm Liam O'Torvall," I said as I sat. "And what might your name be?"

The boy studied me as if he was tryin' to decide whether or no' I could be trusted with his name. He must have been satisfied with what he saw, because eventually he offered something of a response.

"Ram," was all he said.

"How do ye do, Ram?" I offered a traditional pleasantry as I took a piece of roast chicken between my fingers. He nodded and shrugged as he took a larger piece and crammed it into his mouth as if he'd never eaten. "Are ye the owner of this fine property?"

His small blond brows attempted to knit together, but the skin was too smooth and tight to allow a full-blown scowl. "Indirectly."

Now that was an answer for which I was no' prepared. What in the world could the child mean by indirectly?

We sat and ate in silence for a few minutes as I contemplated that riddle. Finally I said, "Mind ye, I'm no' intendin' to invade your privacy, but did ye purchase this cottage? Indirectly that is?"

I watched him closely, judgin' him to be around the age of ten at the time. He looked over at me with piercin' dark blue eyes like he was tryin' to see all the way to the bottom of my soul. He must have judged me relatively harmless because he answered honestly.

"No," was all he said.

'Twas then I remembered hearin' that the king had brought his two sons for a huntin' trip a few months ago. I had no' personally seen them as I was in the eastern territory lookin' at sheep, but as you can imagine, 'twas an event to have royalty visit the Preserve.

The present king's grandfather, gods bless him, set aside these lands as a preserve for wildlife and for the old ways. 'Tis a vast area, surrounded by wall on three sides, several hours ride from the gate at Black-On-Tarry to the circle of the ancient ones or the sea cliffs to the north. I could no' help but wonder how the lad had surmounted the formidable obstacle of the wall, which is a combination of stone and thick hedges, to come here alone, but I was beginnin' to suspect he could be one of the princes. In the flesh.

"So tell me, young Ram. Would ye be claimin' indirect ownership of this fine cottage by right of royal birth?"

The lad's entire body stiffened and his expression issued a challenge. "Are ye goin' to tell?"

"Do ye no' think your mum is, at this very moment, distressed to no' know where ye are?"

I knew he was a good boy at heart when I saw him frown at that. Apparently he did no' want to be home, but at the same time did no' relish the idea of hurtin' his mother's feelin's.

"'Tis no' about her." He glared at me with a defiant intensity that was at odds with his small body and few years.

"What's it about?"

He shrugged and looked away as if he had ceased to be interested in whate'er wisdom I might have to offer or whate'er questions I might have to ask.

"Did ye bring more chicken?" he asked hopefully.

I smiled. "I did no', but my wife has a large pot of stew on the fire at this very moment. There's plenty to go 'round."

"Stew sounds nice."

"My wife is a very reliable cook. But do ye know what's even better than her stew?"

"What?" He could no' suppress the eagerness from his question.

"Berry pie." I watched his little pink tongue peek out to lick his lips. "Come home with me. Have a nice dinner and a good sleep. Tomorrow we will see to it that ye find your way back to Derry. And the next time ye come, ye'll know how to find my house and know that you're welcome there."

He looked around the cottage like he could no' stand the thought of leavin', but must have known that his capture was inevitable and could no' be forestalled forever. He nodded and rose from his chair.

I watched in fascination as he methodically went about makin' the bed, rinsin' the dishes, and takin' care to put out the fire. When done he stood lookin' at me with a mixture of patience and resignation.

"Are ye ready then?" His head turned each way as he looked around the cabin then nodded. "Nothin' to take with ye?" He shook his head. "Well, then. We'll be off."

I let him close the cottage door while I looked for the horse. "Do ye know how to take the hobbles off a horse, lad?"

The boy looked at me like I was mad and appeared to be insulted by the question. "O' course. What do you take me for?"

"I do no' know ye well and certainly meant no offense. Will ye fetch the beast then?"

Without a word the prince walked a short way upstream. The horse brought his ears forward and watched the child as closely as if a wolf was approachin' his flank, but Ram took the chore in stride, quickly removin' the hobbles. I expected that he would lead the horse back to where I waited, but instead he took hold of the pommel of my saddle and swung himself up in an arc of grace that was a thing of beauty. Seein' his easy mastery with the horse, I could see why he would have taken umbrage to my inquiry regardin' his knowledge of hobbles.

He was no' only elf, but royal. O' course he knew his way 'round a horse.

He trotted the horse to where I stood, jumped down, and handed me the reins. Once mounted, I offered a hand and easily pulled him up behind me.

THE WIFE TOOK one look at the lad and fell in love. And why no'? He had the look of an angel, with that white hair curling at will 'round his beautiful face. I had my suspicions, call it intuition if ye will, that his looks were deceivin', that he was no' a bundle of bliss, but I would no' begrudge my love her pleasure. Our own daughters had recently married and become mistresses of their own hearths, which left space at the table ready to be filled by a runaway royal with sharp, inquisitive blue eyes and an air of authority.

She beamed as she watched the child devour two man-sized portions of her lamb stew.

"What were ye doin' out there in the wilds, lad?"

He did no' bristle at her question because he heard nothin' in it save curiosity and a good heart. I might argue with the dadblasted woman from dawn to dusk, but would secretly admit that she did, in fact, have a generous spirit.

He looked at her as he tore off a third piece of soda bread. "Please do no' take this to mean that I object to conversation, ma'am, but I was mindin' my own business."

She harrumphed. "Well, from the looks of it, you were mindin' the business of starvin' to death."

He stared at her for a few seconds while he chewed the bread and then lit the room with his smile. "Your husband was true when he said you're a fine cook. 'Tis perhaps the best meal I ever ate."

My wife took his praise with a pleasure I had no' seen on her face for many years. "'Tis a nice thing to say, but I suspect ye be guilty of flattery. I'm forgivin' your impertinence only because your beauty makes me helpless to do otherwise."

He gave my wife a smile that I suspected would someday cause the knees of many a lass to buckle of their own accord.

"No flattery," he said. "'Tis special. Thank you."

At that she smiled at me like bringin' the boy to our house was the best thing I'd ever done. I found that, e'en in my advanced years, I very much liked havin' her look at me like that.

"Liam tells me your name is Ram?"

He nodded as he chewed and swallowed, then said, "Rammel Hawking."

We procured a clean change of clothes from a village boy near Ram's size and insisted that he take a dip in the tub before nestlin' into bed for the night. When we were sure he was asleep, my wife said, "What are ye goin' to do?"

I had been sittin' in front of the fire thinkin' on exactly that. O' course I had no way to contact the prince's family.

There were no means of modern communication in the Preserve and our only means of transportation was horses, either ridin' them or bein' pulled by them. I did no' relish the idea of leavin', but did no' see that there was another option.

"Tomorrow I will take two gold pieces and try to find transportation to deliver him personally to Derry. I will no' trust the lad's care to anyone else. Much as we do no' like to dwell on it, there is evil in the world. If I was his father, my brains would be scrambled with worry right now."

"Perhaps."

"What do ye mean perhaps?"

"If the king knows his child, he knows he's resource-ful."

I sat back considerin' that point of view. "I can no' argue with that, but he is still of a vulnerable age."

She nodded. "Aye. And I can no' argue with that. I'll pack food for the journey in the mornin'. Will ye go alone?"

"Aye. But if I had my way, I'd be back before I leave."

She smiled at that and gave me an affectionate pat on the head on her way to bed.

By THE NEXT mornin' everyone in the village was aware that the prince of Ireland was a guest in our humble village. They all came out to witness our departure. And I could no' blame them. Black-On-Tarry was visited by royalty perhaps three times in a generation.

The boy took it in stride and I supposed he was accustomed to havin' even larger crowds gather to stare at him. The gate opened for us and we walked out. Ram, wearin' clean trousers, a hemp tunic and his own fine boots. Me with my walkin' staff, a skin of water, a sack of food, and two gold pieces, one to procure transportation to Derry, one to return, gods willin'.

After three hours we reached a road built for automobiles. I glanced down at the boy beside me. He offered no complaint, but I could tell by his movements that he was exhausted. 'Twas a long walk for such a small body.

When I told him to sit for a minute, he dropped to the ground where he stood. I handed him the skin of water and he drank with an eagerness I had forgotten in advanced years.

I heard the sound of a car approachin'. When it neared I waved to the driver. The man slowed, looked us over, and continued on his way. I supposed he did no' trust the look of us, thinkin' we were rascals dressed in strange clothing. Strange, that is, for his understandin' of the world.

Twice more we were passed by, but the third vehicle slowed and stopped. It was a short truck with an open bed.

"Lost?" said the driver.

"Nay," I replied. "We're seekin' a ride to the palace at Derry. And the lucky driver who takes us there will receive a gold coin for his trouble."

The man looked dubious, glanced over at Ram, then said, "Let me see it."

I held the coin on the palm of my hand so that he could get a good look, but when he reached for it, I closed my fist 'round it and pulled it back. He had regular enough features, but I felt entitled to my reservations, particularly since I'd taken responsibility for a potential heir to the Irish throne.

"You'll get it when we get to the palace at Derry," said I.

Eyein' me like he was makin' up his mind, the man said, "That's twenty miles and out of my way. And I had other plans this mornin'. But I suppose I can be bothered to do a neighborly deed now and again." His eyes flicked to my staff then back to my face. "Get in the back." He pointed to the rear.

I hoisted my middle-aged girth into the back of the truck, while Rammel Hawking made quick work of climbin' up. I motioned for him to advance to the front where we could sit with our backs to the cab.

The entire trip took only an hour even with town traffic so dense I could no' have imagined it. Who would have guessed there were so many vehicles in the whole of the world? Fifteen minutes before we reached our destination, a rain shower got us both soaked. Whene'er the truck was in motion, the breeze against wet clothes made us cold, e'en for Irishmen. I looked down at the boy next to me. His teeth were chatterin' but he was no' complainin', and I was developin' an admiration for his character.

Without askin' I put my arm around his little shoulders and pulled him close, knowin' that burrowin' into the side of my substantial torso would give him a measure of warmth and comfort. He did no' resist, but curled into me, drawin' up both elbows and knees.

When the truck stopped, we were facin' away from the palace so I could no' tell where we were.

"Here you are," said the driver as he got out and slammed his door.

My body was stiff after sittin' in such an unnatural position for so long. So it took me a bit to convince my body to respond. Ram was already on the ground waitin' while I coaxed my body to a standin' position. It took a little longer than that to make my knees walk me to the end of the truck bed and devise a way to get off the bloody vehicle while the driver watched as if it was a show.

When finally I reclaimed the ground, I got my first view of the palace. It almost took my breath away. 'Twas a mass of gleaming windows and golden stone such that I thought surely people on Earth put the gods to shame by buildin' such a spectacular place.

I looked down at the boy, tryin' to imagine him residin' in such a place. "Tis your home, lad?"

Ram looked up at me. "Aye," was all he said, but I distinctly caught the tone that revealed he was no' the least happy about that fact.

The driver held out his hand. I put the gold piece in his palm and said, "Spend it wisely."

To that he replied, "Fuck off," and climbed back inside the dreadful contraption.

The guard gate was perhaps thirty feet away, but the guard was already starin' at Ram, his expression frozen in open-mouthed astonishment. By the time we approached the gate, he had closed his mouth. Apparently the royal family had no' reported their child missin'.

"Let us in," Ram told him. The child had taken on an air that said he knew he would be obeyed.

"Aye, Your Highness," said the guard, lookin' at me warily.

When I attempted to follow the child, the guard stepped in front of me.

"Him, too," the lad ordered.

The guard stepped aside, but made it clear that he did so grudgin'ly.

The walk to the seat of Irish kings was uphill from there on a wide stone boulevard that looked clean enough to eat from.

Guards posted at the front entrance eyed me like they believed me to be a person of nefarious purpose. I nodded and smiled in response.

The front door, almost as big as the gate to Black-On-Tarry, opened and a man in service costume appeared at the door. But within seconds of steppin' into the grand foyer, a woman passin' by shrieked and ran off.

I thought I heard the child mumble, "And here we go."

Standin' at the front door, I turned to the man who'd opened it. "Now that I've seen the young prince home, I'll be on my way. Good day."

"Sir," said the man, "please do no' leave just yet. I'm certain that…"

His sentence was cut short by a shriek exponentially louder than the first. Following the sound I looked up to see a woman hurryin' down the stairs. She was easily the most beautiful creature imaginable. Even with red rimmed puffy eyes, she was like a myth come to life. When she reached us, she fell to her knees, grabbed the lad and sobbed.

Though his face was smushed into her shoulder, he looked sideways at me and I was fair sure 'twas embarrassment I saw.

"Sir." I turned on the chance 'twas I who was bein' addressed. "The king would like a word if you'd be so kind."

I glanced at Ram, gave him a little nod, and followed the man forthwith. After some minutes' walk, I was ushered through a reception area almost as large as my village. There were six pairs of desks facin' each other at the edges of the room. As I passed, all of the occupants stared as if I was a leopard on a leash.

At length a door opened. The fancy man stood back and gestured for me to enter with a little flourish. I looked back when I heard the door close behind me. There was no mistakin' the air of authority that floated 'round the king like a cloud.

Handsome as I'd been told he was by folks in my village, he came forward to meet me with his hand extended. "Ethelred Hawking," said he in a matter-of-fact tone.

I took his hand. "Your Highness. I'm Liam O'Torvall." Permittin' myself a hint of pride, I felt my chest swell a bit when I added, "New mayor of Black-On-Tarry."

"Black-On-Tarry," he said gesturin' to one of two large leather chairs that sat next to the small fire. The door opened and a man servant appeared inside. "Would you care for some whiskey, Mr. O'Torvall? By the look of it, you were caught in the rain bringin' my son back to us."

"Aye. I'd be grateful if you have a finger or two to spare. In fact we did encounter a shower."

While the man poured from a crystal decanter with facets that picked up every nuance of light and color in the room, the king studied me.

"If you do no' mind the inquiry, how did you travel from Black-On-Tarry?"

"We walked to a road built for motor vehicles and waved down a ride." I waited to take a sip of whiskey until the king raised his glass, thinkin' that would be the mannered thing to do. "I gave a truck driver a gold coin to let us ride in the back of his contraption."

Hearin' that, the king spluttered and choked on his whiskey. The manservant rushed over with a length of fine white linen and attempted to assist, but the king, seemin' annoyed for some reason, dismissed him and told him to leave us alone. The man bowed slightly and left quiet as a mouse.

When the king finished dabbin' at his clothes and recovered his demeanor, he looked me full in the face. "So my son rode in the back of a truck, in the rain, for twenty miles?"

I shook my head. "Did no' rain the whole way."

"Where did you find him?"

"He was at the huntin' cottage your grandfather built. One of our hunters reported thinkin' he saw a child. The next day, which was yesterday, I took a ride out to investigate the sightin'." I couldn't help but smile rememberin' that the lad had been lured into the open by the promise of chicken and cheese. "The prince agreed to come home

17

with me on the promise of lamb stew and berry pie."

The king nodded. "Mr. Mayor, Rammel's mother and I are greatly indebted to you for bringin' him home safe. As you can imagine, the household has been in a state since discoverin' that he'd gone missin'. His mother was… well, she was beside herself."

"Perfectly understandable."

"Indeed. Most importantly, I want to be sure that you are adequately rewarded."

"No reward is necessary. 'Twas an honor to be of service to the Crown. And the lad… he's special."

The king pursed his lips. "At the very least, allow us to give you dry clothes, a gold coin to replace the one spent, and a ride home."

I thought about it for a moment, put myself in his shoes, and realized that, as a father, I would want to at least restore to wholeness the person who brought my child to me safe and sound. With that reasonin', I said, "Aye. I accept. I would like one other thing."

The king sighed and I noticed a small slump of his shoulders. There was no tellin' what he thought I'd be askin' next.

"I'd like to say goodbye to Ram."

I can no' say the king e'er smiled durin' my audience, but he did no' look displeased by the request.

Half an hour later I was dressed in clothes that were fine and strange and waitin' in the palace vestibule to tell the young prince that I valued makin' his acquaintance.

Ram drug his feet and scuffed his boots along the floor as he came forward, as if he was put out by something.

"Goodbye," I said. "'Twas a pleasure to meet you."

"Aye," he said, "and you as well." Then he whispered, "Next time I'd like blackberry pie."

I pulled back to see if he was jokin' and caught the sparkle in his eyes. 'Twas impossible to tell if that sparkle was ignited by humor or by an actual plan to return to the New Forest the next time heads were turned.

AS IT TURNED out, the quip was an actual plan to be shed of Derry in favor of New Forest whenever the slightest of opportunities presented itself.

Twice more in a half year's time the kings' men arrived at our gate to retrieve the errant prince.

Then one stormy mornin', when I had just broken fast and settled near the fire to begin prioritizin' my day with a nap, there was a rap on my door. I pulled the latch open to find Tommy Hillknocker standin' there with the king of Ireland big as life, bein' pelted by rain like he shared mortality with the rest of us.

I opened the door wide.

"'Tis the king," Tommy said.

"I see that, Tommy."

"I thought I should open the gate for him," Tommy added as if his brain was as addled as some suspected.

"Aye. You did the right thing. Whene'er the king comes to call, you have authority to open at once." Lookin' pleased with himself, Tommy nodded. I stepped back and motioned for the king to come in. When Tommy tried to follow, I firmly but politely shut the door in his face. "Your

Highness. You're welcome in my home. However humble."

The king nodded, stepped forward, and removed the black wax coat he wore to keep the rain off.

"Thank you, Mr. Mayor."

"Please have a seat." Frankly, I felt rather grand bein' able to return the favor of offerin' a seat by the fire and a splash of Irish whiskey. "I know 'tis early in the day, but let me fetch ye a whiskey to ward off the chill."

"In truth, that sounds like just what I need. If I could trouble you for that *and* a few minutes' conversation."

"Certainly, sir." I handed him a pewter mug with a couple of fingers of my best whiskey at the bottom. He looked down into the cup like a man with a heavy burden, then drank deep.

"'Tis about my son."

"Missin' again, is he?"

"I'm afraid so. He seems to have taken a likin' to the Forest and 'tis becomin' a problem. I've been thinkin'. I do no' want to cage my child."

When the king did no' speak again for a few moments, I said, "No. O'course no'."

"But I want him to be safe." I nodded. The king's eyes searched mine. "Do you have children?"

"Two daughters. Grown and married, but no' yet parents themselves."

"I have a daughter. Sweet and obedient for the most part. Rammel…" The king sighed. "He's a lot of trouble."

"Aye. To be sure."

"I've talked it over with his mother. He hates livin' at

Derry. But he seems to love livin' here." The king paused and studied the contents of his mug like a witch scrying the future. "We're goin' to agree to let him stay. Two months at a time here. One month at home durin' which his mother can be reassured he is alright and I can arrange enough tutorials to condense his education.

"But we'll need your help because I've promised his mother that he'll be safe. And fed. And clean."

I cleared my throat wonderin' to myself how he could promise that a child livin' alone among the wild things could be safe.

He continued. "I was wonderin' if I could offer some recompense for sendin' someone out to check on him. I know every day sounds like a lot, but if he was hurt…"

The sentence trailed off as the king's eyes drifted toward the fire. In that moment I believed I could see the sadness the man felt for no' knowin' what to do with such an unruly child. He did no' want to break the spirit of the boy. Gods know that would be the worst thing to do to the person who might someday be leader of Irish elves. But the king was clearly fearful that anything might the *wrong* thing.

"Sir. I would no' dream of takin' payment. If you're askin' me to be his guardian when he's in the Forest, 'twould be my honor. The people who live here owe your family dearly for makin' our way of life possible. I'm too old to make the trip myself every day, but I will see to it that someone reliable checks on him and reports that he is well. A couple of times a week I will take supplies.

"My wife will delight in sendin' him food and, I expect, she will no' mind washin' his little clothes."

If 'tis possible for a man to smile sadly, that's what the king did.

"Thank you. Ram mentioned that we should bring your wife to the palace to teach them how to cook." I gave a hardy laugh at that and wished the old girl had been home to hear it herself. "I'd like to borrow a horse and ride out to tell Rammel about my decision."

I cocked an ear toward the window and heard that the rain had stopped. "The trail may be messy, but at least the rain has stopped for now. If you'd like some company, I'll ride along. Let me gather up some provisions to keep the lad's body and soul together till the morrow."

The king's face lit up when Ainsley trotted out one of his grandfather's battle chargers. He laughed out loud. "You're still breedin' them. This fellow is a sight for sore eyes, I tell you."

He grabbed the reins and gave the horse's neck an appreciative rub in a gesture common among horse lovers everywhere.

For a long time we rode with no sound other than the splashin' of horse hooves through puddles. When we were nearin' the cottage, he began to talk, as if to no one in particular.

"Rammel is rash and reckless like his mother. He has a great heart." He looked over at me and smiled. "Also like his mother."

"I saw her, but we were no' introduced. 'Twas evident that she's mad about the lad."

Ethelred sighed. "Aye. He has no trouble attractin'

love. His problem is that he lacks discipline, and with a country to look after, I can no' give him *all* my time."

"If you'd permit me an opinion." The king did no' answer, but nodded. "It strikes me that he may no' just be runnin' away from something. Perhaps 'tis just as likely he's searchin' for something he thinks he'll find here. In the New Forest."

The king said no more, which made me wonder if I'd said too much. But either way, within a few minutes the cottage was in sight and I could see young Ram waitin' for us by the front door. He'd apparently concluded that hidin' served no purpose. So he watched us quietly, without movin' or speakin' until we were steppin' down from the horses.

He lifted his chin at his father. "Da."

"Rammel," Ethelred replied in a stern tone that I knew might be interpreted by the lad as lack of regard. Readin' between the lines, I knew that was no' the case. The king loved his son. 'Twas a shame the child did no' know it. Ethelred handed the reins off to me and said, "I need a minute or two with my son."

"Take your time," I said, turnin' to walk the horses to the stream for a drink.

THE TWO OF them remained inside the cottage for, perhaps, half an hour's time. When they emerged, the king looked ten years older than he had when we'd first met at Derry. Ram looked pleased beyond description that he was no' bein' dragged home against his will. Again.

As the king mounted his horse, I said to Ram, "Ride

home with me tonight. Have a good meal. We'll work out a system to stay in contact. Then tomorrow you can choose a horse to bring back here."

If possible, Rammel was even more delighted at that prospect. He put away the provisions I'd brought, closed up the cottage, and swung up behind me.

All the way back, he chattered about various things he'd discovered in the Forest. He asked about the genus of every tree and bush, asked about the species of every bird whose song was heard, and asked if I knew there was a pack of wolves that roamed further north.

I noticed the last question gave his father pause. "Rammel, when you come home on December 1st, talk all you want about trees and bushes and birds and the like, but do no' be mentionin' wolves to your mother or you'll no' be back come January."

"Aye, sir."

"And give them a wide berth. Consider it a rule. Wolves are no' dogs."

"Well…"

"Non-negotiable."

"Aye, sir."

Perhaps the threat of losin' his Forest-visitin' privileges would be just the thing to keep the young scoundrel in line.

The king did no' kiss or hug his son goodbye. He gave a nod, then disappeared beyond the gate without turnin' back.

That night, after Ram had eaten his weight at supper and gone to sleep, no doubt weary from the events and emotion of the day, I fondled my wife's ample and shapely arse, then left to go to the meetin' I'd called at Ren O'Malley's house.

I had hastily requested that the heads of certain households gather to discuss the precious responsibility that I had accepted on our behalf. It seemed that, in the case of Rammel Hawking, it would take a village to raise a child.

The idea had come to me that we could combine checkin' in on him with providin' an education that could prove useful. For instance, Ren O'Malley's family had been craftin' fine bows and arrows for two hundred years. On days when Ren was assigned to make the trip and look in on young Rammel, he would stay long enough to teach the boy a thing or two about archery. Truth be told, the mention of the wolf pack concerned me more than I'd admitted to the king. It would no' hurt the lad to have some weapons and know how to use them.

Of course gun powder and the like were no' allowed in the Preserve, but that did no' mean he should be altogether defenseless.

Since Gordy Darnell was the one who first spotted the boy, 'twas only fittin' that he be the one to teach huntin' skills. The Widow Brennan was an authority on plants. She could teach him which ones were to be left alone and which ones would be good for everything from cookin' to the soothing of rashes. If the boy should prove to be interested in playin' stringed instruments, Cleary Dothan would make a right royal tutor. And so on and so on.

I, myself, made plans to go twice a week, take a book,

and perhaps discuss the book I'd brought before. Mrs. O'Torvall was insistin' that she go along on one of my semi-weekly sojourns so she could see for herself that Ram was hale and hardy. How could I say no? E'en after so much time together, I still enjoyed her company.

CHAPTER 2

Ram

I WAS THIRTEEN years old when Black Swan came callin'. 'Twas none too soon. I'd spent a chunk of childhood alone in a tiny cottage in the New Forest. I was the next thing to a feral child and liked it that way.

My father, the king, was an asshole. At least I thought so at the time. Still, he was a sweetheart of a man compared to my prick of an older brother, who was nothin' less than insufferable. My parents tolerated the unusual arrangement of bein' a ten-year-old hermit because I made things difficult, shall we say, when I was home.

I figured out early that, if I did my utmost to try and raise Hades up through the palace foundation, they'd be glad to see my hind view headed out the door. I felt bad for my poor mother because I knew she loved me and wanted me home. To some extent I also felt guilty about leavin' my little sister without backup for long stretches of time, but everyone loved her so I knew she'd do alright.

Once I'd learned to fish and hunt for myself, Liam and Moira O'Torvall made sure my diet was complemented with vegetables and bread. And pie. All in all I was well fed and no' so dirty that disease was imminent.

So far as education went, I got crash tutorin' crammed into short visits to Derry. And, although I would no' have wanted it known at the time, I did no' completely waste my time in the Forest. I acquired skills that included extreme woodscraft, bow huntin', and guitar. I even read books. A lot of them. For a little village lost in time, collectively they have a lot of books and Liam had something to say about every one of them. I did no' object too much. 'Tis a law of nature that hours have to be filled with something.

One cool and rainy day I was doin' just that, readin' a book brought by Liam with an implied promise that he would be askin' me for my thoughts two days hence. I was just gettin' to a part where a fairy was found hidin' in a cellar when there was a knock at my door. The rain had covered the sound of someone approachin' the cottage, so I was startled to say the least. I had already been visited earlier in the day and was no' expectin' anyone.

A stranger was standin' on the other side of the door with rain pourin' off the brim of his hat. I practically had to crane my neck to look up at him because I had no' yet experienced a growth spurt. My first thought was to wonder how he'd managed to get inside the Preserve wall. My second thought was to assume he was lost.

"Are ye lost?" I asked.

I saw the ghost of a smile crinkle the small lines near his eyes. "Indeed not, Rammel Hawking. I'm here for you."

I do no' know if you have ever had the experience of

hearin' someone speak your name followed by those exact words. But when a large stranger dressed in black comes out of nowhere and presents himself in a pourin' rain sayin', 'Rammel Hawking. I'm here for you', it's near paralyzin'. Especially when the message is delivered with an English accent.

My response was to stare and make no move whatever.

"I'm Alder Rathbone. May I come in?"

Well, I knew it was no' well-mannered to leave a man waitin' on my porch with the wet threatenin' to soak through his skin, but his presence and his words raised questions in my mind about the prudence of lettin' him in. Still, I was no' inclined to admit, even to myself, that I might be afraid of anyone. I looked behind him and was about to say he could tend to his horse in the barn first, but there was no horse.

Lookin' down I saw his boots were soaked right through, which could only mean he'd walked. My eyes jerked up to his face. He must have been miserable with the chill and damp, but there was no mistakin' that he was the sort of man who did no' complain or feel sorry for himself.

I stepped back and opened the door wider to let him in.

As he began to take off his hat and coat, I said, "I'll make tea and bring it by the fire."

He gave me a look that said he was impressed with my manners. "That would be nice."

I set the kettle close enough to the fire to boil the water

then brought a tray with cups and sugar. Since the bugger had taken the liberty of sittin' in my big chair, I moved the big chest closer to the fire. The tea service and I sat on the chest together, waitin' for him to explain himself.

He stared at me as if I was bein' evaluated, for what reason I did no' know, his brown eyes reflectin' the firelight, since 'twas a damnable dark day. After a time that seemed to drag by, he said, "I'm a recruiter. I work for a secret organization, which name I will not divulge until you agree that you would like to come to work for us."

"Work for you?" I scoffed. "I'm thirteen years old." I laughed.

"So you are," he said. "It's by design that I am here now. Not when you're twelve or fourteen. But *now*."

I was beginnin' to wonder if the fellow had any success at recruitin' because, to my mind, he was doin' a piss poor job of it. I decided to let it play out and hear what he had to say. Havin' unexpected company was surprisin'ly entertainin'.

He'd left his coat at the door, but no' before retrievin' a tube that he kept by his side. It was apparently designed to keep papers safe from weather. He opened the end of the tube and pulled out documents that had been rolled together.

"I have a contract with me. It's already been signed by your parents, but won't be valid unless you sign as well. We propose to give you the best education available anywhere, not just academic. You'll also learn a wide variety of fighting skills."

"You're from the army?"

He chuckled and shook his head. "No. The organization I work for is not associated with government in any way. We're more like a philanthropy. We protect those who cannot protect themselves.

"I'd like you to consider giving us your next five years. At the end of that time you can choose to go to work for us or not. In the meantime you'll be among others your age who have been judged by us to be potential elite."

"Elite?" I sneered. "I'm already *elite*. I'm a prince."

"If you come with me, you'll leave your royalty at the door. All the boys we recruit are special, but no one is in any way more important than anyone else."

Something about that struck a chord in my heart. I was intrigued by the idea of bein' like everyone else. Since my life to that date had been the exact opposite, that may have been just the carrot to make me reach for the stick. I suspect 'twas part of the reason I found the solitude of the New Forest so appealin'.

"How did you get into the Preserve?"

He chuckled softly and a twinkle sprang to his eye that said he was unexpectedly amused, as if he had no' guessed askin' how he came to be there would be the next question out of my mouth.

"Walked through the gate. But what you really want to know is, why did they let me in?" He still looked amused. "I have my ways."

"Let me see the papers you're guardin' so carefully."

The tea kettle chose that moment to set off a howl. I quickly tended to my guest, fixed my own tea to my likin' and settled down to read the stranger's strange proposal.

There were provisions for visitin' my family from time to time, holidays and such. At that time I felt that I had two families, my blood who lived in the palace at Derry and the one comprised of simple villagers in Black-On-Tarry who seemed to accept and understand me for who I was. The fact that I was already thinkin' ahead to where I would spend my time off meant that I was hooked. The man had known exactly what to say, that I would be with others like me and be treated just the same.

"Any questions?" Mr. Rathbone had settled into my chair like he'd been sittin' in it forever. Bastard.

"Just one. Are you also recruitin' girls?"

I mean I'm no' stupid. I'd recognized that I had a set of highly specialized equipment, and it was wakin' up to the fact that it had its own destiny. And that destiny involved females. I was no' precisely sure about the logistics, but I had seen enough of nature to get the idea. 'Twas an experience about which I was keepin' an open mind. To be sure.

Rathbone smiled. "No, but we've been doing this long enough to know that it would be ill-advised to isolate our recruits from the gentler sex."

"Gentler sex?" I cocked my head, thinkin' about that. "Is that what they are?"

It had no' been my experience that Moira or the Widow Brennan or my mother or sister were particularly gentle. So I wondered where the expression originated. I finished my second cup of tea and signed my name to the bottom of the document without askin' further questions. That may seem foolhardy to some, but my intuition was insistin' 'twas the thing to do.

'Twas plain to me that my parents had signed the papers. I knew the look of their handwritin'. So I signed under their signatures, handed him the document, and watched as he carefully rolled it up, put it back in the tube, and replaced the end cap, thereby sealin' my fate or so it seemed. I remember thinkin' it was such a performance that it might have been the devil after my soul.

"When will I go?"

"Seize the day, Mr. Hawking. There shall never be a better time than the present. Gather your things."

I looked 'round the cottage. What would I want to take? The bow? No. I'd leave the bow. The books? No. From the sound of it, there were goin' to be more books than I would want. The guitar? Oh aye.

"Clothes?" I asked.

"Up to you. You will be given a stipend with which to buy apparel and niceties not otherwise provided."

By the time I'd put my stuff in the duffel I'd brought from home three years before, I realized I was fairly mobile. Except for the guitar.

I saddled the horse, laid the duffel over his rump behind the saddle and tied it down, then asked Mr. Rathbone if he'd like to ride. He looked up at the sky, which was gray, but no' rainin'.

"No. I'm happy to run."

I thought that was a curious thing at the time. Little did I know that in a few years, that would no' begin to qualify as a curious thing.

"In that case," I said, holdin' the guitar case in his direction, "would you mind handin' this to me after I'm alight?"

"Not at all."

When I was settled, he lifted the case to my waitin' hand and we were off. I trotted the horse all the way to Black-On-Tarry and he kept up without lookin' like he was breathing particularly hard. This was a fact that I found interestin', considerin' that he was ancient. Probably over thirty!

I SAID GOODBYE to Liam and Moira and promised to visit. By the time we reached the gate I was beginnin' to wonder if I was doin' the right thing. I looked back to see the two of them standin' in the middle of the street, holdin' hands. I waved. When they waved back, it made me feel sad, like maybe I was leavin' no' just Black-On-Tarry, but my childhood behind.

There was a sleek black car on the other side of the gate that reminded me of a royal motorcade, but the similarity ended when it stopped fifteen minutes away at a whisterport. I kept tellin' myself that my parents would no' have signed off on a deal to sell me into slavery and hoped to Paddy that 'twas true.

"Where are we goin'?" I asked Rathbone.

"Germany."

"Germany?"

He did no' bother to answer. He just handed my guitar to the pilot to stow and settled into the co-pilot's seat like he planned to travel sleepin'. My guitar was stowed in the rear, but the pilot gave my duffel a seat. Fastened the belt and everything.

He grinned at me. "Balancing the weight. I figure it

weighs about the same as you." Then he laughed. I was a little insulted. I weighed a lot more than the stupid bag. "Flight will be about four hours. Snacks in the cooler behind you if you get hungry."

That was almost enough to make me forgive him for the impertinence because, as a matter of fact, I *was* hungry.

I wondered where in Germany we were headed, but decided I was no' goin' to give Rathbone the satisfaction of appearin' anxious by askin' too many questions. Whisters fly low enough to make a super visual ride, but it was gettin' dark by then and I knew I would no' see much.

Since the light was fadin' I unbuckled and dug into the cooler to have a look at what they packed while I could still see.

"Is this just for me or am I sharin' with you?" I asked the two men in the front.

They looked at each other and shared a chuckle. "It's just for you, kid," said the pilot, who had yet to properly introduce himself.

That was music to my ears because dividin' the food into thirds just simply would no' do.

I pulled out a weinerschnitzel sandwich, crisps, and something called a root beer. My thirteen-year-old self was very pleased to see they were providin' beer. I was prematurely congratulatin' myself on makin' a good decision.

I WOKE UP when I felt the whister touch down and looked around. We were on top of a buildin' that appeared to be about the same age as the palace at Derry, but no' nearly as large and no' nearly as grand. 'Twas surrounded by a high wall, lights spotlightin' the surroundin' area which seemed to be a dense forest.

"Welcome to Grunewald Unit, Mr. Hawking."

The pilot gave me a salute and winked, which to tell the truth, was a little unsettlin'.

I followed Rathbone down a flight of stairs that looked far too modern for the exterior of the buildin'. The same was true of the hallway down which we turned, appearin' for all 'twas worth like a dormitory or some such. We stopped at the fourth door on the left. It bore an engraved plate that read 'Rammel Hawking'.

"Great Paddy," I said. "'Tis my name."

"It is indeed, Mr. Hawking. You'll need to watch the language. You'll find your teachers object to extraneous dialogue and swearing is at the top of the hit list." He opened the door for me, but did no' enter. "Move yourself in and get a good night's sleep. Someone will be here at five in the morning to take you to breakfast, show you around, and go over the rules."

"Five?!?" I thought I saw a ghost of a smile flit across his angular face, but could no' be sure.

"And not a minute later. There's an alarm next to your bed. You'll find things will be much more pleasant if you learn how to use it. Good night."

"Wait." He stopped and turned back. "What's the name of this outfit I signed on with?"

"The Order of the Black Swan."

At that he turned and left, leavin' me thinkin', *What kind of fuckin' name is that?*

CHAPTER 3

Lan

Five years later

I HAD FINISHED my education and chosen to sign on with Black Swan. The ink wasn't dry on the paper before I was out the door. First assignment was Grunewald, the unit that serviced Berlin. It was close enough by whister to patrol, but far enough away to be secluded. The building was a renovation, or adaptation really, of an eighteenth century grand house, set in the middle of a forest preserve that was off limits to anyone not Black Swan.

I had seen a lot of the world by then, but had never been to Berlin. I knew why we had a unit there. Because wherever you find prevalent nightlife, you find active nests of vampire. I didn't have any personal experience with leeches at that time. But you don't have to experience a thing personally to believe people when they tell you it's nasty.

I had never heard anything about vampire until six months ago. They trained our minds and bodies to be precision instruments and occasionally said something vague about protecting the innocent. But crap on a croissant. We had *no* idea we were preparing to be the only barrier between humanity and monsters that turned out to be real. When we met civilian juvies, we told them that we were in military school. Hel. Close enough. Right?

Anyway, six months ago they clued me in. There are vampire out there. I had two choices when I turned eighteen. I could sign on as a vampire hunter or go home and keep my mouth shut about everything I'd learned. I was told that, if I chose the first option, I'd find that my training hadn't even begun. I didn't believe that. I mean how much harder could it be? Really.

They said they took the mouth shut part of option two very seriously. No threat was spelled out, but it was certainly implied. I had six months to decide. So. Sure. I thought about it. A lot.

The day before I turned eighteen I still hadn't decided. I returned to quarters around ten o'clock, closed the door, switched on the light and nearly jumped out of my skin.

My uncle was sitting there in the dark waiting like some creeper from a film noir movie. He laughed when I jumped.

"Right. Real funny. What are you doing in this part of the world?"

His smile slowly faded away. "Sit. I want to say something."

Uncle Al wasn't the sort of guy you said no to. I sat in the chair closest to the sofa where he'd parked his overbearing ass. He didn't speak at first, just stared at me, and I have to tell you it took every bit of the self-discipline I'd learned to keep from squirming under that kind of scrutiny. But I knew it was some kind of test. I was supposed to be patient and wait it out. So I did.

"You're going to be eighteen tomorrow."

I smirked. "So I hear."

He nodded. "Are you decided?"

I looked away. "Honestly? No. I've been hoping for a sign."

"A sign, huh?"

My uncle didn't seem to think that was a reliable approach to decision making.

"Well, I don't know what kind of sign you're expecting. I thought I'd stop by. Won't be here tomorrow. So happy birthday."

"Thanks."

I stood when he got up to leave. He turned toward the door, but turned back like he'd forgotten something. I could almost see him mentally patting his pockets.

"Anything you want to ask me?"

I wouldn't have thought so, but since he put it that way. There *was* something.

"I guess it's clear what choice you made. Any regrets?"

He grinned. It was a thing so rare I couldn't think if I'd ever seen him look pleased before.

"A good question for a seventeen-year-old."

"Almost eighteen."

"Indeed." He nodded. "The answer is no. Not one. Hope that helps."

I thought about it for a second. "Would you feel the same way if you died tomorrow?"

His grin got even bigger. "Definitely."

With that he left without looking back and, in fact, it did help. Immensely.

TEACHERS ARE KNOWN to go on every year about how you'd better get ready because the next year is going to be *so* much harder. But it never is. It's always the same thing. So when I signed on to Black Swan for life and they told me it was about to get *real*, I just smirked on the inside and thought, "Yeah. Yeah. I've heard it before."

Looking back now I could slap my little bratty self for acting like a punk. Even if I kept it on the inside. For once the future of dread hadn't been overstated. It had been understated.

The next four years were rigorous enough to make the first five look like a glide on a paddle board over a smooth-as-glass lake. Naturally, once we understood that we were going to be vampire hunters, and what that meant, we began to pay attention in earnest. But here's the bare truth of that. Nothin' they can do or say can truly prepare you for what it feels like the first time you are face to face with a pale-eyed leech who wants to rip you apart with virus-dripping fangs.

My internship was mostly served as backup to the Grunewald Unit knights. I went to Brazil for a few months and did an awful rotation in Central America looking for Chupacabra. Ew. Things give me willies when I think about them. Yeah. They're even worse than vampire.

I was always sent back to Berlin though. Like it was home base. That was okay with me. There was a lot of action and the Grunewald knights were good solid teachers. They taught me about slaying vampire and they taught me about camaraderie.

Then, of course, there were German girls. I mean, you've gotta love girls who have beer with breakfast. Right?

It was a good place to pay my dues and hone my skills.

Three years later, I was told that I was being sent to Jefferson Unit. Rumor had it that I was going to be a vampire slayer in New York, New York.

I wasn't very impressed when the jeep stopped in front of J.U. It was the farthest thing from Grunewald Castle. A plain brick building with not a single window showing. Looked more like a prison than a Black Swan facility.

Don't get me wrong. I don't require frills to complete me. It was just an observation. I stopped at the intercom.

"Knock. Knock."

"Who's there?"

"Landsdowne."

"Just a minute."

I heard the buzzer and pushed on the door. My first thought was that there was an awful lot of activity for a place that looked so quiet on the outside. I hoisted my duffel up higher on my shoulder and stopped a kid going by.

"Sovereign's office?"

"Down one level and turn right."

I nodded my thanks and headed toward the elevators. The central area was impressive with its three-story ceiling, modern gleam and polish. The place looked like a prison from the front, but once inside it was open and light with a view to what appeared to be a park on the other side of tall windows.

When the elevator opened, I checked to make sure the down arrow was lit, stepped inside and pushed S1. A couple of girls, well, young women I guess you'd say, got in after me in workout clothes. One of them looked me over, taking in the duffel, "Transferring in?"

"Yeah."

She smiled. "I'm Elsbeth. I work in medical." The elevator opened. When I realized they weren't getting off, I finally got the hint and exited. "See you around."

The sovereign's office wasn't hard to find. The reception area was glass to the hallway, but I checked the plaque just to be sure. Sol Nemamiah, Sovereign.

There was a kid at the desk, young enough to be a student. He looked up when I walked in and dropped my duffel.

"Transfer from Berlin," I said.

"Go on in." He pointed to a closed door.

I opened the door, hoping the instruction wasn't a new-guy-hazing prank.

The first thing I saw was a mess of blond hair. I knew he was an elf because he had some of that hair tucked behind the ears. I guess he could have been fae, but I didn't know of any fae knights.

When he turned around, I had three thoughts. That he was just about my age. That his eyes sparkled with elf mischief. And that the only word to describe him was beautiful.

Now don't get me wrong. I have a strong preference for the opposite sex and don't usually think about whether other guys are attractive or not. But this elf had it going and I would have had to be blind to not notice.

I looked past him to the man behind the desk. You could tell it was the Sovereign by the way his jaw seemed permanently clenched. He pointed at the elf. "Rammel Aelshelm Hawking, meet Basil Rathbone Landsdowne."

The elf stuck out his hand. I took it and shook. That's when it registered. I laughed and blurted out, "You're P.P."

"Excuse me?" he said, with his brow knitting.

I looked at the Sovereign and thought better of saying more. "I'll explain. Later."

"You two are getting a try out as partners, attached to B Team, starting," he looked at his monitor, "Thursday. Mr. Hawking, Mr. Landsdowne's quarters are next to yours. Show him the way."

"Aye," said the elf as he moved toward the outer office. He held the door open to the hall and gestured toward the elevator. "Welcome to worm patrol."

"Worm patrol? Sounds like I should turn around and ask for reassignment."

He laughed. "I've been told that's what they call rotation in the Big Apple."

"Oh."

Once inside he pushed the third floor button and leaned back against the wall facing me. "So what was the peepee thing?"

I grinned. "Not peepee! P. P. Your reputation is widely

known. Parties and pussy."

He cocked his head and gave a tiny smile. "'Tis what they say about me?"

"Yeah, man. It could be worse. They could be sayin' you're a limp dick wanker who's scared of girls."

He combined a grin with a sly look that I'd come to think of as Ram's trademark smile. "Spent a lot of time alone as a kid. I suppose there was some pent-up party in me. Maybe I've over-compensated. I would no' want P.P. on my tombstone." The elevator car stopped and the doors opened. He held his hand on the door seam while I hoisted my duffel and stepped out. I walked next to him down the wide hallway. It was carpeted with a rich red pattern, like a five-star hotel. The plus column features of J.U. were definitely all on the inside.

"So," he continued as we walked, "your name is Basil Rathbone…"

"Landsdowne. My mother named me after some famous swordsman." I chuckled, looking down at the carpet. "Maybe she set me up for this gig. You think?"

"Could be. I met a guy named Rathbone when I was thirteen. He recruited me. Big fella. No' quite a giant, but really big."

"Yeah. That was my uncle. He's not *that* big. Matter of fact he's just about the same size as you and me."

"No shit?" he asked. I nodded. "I guess things looked bigger when I'd just turned thirteen." He stopped in front of a door with my name on the plaque. "This is you. That's me one door down," he said as he pointed down the hallway.

"Okay." I waved my new ID in front of the sensor and heard the internal click.

"Dump your stuff and I'll show you 'round."

"Sure. Give me five." The place was a lot bigger and nicer than I expected. In fact, it was a step up. I could stand being called "worm patrol" if all the perks were like that.

I followed the elf's suggestion, dumped my duffel, looked around and walked back out. He was leaning against the wall facing my door looking at his fingernails. He seemed to read my thoughts when he said, "'Twas exactly my reaction when I was moved up here a day ago. 'Tis the big leagues. Compensation for risk I guess. If we pass probation, we're goin' to be knights."

I let that sink in. "Knights," I repeated.

I've been lookin' at that plaque on your door. "What do you go by?"

"Basil."

"Noooooo." He drew the word out, shaking his head. "That will never do. Try it on for size. 'Hold the fucker at bay, Basil.' 'Basil, jump back. He's goin' for your dick!'" I had to laugh. It looked like I'd scored a partner who was entertaining. "See? It just will no' do."

"So you want to rename me? What do you suggest?"

"Shorten your limey last name. Lan. I like the sound of it. Girls will, too."

"Oh, yeah? What do you go by?"

He smiled. "Ram."

I nodded, somehow knowing that it suited him perfectly. "No promises but I'll try it out for a couple of days."

Walking out of the elevator into the Hub, I said, "Have you met the guys we're paired with?"

"Yeah."

He didn't elaborate. So I decided to save the interrogation for later.

RAM GAVE ME a tour of the facility. He was thorough when he was on a mission, left no corner unexplored. He introduced me to more people than I could remember then took me back to the Hub.

Opening his arms as if he was embracing the space, he said, "The perfect end to the comprehensive tour. The lounge. Off limits to students. What'll you have?" he asked, sitting down at a table near the double-sided fireplace and gesturing at the bar attendant at the same time.

"What do you suggest?"

Ram grinned. "Keep it simple. Irish whiskey."

"Oh, no," I said, shaking my head. "I haven't eaten in a day. No alcohol on my empty stomach."

"Great Paddy, man! What kind of a shit host am I?!?"

"Well…"

"Let's get you some food. What do you…? Hold on. Let me guess." He tapped his fingers and jiggled his right knee, his brows knitted like he was trying to divine my food preferences. "I'm guessin' you're a French dip man."

It wasn't something I would have thought of, but once he said it out loud, I couldn't imagine wanting anything else.

"Yeah." I grinned. "That actually sounds great."

"With tomato soup."

"Okay."

The bar attendant arrived. "I'll have my usual. My friend, Lan here, will have a cup of tomato soup, Caesar salad, and a French dip. Do no' dawdle and do no' be stingy with the beef. The lad is hungry and very likely still growin'."

I had my doubts that I was still growing, but I had no doubt that I'd been partnered with a force of nature. But that was okay because he gave every indication of being a force of good nature. It was too soon to judge, but I was already feeling like, when it came to partners, I could have done a lot worse. Only time would tell, but I might have won the lottery. And I might just survive Black Swan, with a guy like him at my side.

"So take your mind off your empty belly by tellin' me about yourself. For starters you sound American. You from here?"

"Born in Santa Clara. You know where that is?"

"Everybody in Black Swan knows where that is. Crawlin' with vampire. Where did you do secondary school?"

"San Francisco. You?"

"Berlin."

"I did my internship there! Must have just missed each other. Es ist eine seltsame Welt."

"Aye. 'Tis a strange world."

"How do you like it here so far?"

"Think we might have landed on our feet."

"Yeah. Seems alright. So far." The attendant set a whiskey down in front of Ram and put a water down for me. "So. About the other two assigned to B Team?"

Ram shook his head. "Met 'em briefly. My first impression is that they come with sticks up their asses. Sittin' up just a little too straight if you ask me. One of them is a berserker."

"No way! I thought they were all gone. Stuff of legends and all that."

Ram was shaking his head. "He's real and big as life. And I mean *big*! I guess you'll meet them soon enough if they're sendin' us out startin' day after tomorrow."

"Kinda hard to believe. Goin' out unsupervised, I mean."

"I hear you. But we have a day to fatten you up for the leeches and maybe get laid a few times."

I spluttered into my water. "A few times?"

AT THAT POINT, I thought he was mostly bluff and bluster, but it turned out that he could have had a new sexual experience every hour if he'd wanted. Girls did things trying to get his attention that made me feel embarrassed for them. The notice he got for being beautiful made it hard to be inconspicuous, which is what works best for vampire hunters. He took to wearing a black knit hat that covered the ears and most of that blondeness. Seemed like those two things combined were like catnip to women. But you know what? After a couple of days I couldn't even imagine another partner. When Black Swan put us together, they must have used some kind of magic. They knew what they were doing. We complemented each other's strengths and weaknesses. And it's no small thing that he made things that should have been drudgery or tedium seem like fun.

We needed that counterbalance because there was plenty about our lives that was *not* fun.

It turned out that Ram was kind of right about the other partnership that made up B Team. Storm and Kay were straight arrow types, but I didn't object to that. Straight arrows are predictable. Well, I mean, so long as they don't let their berserker out.

Certainly everybody can't be Mr. Party like Ram. Sometimes a situation calls for a serious attitude. Vampire hunting is one of those situations. The most serious one of us, Storm, was the one we started listening to, like our lives depended on it. And I guess they did.

Ram was technically the most senior member of B Team because he'd arrived a couple of hours ahead of them, but it wasn't a distinction he cared about. He seemed more interested in getting the job done and staying alive than being in charge. So I had no problem with his priorities.

Kay got stuck with the nickname Ram gave him, just like I did. Not that I'm complaining. I wore the name "Lan" like I'd never been called anything else and the fucker might have even been right about guessing that girls would like it better than Basil.

Yeah. Storm and Kay were good guys that I learned to love and they did their share of snatching my hiney from the jaws of death.

Until they didn't.

WHEN PROBATION WAS over, the four of us went through the knighthood ritual together. The hardest thing I ever did was to get through the ceremony without laughing. Every time Ram caught my eye he'd give me a look that made me want to double over in giggles. So much for decorum and solemn occasions that call for reverent behavior.

I remember how much pride I felt the first night on rotation as a fully fledged knight of Black Swan. I think my chest swelled to twice its normal size when someone called me Sir Landsdowne. It's a fine thing to be a titled part of such an old and honorable organization, but guys who do what we did need sweet perquisites. 'Cause nothin' about it was easy.

Three nights a week we'd report to the roof Whisterport and catch a ride to Manhattan, which was infested with vampire like maggots on a carcass. They were so thick it was hard for me to understand how people could be oblivious. It's amazing that human minds allow people to see only what they believe in and ignore everything else.

Even though the four of us learned to work together almost telepathically, like part of a single machine, morale was slipping. None of us wanted to be the one to say it. So we kept quiet. But Black Swan was losing the war against vampire and we all knew it.

Sometimes I wondered why they didn't send more knights to Jefferson Unit. I guessed it was that everybody was having a problem with escalation. I could guess all I wanted. Decisions about such things were way above my pay grade.

I just knew that any night that ended with us waiting for the cleanup crew to come dispose of a corpse or two felt like a victory. You might think that's kind of a sick way to live. After all, you could spin it that the leech had once been human and was turned through no fault of his own. But it was just fucking impossible to feel sorry for vampire.

Sometimes we waited for cleanup over what was left of the body of a woman. Those were the nights that were really depressing. The remains had to be disposed of without notifying anyone, which meant there would be no graves or memorial services and their families and friends would simply never know what became of them, would maybe even hold out hope that they'd come back. I used to think that, in a sense, that was more merciful for them than knowing the truth, but still, it'd be hard.

It started to seem like for every one we took out, two more took his place. The population of young men was being thinned by being infected by the virus. The population of young women was being thinned by being killed by vampire.

People were afraid. The smart ones were trying to leave New York like refugees. People with families tried to keep their kids on lockdown at night. But those at greatest risk were also the most reckless and least likely to believe something bad might happen to them.

As for the job of trying to give young humans a chance to live long enough to gain some wisdom, well, at the time I would have said it bites. We'd chase down vampire only to have them vanish. Poof. Like magic. We couldn't find where they were hiding and it was becoming increasingly frustrating.

Let me tell you, it's not easy to maintain a state of alert vigilance for hours at a time, every muscle tense, every synapse firing, unless there's an apparent reason for it. Victories weren't nearly plentiful enough to keep us at a safe state of readiness. I know that sounds like excuse-making, but the only way we could get a break was to divide the team, trying to stay close enough to provide backup for each other without making it apparent that we were together. Ram and I had perfected the art of splitting up. Or so we thought. We got to be good at looking like we were alone, while never losing sight of each other. For one thing, we'd usually be on different sides of the street.

At six feet tall, Rammel was the smallest of us, but he was also very quick. And very lethal.

Three times he risked himself by pulling a leech off one of us a second before we were on the way to Palesville. Twice more he interrupted an abduction in progress and sent young ladies home to rethink being out at night. Every time Storm wrote him up in a report that resulted in some honor or another, but Ram always declined formal decoration.

It was strange that somebody so charismatic shied away from notoriety, but I knew he had his reasons.

It makes me laugh to myself to say it, but his heroics were the one and *only* thing he was humble about. The thing is, he had plenty of reason to think he was all *that*. I never told him, because his ego certainly didn't need inflating, but I couldn't imagine a better friend and I was *so* proud to be his partner.

I wish I'd said that when I could have.

CHAPTER 4

Ram

O'COURSE WE KNEW that our vocation was dangerous, but we still had a little bit of that delusion of invincibility because we were young and strong. Till the day I die I will wonder if I could have saved Lan. If I'd been a second quicker to notice the danger or a second quicker to react? I'll never know, which is why it will never stop hauntin' me.

It happened one night when we'd just been dropped off in Midtown. We had no' even split up yet, but were walkin' along makin' plans to meet at a favorite bar two hours into our shift. We were passin' by a tight alleyway, when I heard a muffled yell. The others kept walkin' 'cause they had no' heard a thing. I guess elf ears have value beyond good looks.

I stopped the others with a look as I withdrew a stake from the inside of my leather jacket and pointed into the alley. I saw Storm's head jerk toward the corner and I knew he was calculatin' how much time it would take them to get 'round to the other end of the alley. Since we were off Broadway, the block would be short between where we were and the other side. So, without a word, he and Kay took off runnin' while Lan and I began to ease toward the sound.

There was no' much light, just what was comin' from where the pass through deadended at the streets on either end. Lan was on one side movin' forward slowly, but huggin' the wall, keepin' to the shadows. I was on the other. Our eyes were adjustin' to the dark, but no' fast enough, especially since the vampire were wearin' dark clothes.

When we came on the scene, there were five of them feastin' on two girls, who had probably thought they were out for a fun girls' night on the town. The sight was shockin'. No' because we'd never seen vampire eat before, but because we'd never seen so many vampire together in one place before. They tended to be solitary hunters. If they banded together, 'twas typically in pairs. At least in our experience.

I nodded to Lan, but was no' at all sure that he could see me in the dim light.

Let me preface this next statement by sayin' that there are no' rules of gentlemanly conduct when it comes to vampire. Our job was to neutralize them as quickly and efficiently as possible. The idea of tradin' blow for blow with vampire and waitin' to see who would be the last standin'? Well, 'twould be ludicrous. The only thing separatin' us from them was the tiniest graze of a fang with virus-infested saliva on it.

At first I thought we'd been lucky because the leeches were concentrated on feedin' and no' payin' the least attention to the fact that other predators could be found in the city. Namely us.

I crept up behind the two closest to me and dispatched them before what was left of their minds registered that I was there. I had a stake in each hand. I plunged one through the back of the leech closest to me. We'd been unknowin'ly practicin' how to do that for a decade and unerrin'ly hit the heart, even as teenagers without havin' any understandin' of what we were trainin' for. I shifted the stake in my left hand to my right just as the others realized the party had been interrupted, but it was too late.

Lan had engaged two while Storm and Kay were interceptin' the fifth, who'd run the way they were comin'. Normally Lan would have made short work of the bloodsuckers as I had. He killed one, but before he got the other, the girl on the ground, the one who was still alive, reached out and put her hand on his calf. Lan looked down to see what had touched his leg. The distraction was just enough to give the vamp the openin' he needed to grab Lan and bite into his throat.

Believe me, it may sound detached, the way I tell this story. But 'twas no' easy to relive on any terms. When I think back on that night, the memory feels like the whole thing was impressed on my mind in slow motion. I rushed the leech that had his arms around my partner from behind. Lan's arms were pinned down and he had this look on his face like he did no' know what was happenin'. I'll never forget it. Sometimes I wake up at night and, even though the images flee like smoke on wakin', I know I've been dreamin' it because of the residual feelin's. As nightmares go, that one is quite persistent.

I caught Lan as his legs gave way and eased him down to the street.

By that time Storm and Kay were standin' over us. They had taken care of the vamp who tried to flee and then mercifully dispatched the girl who was still alive. 'Twas the best we could do for her because there was no possibility of a good endin' to that. She'd either die a painful death while the virus made its way through her system burnin' like poison or she'd be one of the rare females who turned. Either way, her life was over. We knew that intellectually, but 'twas still a duty we all dreaded carryin' out.

Lan could no' really give any last words because his throat was filled with blood. When he tried, the only thing that came out was a horrible gurglin' sound. I'm no' capable of expressin' how much I hate rememberin' him like that.

I KNEW FROM the first day we met that he and I were goin' to be friends. I could no' have guessed how close we would end up bein'. I loved him like a brother. Correction. Considerin' how I felt about my older brother, I should say instead that I loved him and leave it at that. What I regret more than anything is havin' never told him that I was proud to be his partner.

As you already know, Black Swan has a tradition of givin' leave to remainin' team members when one has been lost in the line of duty. I guess at some point they figured out that a healin' time is required. But first, a formal inquiry is conducted. The unit sovereign and shrink hear testimony and do an evaluation. All three of us would have gladly taken beatin's instead of havin' to rehash what happened that night.

We had flown to California with Lan's ashes and attended the memorial service. Hearin' his mother cry was brutal. Lyin' to her about how we knew him was even worse.

After we arrived back at J.U., we had to face the inquiry.

I've never felt so low before or since. My heart felt like it weighed a hundred pounds. It was hard to walk. Hard to breathe. Hard to imagine a future without Lan in it. I knew Storm and Kay were grievin', too, but Lan was no' their partner. We'd spent three years together. No' every minute, but in addition to trainin' together and patrollin' together, we shared a lot of time off.

Maybe I was a bad influence on him. I know my behavior shocked him at times, but I never went so far that he did no' forgive me for embarrassin' him or gettin' him into a situation no' of his own choosin'.

Sometimes things come in pairs of opposites. The worst thing that ever happened to me was quickly followed by the best thing that ever happened to me.

CHAPTER 5

Ram

I GLANCED OVER at Monk. He was sittin' off to the side, listenin' to us tell the story, no' sayin' a word or givin' anything away. I guess he was hopin' we'd forget he was there, but if he really thought that was goin' to happen, he did no' know Black Swan knights as well as he thought.

We'd each told what we remembered about that night. I guess they'd done a good job of trainin' us to be good witnesses because our stories matched exactly. To my very great relief it seemed like the ordeal was nearin' an end. I was packed and could no' wait to get to my cottage in the New Forest and close the door. I thought the best way for me to process what had happened was alone.

'Twas what I was thinkin' about when I was hit with a blast of hot air. I stood and looked around for the cause. My remainin' teammates were doin' the same thing and we all had alarm written on our faces.

At first we did no' see anything out of the ordinary, but then there was a burst of light and a loud pop. Something materialized out of thin air and fell to the floor. If I was a squeamish sort, I'd say it made a sickenin' sound when it plopped on the flagstone.

Nobody moved. We just stood there starin' at it. I mean, we'd seen a lot of strange stuff. No' just vampire. Occasionally Black Swan sends knights to investigate other things no' supposed to exist. But this was a new one.

I stepped toward it cautiously and leaned closer to get a better look.

"What is that?" I asked.

Whatever it was, it was unrecognizable. I mean we could see it was a creature, but it was so torn and bloody 'twas hard to make out much beyond that.

Kay looked at Storm and said, "Shaped like a human."
Well, duh.

Sol looked at Kay and said, "Not much of a recommendation. So are lots of things that aren't."

At first I thought that the feelin' I was gettin' was the after effect of adrenaline. Seemed just that unpleasant, but different. I mean, when that gruesome thing lyin' on the floor started moanin' and tryin' to move, it made me feel sick. No' that I really had experience with human-type illnesses, but I'd seen enough to guess that it was no' fun.

I did no' know what the thing was. I just knew it was no' good and it was too much of a coincidence that it came out of nowhere and landed in J.U.'s Chamber.

'Tis hard to explain my reaction. It felt like the creature was clawin' at me from the inside. Plus the fact that I'd got hard lookin' at a pile of goo was both disgustin' and disturbin'. Gave me plenty of reason to hate that thing and believe 'twas an evil in our midst.

So, as usual, I said what was on my mind. "I have a

bad feelin' about this. I think we should kill it. Kill it now."

It seemed like a good idea at the time.

Storm had moved closest to it and it looked like the thing tried to reach out to him. He got down on one knee and looked like he was goin' to try to pick it up. I thought he'd gone mad, and I was no' the only one.

Sol said, "Don't touch it! We don't know what it is. It could be anything... a disguised machine or a suicide mission carrying explosives or toxic chemicals. Or a spell!"

I thought that last one was a bit of a reach, but I suppose 'tis his job to consider all possibilities.

Storm acted like the sovereign had no' said a word. He just quietly went about doin' what he was doin' and said, "Call the infirmary. Get them ready for an incoming emergency."

As I've already said, that was no' my first choice, but I'd been teammates with Engel Storm long enough to respect him more than anyone I knew, since Lan was no longer alive. So if that was his play, I was goin' to back him up.

I started toward the wall phone.

"Ignore that!" Sol demanded. "Are you not hearing me?" He wheeled on me. "Hawking, don't you move another step!"

I hesitated for a couple of seconds. Disobeyin' a direct order from a sovereign was a serious offense, but somehow, on the heels of Lan's death, such things did no' seem important. Storm was the one I counted on in the field. It felt like my first allegiance was to him. Always.

Still, I tried to make light of it by sayin', "Sorry. You

know we do no' do orders."

"I'm not joking!" Sol looked at me like I'd lost my fuckin' mind. And maybe I had. "Two minutes ago you were voting to kill it now."

That was true. I did no' have an explanation that any-one outside B Team would understand, so I did no' bother to offer one. With a defiance that some might say was no' that surprisin', I punched in the code and said, "Stormy's call."

By that time Storm was strugglin' to get the thing in his arms and get to his feet which, again, made me dubious about the nature of the creature. I mean Storm was a very big guy who could bench press me on a bet. One thing was for sure, the creature was heavier than it looked.

Seein' that, Kay squatted down on the opposite side of it, facin' Storm, and said, "Might be better to have them send a gurney. You could be causing more damage." He glanced down for just a second, then added, "If that's possible."

Storm shook his head. "No time."

Kay nodded, comin' to the same conclusion as myself. Whatever Storm was thinkin', we were on his side. Kay helped lift the creature so that Storm could get a good enough grip to carry it. "Hope you know what you're doing."

KAY AND I walked behind Storm. He was clearly strugglin' with both the weight and the mess. No doubt it was slippery with all those fluids oozin'. He was breathing heavy, but I could hear him tryin' to say soothing things to the bundle of goo in his arms.

When we were close to the infirmary Kay and I jogged ahead. They should have been ready for us because they'd been warned we were on the way.

I crashed through the swingin' doors and yelled, "Where do you want us?"

Within seconds the med team had moved the creature from Storm's arms to a gurney. The medics hustled away askin' questions about the nature of the injury. *Great Paddy!* How were we supposed to say how it had been hurt? We did no' even know what it was!

They disappeared behind double doors and made it clear we were no' welcome beyond.

Storm just stood there starin' at those closed doors. Made me wonder if he was touched with the PTSD. I nudged his shoulder and said, "Good call. They're takin' care of it. Now let's go get a drink and say goodbye. We will no' be seein' each other again for a while."

Kay said something about drinkin' and bein' Irish, but slapped me on the back and started away with me. He happened to look down at his clothes and seemed to realize, for the first time, that he was wearin' a lot of gore.

"We might want to grab a shower and a change first," he said.

He must have been talkin' about Storm and himself when he said "we" because my clothes were fine. I turned 'round to say something to Storm, but he had no' moved. He was just standin' there still starin' at the door. At that point I was beginnin' to be concerned.

"You comin'?" I asked.

Kay gave me a look that said he was also worried about the uncharacteristic behavior.

Storm did no' move nor did he answer.

So Kay walked back to his side and said, "Hey. What's up? We've seen stranger stuff than this."

I concurred by addin', "Lots stranger."

Storm blinked, looked down at the bloody mess on his clothes, and said, "These are gonna have to be burned."

Kay nodded without takin' his eyes off his partner. "Yeah. Probably. Let's get cleaned up and grab a whiskey."

Storm looked between the two of us and said, "Thanks for the backup." But he still did no' look like he was fully present and accounted for.

I could see that Kay wasn't buyin' it either, but he let it pass and, seein' the wisdom in that, I decided to do the same.

"I'm gonna hang out here a while and see what happens," Storm said. He looked back at the door. "You know. Curious."

I leaned against the wall thinkin' I might as well get comfy, but Kay shocked the fool out of me by sayin', "Okay. Call if you need us. We'll be close."

I could only guess that Kay was cravin' whiskey like I was. I turned to start toward the door when Sol came stormin' through lookin' like he was takin' scalps. If we'd left two minutes before, we would have got away clean.

"Stop right there!" He stalked toward us while the door closed behind him and motioned us toward the empty waitin' room. We did no' sit down and neither did he.

"Look", he started, "I know you three are going through a rough patch. I've been there. Lan meant something to you. I understand that better than you think. Teammates always feel that way, but you just took it upon yourselves to make a decision that could endanger everybody in this unit."

I did no' roll my eyes, but that sounded like exaggeration to me. Nonetheless, even I know no' to poke the sovereign when he's on a tirade. Especially no' that particular sovereign.

"I know you've got problems with authority. Hell. That's half the reason why you're here. But you either compromise with the management – that would be me – or you're no good to this organization." He looked at each of us, one at a time, like he was tryin' to drive his point home. "Is there any chance I'm making myself clear?"

Kay and I nodded, but Stormy just stared at Sol. Actin' the stubborn fool if you ask me. I mean it does no' cost much to let Sol think he's in charge and it keeps him out of our way.

Sol ran his hand over his buzz cut and said, "We have to finish the inquiry."

I blew out a big breath that barely disguised the 'Great Paddy' on my tongue. I needed a drink.

He must have seen something in our faces because he said, "But we can do it another day."

Let me tell you, Sol bein' a softee is almost scarier than Sol on the warpath. Makes you wonder what's comin' next. I figured, whatever it was, would go down easier if it was chasin' after a glass of fine Irish whiskey.

Storm insisted that he wanted to stay a while. And I noticed that I was feelin' better ever since the bloody visitor had been taken behind closed doors.

Out of sight. Out of mind. Or so I thought.

CHAPTER 6

Ram

THE NEXT MORNIN' Storm came out to say goodbye when Kay and I were takin' off for leave.

"Come home with me. We've got plenty of room and my family is crazy about you." Kay tried one last time to get Storm to change his mind about stayin'.

"Yeah. I appreciate it, but I'm gonna take my leave here," Storm answered.

"You sure?" Kay said. Storm nodded. Putting an affectionate hand on his partner's shoulder, Kay said, "You know that 'Confucius say' about being responsible for someone if you save their life?"

"Yeah?"

"Well. It's not true."

Storm laughed good-naturedly. "I'm good. It's what I want. Go home. Make home movies of you having marathon sex with your girl. Eat nachos and tacos and burritos and whatever else. Annoy the hell out of your sisters. And I'll be here when you get back."

Turnin' to me, he said. "Rammel. Take care. Don't forget how to get back here."

I went through the motion of smilin' without feelin' it and wondered if I'd ever feel like smilin' again. "Aye. See you in October."

"October," he repeated and I thought it sounded as wistful as I felt.

I caught a company plane to Edinburgh. Farnsworth had arranged for a private charter that would get me within strikin' distance of the New Forest. I was the only one on the plane, which was good by me. I was cravin' my own company something fierce and just wanted to be left alone while I sorted out my feelin's about Lan bein' gone and how he'd died.

When Storm saw us off, we all knew that there was a question mark about the future. Some guys did no' come back after losin' a teammate. I did no' know how I'd feel about it after three months away. At that point, I was just takin' it one day at a time.

LIAM KEPT MY white mare for me, made sure she was cared for and exercised. She was a magnificent animal and I enjoyed the ride to the cottage. She was eager for a run and I thought the poundin' reverberatin' through my body would do me good. It did. But no' nearly as much good as steppin' off the horse in front of my cottage. It felt like the first time I'd taken in a full breath, all the way down to the bottom of my lungs, since I'd looked across that alley and seen Lan bein' murdered.

I listened to the quiet. No sounds but birdsong and the rustle of leaves. I would no' want it told widely, but knowin' I was completely alone, I buried my face in the horse's neck and cried like a baby. It felt like the hole that had opened up inside me would never be filled. It would always be a giant gapin' wound.

And I wished it had been me, instead of Lan. If life was bein' passed out to the deservin', he was a hel of a lot more deservin'.

I passed the time much as I did when I'd been there as a child. I hunted. I fished. I read. I played the guitar. I observed the creatures in the woods.

When I had bad dreams about Lan's death, I got up in the night and poured myself a shot of amber gold elixir. I did no' drink straight out of the bottle because I know 'tis a slippery slope. Especially when you're alone with nothin' for company but your own demons.

I was certain the New Forest would take me in its embrace and give me healin'. It had always been my refuge. No' to get overly poetic, but to me it had been the essence of *home*, a light in the dark. And it had never failed to give me comfort.

Until then.

After six weeks of wrestlin' with the horror of losin' my partner and best friend, watchin' his throat ripped away from his body five feet away from where I was standin', horrified and useless, I came to the unavoidable conclusion that solitude was no' workin'. I thought perhaps a distraction might.

Instead of drinkin' alone, perhaps drinkin' with others...

So I tidied up the cottage, stuffed the duffel, and headed back to the modernity of nightlife in Belfast. I got a room over one of the rowdiest bars in the whole of the town, thinkin' that I would no' sleep deeply enough to have nightmares. It was sound logic and might have worked except for the fact that I was drinkin' and fuckin' at night then sleepin' all the day long when it was relatively quiet.

After a couple of weeks of that I was restless and ready to move on. I paid the bill, gathered my belongin's, pulled my cap down low and walked to the motorway. After a time I caught a ride with a truck driver.

Openin' the passenger door, I said, "How far south are ye goin'?"

"Goin' home," he said. "I can take you as far as Ballynahich."

"Much obliged," I said, climbin' up.

Within minutes of findin' shelter inside the vehicle, the drizzle turned into a peltin' rain and I was grateful to be out of it. The windshield blades were workin' hard to give us visibility, but 'twas a losin' proposition.

"You know," he said, glancin' over at me, "you look a little like the younger prince."

I smiled. "Yeah. I'm told so often. I think I'm better lookin' than the royal fucker though."

He laughed and said, "I'm Kevin Durry."

I hesitated, no' wantin' to give my name. Before I knew it I heard myself sayin', "Basil Landsdowne." It gave me the eeriest feelin' to have claimed to be my departed partner, but at the same time I had the strange sense that he was somehow kept alive by my speakin' his name out loud.

"So what's waitin' for ye down south?"

"Hopin' to make my way to Dublin."

"Got a job waitin' there?"

I shook my head. "Whiskey and women."

He laughed. I took him for forty, give or take. "I remember a time when those two pursuits were the most important things in my life."

"Yeah? What about now?"

"Got a wife and two boys. Got a cat, but I do no' claim it. Belongs to my wife." He chuckled. "'Tis a solid life. A good life. And I have a new perspective on what's important."

"Sounds like you're a lucky man."

"INDEED. I COULD no' ask for more." He turned to me with a mischievous gleam in his eye. "Unless 'twas a palace in Derry, o'course."

Busted. I looked at the road ahead. "I'm sure 'tis no' all 'tis thought to be."

Out of the corner of my eye I could see that Kevin Durry was nodding. "Nothin' ever is."

"But still, is there no' something more you dream about? Havin' or doin' or bein'?"

"Well, everyone has something like that I suppose. I always wanted to play the fiddle, but I'm thinkin' 'tis too late for that."

"Maybe. Maybe no'," I answered.

He let me off. "Here we are. Best of luck to ye, young… Basil, was it?"

"Aye. Thanks again, Kevin."

He drove away, revealin' that he had let me off across the street from an establishment named the Ramery Inn. For the first time since Lan's death, I laughed out loud.

I trotted across the street and got a room. I was still damp from the drizzle earlier. Dry clothes, hot tea, and a nap in clean sheets seemed like a brilliant idea. 'Twas the first time since Lan's death that my first impulse was no' whiskey. I'm no' much of a philosopher, but I took it as a sign of spiritual progress.

It took three more rides to get to Dublin's Temple Bar on the Liffey. As it turned out, my relief from the urge to drink was temporary.

'Twas no' my first time in the capital of drink, song, and girls. I knew my way 'round and knew exactly where I would stay. There was a pub a few blocks away from the tourist haunts that had rooms above. There are no' that many tourists in mid-September, but there were always some.

I spent the next two weeks lookin' for ways to keep my mind off what had happened. I drank. I whored. I fished. I even went to the zoo. Nothin' alleviated the lost feelin' that had settled into my gut and taken up residence.

Finally I came to the conclusion that runnin' was no' helpin'. Black Swan spelled out how grief leave was supposed to be spent. It was even in a manual. Associates of the slain were supposed to go home, spend time in familiar surroundin's amid familiar people, like friends and family. 'Twas supposed to be a reminder of what we're fightin' for I think.

I wondered if there was something wrong with me

because that's the last thing I wanted. Still, bein' impulsive was no' gettin' me any closer to peace or makin' a decision about whether or no' I wanted to go back to Black Swan.

I wandered the streets around Temple Bar with my black knit cap pulled low and hands in my pockets. I walked along the river, strolled the university grounds, and felt nothin' so much as the feelin' of loss that was beginnin' to be as much a part of me as my hands or feet. Nothin' interested me. Nothin' cheered me. Nothin', no' even whiskey, took the edge off the pain. Orgasms gave me a few seconds of pleasure and blessed nothin'ness, but before I could even get my pants zipped, the plague of sorrow was back like a devil sittin' on my shoulders.

Every now and then the sound of laughter would make me raise my head to see who 'twas that was enjoyin' life. I hated people who laughed. Everything about that seemed wrong. Lan was dead.

I asked myself what I would do if I decided no' to report to Jefferson Unit on October 2nd. My life, since the age of thirteen, had been spent in preparation to be a Black Swan knight. And regardless of the fact that I had failed to save my partner from the end all knights fear, and expect, I knew I was good at it.

Concludin' that driftin' in a whiskey haze was *never* goin' to make things better, I took a taxi to the airport and, for the first time in my life, got a ticket on a commercial airline. For New York.

While I was waitin' for boardin', I called Farnsworth and asked for a favor.

KEVIN DURRY ANSWERED the knock at his door, wondering who might be calling on a Sunday morning. A studious-looking man stood on the stoop holding a beautifully polished violin in one hand and its case in the other.

"Mr. Durry?"

"Aye?"

"I'm Miles Copeland, your teacher. You've been given a fine instrument and music lessons for life or as long as you wish, whichever comes first."

Kevin Durry stared at Mr. Copeland for a full minute before he started to laugh. "Come bearin' dreams, have ye? Well, then, do no' just stand there. Come inside. I have some fiddlin' to learn."

AER LINGUS LANDED at JFK a little before two in the afternoon. I looked out the window, thinkin' that the gray sky looked just the same on the other side of the Atlantic. I let a taxi driver stow the duffel in the trunk of his cab.

"Club Quarters hotel. You know where it is?"

"Yeah."

Frankly I was impressed by that because the Club Quarters was a tiny hotel and off the beaten track. I had noticed it when we'd been on patrol in the area and 'twas the only reason I picked it.

The closer we got to Manhattan, the greater was my sense of dread, and I was startin' to think I'd made a bad choice. Still, I figured the only way I was goin' to decide whether or no' I'd quit Black Swan was to confront the nightmare.

I guess I was lucky they had a room. It had no' occurred to me that they would no' until the desk clerk said, "You're in luck. We've had a cancellation."

"I'm in luck," I said drily, no' feelin' so in the least.

A bell hop, younger than I, showed me to the room.

I said, "Just a minute," then fished through the stuff in my duffel. I retrieved my Dopp kit, then handed the entire duffel to the kid. In truth he was probably only a couple of years younger than I, but I think Black Swan knights tend to age faster on the inside. At least that's how I was feelin'. Old. "Take this and get everything laundered, even the duffel." I handed him an Irish fifty pound note and said, "There'll be another one of those if you can get it done by ten o'clock tonight."

He turned the note over in his hand as if he thought it might be play money.

"Oh, sorry. I did no' change money. I'm sure there's a currency converter near here, but 'tis worth about," I stopped to do a mental calculation, "seventy-five dollars."

His face lit up. "Thank you, sir. You will have these back by ten tonight."

"Good man," I said.

Then he was gone and I was left with nothin' but my own thoughts and traffic noise driftin' up from several stories below. Old single pane windows do no' shut out a lot of noise nor keep in a lot of heat. I headed downstairs to the street in pursuit of the thing that had brought me there.

The alley where Lan had died was only three blocks away. I'm sure I was stiff from long hours on the plane and the walk would probably have felt good if I'd been aware of my body.

I spent a lot of time in midtown, but rarely saw it in daylight. The city felt like an entirely different place. Or maybe 'twas just knowin' that vampire were no' out and about.

Within a few minutes I was standin' on the very spot where it happened. I was first struck by the fact that it was clean. Five vampire, two girls, and one knight lost their lives, but there was no' a hint of it. I supposed that was the whole point of havin' a well-trained, well-paid cleanup crew.

I do no' know if it would have made me feel better to find traces of blood. Probably no'. Still, it seemed wrong that every sign had been erased.

A sudden gust of cold wind blew through the alley. I pulled the collar of my boiled wool jacket close to my throat and slid down the brick wall until I squatted with my back to it. I do no' know how long I stayed like that, relivin' the scene in my mind. But the light was fadin' when I stood up.

There was a deli across the street that had counter seats facin' the windows. I walked over, ordered a corned beef on rye big enough to feed two grown men or one Black Swan knight, and sat down where I could see the alley. I stayed there and watched it get dark. The lights of the city came on when dusk turned the sky charcoal gray.

I can no' say where my thoughts took me durin' that time. I think I mostly thought about my partner, what sort of man he'd become right in front of my eyes, as we grew up together. I stared straight ahead at that alley replayin' all the things we'd shared in my head, work and play.

I heard someone say, "Closing down, sir."

I looked up at the fella speakin' and nodded. "Okay."

It was late enough that the street was quieter. I walked across and stood in the alley again, thinkin' that, at the very least, there ought to be a plaque with his name on it.

I do no' know if I said it out loud or no', but I was askin', "What would you want me to do, Lan?"

And I heard his answer clearly as if he'd spoken to me in physical form. I will never know if 'twas my imagination or my friend speakin' to me from beyond. But I heard him say, "Go back, Ram. If not for you, then do it for me. There's a job to finish. And a whole lot of living still to do. Don't let my death define either my life or yours."

The pall that had hung so heavy seemed to give way in that moment and I felt myself take a breath in. All the way to the bottom of my lungs. It was as if I'd decided to live after all, and a peace settled over me that I had thought I'd never experience again.

Lan's death would no' define his life.

'Twas then I felt it, that sixth sense that hunters develop after a while. I knew without physical sight that there was a vamp close by. My head had been in such a fog I'd let myself get caught in Midtown after midnight without a sign of a weapon.

I looked around. The light was dim, but next to the dumpsters somebody had left some wooden pallets that had seen better days. They were broken up in places so that some of the wood slats naturally broke into pieces shaped like sharp-pointed stakes, just big enough to fit well in an elf's hand. I slid over and broke one off as quietly as possible.

The vamp had his back to me. He was haulin' a pedestrian into the alley, his hand over her mouth. I had to calculate the exact distance with which to drive a stake through his back. Just enough to pierce his heart without goin' all the way through and injurin' the girl.

Fortune was with me. Or maybe 'twas Lan's spirit. I swore I heard him laughin'. When the leech dropped, the young lady turned to look at me with a face that was probably cute when no' lookin' speechless terrified.

"Go on," I said. "Run fast. Get far, far away from here. Stay in crowds of people. Do no' be out alone late at night and do no' tell anyone what you saw."

I knew it was ridiculous to say that. They always told what they saw. Luckily nobody believed 'em. But just in case, I needed to get the cleanup crew there fast.

Pullin' my phone out of my pocket, I dialed the number marked AAAAA in my contacts.

"Hawking," said the voice on the other end. "Aren't you on leave?"

"No' right this minute," I said. "You got the location?"

"On our way."

"Hurry up about it. We've got a victim on the loose."

I did no' go back to Jefferson Unit until the day they were expectin' me back. I did touristy things in clean clothes that had been promptly delivered to my hotel room in exchange for a second fifty-pound note.

Over the next few days, I climbed to the top of the

Empire State Building. Went to the Metropolitan Museum. Went to see AC/DC at Madison Square Garden and bought one of every tee shirt. Went to Bloomin'dales and bought myself a handsome pea coat.

I also took care of family business. Talked to my mother because I had no' answered her calls for weeks. I knew 'twas bad to keep her waitin', but I had no' been in a place to talk. She's flighty, gets her feathers in a ruffle easily, but 'tis also easy to calm her down once she knows all is well.

I'd also ignored several calls from Kay, which really was uncalled for, but I just was no' ready to rejoin the livin', as they say.

Three days after the incident that I think of as Pallet Stake, I passed a stack of *New York Tells* on a street corner. The headline read "Vampire Stalker in Midtown". There was a grainy color photo of a slatherin' bald nosferatu with yellow eyes and fangs in the wrong place, on smaller incisors instead of cuspids. Cripes.

Underneath that was another sightin' of Big Foot in Central Park. Well, who knows? Maybe there is something akin to a large hairy primate livin' in the park.

When the day came to report to Jefferson Unit, I took the elevator up to one of Black Swan's rooftop whisterports. Emotionally I felt battered around the edges, dented in places, sore, sad, and still a little lost. But I was alive and more determined than ever to stay that way.

I dialed Kay's number and he picked up on the first ring.

"Son of a bitch."

"I guess that means you know 'tis me callin'."

"Did you lose your phone? For three months?"

I sighed, knowin' that I deserved a punch in the nose. I was also touched, hearin' the concern in his voice.

"I was in a bad spot. Sorry for the radio silence."

There was a pause while Kay seemed to be comin' to terms with my apology.

"Where are you?"

"On a whister." I looked out the window. "About ten minutes from…" I realized I'd almost said home, "…J.U."

"You owe me a drink and an explanation. I'll be waiting in the lounge."

"Aye. Missed you, too."

"Shut it."

I chuckled and ended the call.

No' wantin' to put any more strain on my relationship with my teammate, I did no' bother to drop my duffel off at my apartment. I went straight to the lounge, let it fall to the floor next to Kay's chair and flopped into the cushy chair opposite him. It curled 'round me like a lover.

"When did you get back? You seen Storm?" I asked before he could start chewin' on my ass.

"Came in last night. Yeah. I've seen him. And we're on call for dinner tonight. Turns out that thing was a girl."

"No way."

"Exactly what I thought. He says she's healed and cleans up real nice."

"So… what? How did she materialize out of thin air? What's the story?"

"He says she was forced into some kind of experimental device to escape assassination. Believe it or not, she's from another dimension."

"I do no' believe it."

"It's true anyway. The machine that brought her here tore her up pretty bad. Well, we knew that part. Right?"

Now here's the thing you may no' know. You may think that vampire hunters who work for an outfit that specializes in paranormal investigation are open minded about stuff they've no' previously heard of. But nothin' could be further from the truth. Sometimes I think we're the biggest skeptics of all.

So, naturally, I scoffed. "Another dimension."

Kay just nodded with his eyebrows raised. "I know."

It suddenly dawned on me. "Do no' tell me he's been here the whole time, still starin' at that door."

"He has been here the whole time, but he's been doing a lot more than staring at a door. He's been acting as Black Swan's emissary, visiting her every day, gaining her confidence like he was some kind of spy. I gather she was held as a prisoner right up until today. They had a hearing and gave her probationary freedom of the building and grounds."

Kay leaned forward and lowered his voice. "Word is that Monq is going to give her the potential employee evaluation."

I stared at Kay. "I challenge anybody, right here and now, to find a world stranger than this one."

"I cannot accept that challenge, Sir Hawking. This one is about as strange as I can handle."

"Very well. Dinner it is."

"Good. And, if you ever ignore my outreach again, I will beat down your worthless Irish ass."

"Fair enough, brother."

Kay's face softened. "Guess you decided to come back."

"Honestly, 'twas touch and go right up until this week. But here I am."

"I'm around if you ever need to talk."

I managed a small smile, nodded, hoisted my bag, and gave a salute on my way out.

CHAPTER 7

Ram

K AY CALLED AT 7:00.
"We need to be early for dinner. Storm wants us to make a good impression."

My response was a snort and a huff. "Then he should no' be invitin' me."

"You can manage good behavior for an hour. Meet me at 7:30. We'll have time for a drink before dinner."

"I'm no' havin' drinks before dinner."

There was a long pause. "I'm sure there's a story there. And I'd like to hear it. So meet me for before dinner coffee."

"Whoever heard of before dinner coffee?"

"Just do it."

"I'm lettin' you get by with the attitude only because I feel guilty about lettin' your calls go to voicemail. But that only goes so far."

"Understood. See you at 7:30."

I was no' especially interested in Project Good Impression, but I took a shower and pulled out clean clothes. Some faded jeans. One of the AC/DC tees I bought at the concert. And my scuffed up square-toed boots.

I sat down in my usual chair, next to Kay. Truthfully I was grateful that there would be four people at the first meal back at J.U. Three would have been really hard. It made my eyes sting just thinkin' about it.

He ordered a sissy white wine. I ordered water.

"What's up with that?"

I knew what he was talkin' about. Let's say 'twas somewhat unusual for me to ask for water. I shrugged. "Had my fill of the nectar of gods. At least for the time bein'."

Kay nodded thoughtfully and was just about to reply, when we heard Sol's voice on the P.A. system. We turned to see him standin' with a mic in his hand.

He cleared his throat and everyone got quiet.

"As you know, our job involves unusual events. Sometimes they challenge our understanding of reality. One such event has taken place here at Jefferson Unit.

"For the past three months we've been hosting a visitor from another dimension. She's spent her time here recovering from wounds received as a result of pioneering a scientific exploration that was heretofore thought impossible. I trust you will make her feel welcome, as she'll be staying with us for a while. You'll get that opportunity because she'll be joining the Mess in about ten minutes. That is all."

I turned to Kay and deadpanned, "Unicorns have been spotted in the Courtpark. Give them carrots, but do no' ride. That is all."

Kay laughed. "Well, everybody can't be as entertaining

as you, Ram."

"Is that a compliment?"

"Not exactly."

I looked around the room, drummin' my fingers on the white tablecloth. I'd been asked to come to dinner early, which I had. Now I was ready for the next thing, which I hoped was dinner.

"I'm hungry. You hungry?"

"I could eat."

"Well…"

"No. We're waiting for Storm and his big surprise."

I went back to lookin' about. 'Twas then I felt the air leave my lungs and my heart started beatin' like I was in full-on chase.

Everybody stopped and stared when Storm entered the room with his hand on the small of her back. I watched her look around quickly and then smile at Krisp. She followed him, movin' with a graceful roll of her hips that made my mouth water. My eyes locked on the way the silk skirt moved when she walked, her head up like royalty.

She was tall with rockin' hair, worn down and fallin' in curls over her breasts. I usually went for brunettes, but it only took a second for me to realize that I prefer a mix of red, brown, blonde, and was that pink? If I had no' already been sittin', she would have knocked me on my ass. I knew I had to get ahold of myself and get my breathing under control before she reached the table or she was goin' to think I was a creeper.

Kay stood up when they reached the table. It was a good thing I had the prompt because I seemed to have forgotten who I was and what I was doin'.

I saw her eyes wander over Kay and then me, quick enough to make an assessment without appearin' rude.

Storm said, "This is Elora Laiken." He said it like she belonged to him, which made my blood heat up. Inexplicably. Even I knew that was an odd reaction. He nodded at us. "These are my teammates, Chaos Caelian and Rammel Hawking, a.k.a. Kay and Ram."

Kay said, "Wow. You've changed a lot since the last time I saw you."

She raised her chin, givin' every impression that she thought herself the same height, and smiled at him. "Have we met then?" She extended her hand in a gracious and ladylike way. She had the sort of manners my mum would approve of.

Next she turned her attention to me, again holdin' out her hand. I took it, feelin' electric tingles run up my arm and continue to invade my entire body.

When I nodded slightly and said, "Hello," she jerked her hand away like she'd been burned. The friendly look in her eyes was replaced with a glare.

Now I'm no' one to get embarrassed easily, but I could feel a rush of blood to my face. Since when does sayin' hello get that sort of reaction?

I settled on a simple and direct inquiry. "What's wrong?"

If I had to choose a word to describe her posture and demeanor, I'd say she looked haughty. And pissed!

"Your voice is what's wrong, Mr. Hawking. It sounds very much like one I've heard before saying, 'Kill it. Kill it now.'"

Ah. The old chickens comin' home to roost. She no' only remembered what was said, but had put my voice to it as well. *Great Paddy*, I thought. *I'm screwed.*

I looked down at my feet tryin' to decide on a way forward. When I glanced up, I could see that everybody in the Mess was starin' like it was a show. I let the room know exactly how I felt about that.

"Hey!" I shouted. "Find something else to do, for Paddy's sake!" Turnin' back to my teammates, I lowered my voice and added, "Wankers," so only they would hear.

It was gratifyin' to see the spectators choose the prudent course of action and return to mindin' their own fuckin' business. Sometimes it pays to have a reputation for bein' unpredictable.

I'm no' much of a game player. I take life straight on. Saves everybody a whole lot of time and energy if you keep your cards above the table and act like you're no' afraid to play 'em.

I leaned into her, smilin' on the inside because I could see that it disarmed her and put her a little off balance. I looked straight into turquoise eyes that I could get lost in and lowered my voice to a level of intimacy.

"Naturally I regret that, my girl. Please accept my apology."

I said it with sincerity and hoped she heard that because, in fact, I was sorry about what I'd said. No' nearly as sorry as I would have been if I'd been taken up on my advice to kill her. I guess I have Storm to thank for the fact that termination was never really considered.

She did no' answer at first, just stared at me like she'd never seen an act of contrition. The fact is, I felt I'd never wanted anything in my life as much as I wanted her forgiveness. I would have begged for it if it came to that, in front of everyone.

I leaned in even closer and whispered, "Do no' be mad."

I could tell the moment she decided to let the grudge go. She relaxed in a way that made me want to drag her close and make her body mold to mine. I could no' help but smile. In fact I had to resist the urge to grin. But something told me it would be a mistake to let her see how much power she had over me. Already. Within a few minutes. That could only mean one thing. My mate had found me. And she'd crossed worlds to do it, at great expense to her beautiful self.

The other revelation, fast on the heels of the first, was that she was no' elf, but human. 'Tis rare, but it does happen. I never imagined that it would happen to me, but I'm no' questionin' the Fates.

I leaned in again. Wantin' to impress her with the fact that I'm a bona fide knight of The Order of the Black Swan, I said, "If we're goin' formal, 'tis Sir Hawking when we're on these premises, but I'd like it if you'd call me Ram."

She took a little step back from me which only served to excite my inner predator. I could feel Storm and Kay watchin' the exchange and wished to Paddy they were doin' something else, preferably somewhere far, far away.

She said, "Okay."

'Twas the sweetest acquiescence I could hope for. I had the urge to repeat it and savor the sound in my mouth. But I did no'. I forced myself to look away and sit down. As nonchalant as if she were any other female.

"Let's eat," I said.

Storm pulled out her chair, which made me grind my teeth. I should be the one doin' that.

I sat in my usual spot, Kay on my left, the wall on my right. Elora Laiken was in the chair across from me that used to be occupied by Lan. Somehow havin' her there kept me from crumblin' into a mess.

I'd spent three months lookin' for a distraction and, by Paddy, here she was. The grand lottery of all distractions in one heavenly body.

I brought my attention back to the conversation when I heard Kay say,

"So, welcome to Jefferson Unit."

She gave him a friendly enough smile and said, "Thank you. Until today I haven't really seen anything except the infirmary." She looked down at the table, then quietly added, "And the Chamber room."

An image of what she'd looked like when she was an indiscernible thing flashed into my mind and I wanted nothin' more than to kick my own ass for no' recognizin' that the awful feelin's were nature's hard-wired empathy for the pain of a mate. 'Twas when I first realized nothin' would ever be the same again.

It also made me wonder how much of the pain and feelin's of loss I'd suffered the past three months were from grief over Lan's death and how much of 'twas about walkin' out on my mate when she was in unimaginable distress. *Great Paddy.* 'Twas in that moment I knew I'd no' ever deserve her if I did my utmost for a thousand years hence.

After the four of us gave Krisp our orders, Kay asked her, "So far what's the biggest difference between your world and ours?"

Without a moment's hesitation, she said, "Vampire. That's plural." She looked around the table. "The plural of vampire is vampire, right?"

So she'd been readin' the manual.

Kay asked, "How do you know?"

"Black Swan Field Training Manual, Section One, Chapter One, Number One," she said as matter of fact as if she had a photographic memory.

Kay shook his head. "I mean, how do you know there aren't vampire in your dimension? Only a tiny fraction of our population knows that our world is crawling with them."

"Crawling?" she asked.

"Okay. Maybe crawling is a bit much. I guess it just seems that way to us sometimes."

Aye. 'Crawling' was an exaggeration, but it *did* seem that way to us sometimes. Honestly, I could no' help but marvel at how the general population could be so clueless about what was goin' on right 'round them. It was almost like they purposefully fitted themselves with blinders.

As you can imagine, I had no' been able to take my eyes away from Elora Laiken since she arrived in the Mess. I mean, there's only one first time for meetin' your mate.

Right?

All of a sudden she was lookin' straight at me, askin' why I was starin'? My first thought was to say, "How could I no'?" But before I answered, Kay spoke up.

"Don't let him bother you. Elves are not known for manners."

Just what I needed. My own teammate, who was happily engaged to be married, was tryin' to sabotage my only chance to make a memorable first impression. I was hopin' to get the message across that he was out of line. So I said, "Oh. And berserkers are the essence of Miss Emily Post, I suppose?"

I was glarin' at Kay when I heard her say, "What do you mean, elves?"

Kay smirked at me before lookin' at her and sayin', "You know. Elves. Pointy ears? Big feet?"

At that point I could see my back-off message was no' gettin' through to the big lummox and I was feelin' the temperature in my blood risin' fast. Great Paddy! What was the bloody man thinkin'? I mean, my feet are no' especially big for an elf and I might add that, unlike humans, I do no' get knocked down easily. O' course, since I also have a dick to match, 'tis something else I have on humans.

While I was contemplatin' punchin' Kay's block so he'd have to walk sideways for a while, I heard her say something that I never could have anticipated or prepared for in a hundred years. I know I was already heated up by Kay's shenanigans, but when she said, "You mean like in fairy tales?", it pushed my temper right over the edge.

I did no' know exactly what she was tryin' to say, but it sounded like she was thinkin' I was a fairy. *Great Paddy's balls in a bag!* My mate, who gave no indication of recognizin' me as her mate, was thinkin' I was a fairy? 'Twas hard enough that she did no' fall into my arms, as any elf would have done. No. The Fates seemed to have chosen me to play with. My mate was no' only human, but from another world. And I could tell that she did no' see me as anything special. The best I could hope for was to set that straight.

Sometimes my body gets ahead of my brain, as happened in that case. I was so anxious to correct the misimpression that I stood up too quickly.

"I am no' a fairy!" I heard the indignation in my voice and immediately regretted soundin' like I was scoldin' her. If she did no' think me an asshole for that, the fact that I'd stood too quickly and knocked over my chair in the process... well, I did no' want her to think of me as a hothead even if she had just called me a fuckin' fairy. At least no' at our first meetin'.

I looked around and noticed every bugger in the Mess had gone quiet again, starin' at me like 'twas a show. I pushed down the impulse to yell at them again, picked up my chair and took a seat. While I was contemplatin' that my mate had taken me for the worst creature in the world, I heard Storm tryin' to make a half-arsed explanation.

"Elves and fae have been at war for over a thousand years. They hate each other." He glanced at me, then added, "A lot."

She looked confused, either like she did no' understand or did no' believe. Without knowin' her better, it was impossible to tell. She studied me as if she was tryin' to come to a conclusion. When she finally spoke, she asked Kay to change places with her.

She came 'round the table and seated herself next to me, which felt like all the wrongs of the world had just been righted, then stared at me close up. Her hand came toward the side of my face, but she stopped, slid her eyes to look into mine and asked, "May I?"

I swallowed hard, havin' no idea what she was askin', but also knowin' that the answer was aye to whatever 'twas.

I did my best to control the shiver that gripped my body when I felt her touch my hair. She lifted it away and when her finger touched the tip of my left ear, there was no amount of will that could suppress my body's reaction. Settin' my conspicuous shudder aside, what happened next was a moment frozen in time in my mind.

Great Paddy. She lit up the room with a grin that made me think she'd finally recognized me as the *one*. I was ready to haul her into my lap when she said, "In your world, do you not have a collection of stories called fairy tales?"

I was no' sure how to react or why she'd given me such a heart-stoppin' smile, but I knew she still did no' know. I shook my head, feelin' both disappointed and more than annoyed that the word 'fairy' had been introduced to dinner conversation for a second time in one evenin'.

For once I chose my words carefully. "Sounds most

disturbin'."

She smiled and said, "Well, there are some that are rather unpleasant, but most are magical and charming. These stories feature mythical creatures that do not exist in my world. Creatures like fairies, elves, dragons and ogres." She continued to stare at me for another minute, then, lookin' around the table, she said, "Are there also dragons and ogres here?"

I looked at Storm and Kay. They looked at me. All three of us were shakin' our heads. Kay appeared to be tryin' no' to laugh. Storm appeared to be exercisin' patience. I was just shakin' my head and wonderin' what the Paddy I'd got into with this woman. I mean, I know what a dragon is. 'Tis a mythological fire-breathing, flyin' reptile. So I made the only logical reply open to me.

"What's an ogre?"

She thought about it for a few seconds and, when she turned those turquoise eyes on me, I was givin' myself the high fives that I had been the one to ask the question and make her look my way. My eyes drifted down to the light freckles sprinkled across the bridge of her nose. They were the kind that'd be hard to see if you were no' close up, where I wanted to be for the next several eternities in a row. Simply enchantin'.

My eyes were drawn downward when she opened her mouth to speak. "It's a big ugly brute."

"Well," I said, "then we may have been wrong. Sounds very much like a description of Sol."

Storm nodded, Kay laughed, and Elora just seemed to be waitin' to see what would happen next.

Kay waxed on. For the one of us who was usually the quietest, his tongue seemed to be doin' jigs and cartwheels for my mate. "It does raise an interesting question though. If there are no elves in your world, then how do you know about elves?"

Our server interrupted the query by arrivin' at that moment. I noticed that she had no' asked to return to her chair across the table and took it as a sign of growin' acceptance, if no' affection. I might no' be able to touch her, but I was close enough to smell the scent of, well, shampoo or soap or perfume or maybe just her. I did no' care whether or no' 'twas identified. I just wanted to keep breathing her in.

She was like a drug to me. I wanted more and more and could no' imagine doin' without.

"Are these nuts on top of my chicken?" she asked.

"Uh, yeah," Storm answered, lookin' amused. "Pieces. I think it's pecan. Looks good. Give me a bite and I'll tell you for sure."

Without a word she went about complyin' with his request, extendin' a fork laden with pecan-crusted chicken across the table. He took it in his mouth and hummed approval.

"Oh, yeah. Pecan pieces. Do you like it?"

She tasted it and smiled. "I do. So what do you have there?"

"Seared salmon with an Alfredo pasta. Want a bite?"

She nodded, lookin' eager as a child at her first fair. "That is good. Can I have that tomorrow night?"

Storm chuckled. "Of course. What have they been

feeding you in the infirmary?"

She shrugged. "Mostly stuff without color that doesn't require much chewing."

Storm looked serious. "Sounds like they didn't make a distinction for you, but just gave you the regular hospital diet. Sorry. I should have been paying more attention."

"I didn't complain."

"I know," he said, looking at her like she was a miracle.

And I was feelin' a heady resentment comin' on all the while a little voice kept chidin' that 'twas my own fault for walkin' away from her to go drinkin' and... Great Paddy. I'm a worthless bastard.

She went 'round the table, took bites of my lollipopped lamb and Kay's twenty-one-days marinated steak. Rare, of course.

When that game was done to her satisfaction, she brought the conversation back to Kay's question about elves. They talked at length about elves as if they were debatin' angels dancin' on pinheads.

Ridiculous.

When she finally changed the subject, 'twas without segue. "What's a berserker?" After a concise and clinical explanation a la Storm, she said, "So you're saying berserkers go out of control?"

I laughed, intendin' it to sound derisive because I realized it was my chance to repay Kay for the 'big feet' comment. "Out of control? Wacked up insane motherfuckers is what they are."

She turned and stared at me. I shoved a bite of lamb

into my mouth, hopin' it made me look unconcerned about the fact that my teammates were also starin'.

"What?" I challenged them both, sittin' together across the table, but she distracted us all before they answered.

"Where I am from, your accent would be typical in a place called Ireland. Is there such a place here?"

'Twas oddly comfortin' to know that Ireland existed even in Elora's dimension of origin. "Aye. 'Tis my home. We've had a truce with the fairies for two hundred years. We do no' go to Scotia uninvited and they do no' cross the borders of Ireland or Wales. Except on preapproved business." I could no' stop myself from askin', "Do you like my accent?"

She smiled shyly as her eyes slid sideways toward me and said, "Sure." Then she gave a most beguilin' little shake of her head. "Musical."

"I'd like to hear these fairy tales," I said, "but would like them all the more should they be called elf tales."

She laughed out loud and I reveled in hearin' the sound for the first time.

TWO MORE TIMES during dinner she turned to me with a funny look on her face, and pushed my hair back to look at my ear, like she thought it might have magically changed since the last time she saw it. No' that I minded. I would have leapt at any excuse to have her focus her attention on me. The fact that she touched me in the process was a boon. Both times gave me shivers that probably reached my toes, but the sensation concentrated at my groin, so I can no' say for sure.

Several knights stopped by the table. While Storm made introductions, I glared at each and every one, but they were too interested in the new arrival to notice my very sincere, if silent, warnin'.

The woman was a charmer for sure. She could no' be faulted for manners and I could no' help thinkin' that even my mother would approve of Elora Laiken. Except that she was human, o' course. She shook hands, smiled, and repeated every one of their names like she intended to remember.

WHEN DESSERT CAME, the reception line scattered. At least they had sense enough to know it would be rude to interrupt sweets. And 'twas one of my favorites.

I dug in, but then saw that she was simply starin' at the plate.

"Do you no' like it?"

She dropped her chin and looked at me, quietly sayin', "What is it?"

"Black Forest Cake with raspberry sauce."

Her brows came together in a charmin' display of confusion. "I know what raspberries are," she said.

"Aye. One of nature's best expressions of juicy goodness. The stuff under the sauce is chocolate cake." She looked dubious. "Chocolate is strange to you?" She nodded.

I leaned toward her and matched her quiet tone. "Just take a bite. Chances are good that you'll like it."

The slight adjustment of the set of her mouth told me she was no' goin' to back down from a challenge, even one that was as slight and silly as darin' her to eat cake. The other two chimed in, sayin', "Yeah. You've gotta give it a shot."

She picked up her fork and glanced around the table at the three of us all watchin' and took a weensy little bite. I shall never forget what happened next if I live to be a thousand. She closed her lips around that cake and moaned. MOANED, I tell you. 'Twas like nothin' I'd ever heard. My cock jumped to attention like she'd taken it out of my pants and begun strokin'. That was alarmin' on so many levels. I mean I'm healthy to be sure, but I'm a decade past bein' randy as a lad.

I had forgotten all about eatin' my own cake as, apparently, had Storm. I say 'apparently' because he had an untouched piece to offer when she'd finished scarfin' down her own like a rugby player.

She looked down at the offerin' and flushed just a bit before askin', "Are you sure?" But she attacked the cake like she had no' eaten in weeks before he reconfirmed his intention to give up the treat.

I was captivated by the sight of her inhalin' Storm's cake, moanin' and makin' excruciatin'ly sexy yummy sounds the whole time. She looked at the plate like she'd love to pick it up and lick it, just before her head turned toward me. I could only hope that someday she would look at me with the sort of desire she was showin' my dessert.

"I'd be honored to have you try mine as well," I said as I picked up the little plate.

She opened her beautiful mouth and was clearly about

to say aye, at least that was my impression, when she realized my teammates were havin' a laugh at her expense. She blushed in embarrassment which brought out my protective instincts and made me want to hang both the buggers by their balls.

"Do no' mind them," I said. "After what you've been through, you should have as much chocolate as you want, whenever you want it." I wanted to go on adding, *"And anything else your heart desires. Please let that include me."* But I knew that would sound wacked to a human. So I let the gift of cake be a pale proxy for a declaration of intent.

"No, thank you." She gave me a smile that was somewhat more reserved and tense. "I've had enough."

"No such thing as enough," I said. "Less is no' more. More is more." That got me a bigger smile.

WE PARTED WAYS at the Hub. The three of us were goin' for our usual after dinner drink, which was a ritualized indulgence on nights off. I offered to see her to her apartment, but she said, "No. This will be my first time on my own and I'm looking forward to being unescorted. Thank you, though."

I nodded and watched her walk away, all the while thinkin' that I had suggested killin' my own mate the night she'd arrived broken, torn, and covered with so much blood it was a miracle she'd survived it.

I realized I was grindin' my teeth recallin' what Storm had said about spendin' time with her every day, watchin' her recovery, gettin' to know her. Paddy. I'm a livin', breathing idiot. I'd been tryin' to play my blues away while

Storm was situatin' himself as her… well, I was no' sure what, but I could say for sure that I did no' like the easy familiarity with which he regarded her. And her him. Did no' like it in the least.

I walked after my teammates. Kay turned around when he saw that I was laggin'.

"You coming?" he asked with a hint of classic Kay everything-amuses-me.

I was no' really grousin' about his laid-back style. No' since I'd seen the other side of that coin.

I'd been lost in my effort to place that beguilin' scent of hers. What was it? Oh aye. Wild jasmine in full bloom. So intoxicatin' it could bring a grown man to a standstill at fifteen feet. My thoughts immediately jumped to a listin' of her physical virtues, the long legs, curves, and, oh, that hair. I'd be dreamin' about buryin' myself in that hair.

Could no' help but smile at that image.

Kay interrupted my private thoughts for the second time in two minutes. "What's so funny?"

I suppressed the urge to tell the fellow 'twas none of his business and attempted to appease him by sayin', "Just thinkin' about how much cake she ate. Never seen a body enjoy food so much."

"Um hum."

There was a distinct element of distrust in his tone, but I did no' care. 'Twas a right special occasion even if I could no' make a public celebration of it. No' yet anyway.

CHAPTER 8

Ram

I WAS ON my way down to the meetin' in the Sovereign's office. After a sleepless night, thinkin' about the beautiful human, I was hopin' to grab a coffee and wake up a bit first. To my surprise and great pleasure, I found the object of my every desire emergin' from the apartment next door. I had no idea they'd put her next to me.

"Good day." I gave her a smile that'd never failed me with the lasses then added, "Ms. Laiken."

"Call me Elora." She smiled in return and it seemed genuine enough. I was thinkin' 'twas a good enough start, but when she pulled the door closed, I saw her glance at the faded rectangle where Lan's name plate had been and she winced. Her colorin' came up, turnin' her face pink, and I could see she was uncomfortable. "I know this was your, uh, friend's quarters. I hope you don't mind. It's just temporary."

By that time I was beside her. "'Tis fine, Elora. Tis no' like he's usin' it." I knew that was the wrong thing to say as soon as her eyes went wide and I realized how callous it must have sounded. So I tried to clarify with a wordier explanation. "Lan was no' the sort who would want a memorial made of his quarters. He loved women and would relish knowin' you're the one sleepin' in his bed. Temporary or no'."

She cocked her head to one side as her eyes narrowed with mock suspicion. "So. You're a silver-tongued elf."

No' lookin' at her sweet mouth after hearin' a mention of tongue would have been utterly impossible. Perhaps Kay might have had the willpower for such a feat, but no' I. With effort I drew my eyes back up to hers.

"No." I smiled seductively. At least I hoped so. "My tongue is sweet. Regular and pink. Will you come have a taste then and see if I'm true?"

I leaned in to kiss her, but she took a step back lookin' like she was certain I was daft.

"Anyway," she said, "it was a generous and gracious thing for you to say. About me occupying Lan's apartment, I mean."

"Well," I rocked back on my heels and laughed softly, "that's another first. I assure you I've never been accused of bein' generous and gracious before."

She studied me for a second before sayin', "Perhaps people don't know the real you." Yeah. Or perhaps they did. But if she wanted to think better of me, I was no' goin' to be the instrument of obstruction. "What's the other first?"

"Beautiful stranger from another world."

"Oh."

I had no' intended my compliment to dampen the mood. I was in the process of tryin' to learn to read her and, if I was guessin' right, references to the home she'd involuntarily left behind were on the taboo list. 'Twas time for a shift of topic.

"So, where are you off to?" I asked. We started toward the elevator, but I was gratified to see that she was in no bigger hurry than I was.

"The Hub. Coffee bar. Only I'm not getting coffee."

"Let me guess."

She did a little thing with her hand that I took to mean something like, "Go ahead and try."

"Judgin' by the way you devoured the Black Forest cake last night which, by the way, was quite something to see and hear, I'm thinkin' you'll be after more chocolate."

She grinned in a way that let me know I was right. "Hot chocolate. It comes in liquid form. I discovered it at breakfast this morning and am thinking about forming a Cult of Chocolate."

"It also comes in cold liquid form as chocolate milk. Humans are addicted before they have teeth."

"Good to know." She said it seriously as if she meant that she was actually glad for the information.

"So you were already out for breakfast earlier?"

"Yes. Storm took me on a tour."

I felt every muscle in my body tense so that the best I could manage was a stupid, "Oh?"

She'd had breakfast with stick-up-the-butt and learned all about hot chocolate from him.

I was schemin' up ways to get him out of the picture, when she asked, "Where are you, um, headed?"

"Something no' nearly so fun as chocolate." The elevator doors opened and my mood turned sour in spite of Elora's presence. "A discussion about replacin' Lan with a new fourth team member."

"Oh. Storm said something about a meeting. Sounds dreadful. For all of you."

"That about sums it up." I did no' want to leave our chance encounter like that, so I coughed up a bit of man-on-the-street philosophy. "Life goes on, right?"

I managed to say that out loud, but it felt like it landed at my feet with a leaden thud.

She nodded, but looked sympathetic. Lovin' the fact that she seemed to have a compassionate nature, I said, "I'm goin' down another floor. You know your way? How to get there and back?"

"Oh yes, I've known how to get to the Hub ever since the day of my hearing." She stepped out and turned to give me a little smile and a chest-high wave with her right hand that was adorable as kittens.

I nodded goodbye but held the elevator for a few more seconds for the pure pleasure of watchin' her walk away. I knew I'd never get enough of that so long as I lived. My thoughts were consumed with images of Elora Laiken comin' and goin', when I remembered that she'd said something about a 'hearing'. As soon as the dadblasted meetin' was over, I was goin' to the library for a copy.

CHAPTER 9

Ram

WHEN I GOT off the elevator on sublevel two and started toward Sol's office, my thoughts turned to the reason why I was there and my feet immediately started feelin' heavy. I pushed on, slowly, wishin' I'd got up early enough to have coffee first. Wishin' I was any place in the world except a few steps away from a discussion about replacin' my partner. Everything about that felt wrong. As if it was no' hard enough buryin' Lan, now we were tryin' to erase his memory altogether by puttin' some fucker in his place.

MY TEAMMATES WERE already there, lookin' grim, which was appropriate. Lan was more than a friend to the two of them as well.

I grabbed a coffee in the outer office, then took a seat on the couch next to the wall. I was glad that seat was still available because I wanted to be in the furthest possible place away from the proceedin'. That was an empty desire because Sol's office was no' that big. Still, I could detach a little.

Sol watched with an unspoken reprimand on his face as I sat down. *Paddy.* I was only three minutes late. Kay sat at the other end of the couch nearest the exit. Storm closed the office door and stood with his back against the wall facin' the desk that represented the seat of power at Jefferson Unit.

After clearin' his throat, Sol said, "You know the purpose of this meeting." I slouched down into the couch to register my disdain for the purpose of the meetin'. The sovereign's eyes tracked the movement and he looked at me pointedly. "I'm not unsympathetic to your feelings. Like I told you before, I've been in your shoes. But the fact remains that a patrol team is four members, not three. There are centuries-old reasons for that. Good ones. So let's strap on our character and get on with it."

I snorted and looked out the window. People often overlook the merits of a good snort. Nothin' else matches its derisive qualities. I first began to pursue the snort as an art form in response to outrageous modes of conformity expressed by my father and brother.

I wondered if Sol's function as sovereign made me prickly because it was far too close to the authority expressed by kings and king wannabes.

O' course he was right. About all of it. Plus, he had a job to do and it was unfair of me to make him the scapegoat for my feelin's, but puttin' things in a more mature perspective did no' make my heart any more interested in discussin' another partner.

Like the professional he was, Sol continued, refusin' to take the bait of my rebellious antics, which was a shame because I'd have much rather talked about my lack of character than replacin' Lan.

"I've got a short list, but of course the three of you have final say about your fourth."

After a few beats Storm crossed his arms and jerked his chin toward the paper sitting on Sol's desk. "Who are you thinking?"

"First is Ghost, naturally."

An involuntary chuff was forced from my lungs. I mean, I'm fairly easy goin', but I did no' like that guy. 'Twas no' just his looks either, although 'twas hard to look at his albino pink rimmed eyes. There was something about him that went beyond creep and my instincts told me I'd never trust him to have my back. My initial reaction was to say I'd quit The Order before I partnered with him.

Sol gave me a look and then read the other three. "Finnemore. Sanction. Blytheson."

I looked out the window, which was no' a real window since we were in sublevel two. It was actually a monitor showing a camera view of the courtpark two floors above us. Still, it was more interestin' than anything goin' on in the room where I sat.

The only sound in the room was a big sigh from Kay. Storm was either lookin' at his feet or the carpet. I glanced at Sol with a look of malice I did no' feel towards him, just the situation. I knew it was immature as hel, but if Lan was replaced, I'd have to face the fact once and for all that he was gone and no' comin' back.

I had turned back to studyin' the camera view of the

courtpark, when I heard Storm say, "Let us have a day to mull it over. Sleep on it maybe."

Sol answered without hesitation. "Sure. Same time tomorrow."

I was out the door and headed toward the elevator when I heard Storm call from behind. "Where you going, Ram? We've got to talk about this."

I kept goin', pushed the button, but waited for Storm and Kay. When they caught up, I said, "I'm thinkin' we can talk just as easily with six tablespoonfuls of fine Irish Whiskey poured over ice."

Nothin' more was said until after we were sittin' in the plump corner chairs next to the gas fire. The day was overcast, which seemed fittin' somehow. The lounge was deserted except for us. And the bartender.

"What'll it be, gentlemen?" The barkeep's eyebrows were raised, probably because it was early in the day for drinkin' and he had no' expected to be workin'. But spirits were invented to give balance to a sober occasion like that one.

We sat in silence, each with his own thoughts, until after drinks were served. Kay thanked the bartender and said, "Keep 'em coming."

After a couple of minutes, Storm said, "Okay. Let's come up with ground rules. I say that, if all three of us say no to somebody on the list, we draw a line through his name." Kay nodded. I let Storm pretend to be 'leader' more often than no' because I was too lazy to care about callin' the shots. I figured if he wanted responsibility, let him have it. "Finnemore. Yes or no."

"Finnemore is a wanker," I said. Actually Finnemore was a likable guy and a worthy knight. I had nothin' against him except that he was no' Lan.

Storm gave me a look callin' me out on the petulance, but I did no' own it as I should have. I gave him a defiant stare-down like an adolescent. He responded by treatin' me like I was one.

"Yes. Or. No."

I raised my eyebrows in challenge and mocked the fake patience. I might have been actin' like a fool, but I was still a knight. "That. Would. Be. A. No."

Kay glanced at me and nodded, "I agree. It's a no. But, look, Sol's right. This is no fun for any of us. Also, it's time somebody said it out loud. Lan's death was nobody's fault. Not his. Not ours. We all wish there was somebody to blame so that we could...." He paused and sighed. "Well, so we could blame them. But there isn't. Let's put a lid on the tempers and move on."

Storm looked at Kay for a moment and then said, "Unanimous. Finnemore is out. That leaves three."

After also eliminating Sanction and Blytheson, that left Ghost, who also was considered, theoretically, to be next in line for the job.

Storm read right off the sheet. "Gauthier Nibelung, a.k.a. Ghost. Age thirty. Field active eight years." Storm set the paper down, rather than read the rest of the resume. "He's in line. He'll be expecting to be called up. And he probably deserves it." Storm ran a hand through his hair and sighed. "What do you think?"

"I think this fuckin' stinks," I said.

"Sol agreed to give us the night to think about it. Why don't you meet me at my place in the morning? I'll have coffee. Get egg sandwiches or something sent up. We'll have another chance to talk it over before we give Sol our decision."

Kay nodded. "Okay."

I looked 'round the room and said, "I'm goin' for a workout."

"That's a good idea," Storm said. "Clear your head. And, Ram…" I looked up at him. "We don't like this either. If they'd let us patrol as three, Kay and I would agree to it, even knowing it's risky."

Why'd he have to go and say that?

I felt my eyes fill up. I jerked my head away. I mean, those two guys were my teammates, but that did no' mean I wanted them to see me cry. I was strugglin' to keep tears from fallin' when I felt them spill down my cheeks. I swiped the sleeve of my shirt over my eyes, hatin' my body for betrayin' me so. "Gotta get out of here." I practically ran for the elevator, keepin' my head down and hopin' my face had no' gone girlie pink. *Great Paddy.* I was losin' it.

JEFFERSON UNIT PRIDED itself on its fitness center and rightfully so. It was huge, took up the lion's share of sublevel three.

I grabbed three guys out of the weight room to have a spar with me. The distraction of hittin' a willin' body was just what I needed to take the edge off.

On the way down to the spar room with the fancy suspended floor, Paltrorn said, "So you had dinner with the new arrival last night."

"New arrival?"

"Don't play dumber than you are, Hawking. I'm talking about the gorgeous babe."

"Oh, aye. I did have dinner with her." I stopped in front of the closed door and faced him. "If the next words out of your mouth are disrespectful in any way, this spar is goin' to leave you needin' sheet time."

I punctuated that with a warnin' look as I grabbed the door handle and pulled it open with a swoosh. *Message delivered and received.* And who should be sittin' in the middle of a mat doin' stretches, wearin' clothing fit so snug that no curve or attribute was left to imagination? 'Twas the devil herself. My mate.

Baglio whistled under his breath and got the same look I'd just given Paltrorn.

I walked straight to the mat, took the eighteen-inch hop without effort and crawled through the braided wire.

"Hey," I said.

"Hey," she replied in kind. Glancin' at the men behind me, she said, "I was just going."

"No need. We were just goin' to spar a little. Stay and watch."

"Um. Alright. Maybe for a minute."

The four of us laced on gloves, paired up, and engaged each other Swan-style martial arts. Elora was a distraction, no doubt about it. I could no' help but glance her way to see if she was appropriately impressed. After a few minutes, she came to the ropes and seemed to be tryin' to get my attention. My sparrin' partner looked at me like,

"What the hel?" So I put him down with a punch, and turned to her with a smile.

"What can I do for you, darlin'?"

"Might I try this?"

I could no' have been more confused if she'd asked to take her tights down and pee in the middle of the mat. Honestly, my thoughts were such a scramble, I could no' immediately think of a response.

O' course I did no' want to say no to her. Ever. So I decided the only thing to do was to let her take a turn and control the situation so she did no' get hurt. I could no' help but grin. It was sort of cute that she wanted to try fightin'. *Go figure.*

"Sure," I said, "if you promise to go easy on me. I'm a workin' lad." I nodded toward Baglio. "Give her your gloves, will you, mate?"

Baglio looked at me like I was standin' at the gate of the looney bin askin' for a half day leave, but he shook his head and began pullin' on the laces with his teeth.

While he helped her get into the gloves, she said, "What are the rules?"

"The rules?" I inquired stupidly.

With a little smile, she said, "No rules. Okay. What's the goal of the exercise?"

"The goal?" Great Paddy. I was gettin' stupider by the second. "Um, to keep us in fightin' shape?"

Since women were never on the exercise level at the same time as knights, that alone was an oddity. But if you add to that a woman sparrin' with a knight, you can imagine the significance of the event.

"Okay. The rules. Easy. Simple. No bitin'. Vampire hunters have a thing about teeth. And keep it above the belt." I grinned in spite of the seriousness of my declaration. "I need the boys in workin' order."

"The boys?"

I walked close and leaned into her so that only she would hear. To her credit, she did no' back away. "Cock and balls."

She jerked her face up to me and reddened slightly. Paddy, that spark in her eyes made her so beautiful, it was everything I could do to keep from draggin' her into me and kissin' her into belief. I was gettin' the feelin' that there was a lot more about this girl to be discovered.

When the gloves were secure, she first dropped her hands to her sides. My first hint that I was out of my depth was when I saw the fire light behind her eyes. That smile told me that maybe I'd been played.

She raised her hands and took on the demeanor of a seasoned fighter just before she began to circle me. Instinctively, I moved when she did, mirrorin' every step. If I stopped, she angled her body away defensively. 'Twas clear she'd had some trainin'. Keepin' her from gettin' hurt could prove harder than I thought.

The look of concentration on her face would have been alarmin' if she'd no' been female.

I heard a blast of cursin' behind me comin' from someone doin' a damn good imitation of Storm. It could no' be Storm because he held swearin' in about the same csteem as the sovereign, meanin' he did no' approve. There were also a few real words thrown into the tirade like reckless, stupid, immature, and punk.

Glancin' over I saw that it was indeed Storm standin' off to the side with Kay and, apparently, they'd brought a crowd with them. Seemed like a good time to wind things down.

I thought I'd reach out and give her a little tap on the outer left bicep. No' enough to bruise, just enough to be a good excuse to quit. I faked goin' left then stepped in for a baby jab.

It never landed.

Actually I was no' sure what did happen until I watched the video days later, when I could breathe again. All I knew was that one second I was in the process of deliverin' a playful jab. The next I was in the air fallin' backward on the way to bein' slammed into the mat.

The air was forcibly evacuated from my body and was refusin' to return. I thought I was goin' to die, but entertained the surreal thought that at least I'd die lookin' at her. She was bendin' over me, lookin' scared, like she had no idea she was capable of doin' damage.

When my lungs recovered from the shock enough to start workin' again, I sucked in a tanker full of air, but it hurt like the dickens. Knowin' I was no' goin' to die was something of a relief, but the pain that accompanied that breath was anything but comfortin'. I've had the air knocked out of me before and know what to expect. This was no' it.

I tried to sit up, but the zinger punched a yell out of my mouth that startled even me. I lay back, Elora was still bendin' over me with a worried look.

"Bloody Paddy's Day, woman! I told you to go easy on me. I think you broke a fuckin' rib!"

Her mouth worked silently for a minute before she got out, "Ram, I'm…oh, gods… I'm so sorry. This is not…. I've executed that move a thousand times and I've never injured anybody. What can I do?" She started tuggin' at the glove laces with her teeth, but then Storm came into view, standin' behind her.

"Stay still, Ram," he said in that calm, okay-everybody-I'm-in-charge way of his. "Med's coming. Let them take a look before you move."

If you've never had a broken rib, there's no point tryin' to explain, past sayin' it hurts. The new wrinkle was that 'twas just as bad seein' those turquoise eyes droppin' tears on my chest.

Bein' someone's mate was new to me. I mean, o' course you hear all the stories, but nothin' prepares you for the compulsion you feel to make things right for your female. I could no' stand seein' her in distress.

"Shhhh. 'Tis probably no' more than bruised ego. Stop now before you make me cry, too."

When the doc arrived, Storm pulled Elora up and away to make room. He knelt down next to me and pushed 'round tryin' to see if he could make me scream. I swear all medics are sadists.

"Get me a wheelchair," the doc said. "It's probably a broken rib, but we're going to need an x-ray to tell how bad and how many."

I heard a murmur wave through the spectators just before a loud gruff voice said, "What the hel happened here?"

Sol swearin'? That was two for two in less than an hour.

I may no' be rememberin' perfectly because it was difficult to think about anything except the pain in my ribcage when I breathed in, even worse when I breathed out, but Storm seemed to be managin' the situation and was maneuverin' the sovereign out of the room.

The only thing I had to say to that was, "Good."

The medics trotted me through the routine in the infirmary. Like I said, it was a busted rib.

I was sittin' on the side of a bed. The tape helped and so did the pain meds, undoubtedly. Still, I was experimentin' with findin' a way to avoid breathing.

Kay and Storm came through the door with an athletic force that reminded me of what I must have looked like an hour before. Elora was with them, but lingerin' on the threshold.

Kay shook his head. "What were you thinking?" Without stoppin' for a reply, as if he assumed I was no' thinkin', he went on. "It's a fracture. Six weeks off rotation, with NO strain on the rib. We're going to get you up to your own bed so you can sleep for a couple of days."

Storm brought the wheelchair over, locked it in place, and presented his forearm for me to grab onto. That was a lot of information to process through the haze of pain and pain meds. Off rotation another six weeks? That meant the decision about replacin' Lan could also be delayed six weeks. Worth the price of a broken rib every day of the year. I should find a way to thank the lass proper.

I had to lean 'round Storm to keep her in sight, which was no' comfortable, but definitely worth it. She was still standin' there in the doorway chewin' on her bottom lip like she was afraid I'd be prosecutin' for assault. Cute.

"You hungry?" Storm asked.

I shook my head no. "Loopy. Sleepy."

Kay helped me get a shirt on, then pushed me through the halls, through the Hub, and into the elevator. Yeah. O' course it was humiliatin' to know everybody was sayin' that a decorated knight was laid flat by a human female. *Paddy.* I would never live it down. But I had bigger problems. Like tryin' to figure out how she did it.

Kay backed the wheelchair into the elevator, then Storm and Elora got on. She skittered to the side of the car and put her back against the wall. When I looked up at her, I saw only sympathy on her face. She mouthed, "I'm sorry."

I started to shrug, but the movement made me wince, which in turn made her drop her head.

At my door I punched in the code and the three of them entered. Kay helped me out of my pants and into the bed.

"Your pain med is in the kitchen," he said. "Take one every six hours *as needed*. Do not take more than that. I'm leaving your phone right here by the bed. If you need anything, call one of us and we'll be here in five minutes."

I nodded. He turned to leave. "Kay." He stopped. "How'd she do it?"

"Don't know, but we're going to find out. Monq thinks her body was designed for the particular physics of her native world. The translation to our dimension is what tore her up so bad when she arrived. She might be a bit stronger than she looks."

"You think?"

Kay laughed. "Get some sleep. Take care of yourself."

"Okay." Already half asleep I said, "This bought us another six weeks."

Kay nodded thoughtfully. "That it did, Rammel."

I WAS DREAMIN' about Elora Laiken bendin' over my bed, her hand on my shoulder, callin' my name while the perfume of jasmine teased my sex. I grabbed her arms to pull her to me so that I could feel the sweetness of her body coverin' mine. I came partially awake when I heard her give a little cry. That was a split second before she landed across my ribcage. At that I came fully awake instantly, I assure you.

She scrambled off the bed while I held my bum rib.

"Rammel Hawking! Look what you've done. Probably made yourself worse."

"Look what I've done? I thought I was dreamin' because, silly me, I did no' expect to wake and find you bendin' over my bed in the middle of the night." After playin' that back in my head, I decided 'twould be better clarified. "No' that I mind wakin' to find you bendin' over my bed in the middle of the night, mind you."

"I'm here to make sure you take the right amount of medicine at the right time. I convinced your friends to leave the door open so I could check on you. The last thing I wanted was to make this worse. It's all... very embarrassing."

"Aye," I said as I threw the covers back and began the process of risin' as gingerly as possible.

"What do you need?" she asked.

"Bathroom."

"Let me help you. Take my arm." She crooked her arm at the elbow to form a brace the same way Storm had done in the infirmary. I tested my weight on her arm and she did no' seem bothered.

"You're goin' to help me pee?"

"You wish," she said, but continued walkin' with me until I reached the door.

When I came out of the bathroom, she was nowhere in sight, but she appeared in the doorway within seconds.

"Hungry?" she asked. I shook my head. "You can take two more pills if you want."

I nodded. She set a glass of water on the night stand and handed me two pills. I downed them and said, "Thanks be to glory."

"I'm Elora."

I looked up at her. "What?"

"Never mind. It was a joke. A bad one, I guess."

"Do no' be mad about me askin', but why are you here?"

"Bein' your nurse is... well, it's the least I could do, considering." She sighed, then said, "Do you want anything else before you go back to sleep? I brought an extra club sandwich. It might not be good anymore. I don't know."

I shook my head and settled back. When she pulled

the covers over me, I thought I might have died and gone to Summerland.

"You should sleep until morning. I'm going back to my place now. Here's my phone." She punched her name and number into contacts. "If you need something, I'm right next door."

"Elora. You do no' owe me a debt. You did nothin' to be embarrassed about either."

"Good night," she said. I may have heard the door close or I may have already been asleep by that time. I can no' say.

CHAPTER 10

Ram

I WOKE UP thinkin' I felt better until I tried to move. I knew I needed to set part of my mind to work managin' pain. And I was hungry.

I spied a glass left next to the bed and wondered if I had no' just dreamed that Elora had been in my apartment, takin' care of me. I remembered she'd said something about a club sandwich and, sure enough, there was a club sandwich standin' sentry on the kitchen counter, although it surely had seen a better day.

So 'twas no' a dream.

When I pulled the lettuce and tomato off, what was left was passably edible. Meat. Cheese. Bread. What's no' to like? I pulled a large juice box out of the refrigerator and sat down to see if I had messages. All clear.

I was plannin' to call Storm to find out how much trouble I was in for sparrin' with the outworlder, but there, plain as day, was a listin' for Elora Laiken right before Engel Storm. Aye. I alphabetize by *first* name. Sue me.

Maybe I'm a fool for love, but I can no' remember ever havin' a bigger thrill than seein' that she'd put her number in my phone. While I was sleepin'! I'd never in my life wanted to brag to other boys about what passed between myself and a female, but on that occasion I wanted to run down the hall shoutin', "SHE PUT HER NUMBER IN MY PHONE!"

If my fuckin' rib had no' been broken, I'd have laughed out loud.

Naturally, I dialed her number. I mean, 'twas the reason she gave it to me. Right?

"Hello." She answered on the first ring.

"You left your number."

"I know. How are you? Do you need anything?"

"I need help takin' a shower."

I heard a surprisin'ly girlish-sounding giggle. "You have other friends for that, Sir Hawking. I meant do you need anything like breakfast?"

Well, it never hurts to ask. "Havin' breakfast now. Club sandwich sans lettuce and tomato, at least I think 'twas what they had once been. And thank you. For takin' good care of me."

"Please do not thank me. I feel wretched about the whole mess, but we're taking steps to make sure it doesn't happen again."

"What kind of steps?"

"They've arranged to close the fitness level for the next couple of hours. Storm, Kay, and Monq are setting up a series of tests to quantify my, um, strengths…and weaknesses, I suppose."

"And this is when?"

"Half an hour."

"I'll be there."

"No. Isn't that too much activity too soon?"

"Rib's taped up nice and tight and tidy. Good as a cast. I'm no' proposin' bench press, just walkin' to the elevator. Believe me, I've lived through worse than this."

"But that's a story for another time?"

"Could be, if you're a really good girl."

"I am that, but I won't be asking for *your* definition of a really good girl." I started to laugh and hated myself for bein' forgetful. "How about a bargain? I'll walk you down if you promise to come back and be truly inactive for a reasonable time after lunch."

"Like a nap?"

"Exactly."

"Will you join me?"

"No."

It never hurts to ask. "You drive a hard bargain. Naps alone it is then."

"Hallway. Twenty minutes?"

"You want to help dress me?"

"No."

"Okay. Hallway. Twenty minutes."

I was movin' slow, but I did manage to clean up and get dressed in the time allotted. In fact, I stepped into the hall at the same time she opened her door. I smiled.

She laughed. "So, how are you feeling? Really."

"No' bad. I will no' be takin' any more sleepy medicines. I can sleep when I'm dead."

She nodded. "Storm said you were tough like that."

I could no' have been more surprised if a human girl

had broken my bones sparrin' with me. "He did? Are you sure it was Storm? He's no' handy with the compliments."

"All the more reason for you to be flattered."

I nodded. "True enough."

"I noticed your fine collection of stringed instruments. Do you play them all or are they for collection?"

"Collection?" I smiled at that. "No. I play. I come from musical people."

We got on the elevator and punched sublevel three. I could tell by her body language that she was uncomfortable standin' in the elevator car alone with me. I wondered if that meant she was interested. *Paddy*. I was lost as to how to woo a human woman. In my defense, I'd never had to. How ironic that the first time a woman was no' throwin' herself in my path was the first time I was wantin' that very thing more than life?

When the elevators opened on sublevel three, two upper classmen held up their hands to block our exit.

"Sorry. This level is closed for the next two hours, sir," said the one on the left, lookin' directly at me.

I waved toward Elora and made no effort to suppress my sneer.

"She's the reason this level is closed! Kindly remove your dunderheads from your little, juvie asses and stand clear."

When the doors started to auto close, I reached out to stop them and really, really wished I had no' when the pain shot straight to my rib. Fortunately the kids took my expression as an indication that I was out of patience, which I was, in addition to wantin' to scream from the pain. I was spendin' the mornin' drug free after all. Among other things, I wanted my head clear durin' Elora's "tests".

A look passed between the boys. I guessed it was a silent agreement to acquiesce because they stepped back.

I put my hand on the small of Elora's back in a universal gesture of male claimin' as we moved past and said, "Now you can make sure nobody else comes through unless 'tis the sovereign himself."

"The sovereign is already on this level, sir."

"Very well. Then change that order to *no one* comes through." They nodded. For good measure, I had to add, "If you two are the future of Black Swan knighthood, we're in a lot of trouble."

When Elora looked at me like I was bein' overly harsh, I winked so there would be no question in her mind that my comment was more hazin' than serious.

Sol, Monq, Storm, and Kay were in a little huddle discussion.

"Oh look," I said to Elora. "They're waitin' in the weight room."

She laughed. You've got to love a girl who appreciates the fine art of punditry.

"Rammel." Storm raised his chin. "Thought you'd be sleeping."

And from the look of it, he wished I was.

Elora said, "He can sleep when he's dead," at the same time I said, "I can sleep when I'm dead."

We shared a look with each other and a chuckle, which seemed to annoy Storm.

"Sir Hawking," Monq interjected. "We're going to ask

the lady to perform a series of physical tasks to determine how her constitution reacts to the physics governing our dimension."

To Elora, he said, "The first item is weight. As a purely informal exercise, let's each venture a guess as to how much you *think* she weighs. Take her height, muscle tone, and bone structure into account. Who wants to go first?"

Monq raised his clipboard, ready to write.

"Hundred fifty," said Kay.

"One thirty-five," said Storm.

Monq looked at me. I used the opportunity to look Elora over, nice and slow. "Somewhere between."

"Name a number," Monq said.

I pursed my lips and settled on, "A hundred and forty."

"My dear." Monq gestured to Elora.

She took off her shoes and stepped onto the scale.

After changing the bench mark twice and adjusting the slider Monq announced, "Two hundred thirty-six."

Kay whistled. I took another look. My mate weighed more than I did. *Great Paddy fuck a duck.*

"That explains a lot," Storm put in.

"What do you mean?" asked Monq.

"The night she arrived I had a hard time picking her up. Kay had to help me. I knew she felt really heavy, but I thought maybe it was partly because she was unconscious and partly because she was... slippery and hard to hold on to."

"And none who work in the infirmary ever mentioned this?" I was lookin' from Monq to Sol. They had to be aware of her weight because they'd moved her from gurney to bed, and probably back again.

"Maybe they thought we already knew." Monq looked at Elora, waving his clipboard to emphasize his point. "Anyway, it's an indicator of cell density, but it's just a number."

"If you're worried that I may be self-conscious about my weight," Elora gave him a crooked smile, "there's no need. I have more pressing issues."

"Yes. So let's get to that," said Sol. "We have less than two hours to learn what we can."

Storm stepped toward Monq and Sol, sayin', "In two hours she can get through a complete circuit of weights and machines."

Monq nodded. "Then I'll compare those results with what would normally be expected of a twenty-three-year-old female in good physical condition."

AN HOUR AND a half later, they listened as Monq rattled off how much her numbers exceeded currently held records of *males* of *any* age.

I laughed out loud.

When Elora looked at me with a question on her face, I touched my rib and said, "I just realized you actually *did* take it easy on me. I could've ended up squashed like a bug. I should be thankin' you for exercisin' restraint."

"That covers strength," Monq said. "Ms. Laiken, will you indulge us with a treadmill test for speed?"

She nodded and climbed onto the newest state-of-the-art equipment, which topped out at twenty miles per hour.

We could all see that, at that speed, she was practically fallin' asleep.

"We're going to need to test her out on the track," Monq affirmed.

All five men proceeded to argue about the best way to do that when they were brought to a halt by Elora's rather loud and obnoxious whistle.

"I gave you two hours." She was lookin' at Storm. "Now it's your turn to have your fight style critiqued."

Storm looked flummoxed. "Well, I…"

"That was the deal," she said in a no nonsense tone.

I could no' help but grin. Storm made a deal to have his fightin' style critiqued by my girl? "Oh, this should be good." Yeah. I said that out loud.

FIFTEEN MINUTES LATER, Storm and Kay were dancin' around with half-assed written all over them. I wondered if she would detect the total lack of sincerity. They were no' even botherin' to wear gloves. Playin' her is what they were doin'. I was curious to see if she could tell when somebody was havin' her on.

I did no' have long to wait to find out. No' a full minute into the charade, she stopped them.

"Okay. Knock it off," she said. "You're putting on a show and nothing's going to be accomplished that way. Take this seriously or, the next time you want to make a deal with me, I'll call you a liar."

Storm blinked a couple of times, nodded at Kay, and smashed his gloves together in a, "Let's go," gesture.

Thirty seconds later she stopped them to give Kay

some detailed instruction about redistributin' his weight.

"No," she said. "When I call out a direction you take a step, then come right back to base."

"Base?" he asked.

"That's what we're going to call the balanced posture to which you will always return. Forward." Kay took a step forward then back. "I know you're a big guy, but I also know you can move faster than that. Stop the kidding around and show me. Forward."

She put him through his paces. After three tries of every direction she called, he started to catch on. And by Paddy, I could see from ringside that he would be benefittin' from the tips once we took to the streets again.

'Twas makin' me wonder who she'd been before her crazy ass arrival in the Chamber of Jefferson Unit. And I was goin' to find out everything there was to know.

When Kay faced off against Storm again, he was takin' the process more seriously.

Next time she stopped them, her comments were for Storm. "Take a fighting stance." He did. She pushed down on his left hand, up on his right. "Hold that posture." She went behind him and took hold of his trapezius muscles with her hands. "Keep your hands there and release this tension here. Send it down into your shoulders and upper arms. That's where you need the tension for extra power. Keeping the strain up here," she pressed into his muscles with her fingers, "is just slowing you down and decreasing your stamina." She backed up a few steps and nodded to my teammates. "Now. Go again."

They practiced what they'd learned for a couple of

minutes.

"Okay. That's enough for a first lesson," she said. "Practice that twice a day for the next eight days. Then I'll give you something else."

I found it tantalizin' that she could be so bossy and so sexy all at the same time. I was lost in reviewin' the curves and planes of her body when I heard Storm tell Sol, "By the gods. She knows what she's talking about."

While they were busy discussin' how amazin' it was to learn something new, I watched Elora walk away. Sol jumped in with his plan to exploit her for whatever could be learned and used to Black Swan advantage. Understandable that the interest of The Order would be his priority. But my priority was Elora Laiken and I'd make sure she did no' do anything she did no' want to do.

When they turned around to talk to the newly proclaimed mistress of martial arts and saw that she was gone, they looked at me like I'd been responsible for makin' her disappear.

"Where is she?" Sol demanded.

"Do no' know," I said. "But she went that way." I pointed toward the hall that led to the elevators and then headed that way. I did no' have to turn around to know that Storm and Kay were close behind.

I spotted her at the Hub Bistro, readin' the daily specials on the blackboard. I walked up to her back, leaned over her shoulder and said, "Can we join you?" close to her ear.

She lifted a shoulder, but did no' look back at me. "It's a free country." I noticed her body stiffen slightly before she turned and looked between the three of us, "Isn't it?"

If my heart had no' already melted for her, it became mush in that moment as I tried to imagine how hard it would be to get deposited in a strange world no' knowin' anybody or even how things work. I felt a lump in my throat, but said, "Aye. 'Tis a free country."

Monq had come by to check on Elora just as she asked that question. "Well, that kind of has to be qualified," he interjected. "You can't come or go without a passport. You can't drive without a driver's license, registration, auto insurance, and proof your vehicle is up to code. You can't work or even get health care without a social security number. You have to pay taxes on everything including air and water. The closest distance between points A and B may involve paying a road toll. There are over three hundred thousand federal laws. You have to educate your children according to legal standards set by someone who's not you. There are laws about who can marry whom. But other than a few more such trivialities, it's a free country."

Apparently he'd satisfied himself that Elora was okay. So, with that, he nodded and walked off.

I looked up at the board above her head and back down into her vulnerable expression. "So what will you be havin'?"

She turned around. "Deciding between cream of mushroom soup and a hamburger."

"Get both," I said.

"That would be wasteful."

"No' at all. We'll eat whatever is left."

With no' another word, she stepped up to the counter and placed an order for the soup *and* the hamburger. But when the girl started through the list of options, Elora lost her confidence. I stepped up beside her and said, "She'll have it rare, American cheese, lettuce, tomatoes, pickles, yellow mustard, no sesame seeds with half and half fries." Elora looked nothin' but grateful for my intervention. "Let's start there. Before long you'll know exactly how you like it."

"Thank you," she said quietly, lookin' 'round like she would no' want others to know she was no' yet adept at orderin' lunch.

"You're welcome." I smiled. "You want juice?"

She shook her head. "Chocolate milk."

"Excellent choice."

That earned me a little smile.

The four of us took a solarium table right next to the window. Some undergraduates had been about to sit down there, but they saw us headin' in that direction and decided another table would suit their needs as well. When the gadget lit up like a carnival win, Storm and Kay went to get the food. I was beginnin' to see there were benefits to bein' out of commission.

"What foods have you tried that you like so far?" I asked.

"Well, everything chocolate."

"Goes without sayin'."

"Green beans with almond slices. Blackened salmon. Pumpkin bread."

"Where did you get pumpkin bread?"

"In the infirmary. They said it's a seasonal ritual. Everybody must eat something pumpkin in October."

I nodded. "Unless you're ready to fight like hel."

Storm and Kay returned with trays of food on the tail end of a conversation about the moves Elora had shown them. They sorted out our orders and sat down across from the two of us.

Storm took a big bite of grilled cheese sandwich and, before he was finished chewin', said, "Sol was going to ask if you'd consider training."

Elora stopped chewin' her sweet potato fry. "Self-defense training?"

Storm traded a cautious look with Kay before continuing. "Well, in a sense. Maybe you could help all the knights," he seemed to be lost in thought for a second, "and students. It might improve our fatality count."

A look of recognition ghosted over Elora's face. "That night in the infirmary…"

When she did no' finish the sentence, Storm answered as if she had. "That was actually a good outcome. The guy you saw lived to tell about an up close and personal vampire encounter." Storm's gaze flicked around the table and lingered on me for an instant. "He was lucky."

"Yes," she said simply.

"You are no' under any pressure to agree," I said.

"No. I think I want to do it and not just because I'd like to feel useful around here. If something I know could help your, um, effort, then it would give me some direction. A sense of purpose, I guess."

"Well said." Kay smiled with approval.

"But do you think the others would be receptive?" she asked.

"If they know what's good for 'em." I punctuated that by touchin' my taped rib.

My teammates smirked at me, but Elora said, "That's not funny."

I dropped my chin and challenged her with a smile. "I say 'tis. And if I can find the humor, so can you."

With her lips still pressed together and eyebrows drawn, she said, "I wouldn't want anybody to be forced. That's my only condition. If they want what I have to offer, it's freely given, but it has to be their choice. That's the only way it works anyhow. And speaking of choice," she pinned me with a look, "you owe me a nap."

"What?"

I laughed on the inside at Storm's look of alarm. Sooner or later I was goin' to have to tell him he did no' stand a chance with the lass. But first I'd have to make her understand that she belonged to me. And I had to find a way to do it without scarin' her off.

"We have another meetin' with the sovereign. He definitely ranks above promises to nap. But it'll probably be short, just officially lettin' us off the hook for another six weeks."

"How are you spending the rest of your day?" Storm asked Elora.

"I have a session with Monq and some personal stuff."

I could tell by the look on Storm's face he wanted to ask what 'personal stuff', but he managed to quash the impulse. "Have dinner with us?"

She turned a completely beguilin' shade of pink. "If it's okay with your teammates." She looked at Kay, then me.

I laughed. "O' course. Goes without sayin'.'"

"Don't make us beg," said Kay and I could have hugged him for makin' her feel welcome, like she had friends in this place that was no' only new to her, but strange as well.

As I'D THOUGHT, the meetin' was short, if no' sweet. Sol was bringin' up a team from Brazil to fill in until we were back on patrol.

"Get your heads around the decision on your fourth before the six weeks is up," he said. "I want you back in rotation six weeks and one hour from the moment of Hawking's latest mishap."

"Hey," I protested. He was makin' me sound like a ne'er-do-well bumbler. I was ignored, but chose no' to make a thing of it.

As SOON As I got back to my apartment, I called media and asked about Elora's hearin'.

The kid replied, "Which one?"

"There was more than one?"

"Yeah. A short one on October 1st, long one on October 2nd."

"Send somebody up with copies of both."

"Now?" the kid asked.

"No time like the present."

"Yes, sir."

Twenty minutes later I was poppin' the first into the

player and sittin' down to watch. There was a big no-neck bruiser of an orderly off to the side, supposedly providin' security. I almost laughed out loud and said to myself, "Yeah. Like that would have slowed her down if she'd taken a mind to run."

I have to tell you that watchin' her anguish was just about the hardest thing I've ever been through. Yeah. There was a lot of information about her life before and the circumstances that had brought her here, but the pain was palpable and sent adrenaline shooting through my body. I watched both recordin's all the way through, replayin' some parts even though 'twas excruciatin' to watch. If she'd lived through it, I could make myself watch it.

The woman was tragedy walkin'. I pledged on the spot that I would treat her like glass and never deny her anything within my power.

THAT NIGHT, AFTER most of J.U. had gone to bed, we clocked her on the track of the Courtpark at a speed of almost thirty miles an hour. 'Twas a record in our dimension. She was really something special. And, human or no', destiny had seen fit to give her to me.

Chapter 11

Ram

I WAS NO' above playin' on Elora's guilt. I'd use any tool at my disposal to get her to spend time with me. I did no' lie, but let her believe that restricted duty was hard on me and, since she happened to feel responsible for that, she acted on her pity by spendin' late afternoons watchin' films with me.

Within moments of the first discussion on what to watch it became obvious that we did no' share taste in flicks. So we agreed to take turns.

I thought that films portrayin' various shades of sexuality might cause her to warm towards me. I did no' select hard core pornography because that would be too obvious. So I went for sex embedded in lots of humor. She frequently pretended to be shocked, which never failed to make me laugh.

She'd say things like, "Ram, this is the worst thing I've ever seen," or "Ram, I wish I could erase that from my memory," but I believed, perhaps projected as Monq would say, that she was enjoyin' the bawdy bits as much as I.

Her turn usually meant movies from bygone eras with costumes and endless talkin'. If it was no' for the fact that I was randy as a goat because of sittin' next to her for two hours straight, I'd have fallen asleep every time.

I learned that she loved music and I loved when she asked me to play for her. One such day, I put the guitar down after playin' and said, "I watched the record of your hearin's, both of them." It broke my heart that she just looked at her feet and said nothin'. I did no' know if she was mad or embarrassed, so I said, "Do no' be mad or embarrassed. I will be your someone to talk to if you need it."

She whispered, "Thank you," but did no' look up.

I KNEW SHE was fascinated with the idea of elves. Hel. I knew that from that first night at dinner when she could no' stop lookin' at my ear and grinnin' like she'd just found sunken treasure. So I got a copy of *Everything You Always Wanted To Know About Elves, But Were Afraid To Ask* and presented it to her as a gift.

"What makes you think I'm afraid to ask?" she said.

I shrugged. "Just in case."

"In case of what?"

"In case you find yourself unable to sleep, dreamin' about me, and want to know something more about my species. Like how to seduce an elf."

She scoffed at the last comment, but then said, "Your *species*?"

I did no' know whether to be offended or no'. "Aye."

She quieted, but still smiled. "Okay."

And we left it at that, but I was hopin' that she would read the part about matin' and put it together that my interest in her went far beyond the obvious benefits that carnal knowledge has to offer.

She did no' want to talk about her previous life, but was curious about mine. So I told her I had two siblings, one who was a joy, one who should have been executed at birth, that I liked horses almost as much as music and that I spent a lot of time in a wildlife preserve growin' up.

One afternoon she asked out of nowhere, "Why did you join The Order?"

I said, "Wild child, I suppose. They promised I would have adventures my brother could no' imagine and that was exactly what I wanted to hear." I left the movie on mute and turned toward her on the sofa. "Tell me something about your life before."

She shrugged and looked away. "Palace life was restricting and suffocating. In some ways I had more freedom when I was a prisoner of Black Swan."

I felt my gut tighten when she referred to her confinement in the infirmary durin' the time I was away on leave. I wanted to protest, to say that Black Swan does no' hold innocent parties prisoner, but it seems that sometimes *we* do. I was ashamed of Black Swan for reactin' to her arrival with fear and I was ashamed of havin' left my mate to fend for herself, broken and alone in a strange world.

The same day we had that conversation, I said my goodbye after procurin' Elora's agreement to let me walk her to dinner, and opened the door to leave.

Storm was standin' there with his hand up in the air like he was about to knock.

His face fell into a disgruntled scowl and he said to me, "Do you no' have a place of your own?"

I gave him a smile that unquestionably laid down the gauntlet. "I like it *here*," I said.

After years together, I knew the boy well and could tell that he was about to punch me, but his eyes went over my shoulder and, apparently, Elora's watchful presence tempered his possessive reflex.

She welcomed him in, but I have to say that watchin' her close the door behind him, leavin' me, her mate, standin' out in the hall? Well, it was hard to swallow. I wanted to plow down the door and make it plain that there would be no more closed doors between my mate and me. No' to mention that there would be no more entertainin' Sir Storm.

The battle lines were drawn between Storm and me, but he met my challenge blow for blow.

One night he had a cupcake with a candle in it delivered to our table for dessert. He pulled a lighter out of his pocket, lit the candle and set the plate in front of Elora.

"Happy birthday," he said.

She looked surprised, delighted, and amazed. "How did you know?"

"I looked up your counterpart's birthday. Figured it would be the same."

"Brilliant!" she gushed. "Storm, I'm so moved that you went to the trouble to learn my birthday and do this for me."

When she bent to blow out the candle, he smirked at me. *Brilliant, my ass.*

She did no' always have dinner with us. She'd made friends with people who worked in the infirmary while she was there and it pleased me that she knew people outside B Team.

One night I was restless and decided to go down for a drink, maybe pick up a game of pool. When I closed my door, I saw Elora headin' away from me, toward the elevator. I jogged toward her silently, no' wantin' to call out as things at J.U. get quiet after ten o'clock. When she got in the elevator and turned around, she saw me comin' and put her hand in the door.

"Much obliged," I said as I walked in beside her. "Where you headed so late?"

She released the door and turned to me. "There's a guy, a knight, who was hurt while I was in the infirmary. He's still recovering. I go read to him at night."

"Read to him?" She nodded. "Does he no' have a TV?"

She rolled her eyes. "Yes. He has a TV, Ram, but that's not the same thing as personal attention."

I supposed I could see that.

"He doesn't have the energy to carry on a conversation, but needs company. This seemed like a good solution."

It made sense in a feminine, and therefore odd, way. "What's that you have there?" I was referrin' to a folder of papers in her hand.

"I type up as much of the stories, fairy tales, as I can remember." I narrowed my eyes at her. "Sorry. I mean, um, elf tales." Her smile was sheepish as if she had forgotten 'twas a trigger for my temper.

"Better. I'll go with you. I'd like to hear these elf tales myself."

"Okay." She looked dubious. "But remember, Ram, this is for *his* benefit."

"What? Are you suggestin' I can no' be selfless?"

She just laughed.

I sat on the windowsill in Touchstone's room and listened to Elora read. I did no' think the story was great, but listenin' to my mate's voice was so soothing I felt a calm settle over me for, perhaps, the first time in my life when in an environment outside the New Forest. The feelin' was so strange I could almost say 'twas alien to my more naturally frenetic state of bein'.

The story was about a young girl, a ragin' bitch of a stepmother, and a bunch of dwarves. The dwarf thing was creepy if you ask me. I would have kept my opinion to myself, but in the elevator goin' back upstairs, she asked, "What did you think?"

I can no' lie to my mate. So I told her the truth. "'Twas a stupid story." Her eyes flared wide for a second, but then she just laughed and did no' seem to mind that I did no' care for the tale. "But I thoroughly enjoyed hearin' the tellin' of it," I added quietly.

The compliment made her turn shy. She was a paradox. This smart polished woman with, well, super powers also had a vulnerability and even innocence about her. Most people, those who think I'm shallow, would question the Fates makin' such a complex matin' for me. I mean most people would no' use 'sensitive' as a descriptor when they think of me. But I would do whatever needed doin' to meet her needs, however complicated they were.

After that I joined her every night to hear another story.

And almost every day with Elora brought a new revelation or surprise.

"YOU WHAT?" I was almost shakin' from hearin' her tell me that she had personal encounters with that insane beast downstairs, the one who did a fine impression of rabid.

"You heard me perfectly well. I've been working with him for weeks and we've progressed to the stage where I need to see how he'll react to other people."

I narrowed my eyes at her. "Elora, do no' try to deflect with that haughty superior thing you do 'cause we're stayin' on point and 'tis this, people call me reckless, but even *I* think this is looney. You'd have to have a death wish to go inside the cage with that animal!"

"Come see. You'll change your mind. Promise."

When she looked at me that way, I knew I would never stand a chance of standin' in her way when she wanted something. If she wanted to see me torn apart by that feral hound, I had no choice but to submit.

Then I saw her checkin' a tranq pistol and packin' it in a backpack.

"You know people do no' usually need tranq's big enough to bring down a rhino when they're out for a stroll with their pet."

"Just a precaution." She looked at me sideways and smiled. I knew what was next. "Don't be such an old woman. Come on." She finished fillin' the pockets of her hoodie with some kind of dog treats.

I had to laugh at the situation. "Who would have ever thought that *you* would end up being a bad influence on *me*?"

She stopped me at a corner of the network of hallways in the subterranean storage facilities, pulled the tranq gun from her bag, and handed it to me.

"Elora," I began.

"It's just a precaution, Ram. Promise. The pistol is loaded if you need it. But don't worry. You won't. Just give me a couple of minutes to say hello and prepare him. When I'm ready for you, I'll call out."

I caught her by the arm as she started away feelin' really conflicted between allowin' her to try and prove something with that monster and my desire to keep her safe. "Elora, are you very, very sure about this?" At first I did no' grasp the implication of the sounds I was hearin'. She was makin' chicken noises at me like we were ten years old.

"Bawk bawks? You're no' serious."

Instead of replyin', her bawk bawks just kept gettin' louder and more obnoxious.

"I give you a first rate education in pop culture and then you use it against me?" She was good at it, too. There's an art to bawk bawk delivery. "Oh for… fine. Waitin' here." But no' likin' it. At. All.

I held my breath, waitin' for the inevitable snarlin' and

crashin' against the chain link cage. But there was no' a sound except for the clank of the metal gate latch openin' and closin', followed by Elora's voice loud enough to know she was speakin' but soft enough for me to no' hear what was bein' said, even with *my* ears.

WHEN SHE CALLED my name, I stepped around the corner bringin' the strange sight into my field of vision. She was inside the cage, smilin' like she'd won the lottery, standin' next to the creature that was at present lookin' more like a dog than a Tasmanian devil. She was holdin' a leash and the mutt was sittin' next to her actin' like it was the most normal thing in the world.

When I took a step forward the dog rose to a crouch and pointed his ears toward me with a concentration that was alarmin' in spite of the fact that he was behind chain link and remained quiet. The silence was short lived. As soon as I took another step he barked a warnin'.

Elora snapped the leash and told him to sit. When he did, she gave him one of those treats she'd stored in her pocket. The dog did no' take his eyes off me, but did no' show any further aggression, with her all the while tellin' him he was a good boy. I would no' have believed it if I had no' seen it with my own eyes. I needed to add Enchantress of Wild and Crazed Creatures to her list of super powers.

Then she crossed a line. She got the dog to lie on his back and beg for a tummy rub.

"Now you've gone too far, Elora," I said. "Allow the poor devil to keep a little bit of dignity. After all, he was originally intended to be J.U.'s mascot."

She just laughed. "Come close to the cage so I can reach out and touch you." She reached through a space about five feet high that was just big enough to get her arm through.

When I came closer the dog's gaze flicked to the tranq gun and he gave up a growl that I would have thought was too soft for human ears to hear, but she corrected him immediately. *She has extraordinary hearin'. Good to know.*

She began to pet me, rubbin' her hand across my hair and down my face to my shoulder. "See, Blackie, Ram's a good boy, too." I knew my plight had taken a pathetic turn when I realized I was revelin' in bein' petted and told I was a good boy, too. "Would you back up about twenty feet? We're going to find out if he can maintain his manners on the outside."

"Elora…"

"Keep your gun in hand. It's just a precaution. He'll be fine."

She unlatched the gate and led the dog out, tellin' him to heel, which he did. They walked away from me even though I could tell that no' lookin' back at me over his shoulder was goin' against the dog's sense of self-preservation.

"By Paddy, the beast trusts you," I said under my breath.

When they started comin' toward me, I laid the pistol over my forearm, kind of slow and casual like there was no' a thing unusual about that. Elora walked the dog past me like 'twas an everyday occurrence and then gave him praise and treats. He wagged his tail and grinned like a puppy.

"Well, what do you think?" she asked, giggling when he tried to steal licks from her face.

"I think nobody is goin' to believe it. You're amazin'."

I did no' know exactly how to interpret the look she gave me, maybe pride, or victory, but I knew I would never get tired of seein' that expression on her face.

Blackie did no' want to go back into the kennel, and who could blame him? But he proved that he could be bought for a price and 'twas seven chicken treats.

THAT NIGHT AT dinner Elora grinned as she told the rest of B Team about the transformation.

"You should have seen it. That slatherin' mad beast was gentle as a little lamb," I said.

"I'm not sure which one of you is crazier, my team-mate," Storm looked at me with daggers comin' from his dark eyes, "or the new arrival to this world who may not know exactly how dangerous two-inch fangs can be."

I opened my mouth to reply, but before I could speak I heard her sayin', "Oh look who's talking. How long are vampire fangs? Blackie's fangs are not covered with bacteria that transforms DNA. So of the two of us, who's crazier, Storm? You or me?" I sat back and smirked. My mate had put the great stolid Storm in his place. "Come with us tomorrow." She looked between Kay and Storm. "Let me show you. Blackie needs to get used to more people."

THE NEXT DAY Elora repeated the same maneuver, walkin' Blackie past three of us, without incident.

"Which one of you three brave knights is willing to be the first to pet the dog?"

I'm willin' to admit to a slight hesitation, but I could no' let one of my teammates outshine me in Elora's eyes. So I handed the pistol to Storm and stepped forward.

"Blackie, sit," she said. "Come toward us slowly, no sudden movements. Hold the back of your hand out for him to sniff."

The dog gave my hand a thorough sniffin' followed by a little lick. I took that to mean I was cleared to touch in dog language. I touched his head between the ears and saw that he was relaxed. So I ran my hand over his lush coat that varied from coarse outer hair to silky undercoat.

"Good fella," I told him.

With chicken treats and encouragement from Elora, he allowed Kay and Storm to pet him. Storm, bein' the least animal-oriented of us, was probably least impressed, but he made an effort.

Blackie had just been put back in the kennel when he made all of us jump with a sudden burst of hellhound behavior. He was showin' his very beautiful and lethal-lookin' white fangs, snarlin' and throwin' himself against the chain link.

"Hey. What's going on here?" A maintenance worker had come 'round the corner.

Storm looked from the man to the dog, and back again. "I think maybe you're the one who needs to answer that question. Is that a taser on your belt?" The man narrowed his eyes and looked uncertain as to how to answer. As Storm started walkin' toward him he backed up. "What would maintenance personnel be doing with a taser inside Jefferson Unit?"

"It's for self defense. How would you like to have the job of feeding that monster and cleaning up after it?" He looked both defensive and guilty.

Elora gasped. "You've been using a taser on my dog?"

Before I could process the fact that she'd referred to Blackie as 'my' dog, she was zappin' the devil with his own taser and he was jerkin' around on the ground. Storm took the taser from her hand before she killed the guy. That would have been a mess to clean up.

Kay had already called security. He put his foot on the maintenance worker's chest when he tried to sit up. "I suggest you stay down until security gets here," he said.

'Twas no' long before Kay was tellin' them to take the guy and hold him pendin' further inquiry. The investigation did no' go in his favor, but did make all the difference to 'Elora's' dog.

Elora took over Blackie's care and feedin'. Soon afterward she had the dog off leash chasin' tennis balls down the hallways and he was re-introduced as the Black Swan mascot at Lan's posthumous ceremonial decoration. I can no' tell you how proud I was when she entered the Chamber lookin' like Diana herself.

She grinned before takin' a seat next to me, the dog on her other side.

Before long she moved the dog into her apartment and it was okay with me. I imagined there was little in this world that Elora could no' handle, but whatever was left, the dog would take care of. I suspected he would be fiercely protective of her and, like I said, that was okay with me.

"BLACKIE WENT BERSERK." Her gaze flew to Kay when she realized that might be an offensive thing to say to a Berserker. "Uh, sorry, Kay." He shrugged as if to say that he was no' bothered. "They had this guy in chains, taking him across the Hub. Let me tell you, Blackie did not like him at all."

O' course we knew who 'twas and knew exactly why the dog would object to a vampire bein' near his mistress. We looked at each other unsure how much truth tellin' would be prudent.

I turned my palms up to say I had no objection to havin' her know what she'd observed. Storm looked at Kay who raised a shoulder, then he said, "You saw a very old and notorious vampire named Istvan Baka. He was captured nearly a hundred years ago and has been held in a facility in the Carpathian Mountains."

"What's he doing here?" she asked.

I answered. "'Tis above our pay grade. 'Tis impossible to keep news of his bein' here quiet. The purpose of the visit? Maybe only Sol knows."

CHAPTER 12

Ram

S OL HAD CALLED us, meaning B Team, to come into his office. It had already been decided that Ghost would be takin' Lan's place when I was cleared from the D.L. in ten days. So we had no idea what 'twas about.

More curious was the fact that Elora had been included.

The four of us were gathered in the conference room adjacent to Sol's office.

"Where is she?" Sol asked.

Storm got out his phone and called, but got no answer.

"Probably on the rugby field with her hellhound," Kay said.

Sol opened the door and told the kid at the desk to go look for her at the rugby field.

"So what's this about?" Storm asked Sol.

"We'll wait until Ms. Laiken is present."

That was my cue to take advantage of the coffee and cookie service.

I was halfway through a cup when she came breezin' in, lookin' for all the world like autumn itself with her bright hair and color in her cheeks. How I would have loved to grab her and kiss her senseless. She closed the door behind her and unsnapped Blackie's leash. "Am I late?"

Sol's ears turned pink from wantin' to dress her down right there, but since she did no' work for him, technically, he had to rein it in. 'Twas amusin' beyond description.

The dog, bein' exceptionally smart as well as an excellent judge of character, came right to me, put his head on my thigh, and waited – eyes bright, ears forward, for a pet. As I gave the pooch a rub behind the ear with one hand, Elora sat down next to me and grabbed the half-eaten cookie I was holdin' with the other. Some people might have bristled at such a proprietary display, but 'twas pure pleasure to have her behave in such a familiar way with me. She tried to wash the ginger snap down with my coffee, but pulled back and screwed up her face when she tasted it.

I laughed. "Serves you right. Get your own."

Sol cleared his throat. "Shall we get down to business, children?" 'Twasn't particularly surprisin' that we did no' answer a rhetorical question. I waited quietly for him to get past his little pout and continue. Elora nodded and got up to make herself a cream and sugar with a touch of coffee. "You're aware that we're losing ground with the vampire infestation in New York…"

He had to be talkin' specifically to B Team, what was left of us, obviously. Elora would no' know anything about whether or no' we were holdin' ground with vampire. At least no' to my knowledge.

"So the Powers That Be have decided it's time for extraordinary measures. I was instructed to offer the vampire, Istvan Baka, temporary freedom in exchange for helpin' us restore the balance."

I must tell you, that was a stunnin' remark if I ever heard one. Vampire hunters workin' with vampire? Everything in my gut said no. No. No. But as it turned out, there was more.

"He has agreed to help us in exchange for a private audience, unbound, with Elora Laiken."

My eyes flew to her so fast I saw her stop stirrin' her coffee.

'Twas as if an invisible giant had reached down, grabbed me by the collar, and jerked me to my feet. That's how fast I was up and sayin', "NO!" in unison with Storm.

Sol sat back lookin' like he'd expected that reaction and was plannin' to dig in for a lengthy discussion if needs be.

Kay looked at Sol and said, "How does he even know about her?"

"He saw her when he was here last week. Described her in such detail there was no mistaking who he meant. He actually thought she was a knight. Called her Lady Swan."

As she was reseatin' herself, Elora gave Sol a level look while stirrin' her cup. "I'm in."

I looked at her like I could no' have heard right, but saw out of the corner of my eye that Storm was about to throw a tantrum. Even in the middle of bein' scared out of my mind for Elora, I recognized that there was something funny about puttin' the words Storm and tantrum together in the same sentence.

She was ignorin' us both. "Any ideas why he would make his agreement conditional on talking to me?"

"I didn't ask. Anything more would be pure speculation," Sol replied.

"Elora," I felt my face heat from the sincere feelin' that everything depended on findin' the right words to bring her to her senses, "please believe me. 'Tis one thing to read about vampire in trainin' manuals and something quite different to come face to face with one. And, while we're on the subject," I turned on Sol, "you can no' truly be thinkin' to turn that monster loose in New York City?"

Sol stood up, looking at ease with arms crossed over his chest, and answered slowly. "Seen the news lately? The numbers of missing women have become alarming and we're not getting anywhere. Not to mention the fact that our best team has been off duty for a while." He let that hang in the air for a moment, probably to make us feel guilty. It worked. "We've reached a point where the potential benefit outweighs the risk."

I threw my hands up in frustration and then grabbed for the rib that protested mightily. I decided 'twas time to sit and try to calm myself.

"You've asked Elora to perform a service for The Order. She said yes. I don't mean this to sound disrespectful, but why are we here?"

When Kay said "we", he nodded toward Storm and me.

"Because you're going to escort her there and back."

Storm made a rude noise that sounded a lot like disbelief, but Kay went on. "What does he mean by private, unbound audience?"

"It would be more accurate to say semi-private. There's a very large mirror in his, ah, room that is observation glass on the other side. You'll be able to hear and see everything that transpires."

Elora laughed softly. "Well, we must be certain you all feel more secure." She looked at Sol in open challenge. "I have a condition." We all looked at her. "When we return, I want to be accorded the same freedoms as anyone else. I want to be able to go shopping or to performances of the arts or take classes or whatever. In the future, whether or not I'm 'accompanied' should be my decision."

Sol sat down at the end of the table. "I can't give an answer without consulting with Monq."

"Alright. Get him in here." Elora sounded imperious.

"I'd watch my tone if I were you, young lady."

Elora rose in an explosion of intensity that startled all of us. "I don't work for you, Mister Sovereign. And unless you want to change that and make my employment official, what exactly is my motivation for 'watching my tone?' What am I to fear? *Incarceration*?" The last word was scalding with sarcasm. "It's simple. You need something from me. I need something from you. If such negotiating tactics work for a vampire, why not for me?"

Sol appraised her with a hard glint in his eye and a tick in his jaw. Then he reached for his phone and dialed Monq. "Can you come to my office straightaway?" He said to the group in general, "Wait here," and left the room.

It was a stunner to see my sweet, and normally gentle, woman act like a meth-crazed commando. She just kept gettin' more and more interestin'.

Kay looked at Elora. "No need to hold back. Just come straight out and say how you feel."

"Look," said Storm, "I know this place must feel confining." Elora snorted. "And I agree it's time to adjust your security clearance so you can move around more freely, but this audience with Baka thing... Ram is right." He glanced toward me in acknowledgement and I thought surely we must have been transported to another dimension ourselves. 'Twas simply no' part of Storm's M.O. to say things like, 'Ram is right'. "For once." He had to add that. O' course. "You don't just have tea with a vampire. They're danger in the first degree. Tricky. Lethal. And evil – regardless of what the training manual says. And this is the *oldest* one we know of."

Elora was unmoved. "I'm not being dismissive. I've spent enough time with the manual and the annals to know that what you're saying is true. But I'm not the girl next door." Reconsidering that, she turned and gave me a conspiratorial smile. "Well, I am the girl next door to *you*." To Storm, she stated the obvious. "I'm strong and fast."

"And way too cocky!" Storm interrupted.

"Even if that was true, it's not your call, Sir Storm," she said.

"And you're not worried about the fact that he specified 'unbound'? If all he wants to do is talk, why would he care whether he's bound or not?" Storm asked.

"Good point," I said with a finger pointed at Storm to

indicate that I was in complete agreement. Therefore, she should listen to me.

Kay said, "Putting that aside for now, there's the issue of trance." He looked 'round. "We had nearly a decade of training to resist it. It's not something you can pick up in a weekend workshop. If you're hypnotized, all the strength and speed in the world won't help you."

"Not a problem. I'm not hypnotizable." She looked at me. "Is that a word?" I stared, no' knowin' whether or no' it was a word and no' carin'. Vocabulary was the last thing on my mind. When I did no' respond, she said, "Ask Monq," then looked at her fingernails.

The three of us were exchangin' looks indicatin' various degrees of shock, when Sol and Monq walked in.

Kay got right to it, which was more than fine by me. "Is it true she can't be hypnotized?"

"Yes. It's true," Monq said. "A very useful trait should she decide to proceed with the meeting."

I could no' believe my ears. Monq was supposed to be the smartest of all of us.

Elora looked at Sol. "Did I mention that somebody needs to take care of my dog while I'm gone? Someone of my choosing."

Storm looked at Monq like he was a traitor. "You're going along with this madness?"

He was nonplussed. "Sir Storm, this is an ideal assignment for Ms. Laiken and, so far as security clearance goes, her profile scores indicate candidacy for top level duty." He leaned toward Storm and stage whispered loud enough for all of us to hear. "She outscored you!"

Storm huffed in response. "Why not just bring him here?"

"Baka has proven to be reliable to the letter of written agreement. Once a deal is made, he can be trusted to abide by it, but he will not hesitate to take advantage of any contractual loophole, no matter how minute.

"We brought him here to assess the developing situation before it gets away from us completely, but transporting him, and striking bargains with him, well, there's always a slight chance that we didn't write a flawless contract. The facility in Romania is without equal. Until we need him out, he stays in."

Quietly, Elora turned toward Sol. "So. Do we have a deal?"

He looked her over and said, "Yes. If you take the vow of secrecy. And, by the way, since you work for me now, you *will* give me the deference I require."

"Yes sir," she said, nodding seriously.

"You need to go get your inoculation."

"What's involved in that?"

"You never had shots as a child?"

"You mean with needles like they use in the infirmary?"

"Yes."

"No."

"Well, they administer tiny little doses of the vampire virus combined with an antidote and it instigates an immunity in your system."

"Okay." Then she brightened and turned to the three of us. "Road trip!" She sounded like we were off to

Disneycamp. I was gettin' angrier by the minute because I believed both Sol and Monq had downplayed the danger of bein' alone in a room with the most infamous vampire ever. No' havin' ever faced a vampire, she could no' begin to imagine what it meant. To her the prospect was as much at arm's length as one of her stupid stories. "When do we leave? How long will we be gone and, most importantly, what do I wear?"

Storm lifted his chin at Monq, crossed his arms over his chest. "What if the three of us refuse to go?"

Bam! I thought. A trump card. Way to go, Storm.

"Then we'll send one of the other teams," Sol replied and I deflated just as quickly as I'd been excited.

Storm pressed his lips together, probably to keep from turnin' the air blue. I flopped into my chair in utter disgust, but my rib immediately reminded me there was a price to pay for forgettin' the injury. I winced, but did no' make a sound.

It seemed we had no other options. If we did no' go, some other team that cared less about Elora's well bein' would take our place and that was unacceptable. All we could do was go along and hope for the best.

The Operations Office arranged for papers so that she could travel internationally. I went with her for the first shot in the series.

When she looked alarmed at the sight of the needle, I said, "'Tis no' nearly as long or scary as vamp fangs."

She narrowed her eyes at me and took the shot like a champ. I waited with her for the two hours of observation required. While we were waitin', we started the process of gettin' her outfitted for the trip.

I sat my laptop on the table and answered her questions about what to take. At the end of the two hours, we moved the operation to her apartment.

'Twas heaven bein' close enough to smell her jasmine scent and feel the radiance of her body heat. 'Twas hell to be so close to her and no' reach out to wind that shiny hair around my fist, or bury my face in her neck. Or pull her close to find out if her body would mold to mine the way I fantasized that 'twould. A thousand times an hour.

As she concentrated on laptop shoppin', I took my time studyin' every luscious curve. Sometimes I thought she might be turned on by my attention, because I'd have the pleasure of watchin' her nipples tighten and bud through the lightweight silk knit top, but it could have been drafts.

My hands were so close to reachin' out and touchin' that I had to put them between my thighs and the chair, literally sittin' on them.

I chose to believe that she worked hard to ignore the signals passin' between our bodies because the alternative was that she really was no' that interested. Paddy. I had no idea what I'd do in that event.

I saw that she'd 'gone away' again, lost in thought. I tapped her knee lightly. "Elora?" When her eyes unclouded and she focused on me, I said, "Welcome back."

"Sorry." She smiled. "Where were we?"

"Talkin' about dress-for-warmth technology. I think you'd look good in that color." I pointed at a jacket that was a dark red and slapped away the thought that 'twas the color of new blood. "O' course you look good in *every* color."

"Silver tongue."

I smiled. "Come taste."

It had become a familiar exchange. I could no' wait for the day when she would no' reply with a scoff and a huff.

"That takes care of clothes. Now on to the next homework phase."

"What do you mean?"

"I need to learn all I can about this Istvan Baka. Right now, all I know is that he's an old vampire held captive by Black Swan, he's good at negotiating, and he's arrogance personified."

"How do you know that? The arrogance, I mean."

"That day I saw him in the Hub. It was written all over him."

"Oh. Well, I'm no' exactly the end-all authority, but I've heard he sits in a plush accommodation writin' vampire romance novels under a nom de plume. And that they're best sellers."

She blinked slowly. "You are joking, right?"

"I can see why you'd think so. It does sound fanciful and farfetched. The irony is juicy, huh?" I stood up, stretched and yawned. Either the healin' or the worry about Elora was drainin' my energy. "Probably just a rumor."

That was when I caught her starin' at my abs. "Hey! Caught you checkin' out the machine. Look at this."

I raised my tee and treated her to my version of a belly dance. The fact that I was able to it without pain meant I was almost well.

It took longer than expected for her to pull her eyes away and say, "Ughhhh!" She closed the laptop with a resolute click. "Does it even cross your mind that this is not appropriate behavior? You could use a few months of finishing school, you know that? On second thought, make that years."

"Finishin' school?" I repeated and said, "Now that is a joke!" Would she no' just be astounded to learn that royal progeny get 'finished' to death?

"No, it's not a joke! Blackie has better manners than you do, elf."

I toyed with bein' offended, but decided 'twas a fair comment. After all, part of my rebellion against bein' a royal was to reject cultivated aires.

"Really? That bein' the case, in your book it would be better manners for me to fall on my back with big, naked balls rollin' from side to side, tongue hangin' out, askin' for a nice tummy rub? 'Cause I can manage that. Right here and now." I pointed at a spot on the floor next to her feet and imagined gettin' naked, rollin' around, and beggin' like Blackie did. Maybe he was onto something.

"And besides…" She had a way of sidesteppin' when she did no' want to answer a question, "…doesn't that," she pointed to my stomach, "hurt your injury?" Her eyes then narrowed to slits. "Or have you been faking this whole time to get attention?"

Faking it? I could no' seem to form a thought beyond that grossly unfair accusation. The very person who'd done the damage claimin' I was fakin'! I think my mouth was hangin' open when I saw the mischievous light in her eye and knew she was baitin' me.

"Got cha."

I felt an appreciative smile formin' all of its own accord. "Seems I've taught you well."

She huffed and gave a throaty kind of laugh I had no' heard before, but definitely wanted to hear again. In addition to makin' me rock hard, it made me want to press my face between her breasts and ask her to do it again so I could feel the vibration.

In truth, I did no' know how much longer I could hold out. Flirtin' with Elora was fun. Sure. But no' as much fun as touchin'. Wouldn't you know that the first woman to no' be throwin' herself at me would be my mate?

How's that for karma?

I mean, it had been almost six weeks since I'd had a good body-buffin'. First time that could be said since I was, well, let's just say I was young. As it turned out, everything they said about wantin' your mate and *just* your mate was true. Seemed my only chance of ever gettin' laid again was to wait until Elora realized that we were *supposed* to be together.

Human-elf pairin's were uncommon, but did happen occasionally. I'm no' sure about what Mother Nature was thinkin' on that one because humans are no' monogamous like elves. For one thing.

CHAPTER 13

Ram

S TORM AND KAY were already waitin' at the jeeps in front of J.U., talkin' to the drivers, when I held the door open for Elora. She hesitated.

"What's wrong?" I said.

She smiled at me. "It's an occasion. The first time I've been outside in this world."

My heart clenched in my chest at the simple happiness she expressed from something taken so much for granted.

She stepped through the door pullin' her rollin' bag, and looked up into the night sky. "Look, Ram, the moon is almost full. What a beautiful night."

Storm gestured for Elora to climb into the backseat of the jeep nearest him and she did. He swung himself in next to her before I had a chance to protest, leavin' me standin' there with my thumb in my butt.

I got in the other jeep with Kay, but had a sour feelin' about her ridin' next to Storm.

"What's the matter with you?" Kay said.

"Nothin'." I pouted.

"Uh-huh."

When we pulled up to the jet on the tarmac, I saw Storm lean over and whisper something in Elora's ear. That was when I realized it would be a miracle if I got through this without killin' my teammate.

I hurried to get on board so I could snag the seat next to Elora no matter where she decided to sit. She went straight for the bench seat and strapped herself in. I practically dove for the seat next to her and looked up in time to see the consternation on Storm's face. Now I must tell you, I had no desire to flaunt my success, but I could no' have suppressed a smirk if my knighthood depended on it.

Storm sat down across from us and looked at me like he wanted to scrape me off his boot.

I heard Elora's voice and looked up, but she was talkin' to Storm. "So, what's up with the V.I.P. treatment?"

"The Order owns six of these. We share this one with other installations in North America, but they're shuffled as needed."

"And you're not worried about the carbon footprint?"

Storm looked confused and glanced at me, as if I knew what the fuck that might be, before sayin', "What's a carbon footprint?"

"It's the ecological cost of the amount of fossil fuel being burned."

He shook his head. "We've been on nuclear for a long time."

"Okay." That seemed to resolve that Q and A. "So how long is the flight? And where are we landing?"

"Bucharest," he said. "About eight and a half hours

from now. We'll have some dinner and sleep through the trip. When you wake up, we'll be in Romania."

Once we were at cruise altitude, Minerva came by to rattle off what was stocked in the kitchen. I noticed that Minerva spoke to me and made a point of pretendin' that Elora was no' on the plane.

"Give us a minute," I told her. She smiled her Hollywood smile and moved to the back to discuss the menu with Kay.

Elora leaned into me and whispered. How pitiful was it that her breath on my face was the most erotic thing I've ever felt. My entire body tensed like 'twas turned to stone.

"Would you get me a corned beef on rye with Dijon? And a Diet Coke with lime?"

"O' course. Would you like to tell me why you do no' want to order for yourself?"

"I want to get to Romania alive. So I think it's best that Cat Face not know which food is mine."

I pulled back to see her face and chuckled. "Cat Face, eh? I can get her fired if you want."

Elora cocked her head. "Really?" I nodded. "No. I don't want to get her fired, but she won't be getting a tip from me."

My laughter got a smile out of her and a scowl from Storm sittin' across the aisle from us.

When the food arrived, she took the deli sandwich and left to go sit next to Kay. That was no' part of my plan, but at least Kay was no' a rival. I knew this because he made no secret that he was committed to his girl. Body, heart, and soul. Maybe Berserkers were monogamous like elves.

I'd never asked. We usually practiced the don't-ask rule in B Team, accordin' to the philosophy that if a bloke has something to share, he will do so unprompted.

CHAPTER 14

Kay

E LORA MADE HER way to the back of the plane and sat down in the recliner next to me. The smell of her food made me queasy. So I gripped the whiskey glass a little tighter and tried to let the conversation be a distraction. I wasn't sure why she wanted to talk to me, but I reasoned that I would know in her own good time.

She asked all sorts of questions about my background and I found that talking about Katrina did distract me from thinking about flying.

Finally, after an hour of meandering, we got to the point.

"Do you know why he wants to talk to me?" she asked.

I shook my head. Honestly, I didn't know and suspected that *no* one knew for sure. "Want my best guess?"

"Sure."

"He saw you and was gripped by the bewitchment thing you've got going on."

She gave me a look that could best be described as innocent confusion. Unless my instincts were deceiving me, I had to give her credit. At least she wasn't deliberately turning my team inside out.

"You know. *That* thing." I moved my head in the direction of Storm, then Ram, one at a time.

I watched her carefully. It took a couple of seconds before she caught up with the implication. When realization hit her features, which seemed to hide *nothin'*, a full-on blush changed her face to the same shade of pink as her weird, but gorgeous hair. I shouldn't have laughed, but just couldn't help myself.

She stood up, making it pretty clear that she took offense to my bringing up the pickle brewing. Or maybe it was my laughing at her. Either way, she had nothin' more to say. Just took a pillow and a blanket out of an overhead compartment and left.

I felt a little bit bad about it. I mean Elora was nice enough and she'd taken the time to try to get to know me better. A nicety that, I admit, had not been returned.

But I didn't like what was going on between Rammel and my partner. I'd have had to be blind to not see that no good was going to come from teammates setting their cap for the same woman. Hand of Odin! It was a mess in the making.

CHAPTER 15

Ram

'T WAS LIGHT WHEN we arrived in Bucharest. As light as 'twas goin' to be, that is. The day was overcast, rainy, with poor visibility. Felt just like home in Ireland. Within minutes we knew the day had got more complicated when we learned that whisters were grounded.

Storm paced the tarmac talkin' to Operations on the phone, lookin' pissed. He looked pissed a lot these days. Unless he was talkin' to Elora.

He snapped the phone shut and stomped towards us.

"We're going to Brasov on the train and picking up cars there." Right on cue a van pulled up and stopped next to where we were standin' with our overnight bags.

Elora grabbed her bag out of the driver's hands. "Just a minute," she said, just before she started tearin' through her rollin' carry on to pull out a cowl neck sweater and a hoodie.

"Cold?" I asked.

She looked at me strangely as she was pullin' the sweater over her head. "You're not?"

I shrugged, rememberin' what a proper New Forest

winter felt like.

At least we got inside the van before it started rainin'.

As we drove through the narrow streets of the old part of the city, Elora was lookin' out the window like she'd never traveled before. Oddly enough, her intense interest made me look at the scenery through new eyes, wonderin' what it would seem like if 'twas my first time in Bucharest.

The driver got us as close to the station as he could, but we were still goin' to get wet. Elora took the hoodie and draped it over her head for cover and I could have kicked myself for no' makin' sure she had an umbrella. Some great caretaker protector I was provin' to be.

Silently thankin' Farnsworth for small favors, I was glad we had a first class compartment. Elora entered first and took a window seat. Just as I was about to throw down with Storm over who would be sittin' next to the lady on the train, Kay practically threw both of us out of the way and took the prize seat for himself. 'Twas out of character behavior for Kay, but I just took it as a side effect of hatin' to fly as much as he did.

I stepped in after Kay and did, at least, manage to get the seat across from my girl. She snuggled under the hoodie like it was a blanket, even though I knew it had to be damp from the rain.

While she stared at the passin' scenery, I stared at her, memorizin' every tiny nuance of her expressions. At length she realized I was lookin' at her while she was lookin' at Romania. She raked her eyes over me, turnin' the tables, but I did no' mind a bit. On the contrary, I wanted her to look her fill and feel comfortable doin' it. I knew I was attractive. Sooner or later she'd figure that out.

I was so relaxed, enjoyin' lookin' at my mate that I was half asleep. My third finger had found its way into a hole in the upholstered armrest. I was pushin' in and pullin' out with a rhythm some might say matched slow and deliberate copulation. I could no' suppress a little smile, knowin' that I was bein' suggestive. I am an elf, you know.

I waited for her temper to spark, as it often did when I was bein' vulgar. But she surprised me by quietly matchin' the cadence of the pumpin' of my finger with a mime of scissors cutting.

I laughed silently, feelin' my abs contract, the pale shadow of pain lettin' me know my rib still did no' care so much for laughin'.

There was something in her reaction that I will never forget. She was smilin' with a new gleam of interest I had no' seen before. 'Twas no' a look of lust or affection or even the satisfaction of havin' scored points on me. I would have to say 'twas most like appreciation. At that point, I was hungry for scraps of indication that she was movin' toward seein' me as someone she wanted around.

As for myself, she was so much more than I'd ever expected. Made me think I must have done *something* right in this life.

WHEN WE GOT to Brasov, Storm grabbed Elora's elbow and steered her to the first car before I'd even got off the train. He put her in the back seat, which left me ridin' with Kay and the driver of the other car. I'd never realized what a sneaky bastard Storm could be.

CHAPTER 16

Storm

I DIDN'T KNOW what game Rammel was playing. He could get any female he wanted. And had. The fact that he was going after the one girl I'd ever been serious about, well, it was seriously pissing me off. If it wasn't for the fact that she seemed to like having him around, I would have throttled his little elf ass and thrown him off the back of the train.

They thought they were sly with their little pantomime games, but come on. I was sitting right there. I needed to get his highness alone and have a mano y mano talk.

"Are we eating?" she asked from the back seat.

I looked at my watch, realized I hadn't changed the time since we landed, and tried to look back at her, but it was too cramped. Gods damn little European cars.

I looked at the driver instead. "We need to find a place for lunch before we leave town. Someplace with decent food, but we don't have all day."

"Hotel Bella Muzica," he said.

I nodded, suppressing the compulsion to say, "What ever," which told me I was just cranky in general.

The place wasn't busy because it was in between meals. "Whatever's quick," I told the waiter.

They brought us some kind of stew that I barely tasted because I was in a hurry. I hated rushing Elora, but we needed to get to the blasted Drac Unit before dark.

While the others were finishing, I went down the block to a market and bought the closest thing they had to snacks. Water. Bread. And chocolate for Elora.

When I came back, Ram and Kay were on the sidewalk.

"Where is she?" I said.

"Ladies," answered Kay.

I finally got everybody back in the cars for the hard leg of the trip. It was painfully slow because of steep mountain roads with sheer drop-offs, but we made it just as the light failed altogether.

I was pulling luggage from the car when I heard Elora speaking French to the overseers and I had to wonder what all else I didn't know about her.

We knew we were going to be expected to dress for dinner and, let me tell you, it's not that easy to work a tux into overnight luggage. But Black Swan knights don't say no when Sol Nemamiah tells us what to pack.

Chapter 17

Ram

I STEPPED INTO the room I'd been assigned for the night and started to close the door behind me, but 'twas forced out of my hand.

"What the..?" I turned 'round to see that Kay had followed me in and was closin' the door behind us both.

"Don't think I don't see what's going on, Rammel." My eyes traveled to the closed door and back to Kay, waitin' for him to say what was on his mind. "I'm not choosing sides – because I love you both like the brothers I never had – but Stormy's gonna have other chances to find love. Am I right in understanding that you get just one? Am I right that you're sure she's the one?"

I did no' know whether to be more shocked that Kay had guessed my predicament or that he was spoutin' so many words at once, particularly in the form of an unsolicited opinion. He had my attention and I definitely wanted to see where he was goin' with this line of questionin'.

"Guess there's more goin' on in that big head of yours than I give you credit for."

"Whatever. Back to the point. Just how does it work, her being human and all?"

Well, there was the rub. I could be no less than honest. "Bugger if I know."

"But it has happened before?"

"Aye. But 'tis rare."

"Well, that aside. You don't have a fighting chance." Kay leaned his back against the door and crossed his arms over his abs like he had no plans to be leavin' anytime soon.

"Thanks for the very fine vote of confidence."

"You want to hear me out or not?"

"Go on."

"First, there's a matter I'm afraid you're not factoring in. She thinks she owes Storm her life. And she should think that because…well, she does. If it had been up to you and me, she'd probably be dead."

Crap for breakfast. That was an ugly memory I did no' want to have to confront. Again. But that did no' diminish the truth of it. 'Twas perhaps my worst moment and I deserved to have to live with it.

I sat down on the side of the bed and ran my hand through my hair. "Aye. 'Tis true."

"Did you see the record of her hearing?"

"Aye."

"Then you know she has an over-developed sense of honor. For a woman. Women are usually about practicality – which is probably why the species has survived, but Elora's different. This isn't going to be about who's cutest. And I'm not saying I would know, by the way, so don't ask. If she thinks she owes it to Storm to be with him, she may feel like there's no other choice."

As that began to sink in, my stomach started to feel like lead. I had no' realized there was more at play than attraction. Or that losin' her was any kind of actual possibility. I mean, would Fate really pair me with someone who was no' destined to be mine?

So much for havin' done something right.

"Is there some advice buried somewhere in this breakin' news?"

Kay stood up straight and took a couple of steps toward me. "I'm glad you asked. I saw the little episode on the train." I made my face go deliberately blank. "The finger in the upholstery?" Okay. If he was goin' to name it out loud, I had to grin just thinkin' back on it. "Okay. See? There's the problem right there. Elora's not going to choose a guy with porn mud flaps."

I could no' have been more confused if he'd said Elora wouldn't smoke fairy farts. "Porn mud flaps?"

"Truck flaps with nudie silhouettes in a come-and-get-it pose? You've never seen that? Never mind. The point is she isn't going to be won over by displays of vulgarity."

"Vulgarity." I repeated the word. My mouth was open gettin' ready to protest. That was *no'* how she saw me. We had fun together. Did we no'? But before I could defend myself, he went on.

"Yes. Vulgarity. And we both know you were raised better." Mention of my upbringin' was out of bounds and my teammates knew that. I considered punchin' him and would have if I had no' had the feelin' I needed to hear what else he had to say. "Knock knock in there. Anybody home? She. Is. Human. She's not just going to wake up one morning and recognize you as her mate. You need to get yourself off autopilot and get your head in the game, or by Yuletide there may be some beautiful framed photos of you and me as best men at their wedding. Have you seen the way he looks at her? They may very well get to the altar before Trina and me."

A vision of my Elora wearin' one of those frothy white dresses, lookin' up at Storm with adoration in her eyes had me on my feet and ready to take on all comers.

"That's no' funny, Kay!" But as I said it, I was replayin' things she'd said to me. *'That's disgusting, Ram.' "You're in desperate need of finishing school.' 'Blackie has better manners.'*

Great Paddy's prick on a stick. Kay was simply confirmin' what she'd been sayin' all along. Only I had no' been listenin'.

"No shit? Even if you get her to want you, how are you going to motivate her to choose you over her sense of duty and obligation?"

I had no idea how to begin to answer that. I turned it over in my head a few times before sayin', "Do you know?"

Kay's expression softened a little, as did his tone. "You've got to start thinking like a human." *What?* "Love." Kay said, as if 'twas a whole sentence.

"What about it?"

"You need to find out what romance looks like and sounds like to Elora. What are her fantasies? Does she believe in true love? You'd best stop sitting on your hands and be finding out if she believes in forever."

How ironic that Kay would use that expression when "sitting on my hands" was exactly what I did sometimes to keep them to myself. I had the thought that it might be a sign, but dismissed it as coincidence. Just because I'm Irish does no' mean I buy into every woo-woo bullshit superstition.

No' exactly.

I was resistin' the urge to direct my anger at Kay, but I was feelin' anxious of a sudden and felt like I needed to be alone to think it through. I mean, what the fuck do I know about human romance?

"Great Paddy, Kay, what the fuck do I know about human romance?" I ran my hand through my hair in frustration. Again. "When elves recognize mates, we basically walk up and say, 'Tis you and me. Let's go.' The whole thing is playful. No'…" I waved my hands around lookin' for the right word. "..so bloody serious."

"But you do love her."

"Of course I love her. I love everything about her and do no' even have a choice in the matter. I mean, no' that I would change it. Fuck! I can't think straight." Suddenly it occurred to me that I was takin' advice from somebody who knew nothin' about the subject matter. "But what would you be knowin' about it anyway? You've been with the same girl since you were suckin' pacifier."

"That's true. Just saying that, if I were you, with so much at stake, I believe I'd find a way to figure it out. Look. It all comes down to this. How bad do you want her?"

I was no' enough of a poet to describe how badly I wanted her. There's simply nothin' I would no' do to make her mine. I'd go on quest. Fight dragons… That's when it hit me.

"She *does* believe in forever. All those stories she likes so much end with her sayin' 'and they lived happily ever after'."

Kay smiled. "Well, there you go." The big guy dropped his arms and left the room without another word, leavin' me sittin' on the bed in a room as old and drafty as the ruin where I grew up. I looked 'round.

Okay. So the place where I grew up was no' exactly a ruin, but the converted fortress felt crumbly even to me. I wondered what she was doin', if she'd like to have company. So I walked across the hall and knocked softly on her door. I did no' get an answer so I supposed she was either sleepin' or bathing. I smiled imaginin' the first and got hard imaginin' the second.

I WAS DOWNSTAIRS sharin' a before-dinner drink with Storm and Kay when Elora entered the room lookin' like a million bucks. It did no' escape my notice that every eye turned to watch her cross the room to where we stood near the fireplace.

By the look of her rosy complexion, I saw my second guess was right. She'd had a hot bath that lifted her color. 'Twas a nice compliment to her hair.

Madame Relacque said something to her about buildin' a too-early fire specifically to keep her warm.

"Thank you." Elora smiled graciously. "Between that

and some red wine, I believe I'll be toasty."

Madame Relacque looked confused. "Of course, you can offer a toast if you wish, my dear."

I coughed into my hand to suppress my chuckle. Elora exchanged a look with me and managed better than I to keep a straight face.

"No. I don't want to toast. I meant that I will be warmed by the fire and the wine."

"Of course," said our hostess as she handed Elora a glass of Dragasani poured by our host, who'd overheard the entire conversation. "This was vented by a Transylvanian winery, Nachbil. See if it's to your liking."

Elora breathed in the aroma, judgin' from the rise of her chest and the smile on her lips, and took a sip. "Wonderful," she said, and our hosts beamed.

You know I care no' at all for manners and think that, for the most part, 'tis a batch of silly customs invented to preoccupy prissy poseurs. But in spite of myself, her lovely manner and her lovely manners made me proud that she was mine. Mine whether she knew it yet or no'.

I knew I had a split second to act before Storm managed to rush in between us and spoil the moment. So I stepped toward her. "Would you care to sit here by the fire?" I asked, as I pulled out a chair near the end. She acted like she had no idea about traditions like pullin' out chairs for ladies.

I froze, thinkin', *for Paddy's sake, the woman believes I'm a lunker.* 'Tis fine to hold manners in disdain when your future does no' depend on such things, but clearly Elora held some esteem for convention, which meant I needed to reevaluate its importance. Such a woman does no' want a boor for a mate.

I was thinkin' maybe 'twas time to grow up and try to be worthy of such a prize.

ELORA CHATTED UP one of the locals durin' dinner, but by the time dessert came, I could see that she was tired and tryin' to hide yawns.

Storm turned to the facility sovereign, which in that case was either of two people. The sovereignship of Drac Unit was shared by the Relacques, the married couple who were our hosts. It was a unique arrangement, but seemed to work. Since he was sittin' closest to Monsieur Relacque, Storm directed the question to him.

"What are the plans for tomorrow?"

Monsieur Relacque let his eyes drift over those of us who were interested parties, meanin' those of us who were directly involved, as he said, "We're prepared for the interview to take place whenever it's most convenient for you. We'll serve breakfast in the morning at nine. So, anytime after that?"

I pushed back my chair and stood. "I'll walk Ms. Laiken to her room."

Elora did no' leave me lookin' like a fool. Takin' my lead she said, "Yes. It's been a long day and I want to be at my best tomorrow." To the Relacques, she said, "Thank you for the lovely dinner. It seemed like an occasion. You made a memory I won't forget."

Aye, indeed. I knew that my mum was goin' to cherish this girl.

Storm looked confused and perplexed. Elora gave me a grateful glance as I pulled out her chair, but the gratitude was no' for the gesture. 'Twas because she was fallin' over sleepy and needed a gracious escape.

She was silent as we climbed the staircase and walked down the hall toward our rooms. When we reached her door, she turned toward me. When her lips parted to say something charmin' like, "Thank you for walking me back, Ram."

I pulled the side of her body flush with the front of mine and nuzzled her ear, askin', "Would you like me to tuck you in?"

She released a tiny giggle and said, "Um. No?"

"You do no' sound sure."

I was suspectin' she had enjoyed the warmth of the red wine more than usual. That was confirmed when she made a mock serious face before sayin', "No," in a low voice and burstin' into a series of giggles.

"I like it when you imbibe. Unfortunately, you're countin' on me to be a gentleman." Under my breath I said, "And I never thought anyone would be accusin' me of that!" I pushed her door open and stepped back. "I'll leave my room unlocked just in case you get cold in the night. 'Tis that one." I pointed to the door across the hall.

O' course she thought 'twas banter. I assure you it was entirely serious.

CHAPTER 18

Ram

I WAS SITTIN' in the day room with my eye on the door, listenin' to Storm and Kay chat up two of the knights currently stationed there. Storm had known one of them from school in San Francisco. I spread marmalade on toast, then spooned scrambled eggs on top of that. It was no' dainty, but 'twas a heavenly way to start the day. Especially when paired with good coffee.

Elora swept in lookin' fresh as a daisy in full bloom. The mix of turquoise threads in her sweater made it near impossible to look away from her eyes. Perhaps 'twas the point. Women are always dabblin' in bewitchin' with their fashion schemes. At least she had listened to me about no' wearin' red. A woman like Elora in red would be servin' herself up as a vampire's catnip.

I watched her take a cranberry juice, hot chocolate, and an orange scone from the sideboard. Storm was dividin' his attention between watchin' Elora and listenin' to what his friend was sayin'.

She sat down in the chair next to me. "Good morning," she said.

"Mornin'. You want us to ask for some red wine to go with that or did you have enough last night?"

She snorted softly. "Like you've never had too much of anything?"

I grinned. "More is more."

She broke off a corner of her scone, stared at it for a bit, then put it down on the plate. She took a sip of juice, but just looked at the cocoa like she was no' sure why she'd got it.

I leaned toward her so no one else would hear me. "Off your chocolate this morn?"

When her eyes slid sideways toward me I knew she was nervous. I sat waitin', wonderin' if she'd lie and give me bluff and bluster. But she was no' that sort. Instead, she nodded and smiled a shy little smile like she was embarrassed to be found out.

I reached for her hand underneath the table where no one could see. She wrapped her fingers around mine and did no' pull away. "You do no' have to do this, Elora. I'll pull the plug before you can say, 'Baka, go fuck yourself'."

Her eyes widened for an instant before she laughed and, just like that, the nerves were managed. "Thanks. I'm good."

I was proud of her for agreein' to go through with this, but must tell you that what I really wanted was for her to come to her senses. 'Twas worth another try. "No one would think less of you if you change your mind. I promise."

She shook her head. "Let's do it."

Exactly what I was afraid she would say. "Have you a

stake in each boot?"

"I do."

"When you're ready. No' before. 'Tis all on your terms."

She turned to the knights who'd been talkin' to my teammates.

"Are there any rules I should know about?"

"Rules?" They both repeated at almost the same instant and looked at each other.

"Yes," she said. "Like, time limit for instance?" They looked at each other, their faces blank. 'Twas obvious no one had given thought to the parameters.

"Well, in that case," she went on, "I propose twenty minutes. That seems fair to me. If I don't like the way things are going, I'll end it then. If I think something productive could be gained by staying longer, I will."

"If you want to talk about fair," I said, "one minute is more than fair."

"Let's just settle on something solid," Storm said. "Like no more than twenty minutes no matter what."

Elora crossed her arms and widened her stance. I recognized that body language as meanin' that she was no' goin' to budge on how she would handle this. "Twenty minutes is a loose guideline. If I think something useful will come from staying longer, I will."

Storm narrowed his eyes. "Why did you ask about rules if you didn't have any intention of abiding by them?"

"As it turned out, there *weren't* any rules, were there? We're making this up as we're going, which means I might as well advocate for my point of view."

"Twenty minutes. No more. And if I say you're done, you're done. We're pulling you out of that room without further argument."

She pursed her lips and said nothin' more, but I knew her well enough at that point to know that did no' mean acquiescence. No indeed. What it meant was that she was done arguin'. No more. No less. If Storm was stupid enough to think that meant he had her agreement, that was on him.

The four of us rode the small elevator to the top of the tower. Elora's jasmine scent filled the space and made me a little dizzy. It also made me mad with jealousy knowin' that Storm and Kay could smell it, too.

The doors opened to a small observation area, clinically minimalist. The far wall was mostly a large glass window that looked directly into Baka's room. I could hardly call it a cell because 'twas far too opulent for that.

I did no' know how secure the glass was, but the doorway was protected by a security vault that would be at home in Fort Knox.

Within a second of steppin' off the elevator, my eyes had swept the room for equipment, counted two knights and one control panel attendant, and landed squarely on the vampire standin' at the back of his plush cage. Supposedly he could no' see through the glass, but for all the world he appeared to be starin' at Elora. It made my skin crawl and I wanted nothin' more than to simply grab her and leave the madness behind.

Storm got between Elora and the glass wall so that she had to look at him. "Do not take your eyes off him," he said. "Do not turn your back or sit down. Do not allow him to get closer than five feet." His eyes flicked to me. "They're fast, Elora. Faster than you can imagine. I'm not saying he's stronger than you. I'm just saying that you have to keep your guard up at all times. He's very old and very wily." Her eyes wandered. "Are you paying attention to me?"

She looked at Storm. "Do not take my eyes off him. Do not turn my back or sit down. Do not allow him to be closer than five feet. Got it."

Storm slumped a little. "I hope to Woden you're taking this more seriously than appearances would suggest."

"Serious as a judge."

Storm dropped his chin. "That's *sober* as a judge."

"Whatever," she said.

That's my girl, I thought.

She looked at me as if I'd said that out loud. I nodded just enough for her to see, wantin' her to know she had my confidence, if no' my approval.

"He's the most notorious vampire in Black Swan history," Storm said. "Do not take this lightly."

"I'm not!" she said. "Let's get it over with. I'm ready."

One of the attendants spoke up. "We'll be able to hear as well as see everything that happens in that room. When you're ready to leave, all you have to do is raise your voice and say, "Open!" He turned the arm on the control panel microphone toward his mouth and said to Baka, "Step all the way to the back of the room and remain still while your guest is admitted. If you make a move that might be interpreted as aggressive at any time, we will sedate you and extract Ms. Laiken. Do you understand?"

The vampire nodded solemnly, movin' nothin' but his head, no' changin' expression.

Elora took a step toward the vault door, but turned back suddenly and asked the control panel attendant. "Has he ever attempted escape?"

He looked blank. The others looked from one to another. Storm, Kay and I shook our heads and shrugged at the same time. I did no' recall havin' ever heard a story about huntin' Baka down since his imprisonment a hundred or so years before.

Her voice pulled me from the effort of tryin' to recall.

"You don't know?" The panel attendant shook his head. "Please call Madame du Relacques and ask her."

"Now?" asked the knight who stood over the security panel.

"Yes! Now! I want the answer to that question before I go in there."

He looked at Storm, Kay and me, revealin' himself as every inch the sexist asshole he appeared to be.

Elora was fumin'. And I did no' blame her. After all, she was the one riskin' her neck to do a favor for Black Swan. I could almost see her thinkin' about tossin' the guy out the window into the river gorge below. The image of that gave me a phantom pain in the ribcage. If the fellow knew what was good for him, he'd comply and be quick about it.

Storm nodded and said, "Call her."

Apparently she answered her own phone. We listened to him converse briefly in French before settlin' the in-house phone in its cradle and sayin', "No escape attempts."

Elora nodded and seemed satisfied with that. "Okay. Let's do this then."

Storm, Kay, and I watched as bystanders while the local knights handled operation of the vault and trained weaponry on the vampire. Just before she stepped through, she glanced back at me. I gave her a nod and a wink, even though my stomach was turnin' somersaults. Lettin' her walk through that door was by far the hardest thing I've ever done in my life, goin' against eons of hard wired instinct to protect my mate. The openin' was circular, like a science fiction portal to another world and I was scared shitless that I would no' see her alive again.

The locks sounded loud when they slid back to allow her entry. They sounded even louder, when they slid back into place, lockin' her in with the leech.

"Lady Laiken," Baka said, with just a hint of a smile and a smaller inclination of his head. "I won't bother to introduce myself because, well, because that would be silly. So I will just say welcome to my humble home." He gestured at the relatively small room that had been his world for the past century.

"Thank you," she said politely. "Had breakfast?"

Baka grinned, which was surprisin', at least to me. I had no' expected a vampire, even an old one, to be in sufficient command of his faculties to grasp sarcasm. "Would it make you more comfortable if I sit?"

"Somehow I don't think the word 'comfortable' works for this situation. But, yes, I would like it if you sit."

He moved toward the fire with an exaggerated slowness.

"Join me." He pointed to the stuffed chair facin' the one he'd just taken. "Would you like something to drink? Wine?"

She glanced around the room, which meant she'd broken rule number one and taken her eyes off the bugger. "Sparkling cider," she said.

I leaned back to catch Storm's eye and mouthed, "Sparklin' cider?" I'd never heard her make mention of sparklin' cider before. I was no' complainin' as I would have been if she'd accepted his offer of wine. We should have made that rule number one. No alcoholic beverages. Or doobies. No' that the staff might pass doobies through the little doggie door.

Storm just shrugged to let me know she'd never mentioned sparklin' cider to him either.

"Sir Ansel," Baka said to the glass, "a sparkling cider for my guest, if you please."

Great Paddy, the monster maintained an air of old-world formality that made him seem like a cartoon vampire.

"Who's your decorator?" Baka indicated himself with a self-effacin' cluster of posturin'. "Hmmm," she said.

"Is that 'hmmm' you like it or 'hmmm' you don't?"

"Very. Nice." Her tone was non-committal even if the words were complimentary.

After repeatedly breakin' rule number one, gettin' a good look around at his collections, she said, "You're a musician?"

"Yes."

"And you play all these instruments."

"Yes."

She nodded. "And paint?"

"Yes."

"And you write vampire romances. Fiction I presume?"

He grinned. "Have you read one of my books?"

"I've read all of them, Valerie."

He raised an eyebrow and smiled in a way that I thought might look seductive to a woman. "And was that research or did you enjoy my work?"

She raised her chin. "Loved it. Can't wait for the next installment in the series. What will it be? Love Bleeds?"

"Mocking me?" He was clearly amused, which made me even more nervous. "I'm crushed."

"A sensitive vampire? That has to be an oxymoron.

"Actually, regarding your books, I did notice that there was a lot written about the joys of giving blood to irresistibly sexy, good-looking vampire, but nothing about mercilessly ripping out throats and leaving unrecognizable corpses behind."

He shrugged. "I write romances. I don't like horror."

"That's very funny, Baka. You're a lover, not a fiend. Are you gay?"

Wait! What!?!

Baka was apparently as startled by the question as I was, but he recovered fast and laughed. Long and loud, makin' me wonder what a bloodsucker locked up for a century has to laugh about. Or maybe he was just that delighted to spend time with the most desirable creature imaginable.

When his laughter subsided, he asked, "Why would you think that?"

"Well, let me see. You're into the arts. All the arts. You wear silk. You write romance novels. You have long hair. You're over thirty with a flat stomach. And you have lots of pillows on your bed."

"I guess six hundred years is enough time to get in touch with one's feminine side. I am not motivated to impress others with an unrealistic, arbitrary, or fashionable ideal of masculinity; a superimposed caricature of a man."

When the sparklin' cider was placed in the panel cabinet, the vampire rose and slowly crossed the room. I was relieved to see that Elora regained her wariness and stepped back.

Baka set the crystal stem on the table next to the other chair and poked at the fire. I wondered if she was thinkin' the same thing I was regardin' the absurdity of allowin' a dangerous prisoner to have possession of an iron fire poker.

When he took his seat again, he said, "Regarding my flat stomach, six hundred years ago people such as myself didn't have access to sugar, beer, fried food, or fructose corn syrup. Thank you for noticing, by the way."

"Are these two chairs a permanent part of your furnishings?"

"Yes."

"Do you often have company?"

"Never." She raised her eyebrows as if waitin' for further explanation and he did no' disappoint her. "Even vampire have hopes and dreams. Mine are simple. I dream of having someone to talk to."

Great Paddy, I hope she did no' fall for that.

No. It was worse. She crossed the room and sat down in the chair across from him, breakin' every single rule we'd come up with and more. The sight of my mate in such a vulnerable position as sittin' down four feet away from him? I guess I went a little crazy, but you have to agree that 'twas entirely justifiable. I mean, like every vampire hunter, I'm no stranger to feelin's of fear, but the fright I felt seein' Elora so close to the old leech was on a whole new level.

Apparently I tried to open the vault without knowledge of how it worked and screamed at everybody in the room to get her out. I can no' say what happened after that. They tell me I was hyperventilatin', which was why I found myself sittin' on a counter with a paper bag over my mouth and nose.

When she was safely back on the right side of the vault, I was relieved enough that I could cry, but I was also so mad at her I could spit fire. So mad I could no' even look at her.

"WHAT'S THE MATTER with him?" Elora asked my team-mates.

"He's scared to death! That's what's the matter! Every one of us could just…" Storm clenched and unclenched his hands in the air pantomimin' a right proper stranglin'.

With a suddenness I was no' expectin', he turned on

me, pointin' toward my chest. "For every time I have ever called you reckless or psycho or accused you of having a death wish, I take it all back. She makes you look downright timid."

I could no' believe I was takin' up for her in any way, but I heard myself say, "Lay off. 'Tis done."

"Are you okay?" She looked at me. I just went back to breathing through the paper bag and let my eyes do the talkin'. "Wow. It looks like there was some serious drama on *this* side of the mirror."

"Oh! Sweet. Do you care about us at all?"

Elora's mouth fell open. "What do you mean? Of course."

"Ms. Laiken," Kay began, "emotions were running a little high because of fear. For you. And from this side of the glass, it seemed like you were sort of asking for it."

"It? Asking for it as in getting bit?"

Kay nodded.

Elora looked around the room. "So it's *Ms. Laiken* now is it?" When she saw that every single one of us were mad as hornets, she said, "Okay. I'm sorry if I gave you cause for concern. But I was the one in the situation and I had to follow my own instincts."

"Cause for concern?" Storm was no' the sort to indulge in fits of temper and, I must say, it looked a little off kilter on him. He turned toward the wall and yelled out loud before resumin' the upbraidin'. "Inoculations can't save you if your jugular is sliced in two." *He had a good point there.* He held his hand in front of her face, thumb and first finger twitchin' together. "And you were this

195

close. Even *you* wouldn't recover from that."

The woman had the nerve to look like she was gettin' angry in response. "That's just it, Storm. I wasn't in any danger. I'm sorry you were needlessly worried, but you're going to have to learn to trust me." He hissed out his aggravation then dropped his hands to his sides as if to say he was givin' up. "What if I had told you I was going to rehabilitate Blackie? We both know you would have forbidden me to go near him. Blackie would have been sentenced to live out his life being tormented by that sadist."

"Please tell me you are no' comparing that *thing*," he pointed to the creature behind the glass, "to an abused dog! If you're saying you have plans to domesticate Istvan Baka, then you need to double down on your therapy sessions."

Elora pulled back like she'd been slapped and, as irate as I was, my protective instincts proved stronger. I jumped down from the counter, got in front of Storm and said, "That's enough!" I held his gaze long enough for him to know I was no' jokin' around. I looked down at the paper bag in my hand then threw it down. *Great Paddy. Hyper-ventilatin'? What would be next?*

A nice long descent down an ancient spiral staircase might be just what I was needin' to help clear my head. I let the door slam shut behind me and tried to keep my mind on countin' steps, tellin' myself over and over that the thing that was important was that she was no' just alive, but unscathed.

As much as I tried to convince myself that 'twas over, I

was chilled to the marrow seein' that my mate had such little regard for her own safety. I believe 'twas at that point that a deep abidin' fear settled into my solar plexus, that she could no' be trusted to keep herself safe. And I knew, without needin' to be told, that death or separation from her would result in my own demise.

Half an hour later I answered a knock at my door. 'Twas Kay.

"Get your stuff. Got a break in weather. Whister's waiting for us."

I WAS THE last one on board. I guessed Storm must still be royally pissed because Elora was in back by herself and he was sittin' next to the pilot. I hoped he was stupid enough to hold onto his pout forever.

My heart melted when I saw her look up to see what I'd do, her face a mask of honest vulnerability. I moved to the back, reached out and shoved a wisp of her whister-blown hair back into place, and slid into the seat next to her. She might as well find out now that nothin' she might do would ever make me want to sit anywhere but by her side. I did no' miss the look of gratitude though. And right after we took off, she leaned over and said, "I'm sorry." I managed a little smile in acknowledgement. Then she said, "Do you have a history of hyperventilation?"

Great. Paddy. "Certainly no'."

"No offense intended. I just wondered if it was an un-usual reaction for you."

I twisted my body so I could face her and was about to tell her that I'm no' usually so, um, excitable, but when her tongue peeked out to wet her lips I got lost in lookin' at her mouth and longin' to be bathed in kisses. I thought about kissin' her. O' course that was my inclination, but I did no' want her to accept me from gratitude. As if she was followin' my line of thinkin', she said, "Do you think there will be a debriefing?"

I managed to shift my attention upward to her eyes. Seemed she wanted to lighten the moment. That was okay with me. I would play along. So I said, "Would like that, but I'm no' wearin' briefs. I wear boxers," I leaned in close, "as you know."

She treated me to a laugh, which made Storm turn around and glare at both of us for a couple of seconds.

We were in Bucharest in minutes. It seemed so strange that a trip that had taken hours in a car on narrow windin' roads was reduced to so little time.

I saw Kay havin' a little talk with the hangar manager. When he walked over to us he said, "We're makin' a stop in Edinburgh to pick up folks headed for the Americas."

A couple of people I did no' recognize were already on board waitin' for us. Elora sat down on one of the bench seats next to one of them and was sayin' hello while I was left settlin' myself across the aisle. At least I could keep an eye on her.

Storm went all the way to the recliners in the back. Good.

I got Benson, the flight attendant, to bring me a laptop. I needed to do some research on romance. It was also a sneaky way to watch what was goin' on between Elora and the bloke chattin' her up without starin'. Blatantly. I could glance over the top of the screen now and again with no one bein' the wiser.

After snacks, I watched Elora rise and walk to the rear. She'd had what was apparently a heart to heart resolution with Storm and had decided to stay in the back for a nap. I watched her drag a pillow and blanket out of the overhead compartment, recline the seat to sleeper position, turn her body toward the window and pull down the screen.

I did no' want to resent Storm. Paddy. He was as close to me as a family member. No. That's no' true. In many ways he was closer because of our shared near-death experiences and the times we'd saved each other from bein' vampirekabobs. I could never bring myself to hate Storm no matter what, but he was gettin' on my nerves like a twinge that would no' stop. I could no' cause a shift of his attention toward Elora. The only way that was goin' to happen was for Elora to tell him that she'd chosen me.

So I turned my attention back to the search for romance. One thing was clear. I needed to drastically step up my game.

The first search result was Masspedia. It said, "make plans for romance with romantic ideas for date nights, anniversaries, romantic travel, and romantic getaways". Seemed like a good place to start. At least they made liberal use of the word 'romantic'.

I catalogued each one of those suggestions in my head and started through the other results, noticin' a lot of musical references. I realized that a lot of the 'romantic' music sounded like music Elora would like, music with sweet lyrics and relaxed melodies. It hit me that I had made fun of this music and said only borin' people would find it worthwhile.

I really was makin' a mess of my own courtship. I'd as much as told her that romance is for losers. *Great Paddy, dunk me and hang me out to dry.*

CHAPTER 19

Ram

W E WATCHED THE playback of Elora's "audience" with Baka in the conference room adjacent to Sol's offices. 'Twas difficult to watch, but curiously I was able to see things I had no' seen when I was terrified for Elora's life. Baka's fascination with Elora clearly went beyond hittin' on her, although I could no' say if he was interested in blood, sex, or both. Baka was lookin' at her like she was the end game. And I did no' like it.

I had the stray thought that Sol might no' have considered what would happen if a vampire ingested Elora's blood. He might absorb some of her density and, therefore, enhanced abilities. And then where would we be? Paddy.

I heard Sol talkin' and realized the playback had ended.

"...fulfilled your part of the bargain. You are, therefore, free to come and go on probationary status, but you are bound by your vows of secrecy same as any other Black Swan employee."

"I understand." She smiled, clearly delighted at the

prospect of bein' out on her own. At the same time, the idea of that made me shudder.

"We should go into the city for a celebration dinner," Storm said, smilin' at Elora. I wanted to punch him in the mouth and watch it swell up so that his smile would look as ridiculous to Elora as it did to me.

"The rest of this meeting concerns plans going forward so you are free to leave, Ms. Laiken."

"I'll stay," she said simply, as if she could no' take the hint. I could no' help but smile because I knew she was adept at nuance.

Sol looked surprised. His brow creased slightly with displeasure, but he decided to allow it. "Very well. He'll be arriving tomorrow to coordinate strategy." Sol pointed a remote at the screen and a map of a section of Manhattan came up. I recognized it because 'twas a frequent focus for patrol. "Monq's team has concluded that the abductions seem to be clustering in this area." He pointed the pin light to the corner of 39th and Broadway. "It's a club called Notte Fuoco."

A street view photo of the club came up.

"It's all the rage," he said flatly with dispassionate distaste. "A restaurant and two floors of depravity."

I suppressed a snort at Sol's puritanism. I doubted he was personally acquainted with what the word 'depraved' truly meant, but he'd been a young knight once. If he'd written an autobiography, I had no' read it. So who was I to judge?

"The restaurant is on street level." Street view was replaced with an interior shot taken when no one was there.

"The second story is deejay dance." That photo revealed a crowded, dimly lit room with dancers in bird-cage contraptions suspended from the ceilin' and wave lightin', oscillatin' from purple to red to white to blue.

Elora leaned over and whispered. "Somebody should have told them that nobody looks good in colored lights."

I snickered quietly, but no' so quietly that Sol did no' hear it.

"Something funny about this, Hawking?"

"No' at all, Sovereign. Something caught in my throat."

He gave me a sour look, but that was hardly something new.

"Then there's the basement space they call The Underground," he continued with a photo of tables, dance floor, and stage. "Live music with themed nights. Folk music. Street music. Acoustic. Fifties. Eighties. Its popularity has surprised a lot of people who bet against its success. Or so I'm told.

"This is where Baka comes in. I gather he's been using his time alone to pursue various interests including musical skills. His experience with stringed instruments can be tapped for this effort. The former house bass player was delighted to accept an all-expenses paid vacation until further notice so that Baka can take his place."

I glanced at Kay. His ears were turnin' red. No' a good sign. Believe me.

Storm got to his feet as if he couldn't keep himself sittin' in the chair.

"You are *not* seriously considering loosing that wily

old vampire on New York City!" Storm more or less spoke for all of us.

Challengin' the sovereign was no' unheard of, but 'twas something saved for, shall we say, special occasions.

"No. We're not considering it." Sol nodded at the chair. "Have a seat," he said evenly. When Storm was reseated, Sol said, "It's not under consideration. This is what we're doing."

"Son of a..." Storm began.

"Stop right there, Sir Storm. I'll thank you to remember where you are and to whom you are speaking."

Storm pressed his lips together, but remained silent, looking around the room like he wanted to bolt. Or hit something.

"For the record," Kay said. "I agree with my partner."

"Make that three," I said.

"So. Noted," Sol said. "Istvan Baka will be free while performing the duties outlined in his contract. That is, of course, conditional on his strict adherence to the synthetic blood diet he's been on since his incarceration and reporting to me once a day. When he's recalled, he will give himself up. If he doesn't, B Team will run him down and either capture or kill him."

Kay raised his hands and then dropped them in a gesture meanin', 'I give up.'

Sol ignored Kay. "Regarding the celebration dinner you proposed, Sir Storm, if you're going, you might as well make it a working evening. Take Kay and Ram with you and scout Notte Fuoco."

Storm's face fell in an almost comic way, but I'm proud to say that I managed to suppress an outright laugh.

Sol said, "That is all." And left. Simple and to the point. I have to give him that.

When just the four of us remained in the room, Elora revealed her excitement. "When can we go? Tonight? Let's go tonight!"

Kay shook his head. "Clubs are usually closed on Mondays."

"Tomorrow?" she asked hopefully. The three of us looked at each other and shrugged which meant that none of us objected. I could tell Elora wanted to jump up and down. "What time?"

"Leave at eight?" I said.

"Yes! What should I wear?" she asked, then hurriedly added. "Never mind. I'll ask Elsbeth."

I KNOCKED AT exactly eight. After waitin' for a bit, I knocked again. When she did no' answer, I was thinkin' about pullin' out my phone to call, but then the door opened. I sucked in a breath. The everyday Elora was enough to knock me on my ass. The glamorous Elora robbed me of breath in my lungs and thoughts in my head.

After a few seconds I was clearheaded enough to speak and tried to make light of havin' been temporarily paralyzed. "Excuse me. I'm lookin' for Elora Laiken?"

Her shoulders slumped like she was disappointed. "Okay, so I'm out of my element. Elsbeth did a club night make-over. It's all wrong, isn't it?"

MY EYES WANDERED down to where the ends of her curls fell between her breasts. Before my brain could get control of my hand, I had reached out and taken a lock of silky hair between my fingers. If I did no' have elf ears, I might no' have heard the little catch in her breath that made her lips part slightly and I could no' help a smile. My eyes jerked up to her mouth and I stepped inches closer, herdin' her back into her apartment. "Let's stay in tonight and let me show you just how very *no'* wrong you look."

She put her hands on my chest to stop my forward progress and shut down what could have been a very promisin' night in. "So. Really. This is okay?"

I leaned against the doorway. "Perfect. Let's go."

MY TEAMMATES WERE on whister level waitin' when we arrived. I watched them both do their share of starin'. Storm said nothin', but Kay said, "Like the come-and-bite-me outfit."

He smirked at the look of warnin' I gave him. I did no' want anything spoilin' her night out.

Seein' the skyline comin' up through Elora's eyes was, well, eye-openin'. We had made the run so many times that the scenery was commonplace. We might as well have been on the subway goin' to work. 'Twas refreshin' to be reminded that the city had beauty as well as an underbelly known intimately well by vampire hunters.

THE WALK TO Notte Fuoco was pleasant. 'Twas a balmy night for that time of year. Comfortable enough for lightweight jackets. Elora slowed at displays in windows to satisfy her curiosity. I had to repeatedly clear my throat to remind Storm and Kay that we were no' workin', but there for her.

Kay talked to the hostess about a table, then walked over to where we stood. "An hour. She says we're welcome to stop in at one of the other levels for a look around while we wait."

We went up to the second level first. B Team was in the habit of lookin' for vampire when in Manhattan. So we found ourselves doin' exactly that. I glanced over at Elora and saw that her face was somewhere between pink and red, close to matchin' her hair. I followed her line of sight and realized she was embarrassed about the gropin' and grindin' takin' place on the dance floor.

I was about to suggest we move on when I saw Storm place his hand on her lower back and urge her toward the elevator. I was goin' to have to be quicker if I wanted to shut Storm out of the game.

We bypassed street level and went straight to the basement. 'Twas blues night and the mood could no' have been more different from where we'd just been. The music was slow, subdued, somebody doin' a cover of "The Thrill is Gone".

I did a double take when I realized the bass player was none other than the oldest vampire known to Black Swan. Even behind gray shades, there was no mistakin' 'twas him. 'Twas impossible to tell where he was lookin' behind the glasses, but he seemed to be lookin' at Elora.

Paddy.

Kay got us a table. Elora listened to music, while the

rest of us looked for clues as to why the disappearances were originatin' from that spot. Storm pointed to his watch when it was time to eat.

They gave us the corner booth Kay had asked for. We could have got in a lot sooner, but we were willin' to wait for the spot with the view. Elora might weigh more than the rest of us, but she ate a lot less. Ate less, but enjoyed it more, from all appearances.

Storm was settlin' up when Kay said, "Two and a vic. Eleven o'clock."

I grabbed Elora's forearm and pulled her attention with a look that I hoped was deadly earnest. "Stay here," I said. "Do. No'. Move. From this table until I come back."

We followed the trio Kay had identified out the front door, but they had vanished into thin air.

"I'll go this way," I said.

"No," Storm stopped me. "Stay with us. You know the rules. No less than two."

I wanted to argue, but the reasonable part of me, however small, knew he was right. I could no' strenuously object to Elora bein' unnecessarily reckless with our future if I was no better. I nodded and followed behind the two of them, keeping tabs on our backs.

For some reason, which I could no' explain in a hundred years, we all silently agreed that we needed to go south, away from Times Square. There was no discussion, no argument, no agreement. After so much time as a team, we worked together like a single hunter with six eyes, six legs, six arms. I do no' know if vampire dream, but if they do, I'm pretty sure we're their nightmare.

Findin' nothin' on the first block we ran a grid pattern back and forth turning to check each alley way as we passed it. Nothin'. Absolutely nothin'. Fifteen minutes later we knew we'd lost them and further lookin' was pointless. We came to a stop, breathless, but charged up by the emotions of the chase.

"We lost 'em. Might as well head back and pick up Elora," Kay suggested.

We should have gone back to the Bistro, collected the beautiful outworlder and been on our way. But she was no' there. We asked the hostess to check the Ladies' room. Kay went upstairs to look around while Storm and I tried the Underground. She was no' there and neither was the band that had been playin'.

They'd been replaced by a guy on a stool with an acoustic guitar. I wish I could say I was so concerned about Elora that I did no' notice he sounded lame as a wet noodle, but I can no' lie about music. I imagined she was in the buildin' somewhere. If I had known where she was and what she was doin', I would have been out of my ever fuckin' mind.

My teammates and I had just come together at the street level entrance to confirm that Elora had left the buildin'. Great Paddy. I was just, at that point, beginnin' to learn that the woman simply would no' do what she is told.

I was just takin' my phone out of my pocket when she ran into the bistro lookin' breathless. And beautiful. I hated that she looked beautiful, because I was no' pleased with her. Like Kay had said the night we met, New York is crawlin' with vampire.

I was first to reach her. "What part of stay here and do no' move did you no' understand?"

Instead of objectin' to my tone, which surprised me, given what I knew about her, she grabbed the sleeve of my jacket and pulled me toward the door. "Get them now. Let's talk outside."

"How do you expect me to get them when you're busy pullin' me out of doors?"

I did no' wait for an answer, but caught Kay's eye and motioned toward the door. She pulled the three of us into a little huddle.

"You left with another vampire right behind you. So naturally I followed."

"NATURALLY?!?" I said. "Elora. There is nothin' natural about runnin' down vampire. 'Tis a highly skilled proposition. If everybody could do it, well, I do no' exactly know how to finish that sentence…"

"Just let me finish," she said. "I followed him and killed him before he could become a problem for you."

I'm fairly certain that I lost the ability to feel my face at that revelation. None of us, meanin' B Team, said a word in response. We were probably all three too stunned to make our mouths work. She looked between us expectantly, waitin' for feedback.

Finally, I repeated the news, no' believin' it could be part of my reality, but just tryin' to confirm that I was no' havin' a very bad dream. "You went after a vamp with no back up." 'Twas no' a question so much as a test of veracity.

"Well, somebody needed to do it!" Paddy help me. I wanted to throttle my own mate. She must have seen the emotion overtake me because she said, "Do not start hyperventilating!" That only served to drive my fury right off the livid cliff.

At that point, Kay found his voice. "Somebody needed to do it? Elora, that was truly a dumb ass thing to say, but maybe it fits, because I'm starting to think you are one." The exasperation in his body language and tone of voice almost seemed to match mine. "Why don't you just take us to the scene?"

Elora nodded and started walkin' that direction. As we followed she explained exactly how it happened. I glanced at Storm, who seemed to have been struck permanently dumb. Two and a half blocks away from the club, she turned into an alley as she was sayin', "So I asked to see his fangs and he showed me. Then I gave him wood."

That's when we heard Baka laughin' it up. 'Twas worse than I'd thought. No' only did she leave the eatery when I told her to stay, she went after a vampire, and Istvan Baka went after her. *Criminently.*

"Gave him wood!" It seemed that Baka could no' stop laughin'. 'Twas a testament to the phrase 'need to get out more'. "This just gets better and better. She killed him with a toothpick that she grabbed out of some fellow's mouth as she ran by. Did you know that?"

B Team, all three of us, turned to look at Elora in unison, temporarily forgettin' all about Baka.

She looked between us like nothin' more significant had occurred than a stroll in the park. "What?"

"And did you tell them that Sol is waiting to see all of you in his office as soon as you get back? No matter how late?" Baka continued.

"I hadn't gotten to that part." She said it through clenched teeth. "Yet." Then she gave him the finger.

Storm turned on me lookin' for all the world like that was my doin'.

"Why be glarin' at me?" I asked. "She's the one who gave him the bloody finger!"

"Because. Rammel. Somehow I see *yer bluidy* influence all over this. I don't think she even knew what a rude gesture was before she started spending time with you!"

Well, that was almost certainly true, but that was no' the time to own it.

Baka started laughin' all over again. "Better and better," he said in that weird accent. "I haven't had so much fun in… well… ever." He patted his shirt pocket. "I need to take notes. I'm putting this in a book."

Kay decided to intercede before things escalated. More. "Okay. Everybody settle down. Let's hitch a ride with clean up. We'll get back faster and sort this out."

Elora looked properly horrified for the first time. "You mean ride with the, uh, body?"

Go figure. She'd had no problem killin' the thing, but did no' want to be near the remains.

"If you can kill it, you can ride with it," Storm said, echoin' the sentiment all three of us had no doubt heard in our heads. Then to Baka he added, "You're relieved."

"Fine by me," said the leech, throwin' a grin over his shoulder at my mate. *Great Paddy.*

"By the way, you're all bloody welcome," Elora said before flouncin' away a few yards to lean against the brick wall with her arms crossed in front of her and a pout on her mouth. That was fine by me because I needed a break to cool down and I could keep an eye on her while I was doin' it.

Nothin' more was said when clean up picked us up. 'Twas also deadly quiet on the ride back to J.U. When we got on the elevator, Elora pushed the up button.

"Oh no, you don't," Storm said. "He wants to see *all* of us. You, too."

She rolled her eyes like a teenager, but got in with us.

As promised, Sol was waitin' up in his office, rollin' one of those small black cigars between his fingers, and starin' straight ahead.

"We went…" Storm started, but Sol held up his hand to stop him from sayin' anything further.

"I want to hear it from the young lady."

I knew she would bristle at bein' called 'young lady', but I was so out of sorts, I did no' care. Very much.

She retold the events of the evenin' from her point of view. It would have sounded perfectly reasonable, I suppose, *if* she was an experienced vampire hunter.

"Any of the rest of you have anything to add to that?" I glanced at Storm and Kay. None of us said a word. "I'll let you know if I have further questions. You're dismissed."

Really? I thought. *That was it?*

Storm and Kay got off the elevator at the Hub without a word. They did no' need to tell me they would be sharin' a whiskey or two. 'Twas what I would have been doin' if I

213

did no' feel obliged to walk my girl to her door. I do no' think I'd ever felt so bereft. No' even when Lan died. I was that sure that she was goin' to be the end of us.

When we reached her door, I said exactly what I was thinkin'. "Will you be the death of me then?"

She turned to look at me with sympathy, even if she was completely unrepentant. "I didn't do it to worry you, Ram. I did it because I was worried *about* you."

I could no' stop myself from pressin' close to her. Knowin' how close she'd been to two vampire, on her own, 'twas impossible to deal with the idea. I buried my face in her neck and breathed deep. Night bloomin' jasmine. Too delicious for words. She was warm and supple and fit me perfectly, head to toe. Just as I had that thought, I felt her tense.

I would never take from her what she was no' ready to give. So with a little growl of agitation, I pushed myself away and walked on to my own door without lookin' back.

Chapter 20

Ram

B Y THE TIME I woke the next mornin', I was in a mood to let the past be in the past. It was easy. We would no' be puttin' Elora Laiken in a situation to come in contact with vampire again. Combinin' work with a celebration outin' had been a bad idea that would no' be repeated. Ever.

I'd slept in, had breakfast, and when Elora was still nowhere in sight, I decided to take a peace offerin'. A cocoa peach latte, guaranteed to get me in the door.

"I have news," I said when she opened a crack.

Eyein' the cup in my hand, she asked, "Is that a big?"

I smiled. "Would I bring you anything less?"

Blackie pushed his head 'round Elora's thigh to say hello and wagged his tail.

She opened the door wider and took the cup from me. "You know he likes you."

"I like animals. They like me." I bent down to give the big boy a scruff between the ears, but he flopped over to his back for a tummy rub instead. Well, why would Elora no' have a demandin' pet with a mind of his own? I rubbed his tummy and laughed at him, too.

"Well, there's no accounting for taste." She sat down at the dining desk. "It better be good news because that's the only kind I want to hear today."

"'Tis. Today's the day I report to the infirmary for clearance. In a couple of hours I should be officially off the D.L. Fit and ready to return to duty." She scowled, even though she'd just taken a swig of the drink she called nectar of the gods. "What's wrong? You do no' look happy."

"I have mixed feelings. After what happened last night, well, it punctuated what you've been saying, that those things are fast and strong and that they have big teeth. You lost a partner. The same thing could happen to you or Storm or Kay."

I could no' believe she was bringin' this up, just as I had decided to forgive her and let bygones be bygones. "Elora…" I started, but then I heard what she was sayin' to me. I mean I heard what was in her heart, beneath the words. "And if that should happen you'd feel alone in this world."

She moved to the couch and sat down at the end, lookin' out the slidin' door, but no' answerin'. I took that to mean that I was right.

She was always so upbeat, so together, and enthusiastic. I did no' stop to think about how much pain she was hidin' behind that. 'Twas easy to forget that she'd lost everything that she knew when she'd survived passage to my world.

I sat down next to her. "Look at me," I said. I could tell

she did no' want to and suspected why. "Look at me." I said it softer.

Turnin' toward me I watched two tears runnin' down her cheek. I cupped her jaw with my right hand and used my thumb to wipe them away. "Ah, my darlin' girl. You truly will be the death of me."

'Twas as if I absorbed her sadness into my skin when I came in contact with her tears and I rededicated myself to the proposition of seein' to her happiness. I could no' change what had happened in her past, but I could move mountains to insure her future. If that's what it took.

She pulled away and swiped at her face. "When do you go back to work? Officially?"

I dropped my hand and sat back. "Right away. We've been slackin' long enough, makin' it hard on the others." She nodded, but seemed lost in melancholic thought. I wanted to assure her that I was no' goin' to die young. I had too much to live for. I opened my mouth to tell her so, but learned that 'tis near impossible to lie to a mate. If I was a carpenter or doctor or politician, I might be able to say the words. But a vision of Lan poppin' into my head told me I was no' in a line of work that enabled promises of long life.

So I settled on what I could say honestly. "Listen to my words and please hear me. Most knights die of old age, in comfy beds, with great-grandchildren standin' all 'round. What happened to Lan will make us all the more careful."

She searched my face, lookin' deep into my eyes like she was lookin' for the truth of it. I let her look and read my feelin's to the extent she was able. Then I was ready to re-establish equilibrium.

"Your coffee's cold, but no matter. Come to lunch with me. That French onion soup you like is on the blackboard today. We can take Blackie out for a frisbee afterward if you like."

I was rewarded with two things, the smile I love most in the world and the company I love most in the world sharin' lunch with me.

THREE HOURS LATER, I'd had a decent workout between frisbee with Elora's dog and a couple of hours on bio level. I'd just finished a shower and was gettin' dressed when my phone buzzed on the counter.

The text was from Sol. *My office. One hour. Acknowledge.*

I had to give the devil his due. The man was a master like no other when it came to economy of words, the very antithesis of Irish culture.

I assumed he wanted a final answer as to who would be our fourth, which drew a very large and involuntary sigh from me. Lookin' up at myself in the mirror I smiled, realizin' that I felt nary a twinge from the ribs. All healed. Namin' Ghost as my partner was a bitter pill. I had to look for posies along the path where I could find them.

'Tis an understatement to say that I was surprised to see Elora in the conference room when I arrived. I could no' imagine why she would have been called to sit in. I looked at her, lettin' my curiosity show on my face, but she gave away nothin'. Hmmm.

I stopped at the side service for a cup of tea, knowin'

that there would be the usual banter about pussies and tea, but no' carin'. Sometimes a lad needs tea like his mother made and nothin' else will do. Such an occasion had just presented itself.

I sat down at the table, seein' that Storm and Kay were equally perplexed, and stirred my tea.

"Ms. Laiken is going to give a short presentation. Please give her the courtesy of hearing her out before expressing your opinions." Sol nodded toward Elora. "You have the floor."

I stopped stirrin' and rested the spoon in the saucer. If I had known what was comin' I would have poured a cup full of Irish whiskey instead.

I could see that Elora was nervous. 'Twas the first time I'd seen what anxiety looked like on my girl, but 'twas unmistakable and it had all my neurons firin' on red alert.

She moved to stand at the head of the conference table, in front of the blank presentation screen, and began.

"I would like to be considered as a replacement for Sir Landsdowne. I'm the best candidate and I have several good reasons to support that claim.

"I have probationary security clearance. I'm reasonably intelligent. I'm not just trained in hand-to-hand, I'm the trainer. I also have experience with a variety of weapons. I'm familiar with policy and can recite most of the Field Training Manual on request. I am stronger than the strongest knight has ever been. I am faster than the fastest knight has ever been. I can't be hypnotized. I have had my inoculations. I am resourceful in finding weapons when vampire are afoot and have successfully neutralized the enemy in the field. I've established a working relationship, of sorts, with the point per… uh, vampire. I have bonded with B Team. I know them. They know me. We're comfortable together.

"Last and most important. In this world, those men are the closest thing I have to loved ones. I can't stay behind while they go out nightly to possible mortal combat – possible fatality, knowing that I could be the lynch pin that keeps them alive. It would be cruel to ask that of me."

I was almost too stunned to blink, much less to take my eyes away from her. I must tell you that my initial reaction on the matter was to feel betrayed. It seemed my fears that she would be puttin' our future in constant jeopardy were no' unfounded. On the contrary, it seemed she was set on a course of destruction. No' just of herself, but us, whether she knew that or no'.

When Elora sat down, Sol sat forward, but spoke from his chair. "I've discussed my personal concerns about this proposal and have been satisfied with answers received.

"The short of it is this. Ms. Laiken has added herself to your short list of replacement candidates. Oddly enough, she was not the first to nominate herself for the position. Istvan Baka pointed out last night that she is a one-of-a-kind resource currently being underutilized."

Great Paddy. The vampire wants her in the field.

"However, according to tradition, the choice is yours. I, personally, think she's the best man for the job, but making her B Team's fourth," my head came up when he looked straight at me, "and Ram's partner, will require two of your three votes. Further, one of those votes must be Sir Hawking's. Those are the conditions. What say you?"

Storm was first to speak. Like that was a surprise. "You *cannot* be serious. No. Absolutely no. And that could not be more final."

"One vote no," Sol said without conveyin' emotion of any kind.

"Wrong! That would be three votes no." Storm first looked at Kay, then me. Seems he had jumped to the conclusion we would share his view.

"Hold on." Kay held up a hand. "I say it's up to Ram. Partly because he's the most senior member of B Team and partly because he's the one most affected since she would be his partner. As far as I'm concerned, everything she said is true. Plus, unlike some of the guys who were on the short list, she's *actually* killed a vamp. She did it by herself with no real training and no help of any kind. And another plus that she didn't add is that, from a purely tactical perspective, she offers some unique benefits, as a woman, that could be useful."

Storm's brows were drawn in so tight that deep lines had formed between them. All of a sudden he grasped Kay's inference and drew in a sharp breath. "Decoy?" He spat. "You're suggesting using Elora as bait?" I could see the outrage in the color of his complexion and hear it in his voice. He was as petrified by the prospect as was I. Perhaps he really did love her. "That's the kind of half-cocked idiocy I'd expect from Ram! What is wrong with you, Kay?"

"Look," Kay answered calmly. "I didn't put her up to

this. She volunteered. Apparently we've given her the mistaken impression that our collective asses are worth looking after. She wants to be…"

"…Wendy," I finished that sentence.

"What?" Storm said it like a challenge.

"'Tis a character in one of her stories. A responsible, nurturin' girl who takes care of lost boys."

Storm turned on Elora, who was lookin' at me, considerin' what I'd just said, but no' denyin' it. "Is that true? Is this about some kind of Savior Complex?"

Elora pulled her attention away from me before answerin' Storm with an evenness that made me proud even as I wanted to put her in a tower keep that was only accessible by me. "Wanting to keep your friends alive is not a psychological aberration, Storm. How do you think I would feel if they brought one of you in on a gurney one night, with me knowing I might have prevented that? My training and abilities should be used for a worthwhile purpose. You can't really think I'm better suited to clerical work.

"I get it. You're afraid I might get hurt. Now you need to understand that I feel *exactly* the same about the three of you."

I stared straight ahead, no' really seein' what was before me, only visions of the horrors that were potential results of this insane notion.

"As I see it, the only drawback is this," Kay continued, "and I'm going to be completely honest because it's just us here in this room. Right or wrong, B Team is regarded as cream risen to the top. You know that Lan's place would usually be seen as a reward for an outstanding record. The feeling might be that it isn't fair to give the spot to someone who hasn't earned it the usual way."

"I think that's a very good point," Storm concurred.

Sol turned his attention to Kay. "So, is that a vote yes or a vote no?"

Kay pressed his lips together, sighed, and said, "Yes." He turned toward Storm, knowin' before he looked that his partner thought his position was a betrayal. "Sorry." He shook his head. "On balance, I think it's the best thing for the team and maybe also our best shot at dealing with this outbreak. The city's counting down to panic. So far they haven't put together that what many of the missing have in common is a club in the Times Square district, but they will. We're just running out of time for indulgent choices."

Sol looked at me and said the very thing I did no' want to confront. No' in a hundred years. "Guess that means it's up to you, Hawking."

She looked at me hopefully. My predicament was a true Catch 22. If I said aye, I would drastically increase the chances of losin' her. If I said no, she would be safer, but she'd hate me for takin' her choice and, therefore, her freedom away. Knowin' that for people such as ourselves freedom is a critical factor in happiness, I would therefore be takin' her happiness away as well. And I had pledged myself to the proposition of seein' to that just hours before.

"Goes without sayin', that if she was any other female, this would no' even be on the table. But we know how special she is. I can no' stand the idea of exposin' her to what's out there, but I do no' have reasonable grounds to deny her if this is what she wants. As she said, she is stronger, faster, and is the best of us in hand to hand. She's very likely smarter as well, at least more so than I. So far as bein' my partner, I already know I like spendin' time with her. If she's goin' to be out there, I'm glad I'll be close by."

"So that's a yes?" Sol asked for clarification.

"Aye. 'Tis."

"This is madness!" Storm thundered, then let out a string of curses under his breath that were easily heard by me and perhaps the others as well. For someone opposed to swearin', he could turn the air blue when he was of a mind to do so.

Sol gave him a witherin' look that said he was re-gardin' him with all the esteem one would bestow on a toddler throwin' a tantrum. Under other circumstances I would have found that immensely entertainin'. "I think as a courtesy Gautier should be told before a general an-nouncement is made. Right or wrong, he's expecting to be named. I will inform him of the decision, but with your permission, would like to be able to tell him he will automatically be transferred to B Team the next time there's an opening. Gods forbid. Does everyone agree?" Sol took the silence as acquiescence by abstention.

"Also," he went on, "Ms. Laiken and I have discussed a couple of procedural issues and resolved them. The one that concerns you is The Order's policy on office romance. Since there has never been a female operative in the department of hunters, it hasn't previously been an issue.

As a formality I need your acknowledgement that you are aware of the policy."

"Done," said Kay.

My head felt pressurized like I was under water. This was a Catch 22. It was a Catch 33. I'd barricaded myself into a corner with no escape. *No fuckin' romance? After all the research I'd done to woo the Lady Laiken?*

I was a rule breaker by nature, but I'd always respected Black Swan policies because they were worthy of respect. This, though, was something else. I had to draw the line at the idea of The Order comin' between an elf and his mate. Great Paddy.

"Acknowledged," I said. I did exactly as asked. No more. No less.

Sol turned to Storm. "Nod if you understand."

I imagine we all saw the tick in Storm's jaw muscle. He was glarin' daggers at the Sovereign, who really couldn't have cared less, but Storm managed enough of a chin dip to count as a nod.

Next, Sol's attention rested on Elora. "Lady Laiken, report to the personnel office in one hour and they will go over your benefits package. You will receive the same salary and benefits as any knight on probation."

"What are benefits?" she asked.

"Things like pension, holiday, and sick leave."

"I don't get sick."

"You mean you've never been sick?" She shook her head. "Ever?"

"I've never been sick. Ever."

"Interesting. Your team has one week to brief you on

guidelines and bring you up to speed on weaponry. It will also give us time to make adjustments to your teaching schedule.

"Your induction ceremony will be tonight after dinner. All knights not on rotation will be present. Congratulations. Welcome to Black Swan."

"Are we done?" Storm grated. If anything it seemed his irritation was buildin' rather than subsidin'.

Sol looked at him. "One more thing. The three of you are responsible for getting her up to speed on equipment and whatever street sense didn't make it into the Field Manual."

Storm huffed and stomped out, lettin' the door slam against the wall on his way out.

Sol looked at Kay. "He may be due for a workshop on temper control."

It really was kind of surreal to be hearin' that sort of talk about somebody else. The fact that the subject was Storm, of all people, would have been comical if there was anything, at that moment in time, that could have made me smile.

Kay stood and said, "Don't worry. He'll come round," to Elora, then leaned over the table and offered his hand. "Welcome to B Team, Lady Laiken."

Elora stood and took his hand, lookin' satisfied that at least one of us had some grace. "Thank you, Sir Caelian."

"You know there's a reason why they call us Bad Company," he said. "And it isn't because we're no fun."

She smiled. "I surmised as much and will do my best to uphold the reputation for badness."

Kay smiled and walked away. As usual, Sol had left without a goodbye. When the man was done, he was done. Niceties be damned.

I was still sittin' in the chair tryin' to sort through what had just happened. 'Twas the Fates' version of a drive-by, to be sure. An hour ago I'd thought my biggest problem was findin' a way to make Elora Laiken fall into forever love with me.

Now my biggest problem was how to keep her safe in the field. I'd be needin' to watch for vampire *and* rivals, who just kept poppin' up. 'Twas bad enough when Storm set his cap for my mate. Now a slick old leech was vyin' for her affections as well. *Paddy.*

"Are you going to sit there until bedtime?"

I looked up at Elora. "Had no' really made other plans."

"I need a celebration cocoa."

I shrugged and got to my feet. "Right behind you."

She stopped at the door and turned to me, lookin' more trustin' and innocent than any vampire hunter I'd ever seen. "Thank you for the vote, Ram."

I felt my mouth twitch. "You're welcome. *Lady Laiken.*"

She giggled. Another first for a vampire hunter.

FOLLOWING THE INDUCTION ceremony, Sovereign Nemamiah requested that the gatherin' stay behind for an update on the operation involvin' Baka. The exact reasons for the vampire's involvement had remained above my pay grade and that of the other knights, so far as I knew.

Sol stood on the floor of the Chamber and addressed those of us who were present, includin' the newest Black Swan knight sittin' to my right and smellin' far, far better than a vampire hunter should.

"You're all aware that Istvan Baka has a temporary reprieve to work with us, under contract, on getting the numbers of disappearances under control." He nodded at Elora. "You can thank the recent inductee for securing his help, which has already proved valuable beyond measure.

"Baka was instrumental in creating a network of fool proof hideaways for vampire when he was in New York decades ago. The system connects unused and abandoned subway tunnels to secret street level entry and exit points. He has confirmed that there was such an access point in the old Tri-State Mercantile building currently occupied by the club, Notte Fuoco.

"Obviously all vampire are not coming and going from that point, but put an asterisk next to its importance. It's sure to figure prominently in our strategy to curb the epidemic. You'll be kept posted when new intel is available. That is all."

THE NEXT DAY the new B Team assembled on the Splat Deck for trainin' purposes. Kay was goin' over a variety of weapons lined up on a table in front of him.

"We developed bullets with a core made of hard wood so green it won't catch fire before reaching the target, but we like the splat guns better because they're silent and if an innocent gets in the way, they won't get hurt.

"As you might guess, one of the logistics problems is

how to carry this," pickin' up a splat pistol, "without drawing attention. That's a lot easier to do in cold weather because you can hide a world of sins in outerwear. In warm weather we pretty much have to rely on stakes in boots.

"The silver gel only works on exposed skin. That means if your aim isn't good enough to hit a vamp in the face, it won't do you any good. So we'll start with the fixed targets at maximum range of thirty feet. Have you ever shot a gun?"

"No."

"Okay, well, we all have our strengths and weaknesses. We know you're good at hand to hand."

"And ancient weapons," she added.

"Yeah, but swords and quivers are not exactly low profile. Storm's the best shot." He turned to Storm. "Why don't you show her how it's done?"

"You wanted her on the team. You show her."

Great Paddy. I did no' know Storm was even capable of bein' such a whiney little infant, but 'twas wearin' thin. So thin, in fact, that I had no more patience to bring. I stepped in front of his face so he had no choice but to look at me and see that I was no' pleased with his bitchy little attitude.

"What's this now? A fearless leader or just a pouty lunker who turns crybaby when he does no' get his way? 'Tis done! You get that? Let me say it again carefully. 'Tis. Done! She's one of us. And if you do no' come on board, you're goin' to get us all killed." I jerked my head toward Elora. "That includes her."

His nostrils were flarin' as he clenched and un-clenched his jaw. I could see he was no' ready to step it back. He fumed at me like I was the enemy for a few seconds, but a change in perspective registered on his face and his breathing slowed. I do no' know if 'twas because he replayed my words in his head, but something brought him 'round to reason.

"Okay. Move aside."

Because he sounded like himself, I did.

He picked up one of the splat guns from the middle of the table and went to stand next to Elora. "The gel capsules go in here. There are three shots to a cartridge. When it's loaded, you move this latch with your thumb to bring them forward into the chamber. Here. You try."

Elora watched carefully and repeated the steps right the first time.

"We deliberately designed these guns with a sound identical to loading shells in a shotgun because any advantage is a good advantage. And few things sound more ominous than hearing the sound of a shell moving into the chamber of a shotgun, especially when it's both quiet and dark. Vampire scare fairly easily and then they make fatal errors." He smiled. "We like that."

He took the gun from her hand, spun and fired three shots in rapid succession. All hit the target in the face.

"Whoa. Seriously?" she said.

"Told you he was good," said Kay with pride.

Storm smiled. "Okay. Load again and try to hit my shots on the target."

She loaded the weapon like she'd been doin' it for

years. After Storm corrected her stance, she fired. The first two shots missed altogether. One hit a target in the crotch – two targets away from where she was aimin'. By the fourth round she'd managed to hit *her* target… in the crotch.

I gave Kay a WTF look and said, "I'm beginnin' to sense a very disturbin' pattern here."

He laughed, but Elora slid a sideways glance at me that looked a lot like elvish mischief. "Maybe you should keep it in mind, *partner*."

I laughed softly, hopin' the idea that there's always truth in jokes was a cock-eyed notion.

I stepped behind her, placed my hands on her hips, and urged her to swivel her body to make a slight angle to target adjustment. I ducked down a little to mimic her line of sight and moved her arm up a bit.

"You're hittin' 'round two and a half feet south of where you're aimin'. Maybe there's more of a drop in flight than you're calculatin'. So why do you no' try aimin' just that much higher and see what happens?"

Her next shot hit the target in the chest.

"I'm callin' that progress." I smiled at the little victory.

Kay took the pistol from her and said, "We'll work on it."

THAT NIGHT AT dinner, Kay made Elora feel welcome as our newest teammate. First, with a gift. He'd had Farnsworth find one of those gold plated business card holders and had it engraved with her initials. He handed her a beautifully wrapped gift box and looked on with pride as she opened it.

"A business card holder?" she asked. "It's beautiful, Kay. Do we, ah, carry business cards?"

He laughed and shook his head. "Look inside."

She opened the case to reveal twenty or so toothpicks.

"Just in case your shooting doesn't improve," he said. Elora rose and went 'round the table to give Kay a kiss on the cheek and a neck hug. "Hey. I'm an engaged man."

She reseated herself with a big smile. "Thank you. You never know when such a gift might come in handy."

The second part of Kay's plan to make the evening an occasion included sharin' B Team's most embarrassin' moments, includin' me givin' Storm mouth to mouth. *Paddy*. I had worked hard at purgin' that experience from memory.

We threw everything we could think of at her, hopin' the important stuff would stick. Or come back to her if needed.

"Never allow yourself to be separated from your partner," Kay said. Storm nodded. "And we can't ever let the team be trapped together at a dead end or elevator, places like that."

"And there are better ways to identify leeches than askin' to see their fangs." *Criminently*. That was one for the annals.

"Like what?" she asked.

"You encountered a vamp by himself, but that's unusual. They like to work in twos or threes. The one you followed was hopin' to get a free ride. Like buzzards waitin' their turn for the ones closest to the carcass to get their fill and fly off."

"Ew," she said.

"Are you sure you're no' too squeamish for this kind of work?"

"I guess it's too late to consider that now," said Storm, allowin' his surliness to resurface.

"Back to the subject." I gave Storm a pointed look then turned to Elora. "After a while you'll be able to recognize vampire on sight. They move differently, stiffer I guess you'd say."

"Stiffer?" Kay said. "Funny, Ram."

"Well…" I shrugged as if to say I can no' help that I'm naturally entertainin'. Back to Elora, I said, "In the beginnin' you can rely on us to help identify targets."

She surprised me then by sayin' to Storm, "The day you told me about what happened to Lan, you mentioned aphrodisiacs and I didn't question it at the time. I know there are differences, but in my world, aphrodisiacs were proven to be a myth."

I had no' known about the conversation, but I supposed there must have been quite a lot that passed between the two of them without my knowledge. I tried to make light of it. "I, for one, would very much like to hear how that was proved."

"Um, actually, it was a TV show called 'Myth Busters'. Every episode they would take a commonly held belief and put it through a series of scientifically designed tests to determine fact or fiction. I saw the one on aphrodisiacs."

Storm looked unconvinced. "Like you said, what if it's one of those other-dimension differences?"

"Could be. I'm just saying that aphrodisiacs can be a convenient 'devil made me do it' excuse."

Storm nodded. "Noted."

I noticed that Kay was lookin' at Elora with more interest than usual. "On another note entirely," he said, "I don't want to be the dead messenger, but I think you ought to do something about the hair."

Elora blinked. "Like what?"

"Like cut it off."

"What? Why?"

"Your hair is great, Elora, but you didn't just fight your way into a beauty contest. Your priorities have got to shift from cuteness to battle readiness.

"This must have been mentioned in your hand-to-hand training. If you leave all that hair down, sooner or later it will get in the way, could easily create a blind spot. Wearing it up is almost worse because it might as well be a handle; grab, jerk, pull you off balance at best, snap your neck at worst. I think I speak for all of us when I say I'd rather see you *alive* with shorter hair."

Elora looked from Storm to me for our reactions. I did no' entirely agree because, after all, I wear my hair longer than most. But if it would improve her chances of survivin'...

"Well, when put like that, how can I no' agree?" Even as I said it I was thinkin' about all the nights I'd laid in bed fantasizing about divin' into a tangled mass of jasmine scented silky strands. Or feelin' it trail down my body in concert with feathered kisses from chin to cock. Or havin' it brush against my thighs as I watched her ride me with her head thrown back. I looked at it with longin' and said, "I, too, prefer you alive."

Elora looked down, clearly no' happy with the suggestion. "I'll think about it," she said. Without segue her head came up and she seemed reanimated. "I've had an idea and want to run it past you."

We nodded or gestured for her to continue.

"I was thinking about Baka's gig as bass player for Notte Fuoco. We might expand on that idea. He could maybe arrange for jobs for the four of us. Then we could be there every night. Sort of like under cover without raising suspicion, but keeping each other in sight?"

The three veteran members of B Team looked at each other. 'Twas no' just a good idea. 'Twas nothin' less than brilliant.

"I think you should be a dancer, Kay," I said.

"Funny, Ram. I think you should bus tables."

"Okay. Seriously. If the vamps are coming and going from the live music level in the basement, then, shouldn't that be the center of the operation?"

"Yeah. She's right," Storm said. "She should serve drinks. Right or wrong that's what patrons expect to see female employees doing. Plus it gives her a mobility that we wouldn't have as bouncers or bartenders."

"If she's going to serve drinks, then Ram should bartend. That makes the most sense. They might not be in constant contact, but he could keep an eye on her."

"And vice versa," she corrected Kay, makin' me smile.

"And vice versa," he repeated, lookin' between the two of us.

"We'll be bouncers."

Elora nodded. "Makes sense. You look the part."

"Sol's call. We have to run it by him, but I'd give you dimes to dollars, he's gonna love it," Storm said.

And he did.

ELORA WORKED HARD the rest of that week. She worked on target practice and spent considerable time with the bar staff tryin' to pick up the fine art of professional drink delivery.

When she was no' busy trainin', she was workin' with that dog. Alsatians were versatile dogs, good at just about any task you set before them. So it was no' a surprise that Blackie took to her 'hunt the vampire' game that she'd devised usin' two halves of Baka's shirt.

One afternoon she knocked on my door.

"Come play a game with us."

Now how could I refuse such an invitation? "Sure. Do I get to name the game?" I leered.

"No," she ignored my innuendo. As usual. "I want you to play hide and go seek with my dog. Give me one of your tees from the laundry. Then I want you to go hide somewhere in the building."

I opened my mouth to ask where, but she held up her hand.

"Don't tell me where. I don't want to influence the outcome. We'll give you a, what do you think, ten minute head start?"

"Okay." I went back inside to grab a shirt out of the hamper. I'd just had laundry done so there was no' much to choose from. As I handed her my favorite Black Sabbath shirt, I said, "I need that back. No blood. No rips. No teeth marks."

She laughed. "If he doesn't find you in," she looked at her watch, "half an hour, I'll call you and tell you the first attempt failed." She started away. "Oh. Start in the Hub though. That's where I'm going to set him on you."

"Set him on me?"

Chucklin' she said, "You know what I mean."

"No' sure that I do."

"Come on. It'll be fun."

I GOT OFF the elevators at the Hub, but got back on and went down to the lowest level. I knew exactly where I was goin' to wait. The cage that used to be his prison.

I had brought a book and planned to settle in for half an hour before gettin' a phone call, but five minutes after I was in place, I heard the sound of claws tappin' on the tile floor. By Paddy, the dog had done it and in time that must be some kind of record. He rushed to the outside of the cage and barked a song of victory in between moments of grinnin' at me.

When Elora arrived, she had Storm with her. Blackie looked over his shoulder, waggin' his tail and put a paw up to the cage like he was ready for his trophy photo.

Elora went to her knees and let that mutt lick every inch of her face while she praised and petted him.

I got up and let myself out. "I'd be askin' for a hello kiss myself if you were no' wearin' so much dog drool on your face."

Storm gave me a dirty look. I supposed 'twas because I talked about Elora and kissin' in the same sentence. The lad was goin' to have to get over it.

CHAPTER 21

Ram

LIKE ELORA, I had my own homework to do. If you ask me, my job was harder. It requires a much higher level of education to mix drinks than to take orders for them and carry them to tables. So I started carryin' a little handbook around, studyin' recipes and such. Elora quizzed me before and after dinner every night and I was startin' to feel like a bartender. Perhaps I did no' have the flashiest moves, but the ladies like to look at me and that counts for something. If the Black Swan gig ever dried up and I did no' want work as a prince, which I definitely did no', well, people will always drink.

We hit a snag with the uniforms. Well, no' Elora. She got field operations to modify her skirt so that she could attach a gun to a garter and no one would be the wiser. I'd never thought I had a weapons fetish, but that image never failed to get me hard. My hands itched to reach under that skirt and gently pop that garter. I know. That was neither here nor there. Just sayin'. Some day.

Notte Fuoco dress code was no' so much a problem for me because I could stow a satchel under the bar, but

Kay and Storm had no way to hide splat pistols under black tees and jeans. They were bare ass except for stakes in boots, which was a much bigger risk to themselves.

The Fates must have been doubled over laughin' at me. As a demonstration of 'bein' careful what you're wishin' for', B Team was back on the duty roster. I'd been ready to get back to work and wantin' to see our names posted, but that was before. In my defense, I could no' have guessed in a hundred years that my mate would be the first female knight in the history of The Order. And on B Team!

We had Thursdays and Sundays off because those were the slow nights at the club. And Mondays, o' course because the club levels were closed.

So Tuesday night found me behind the bar tryin' my best to look like a whiskey-slingin' professional. It was no' too hard except for the fact that my first priority was keepin' an eye out for where my teammates were at all times. And, o'course, lookin' for signs of vampire.

I lived for the trips Elora made into the bar to leave or pick up an order. She always had a smile that seemed to say she thought of me as special, but I could have been readin' too much in.

Every hour we got a ten minute break. When the crew arrived to spell us, I turned to Elora and said, "Let's go up to the street. I'm feelin' bat shit claustrophobic down here."

"Sure," she said. "Sounds like a plan."

It felt good to be out on the street. It felt good to have Elora all to myself. 'Twas without my teammates 'round. 'Twas when I had the idea that a day in the city would be a perfect ruse for a romantic date. I could always say I was just givin' an out-of-towner a tour of the city. If she happened to fall in love with me by the by, how could I be blamed?

We turned in response to the noise bein' made by a group of young women who emerged from the club lookin' like they'd had way too many spirits in too short a time. One of them noticed me and, even through a drunken haze, I saw interest click behind her eyes.

She headed straight toward us, pushed her way between my partner and me, and tried to press her comic fake boobs into me. I had taken a step back and was just about to tell her to buzz off, when she jerked right and stumbled into her friends.

Elora had taken her by her sideways ponytail and shoved her aside. "Find something else to do," she said.

The lady, and aye, I use the term in the most generic sense, grabbed onto one of her friends to get her balance while swearin' in a way that would make Paddy, himself, turn away blushin'.

When she looked up at Elora, I could see she was contemplatin' a cat fight. The idea of a drunken girl thinkin' about a brawl with a Black Swan knight, especially my partner, was so ridiculous I laughed in the girl's face and said, "Oh. I definitely would no' if I were you."

Her friends decided on her behalf that my admonition was good advice. She half-staggered as they pulled her away under protest.

Crisis averted, I had the opportunity to consider what

had just happened. 'Twas no' my imagination that time. My mate had acted on jealousy. There was no other reasonable explanation. And that realization must have made me look very much like the Cheshire cat.

When I turned my very delighted smile on Elora, she looked around like she was embarrassed and said, "I really have no idea why I did that. It was wrong. I mean it's not as if you can't take care of yourself or decide whose fake chest you want pressed against you."

"Elora…"

She walked away before I could respond, sayin', "I've got to visit the Ladies' before time's up. I'll see you down there."

"Hold on. Partners stay together. Remember?" I caught up to her before she opened the door to go back in.

Looking agitated, she said, "You are *not* using that as an excuse to come in the women's restroom with me."

I smiled, hopin' to put her at ease. The last thing I wanted was for her to ever feel embarrassed 'round me. No' for any reason. And particularly no' if she was feelin' an instinctive reaction to keepin' other females away from me. What I wanted more than anything in this life was for Elora Laiken to see me as claimed territory. "No? Well, then I'll wait outside." Then I added, "For a count of one hundred."

WEDNESDAY NIGHT, I knocked on her door to signal 'twas time to catch the whister. For the second time, you could have knocked me over when she opened up. Her beautiful hair had been shorn close to her head. 'Twas less than three inches long. Spikey. Messy. 'Twould fit in with club work, but oh. How I would miss that hair.

"Kay's right. Long hair's too easy to grab. I found that out last night."

I nodded just before reachin' up to run my hand over her head, wishin' I'd done that when 'twas still long. "Still beautiful," I said. And 'twas the truth of it.

She closed the door. As we walked toward the elevator, I screwed up my courage and said, "Would you like to spend tomorrow with me?"

She glanced sideways, but kept walkin'. "I would, but I can't. Storm's taking me to the mall shopping and teaching me to drive."

"He's takin' you shoppin' at a suburb mall and teachin' you to drive? Okay. Better him than me." 'Twas a lie. I would have been glad to take her anywhere, partly because I wanted to be with her and partly because I did no' want her with Storm. *Great. Paddy.*

She gave me a playful punch to my bicep. I laughed on cue although I was feelin' like givin' Storm a much less than playful punch to his smug-all ugly face. "Then Sunday. Give me Sunday."

"Sure."

"Ten thirty. Street clothes."

THE NEXT DAY I was incurably irritable and no' fit for company of any kind. Knowin' Elora was spendin' time alone with Storm sat in my gut like a burr under the saddle.

I had dinner by myself at the bar and then headed to

the back of the lounge for poker. On the way back, I passed Ghost playin' darts. He caught my eye and lifted his chin in acknowledgement. Paddy, he was an ugly fucker. I could no' say for sure that I saw hard feelin's in his stare, but I suspected he was no' at all happy about bein' passed over. Especially by a woman.

Truth be told, most males would have a problem with that and 'twas compounded by the fact that she'd skipped the dues-payin' that the rest of us had undergone. Aye. She was the exception to almost every rule in the book and I knew that better than anyone. Still, it might be a hard pill to swallow for a seasoned knight expectin' a bump.

I mimicked his chin tip on the way past and closed the door to the card room behind me.

On my way to my usual seat at the table, Sanction said, "Hawking, I was just saying that we have a guest tonight. Storm has been teaching the Lady Laiken to play poker. Since Bellstrong is on duty tonight, I told him she could sit in, that we're just as happy to take her money as somebody else's."

My mood instantly elevated. That meant that, any minute, she'd be walkin' through the door and sittin' nearby. No sooner did I have that thought than she did come through the door, followed by Storm.

As she took the seat opposite me, I scanned her body slowly. For damage. You know. She appeared to be alright. In fact, she sent a high beam smile my direction that played my body like a xylophone.

Since I'd been off my feedbag all day, I was feelin' more than peckish. I ordered one of the Hub's big club sandwiches made with thick nine grain bread, no' stingy with the bacon. Things were lookin' up.

I could no' wait to see how well Storm had taught her to play and if she'd be able to hide anything from me. She looked at the first hand and grinned at everyone like she'd drawn a royal flush, then folded. I saw a series of glances exchanged 'round the table and, really, I did no' blame them. 'Twas strange even for an outworlder.

By the sixth hand, I had caught on that she was tryin' to disguise the transparency of emotion, usually imprinted on her face in exquisitely expressive ways, by actin'. I had to give Storm credit due if he'd deliberately taught her that. 'Twas workin'. I was sure that, given enough time, I could decipher a pattern, but for one night? She might at least get out of the game without heavy losses.

After three hours, the two of us were in for a big pot. Aye. I won it. And got to learn one more thing about my girl. She was no' a sore loser.

CHAPTER 22

Ram

THE REST OF the week was uneventful, which was good and bad. 'Twas good because my partner and mate had no' been put at risk. 'Twas bad for the same reason. We were startin' to think our brilliant play to stake out the alleged vamp hot-spot was no' so brilliant after all.

No' much could dampen my enthusiasm because I had planned a romantic day in the city with the Lady Laiken and nothin' would take the shine off that.

A cold front blew in from Canada Saturday night bringin' wind with it. And nothin' stings like moisture-rich wind rushin' through the canyons formed by tall buildin's between the two rivers.

She opened the door with a smile that quickly vanished when she saw the look on my face. "What's wrong?" she said, lookin' down at her clothes.

I smiled. "With you? No' a thing in the world. But you'll be needin' a warmer coat. 'Tis colder than a well digger's arse where we're goin'."

"Oh," she said. "And where is that?"

"'Tis a surprise. Grab a hat while you're at it. The hair

bob does no' leave you much protection from a bite of winter."

"Sometimes I think you want to dress me up like a doll."

"Nothin' could be further from the truth. Although…"

"Never mind. I'll be right back."

I waited by the door with Blackie, who, I noticed, was wearin' a leash.

"Goin' somewhere"? I asked. He grinned at me, showin' off his sparklin' white canines.

"How's this?" Elora held her arms out askin' for approval. She was wearin' one of the polartech coats. That should do it.

"Perfect."

"Good. Let's go." She grabbed the leash.

"Um. I had no' planned on havin' the pooch accompany us."

"Oh, I know. I'm droppin' him off at Operations. They like havin' him around and he'd rather be there than alone in here."

"Okay."

"Tell me where we're going." I was mightily encouraged by the excitement I heard in her voice.

"Sightseein'."

"Really? Where?" She was almost breathless. It was adorable.

"Today we're tourists. There's a whister waitin' to take us into the city. There's more to New York than Notte Fuoco and Times Square."

She almost squealed, makin' me feel good about the

time I'd spent researchin' romance. I knew the Yuletide decorations made the city more romantic because the guides said so.

We walked three blocks from the drop to Saks to look at the display windows. I had my hands in my pockets to keep them warm. She linked her gloved hand to the crook of my arm and snuggled in close while I laughed from the pure joy of havin' her so close.

We walked down to Rockfeller Center to see the Yule tree and the ice skaters.

"'Tis a tradition to get hot chocolate when you come to see the big tree."

"I could learn to love tradition." She smiled.

"Very well. Let's put that to the test and begin with women in the kitchen and knowin' their place."

She laughed. I went to fetch chocolate while she went to find a table by the rink where we could watch the skaters. She waved at me to show she'd been successful in snaggin' a place to sit.

"This reminds me of Yule at home." She looked a little sad. "We always had a big tree – well, not as big as this."

I stopped, almost afraid to breathe. It was the first time she'd mentioned something from her life before and I did no' want to say the wrong thing. After mullin' it over, I decided it would be safe to say, "With lights and orna-ments?"

She nodded. "The works. Does your family celebrate Yule?"

"Oh, aye. In a big way. They are very much into good times."

"Well, that explains a lot." She smiled at me with something lookin' enough like affection to make me think my plan was workin'.

"Here's to good times spent together." I raised my paper cup in toast. When the cocoa was gone, I said, "'Tis too cold to sit still. Let's keep movin'."

I noticed that some people were gettin' photos in front of the tree. Seemed like a good idea. So I stopped an elderly gent and asked if he'd take a photo of us with the decorations behind us.

"Come close." I smiled at Elora and she obliged, snugglin' in tight like she belonged there.

"Smile," he said. And we did.

As we walked, she babbled in the most precious way, askin' questions about everything in sight. When we passed the Sherry Netherland on the way to the Metropolitan Museum, she said, "Oh that's where…" But she did no' finish the sentence.

"Where what?"

"Um, I just heard nice things about it."

I had to laugh at the understatement. "Aye. 'Tis probably the most costly hotel in this hemisphere."

I hailed a cab to take us the rest of the way. Elora said she wanted to try it the next time.

"Try what? The Sherry Netherland?"

"Ha! You wish. No, silly. Getting a taxi."

"Oh. Aye." 'Twas turnin' out to be a wonderful day in so many ways. 'Twas a great pleasure to share that she was findin' adventure in simple things taken for granted by most of us.

"The museum is a wonder. You could spend weeks there. Maybe months, but we do no' have long because I'm set on givin' you a 'taste of New York'. One day is no' nearly long enough to see the Big Apple. So we're like butterflies, just lightin' down here and there for a short time."

"Why do they call it the Big Apple?"

"No idea," I answered honestly, wonderin' why I'd never been curious enough to find out.

"Let's ask somebody."

I paid the cab driver while Elora began askin' passers-by if they knew why New York was called the Big Apple. After a dozen or so people had been queried, every one regardin' her with the suspicion usually reserved for census takers, she was ready to give it up.

"Well, what's the point of nicknaming a city if nobody knows what it means?"

I smiled and shrugged. "You make an excellent point. I vow to go on knightly quest for my lady and will no' rest until I bring you the answer."

She grinned and batted her eyelashes.

We climbed the steps and found the end of the coat check queue. I turned to have a look at who else was out on a blustery Sunday and came face to face with a cute toddler, ridin' her mother's hip and primed for a flirt with me. I was engaged in a fetchin' game of peekaboo, when I noticed Elora watchin'. I turned toward her with a smile.

"So you like babies," she said.

"Well, aye. Who does no'?"

"Most people like their own, I guess. You're full of

surprises, Rammel Hawking."

"Back at you, Elora Laiken."

I got our tickets and pulled Elora out of the way where she could have a look at the guide.

"What's your fancy? Sixteenth century violins? Eighteenth century paintin's? Ancient Egyptian tomb raidin's?

She pointed to a square on the brochure. "Arms and armor."

"O' course," I said.

After a couple of hours, she said, "You were right, Ram. It would take months to see everything here. And that's if it was your full time job."

I nodded. "Just so. And we've used up the time allotted for this stop on the tour."

"Oh, no, but…"

"We have lunch reservations at a place that specializes in chocolate."

"Which way to get our coats?"

I chuckled, but cataloged the fact that my mate could be manipulated with chocolate as easily as persuadin' a horse with sugar.

When we started away, I said, "What was the most surprisin' thing?"

"How tiny people used to be."

"You've lost me."

"Didn't you notice that the suits of armor looked like they'd been made for twelve-year-olds?"

"Well, now that you mention it. I suppose you're right."

One thing about Elora, she was as unpredictable as the

weather, which suited me just fine. I counted myself the lucky one to be in for a very interestin', never borin', life.

Outside, she said, "Ooh. I want a turn at getting a cab."

"You'll get your turn, but no' here." I pointed at the taxi stand. "See. They're already lined up and waitin' for us."

"Too easy," she said.

At Serendipity I told her to go easy on lunch and save room for frozen hot chocolate. After we ordered, she turned to me and said, "A Bi-Sensual burger? Is that code for bisexual?"

She was referrin' to my order.

"Certainly no'," I said. "It means twice as sexy." I gave her my best seductive smile, but she looked more dubious than turned on.

When she finished her black bean soup, she left for the powder room, which was civilized talk for the john. I had nothin' to do but turn around and look at the commotion behind me. Six little girls and a chaperone out for some lucky little lady's birthday. When I turned, they stopped and looked at me. So I made a face.

At first, they weren't sure how to react, but then one of them laughed. Within a couple of minutes they were all findin' me hilarious. Unfortunately Elora returned to our table to find me with two long French fries hangin' from my nostrils. It had seemed like a good idea at the time. Until I was confronted by the horrified look of the woman I was supposed to be romancin'.

I quickly pulled the potatoes out of my nose and set

them aside on my napkin. Even I agree that it would be unacceptable to eat food that has been in your nose. In public.

As she studied me, I waited for her to say that she was ready to return to J.U. At length, she smiled instead and said, "You're going to be a wonderful father someday, Ram."

I was no' goin' to be a father at all. Elf-human matches are barren, but I would no' trade what destiny chose for me for anybody else's life. Elora Laiken was a treasure beyond compare.

At that moment the waiter set an enormous goblet of frozen hot chocolate in front of her and I got a glimpse of what it would look like to be loved by Elora. I watched every movement as she dived into the concoction.

Seemed like 'twould be a good time to slip in twenty questions, while she was distracted with chocolate.

"So what's the best dinner you ever had?"

She answered without hesitation. "Castle Kronberg, on the outskirts of Frankfurt."

"What are your favorite flowers?"

"Stargazer lilies with Mexican red roses and tree fern. No baby's breath or leather leaf. Ughh. And I don't like flowers to look 'arranged'. I like them to look like you just cut them in the garden, brought them in and dropped them in a vase."

"Favorite movie."

"*Willow*."

"Why?"

"The love story, of course. And the rascal-turned-hero

adventure."

"Best love song ever."

"'If' by Bread."

Somehow I managed to keep from gaggin'. Visibly. "Tell me about your favorite boyfriend."

She stiffened. Her demeanor changed and she set her spoon down.

"I've never had a boyfriend." She looked at me like she was waitin' for a follow up question. "Okay, I know what you're dying to ask so I'll tell you. I'm not a virgin, but it wasn't an experience I'm eager to repeat, either."

I could have kicked my own arse for stumblin' into mood-ruinin' territory. But her reaction was unexpected and contained the seeds of things I needed to know. My feelin' at the time was that somebody had made Elora believe that sex was something to be avoided. I kept my face blank, but on the inside I was wishin' I could track the bloke down and set him on fire.

I'd vowed to have nothin' spoil the day. No' even me. So I had to do damage control and fast.

"Hey. Let's go do something fun."

"Like what?" She gave me a small smile. "Tell me now."

"Demandin'. I like that," I teased. "The grand dame of modern department stores. Other than Harrods in London," he amended. "You want it. They got it."

"Ooh. My kind of place."

"Guessed as much. Enough online shoppin' for you. Let's go milk the real cow."

The walk to Bloomin'dales was even colder because

the wind had come up. She nestled into my side, makin' me thank the gods of winter for small favors.

"Now I have one question for you," she said. "What do you want more than anything else in the world?"

O'course the answer to that question was easy and immediate. What I wanted to say was, "You." Plain and simple. What I said instead was, "I can no' say."

"I'm betting you plan to have a big family someday, lots of children."

I turned my face toward her. She was so close that my lips were practically touchin' her cheek. I said, "'Tis no' that important, Elora." I hoped she would always remember what I said, that I spoke from the heart, and believe me.

She pulled to a stop and, bein' both strong and heavy, that meant I came to a stop with her.

"Wait, Ram, let's do this."

She was lookin' at a neon palm sign above a door that read, "Fortunes Told".

"Give your future to Gypsies?"

She laughed at me. "That's the most superstitious thing I've ever heard anyone say! Don't be ridiculous. Come on. It's just for fun."

I do no' like dabblin' in the occult, or more likely, gettin' fleeced, but 'twas no' a day for denyin' her what she wanted. So I shrugged and opened the door for her to go before me.

There was no wait. The boy who greeted us showed us into a back room that looked just like what people would expect. We sat down on foldin' chairs in front of Madame

Whatever.

She looked at me. "Fifty dollars."

I fished a fifty dollar bill out of my wallet and set it on the moon and stars tablecloth in front of us.

She folded the bill, put it in her bra, then said to Elora, "I know why you have come."

"You do?" Elora sounded as intrigued as a child and her innocence almost made me laugh out loud.

"Yes. There are three men who are in love with you."

Wait. What? Three?

"You are facing danger from a monster whose eyes are very pale, almost white."

"Aye," I said, beginnin' to fear that she might have enough actual talent to see that we were vampire slayers. "We get that a lot." I was worried that the day was goin' to take a turn for the worse and wanted to get Elora out of there before the fuckin' gypsy began predictin' rivers of blood or some such. I turned to Elora. "Let's go. This is no' fun."

She gave me a look that told me she agreed. We got up to leave and were almost at the door when the gypsy said, "I have a message for the lady." Elora turned 'round. "Choose wisely and love will be new for the rest of your days."

Elora did no' respond. Just pulled her coat close and nestled against me again to keep the wind from gettin' between us.

"Okay, so I admit it," she said. "You were right. Maybe that wasn't the best idea."

"You know I do no' care what we're doin' so long

as 'tis with you."

The way she smiled at me gave me the impression that finally I'd said the right thing.

I never would have believed a person could have so much fun in a store. She wanted to look at evenin' gowns even though she had nowhere to wear one. She wanted to look at gourmet kitchen tools even though she had no intention of cookin'. It was bizarre. But cute.

We were behind a curvy blonde in "JUICY" pants goin' up the escalator to the next floor. And when I say behind, I mean there was no' much to look at but the woman's behind.

I leaned over and whispered. "We should buy you a pair of those very fetchin' britches to show off your gorgeous arse."

She gave me a scandalized look that made me laugh hard, even if it was silently.

As soon as we got off the escalator, she pulled me a few yards away from "JUICY" and said, "First, ugh! Second, as my partner, you can have my permission to put my corpse in those, but only if there will be no open casket viewing. Third…" Though she was makin' a fair to middlin' show of a good scoldin', I could see she was havin' to work at keepin' laughter inside. "…you do not have permission to comment on my gorgeous ass."

I leaned in like the conspirator I wanted to be. "I get it. Over your dead body. You know, scratch the surface and we find your very ladylike upbringin' still hale and hearty and ready for tea with the queen. But I would no' be wantin' anyone else to see your very shapely, juicy arse in those fine britches."

I stood waitin' for her reply with a smile born of talk about Elora's arse. She opened her mouth like she had something else to say, seemed to think better of it, and marched off toward the Ugg boots. I would have loved to know what went through her head that she decided no' to speak out loud.

"IF YOU BUY anything else," I said, shiftin' the box of Ugg boots, "we'll have to ask them to ship."

"What about the super cool leg warmers?"

"Aye. 'Tis fine. Those will no' take up much room."

"And I really wanted a new hat. I don't think I look good in raspberry."

"You're very wrong. You look spectacular in everything. But if you want another hat, you shall have another hat."

After nearly an hour of tryin' on hats, I was regrettin' havin' said that. "If you want my opinion, I love the way you look in the white. It reminds me of my special place in Ireland. The one I told you about."

She looked at me like she was tryin' to decide if I was jokin', then went back to where we'd seen the white hat. She put it on and looked in the mirror.

"Get the scarf that goes with it," I said.

And she did. Which was charmin'.

When we stepped back out on the street it was dark. The wind had died down some, but it felt more damp and, therefore, more frigid. The holiday lights were beautiful at night.

"You promised that I'd get a turn to get a taxi."

I looked up and down the side street. There was no sign of a cab.

"Okay. First lesson. When you do no' see a taxi, what do you do?"

"Walk until you see one?"

"Find a busier street." I pointed. "That way."

She waved for a cab wearin' her white hat and scarf. When he swerved to the curb and stopped at her feet, she practically jumped up and down like she'd just scored at rugby.

Inside the car she was breathless from the cold and excitement and could no' stop talkin' about Bloomin'dales. It was clearly her favorite thing. I saw the cab driver stealin' looks at her in the rearview mirror. Maybe because she was animated in a non-New York kind of way. Maybe because she was the world's most beautiful woman. At least to me.

And two others, I thought with a sour taste.

WHEN WE WERE settled into our seats next to each other on the whister and lifted off, she leaned close and said, "This was the best day of my life."

If I live to be three hundred, I'm sure I will never hear words sweeter than those. What I wanted to say was, "I do no' want to be a vampire hunter anymore. I just want to take you home to Ireland where I can keep you safe and love you every second for the rest of our lives. I want to kiss your freckled nose and your rosy cheeks and your beautiful mouth, worship that body that slays me and

make love to you over and over until you beg me to stop."
But what I said was, "Me, too."

Somehow, I hoped to Paddy she heard the rest that was unsaid, but in my heart.

"You know everywhere we went today, people stared at you."

"You're so very wrong, my girl. 'Twas you they were admirin'."

After havin' her to myself for the whole day, I found that sayin' goodnight was even harder than usual, but I managed to let her go.

"Thank you," she said softly.

"Pleasure was mine." I handed her the box of boots. "You look beautiful in your new hat and scarf."

She grinned and closed her door.

THE FIRST HOUR back at work on Tuesday, I got a text from Elora.

Meet me on street level. Now!

I threw down my bar rag and turned to the other bartender. "You're on your own for ten minutes."

"Hey!" he said, but I was already gone.

I saw her waitin' outside the bistro door. "What's...?"

"Come on," she said as she started joggin'. She went slow enough to look like somebody from our dimension, just like we'd taught her. "I've got to meet Baka and, you know, since you're my partner..."

I had no reply for that.

The vampire was waitin' in the same alley where Elora had killed one of his buddies.

"Hey," she said to him. "What's up? We've got five minutes before we have to start back."

Baka flicked a glance at me, but spoke to her. "I finished remapping the underground. It's pretty much the same as it was in the twenties except that somebody has updated the lighting with low energy, storm shelter fixtures. When I reported to your Sovereign yesterday, he ordered me to take E Team on a reconnaissance tour since you had the day off. I told him I thought that was a bad idea. If we were spotted by vampire we'd lose the element of surprise when we need it.

"He said do it anyway. So I took them down for an hour yesterday afternoon. We didn't encounter vampire, but there are indications that the tunnel system is… in use."

"You mean you saw signs of remains," I said and he confirmed that with a nod. I ran my hand down my face. "And why be tellin' us this then?"

Baka scowled. "Because something about E Team doesn't feel right." He shook his head. "Hunches are the hardest sort of thing to explain."

I looked at my watch and touched Elora on the arm. "Gotta go."

Baka looked between us. "Watch out for the entrance. It's hidden in the wall at the end of the hallway where the restrooms are."

"Show us," Elora said.

When we got back to the basement level, the manager grabbed me. "Hawking, if you want to keep your job for another night, I suggest you get yourself back to the bar now."

Elora nodded at me to go. I was torn. I needed to keep the job and the cover, but did no' really want to let her out of my sight with that leech. I reasoned that she had already been alone with him, in and out of captivity. Plus, I had to show her she had my confidence, same as I would give any other partner.

But five minutes later she came rushin' into the bar with a flush on her face and lips swollen like she'd been makin' out. It had been a long time since I'd felt a fever rage like the one that came over me. Somebody had touched my mate. Somebody was goin' to die.

I know I growled at her, but I could no' help myself.

"What the bloody hel, Elora!"

"Two vampire came in while we were in the hallway. A couple of minutes ago. We've got to find them."

'Twas no' the time for vampire huntin'. 'Twas the time for sortin' out my mate's behavior. But the honor of bein' a Black Swan knight takes precedence over everything else when vampire are on the premises. So I decided to shelve the confrontation for later.

B Team searched all three floors of the club, the restrooms, the kitchen, and the perimeter for three blocks, but did no' find vampire. The manager threatened to fire us all, but allowed us to finish our shifts. We suspected that Sol would find a way to smooth over our lapse in performance. And, certainly, I had more pressin' concerns.

We stopped at the lounge to share a drink before turnin' in. After adrenaline and emotions run high on a hunt, we need a taste to calm down.

"E Team is sittin' outside by the fire pit. What do you say we join them and find out what they learned from their 'tour'?"

Kay and I nodded. The four of us converged on the veranda.

Storm spoke to E Team. "How 'bout we join you?"

"Sure," they said.

After a few minutes of questions and answers about what they'd seen in the tunnels, Ghost stood up and started toward the Atrium door. "Anybody need anything while I'm up?"

Elora said, "Yeah. My Hot Butter Bacardi should be up if you don't mind grabbing it."

"Done," he said.

Half an hour later, I was feelin' warmed by whiskey and a little less crazed by my suspicions regardin' what had happened between Elora and Baka.

"Ram?" Elora's voice was quiet.

"Hmmm?" I was focused on E Team. It seemed to me that they were bein' unusually tight-lipped, like they did no' really want to divulge their impressions, which was odd. Black Swan is a cooperative. That means we cooperate.

"I need help. You've got to get me home. Please." Elora had leaned in to me and whispered with an unmistakable urgency. Then she raised her voice, sayin' to everybody present, "That's it for me. Some of us actually work for a living delivering booze to letches and drunks. Have a good night then."

"Hold on. I'm goin', too," I said and gave a general wave goodnight.

As soon as the elevator doors closed, I looked at Elora. "What's wrong?"

"Not sure, but I'm scared that, I think maybe… aphrodisiac."

I took her by the shoulders and turned her so I could get a good look at her face. *Paddy*. Her pupils were dilated like she was a tweaker. "Fuck," I said as if I could find nothin' less appropriate to say.

The fear I saw in her beautiful eyes sent a jolt of adrenaline racin' through my veins, prickin' every nerve endin' on its way past. I was lost for what to do. If there was an antedote for aphrodisiac, I certainly did no' know it. But I had to do something. Her discomfort was becomin' conspicuous by the way she seemed to be agitated to be in her own body.

"Okay. We'll figure something out," I said. 'Twas meant to be reassurin', but nothin' productive was comin' to me. I wanted to ease the discomfort that was becomin' more apparent by the minute, but takin' advantage of the situation was something I would no' consider.

Her breath was labored by the time we reached her apartment. She stood in front of the door like she could no' remember the code. I knew it. So I punched it in and looked up and down the hallway to make sure no one saw me go in so late at night. The last thing she needed was gossip and cat calls. Humans were notorious purveyors of both.

I pulled her inside. When I turned from closin' the

door she had dropped her coat on the floor. My mind was goin' a dozen different directions, tryin' to light on a solution, but none was comin'.

She grabbed the front of my leather jacket and said, "You've got to help me." Her eyes were wide and wild, castin' about like a mad woman, but what tore most at my heart was the plea, *you've got to help me.*

"What do you mean?" I said stupidly, knowin' full well what she meant and tryin' to stall for an alternative. I'm sure I was lookin' almost as hysterical, myself.

She pushed at me a little, fistsfuls of leather still in her grip.

"Don't you dare pretend naïveté with me, Rammel Hawking. You bloody well know what I mean!"

She released me and closed her eyes as if runnin' her hands down her body gave a slight relief. When her middle finger found its way to her pussy, I began to fear losin' the battle. My dick was respondin' to the teasin' vision with an engorgement like it had never known before and I did no' know if my desire to be honorable could overpower my body's interest in a willin' mate.

"No." If an elf ever faced a moment of greater frustration, I can no' imagine what it might have been. "I do no' want the first time to be like this."

"Ram!" she shouted, lookin' on the verge of a full blown panic. "Either help me or get out of the way so I can find somebody else."

She shoved me aside and started toward the door that had been behind me a moment before. I managed to reclaim my place in front of the door before she opened it and was gone. In the second that took place I'd seen images of my mate out scarin' up fuck partners. O'course 'twould no' be hard for a woman like Elora to find eager candidates. And o'course that was no' an option.

The reasonable part of me decided that, if there was only one way to ease her affliction, I would serve that purpose even though it was no' my first choice. I just had to hope that she'd forgive me when the effects of the drug wore off.

"That's no' gonna happen!" I matched her tone so she'd know I was completely serious. If she was beddin' somebody that night, by the gods, 'twould be me and no other.

"Well then?"

She challenged me to get on with it. Curiously, in that moment, I seemed to forget everything I knew about intimate relations and felt as inexperienced as a backward twelve-year-old. But I knew I wanted to kiss her. I would always want to kiss her. So I would start there.

I took her face in my hands and stepped in, but she was impatient, wantin' something hard, fast and raw.

I held her firm, no' lettin' her wiggle out of my grasp, and said, "Shhhh. Hush now. I'm here. Promise you will forgive me." She moaned. I gave her a little shake so she'd pay attention. "Say it! Say you'll forgive me."

She looked into my eyes long enough to persuade me she was in control of her faculties on some level. She nodded. 'Twas good enough.

Tellin' myself I could no' be a low life cad when I

treasured her more than life, I poured my love and cravin' for her into my kiss, hopin' she would know on some level that there was so much more to my feelin's than carnal interest.

For a moment, I thought love might be the cure, and my kiss might overcome the drug's demon. For a moment, she was quiet and still, but 'twas the proverbial calm before the storm. She pulled me close enough that I could hardly breathe.

"Ease up. I need to get my breath."

She loosened her hold and pushed my jacket off my shoulders so that it fell to the floor beside her coat. Then usin' her mouth to open mine wider, she stole my breath in an altogether different way. Her tongue was tanglin' with mine in a dance of desperation, when I heard a loud tear.

I pulled back and looked down. She'd ripped the Notte Fuoco tee shirt open from neck to waist. Her hands were runnin' down my chest and tuggin' at the waistband of my jeans.

I'd never had a woman attempt to take my clothes from me in such a forceful way before. It was an act so erotically charged that I knew I could no' pull back if wild horses were tryin' to drag me out the door. Once I realized that the decision had been made, no turnin' back, I freed the part of me that I'd been holdin' in check for what seemed like an eternity and let loose the force of my feelin's for the woman whose body was demandin' attention from mine.

I pushed her tank and bra straps down her shoulder

until a plump breast popped free. She looked exactly the way I knew she would, creamy skin, rosy pink nipple. She groaned, grippin' my shoulders and throwin' her head back when I bent to suck that nipple into my mouth and lave it with my tongue.

I had no' thought it would be possible to be any harder than I was already, but a throbbin' impulse was added to the pressure against the crotch of my jeans.

When she reached down, her intention clear as day, I hissed in a breath and angled myself away sayin', "We can no' be doin' that if there's to be anything left for you."

Movin' toward the bedroom, her goin' backward, me goin' forward, we tore away all the clothes remainin' except for cute little short-type panties and knee socks. She looked like a dream and my cock, standin' so straight it was practically pointin' at my chin, agreed.

I pulled the coverlets away, leavin' a bottom sheet. She wasted no time crawlin' onto the mattress and pullin' me down with her.

I moved the crotch of the panties aside and brushed her sex with my fingertips. She gasped and came up off the bed like a wanton never before touched, except that my woman was stronger than any other and almost threw me from the bed.

"Easy, darlin'," was all I said as I pulled the silky drawers down her legs and away from her body.

"Please," was all she could say.

It was plain by her frantic movements that she was losin' the battle with any semblance of control. Her eyes pooled with tears that began runnin' down her face, breakin' my heart as they ran. I situated myself between the cradle of her thighs and, just as she began to beg in earnest, I thrust inside her.

The intensity of her need drove me to a performance level beyond aspirations. I put my hand on the headboard and stiffened my arm to keep from drivin' her into the wall. 'Twas gratifyin' to see the pained expression leave her face and be replaced with a rapture so perfect that it filled me with emotion, more than I thought possible. 'Twas overwhelmin' in every way imaginable.

When her muscles gripped my cock, I let go with a noise that sounded foreign even to me. I lay still, listenin' to her heart rate mixed with mine, her breath mixed with mine, as both began to slow. I knew I did no' have to worry about crushin' her beautiful body with my weight. So I just enjoyed the moment and the realization that "makin' love" was no' just a euphemism for fuckin', but a real thing.

After a few minutes I lifted my head to look in her face. Her eyelids were half closed, but her face bore a little smile as she said, "Ah, Ram. You feel so good."

I kissed the remainin' tears away from her face and, for a time, she was peaceful. Satisfied. I thought it was over and was wonderin' if I should leave or if I stay with her until the morrow. I was mullin' over the choice when the next surge began. At first it sounded like a low groan in the back of her throat, almost too quiet to hear. Within minutes she'd once again become frantic for relief. I was no' yet prepared to offer myself. So I rolled away and used my fingers to ease her way, the whole time tellin' her that I loved her, that I would no' leave her, that she was perfect in every way, that everything would be alright.

Over the next few hours we experienced variations on love-makin' that few couples manage in one night and I was thinkin' I was perhaps the luckiest elf ever born.

Durin' the minutes when light was first breakin', a hint of pink and gold risin' to overtake the gray, I lay facin' her. Her eyelids were heavy, tryin' to close. Between that and the peaceful way she was breathing, I knew it was finally over.

Her eyes flew open wide without warnin', like she'd forgotten something important. With a little smile, she whispered, "Thank you."

I reached over and cupped the side of her face, rubbin' the softness of her cheek with my thumb.

"Darlin' girl," I said. "These have been the sweetest hours of my life."

WHEN I WOKE I was spoonin' with Elora, her very firm and shapely derriere pressed firmly into my lap. Her body heat was enough to keep us warm without the need for covers. What I would have liked more than anything would have been to leisurely savor the experience of findin' myself in a naked tangle with the Lady Laiken. But the cause of my wakeful state, Elora's dog, was becomin' more insistent about his own needs. Hopin' for the dog version of an alarm snooze, I turned back to Elora and thought to ignore him for at least a couple more minutes. But the dog was havin' none of it. He gave me a lick on the behind that caused me to jerk my pelvis into Elora.

She hummed, but did no' wake.

I gave Blackie the dirtiest look possible. Whether or no' he took it as such, no one can say. His response was a wag of a bushy tail and a couple of revolutions to the left. The dog always turned to the left. Do no' ask me why I noticed that, but I had the odd thought that he would no' be very good at reels.

Risin' slowly so as no' to disturb Elora, I pulled the covers over her and could no' help but smile at the sound of her soft snorin'.

Our clothes, both mine and hers, were left in a messy trail. I got dressed and left Elora's clothes folded neatly on the chair next to her fireplace. I did no' think 'twould be very gentlemanly to pick up my clothes and leave hers on the floor.

Since Blackie was whinin' like the situation was urgent, I did no' think it prudent to take the time to go to my place next door and replace the torn shirt with a whole one. So I zipped up my leather jacket and headed for the Courtpark where he could relieve himself and be fawned over by fans.

She was still sleepin' when we got back. So I filled the dog bowl with what was in the bag and went to leave a note on the bar. After some thought and several false starts, I finally wrote, "Do not be embarrassed. – R." As an afterthought when my hand was on the door, I came back to the bar and added under what was already written, "Or mad either." She'd promised to forgive me and Elora was the sort to keep her promises, so I was no' worried. But just in case.

I closed the door quietly, again makin' sure no one saw me in the hallway, and headed next door for a shower.

AN HOUR LATER, feelin' that all was right with the world, I got off the elevator on our floor with a large hot chocolate for Elora. I let myself in to her place and heard the hair dryer blowin' away.

I heard the sound stop and saw her head poke out of the bathroom beyond that adjoined her bedroom. I smiled and held up my gift of cocoa.

When she started toward me, I said, "Brought you a hot chocolate," and held out the cup, but she did no' take it. I was beginnin' to get the feelin' that she was mad.

She grabbed my note from the bar, waved it in the air, and said, "Don't be embarrassed? Don't be mad? How could you?"

I dropped my arm and set the cup down on the dinin' desk.

"I, em…"

"How did I end up drunk, Ram?"

"Drunk?" I repeated strugglin' to get my bearin's. It felt like I had come in on the middle of a movie with no clue what was goin' on.

"I don't even remember having more than one drink." I stared at her, wonderin' where this was goin' and no' knowin' how to respond without hearin' more first. "You brought me back here, undressed me, and left me in bed naked."

"Now, wait a minute." It was just beginnin' to dawn on me. She did no' remember a thing about last night. She was accusin' me of bein' a pervert who would take advantage of a woman who was too drunk to know what she was doin'. "I did no' undress you."

"No? And you didn't leave my clothes on the chair either."

I really did no' want to answer that question because, given that she remembered nothin', it would beg too many other questions. So I said, "I did bring you back here last night. I did take Blackie out for his walk this mornin' because you were no' up to it. And you're welcome, by the way. I did pick your clothes up where you left them on the floor and I did put them on the chair. You're welcome for that as well."

Her features softened as she studied my face and heard the truth in my words, even if it was no' the *whole* truth. Great Paddy. What a mess!

"I'm sorry," she said. "I know there's nothin' worse than being accused of something you didn't do. I just... I've never been drunk before. Waking up and not remembering what happened is a new thing." She glanced toward the bedroom door. "And I don't like it."

Normally I would have pointed out that she had none of the symptoms associated with hangovers, but thought it better to keep my thoughts to myself, in that case.

"Happens to the best of us."

"Well, now I am embarrassed."

I smiled. "I'll do my best to make sure it does no' happen again."

Criminently. I'd been so caught up in the dramatic events that I'd had no time to ask the most important question, which was, how did she ingest the drug? Who gave it to her? Most importantly, why was she a target?

Normally I would have gone straight to Kay and Storm and asked them for help sortin' things out, but there was nothin' normal about the situation. I could no' go to them without compromisin' Elora by revealin' what had happened. And that I would no' do.

I had to try and figure it out by myself. And fast.

CHAPTER 23

Ram

B Y THE END of the second week workin' Notte Fuoco, we were startin' to feel like drinks and bouncin' were our real jobs. The inevitable had happened, my constant vigilance had lapsed, but as luck would have it, I was facin' the bar, wipin' out a glass, when I saw Elora's head pop up above the crowd. I locked on her location and swung myself up over the bar.

Patrons scrambled to get out of my way, but they were no' my priority.

When she passed under one of the spots, I saw her unmistakable hair on the way to the restrooms. With a horror I'll never forget, I saw that she'd placed herself between three vampire and the tunnel entrance Baka told us about. I charged forward reachin' for my splat gun and findin' nothin' there. O' course I had a splat gun. 'Twas just that 'twas stowed under the bar. I did the one thing Black Swan knights can never do. I panicked when I thought my partner might be in trouble.

Gods love her. She'd staked one vamp and engaged a second before I reached her. The third pulled a knife, but in the blink of an eye he found me in front of him instead of his target. Elora.

As the Fates would have it, and it seemed they were targetin' me for their amusement of late, two women chose that moment to come out of the Ladies' room. 'Twas the worst timin' possible.

The vampire did no' consider his actions. Nor did he have a motive for what he did next. He was simply an evil shadow of whoever he'd been as a human, a lost soul without reason or empathy.

He slashed at the woman closest to him. The knife cut through her jugular, which began to spurt like a macabre fountain, just as her friend started to scream.

There are reasons why Black Swan takes so long to train its knights. One of those is so that a knight will revert to his trainin' in combat situations without havin' to rely on instinct. My trainin' had left me with an automatic response to innocents in danger from vampire. The priority was protection. 'Twas always the overridin' mission and, really, the entire point of what we did.

I put myself in front of the woman still standin', even though I had no weapon with which to protect either the bystander, myself, or Elora. I was hopin' against hope that my teammates would hear the commotion and arrive in time to intervene. Hope. 'Tis no' much compared to weaponry.

When I saw the knife comin' toward my neck, 'twas almost as if in slow motion. I shifted my position and turned so that it missed my jugular, but I felt the burn deep in my face travelin' down my chest to my stomach. I'm no' sure, but I think my head banged against the wall behind me.

CHAPTER 24

Kay

W E WERE WORKING the lounge section of the Underground. When I say 'we', I mean Storm and me. He was on one side. I was on the other, but we were always in eye contact of each other.

The first hint of trouble was when people started leaving the dance floor and moving in the direction of the restrooms. Seeing that, the musicians stopped playing. When they did, we could hear a woman screaming. By that time the crowd was thick and elbow to elbow, drawn by curiosity, morbid or otherwise.

It probably took us three minutes to push, press, and toss folks out of the way so that we could get to the scene of the disturbance. And, well, shit. It was bad.

Ram was down. Elora was on the ground holding his head and saying something to him, but it was clear he wasn't hearing her or anything else. Looked like a dead vamp behind her and a civilian who, likewise, met death in an ugly way. The kind of ugly that leaves most of a person's fluids behind.

Storm pointed up. That was all he had to do. We'd

been together so long we could almost communicate telepathically and I knew that meant that he was going up to street level to get a signal so he could call in an emergency. No matter what, the cover up was going to be a nightmare for Black Swan.

I jerked my tee shirt off and went to my knees by Ram, stuffing the cotton along the gash. It was long, deep and ugly, but gods knew that Ram was a fighter even before he had a future to fight for. If there was any chance of survival, he'd pull through. I knew that.

Elora was on his other side. She looked up at me and said, "Stay with him. Promise me."

"What are you doing?" I growled it at her.

"You know what I'm doing, Kay."

"You are *not* going after vampire alone. Geez, you are a dumb ass! What's the first rule?"

"I'm not going alone. Baka is going with me."

I watched her look over her right shoulder and saw that Baka was standing there, looking grim as the Reaper himself. He nodded.

What. The. Hel.

I looked from her to him. I couldn't stop her. There was no point trying. She knew it. I knew it. "Storm is going to seizure when he finds out."

She glanced down at Ram and said, "Keep him alive."

She obviously didn't know how I felt about Rammel or she would not have said such a thing to me. I'd kick in the gates of hel to bring him back if that's what it took. I didn't answer her, but she must have recognized something in my face because I saw both understanding and satisfaction register on her face. Just before she left. With Istvan Baka right behind her.

What a night.

WHEN I'D SAID Storm would seizure about Elora running down vampire, with Baka no less, it turned out to be an understatement. If it had been anybody else besides Rammel, he would have left them on the ground and gone after her sooner.

It took the med van twenty-three minutes to arrive. According to Storm's instructions, D Team, who was technically off duty, arrived to manage the scene. They also brought everything Storm asked for: vests with cargo pockets and a black bag full of arms already loaded with wood core bullets. I guessed we were dispensing with splats.

Ten minutes in we came across Baka, pulled the dart out of him and he sat up like the undead waking in a bad vampire movie. First thing he said was, "Gautier Nibelung." I exchanged a look with Storm. In a way it was shocking to the bone to find out that a knight might be capable of turning on Black Swan. On the other hand, I'd always felt there was something off with Ghost. "We won't find her by ourselves. Too many possibilities."

Well. He should know, I thought.

CHAPTER 25

Ram

T HE FIRST TIME I woke up, the lummoxes were tryin' to force a needle into a vein and botchin' the job. At first I did no' know what was happenin' and then I remembered that the last thing I saw was Elora tryin' to stake a leech without bein' touched by fangs. 'Tis trickier than it may sound to the uninitiated.

O' course the only appropriate reaction on my part was hysteria. I tried to get up, but something was wrong with my body. There was a medic bendin' over me with blood all over his blue scrubs. He was yellin' at somebody. Sayin', "Hold him down until the sedative kicks in."

Then Fortnight and Cheng from D Team were on either side of me pressin' me into the ground so that I could no' move. I looked in Cheng's eyes and said, "Elora."

"Just rest, Ram," was all he said. I made a mental note to punch the fucker out the first chance I got.

THE NEXT TIME I touched consciousness, my first thought was knowin' where I was because of the smell of the place. The infirmary had an antiseptic smell like no other. The next sensation that followed the smell was pain. *Great Paddy.*

I was tryin' to open my eyes and managed to pry them open a slit. I heard loud voices out in the hall and thought I heard one of them shout something about Lady Laiken. If you've ever wondered what's worse, horrible pain or horrible fear, let me settle the question. Horrible fear is worse. I was tryin' to get my mouth to form words so I could ask what was goin' on, when I saw a blurry shape by the bed.

"His heart rate is escalating and we can't have that in his condition. I'm going to sedate him so he'll go back to sleep."

In my mind I was shoutin', "NO!" But no one knew it and within seconds I was asleep again.

The third time I woke it was as if no time had passed since I was insistin' that I no' be rendered helpless by drugs. There's no worse feelin' in the world than helplessness. I'll take pain any day.

I had come to enough for my heart to go straight into overdrive.

When I tried to sit up, I felt a nurse pressin' my shoulders back to the bed. "Sir Hawking, you've been hurt. You need to try to remain calm so as not to tear your stitches."

To someone else in the room she said, "Baxter. Get the doctor."

I fought to get my eyes all the way open, but everything was a blur. "Elora," I said, but it sounded more like a croak than a name.

I tried again and managed something more intelligible. "Elora."

I saw two nurses look at each other and knew something was wrong. That was when I decided I was gettin' up. If they were no' goin' to answer my questions, I would be gettin' my own answers.

Two nurses are no' much of a match for a Black Swan knight, no' even when he has a concussion and one hundred forty-three stitches. They were attemptin' to restrain me physically while beggin' me to stay in the bed, when one of the doctors burst through the door.

I stopped to give the woman a chance to tell me what I needed to know. I repeated, "Elora," to the newcomer.

"Sir Hawking," she began, "your partner has been injured. She is alive and nearby. You can be sure that we're taking very good care of her. And, just like you, she needs to rest. You've got a concussion and a hundred forty-three stitches to take care of. So I need to insist on your cooperation."

"See her." I pulled the I.V. out of my hand and swung my legs over the side of the bed even though it almost made me scream.

"Stop!" said Doc Lately. I ignored her. "If you don't stop, we will sedate you," she said.

The pain was pullin' me further out of my woozy state, which was good and bad. The good part was that I was able to think, sort of. The bad part was that my body hurt like a motherfucker.

I gave the woman a look that stopped her in her tracks and simply said, "Try." 'Twould take more than an inordinately long education and crisp white clothes to stop me from gettin' a status report on my partner. Especially since my partner also happened to be my mate.

"Hold on. We're both reasonable people…"

"Speak for yourself," I said.

"I'm sure we can come to an agreement that will satisfy you."

"I'm no' negotiatin' whether or no' I see Lady Laiken with my own two eyes."

"Okay. If you will agree to let us reattach your IV, and you will sit in a wheelchair, I will personally take you to her room and let you see her for yourself."

I thought about it. Like she said, 'twas a reasonable plan and I was startin' to relax since my fears that Elora might be dead had been put to rest.

"Get this catheter off me and I'll agree."

"Very well," she nodded.

Five minutes later the doc was pushin' me down the hall to the last room on the right. She stepped on a lever and the door quietly swished open. The lights were dimmed and the covers were pulled up to her clavical, but the heart machine was beepin' a steady reassurin' sound and she was breathing on her own.

The doc said, "I'll leave you here for five minutes. Then I'll be back."

After a few minutes I heard the door swish open behind me.

"What happened?" I asked the nurse or doctor standin' behind me without tryin' to turn 'round. "Do you know?"

But 'twas no' a nurse or doctor who answered. 'Twas

Storm's voice quietly tellin' someone, "We'll take it from here."

He came behind me and started to turn me 'round. "No," I said. I want to stay here.

Storm and Kay stood in front of me.

Kay said, "You want to know what happened? We're going to tell you, but not in front of her. She had a bad time of it and we don't want to take a chance on having her overhear the replay."

I understood what he was sayin', but did no' like the choice.

"Rammel," Storm said. "She's alive. You're alive and you're both going to be okay. Let them do their job."

I looked back at Elora, even though twistin' my body was mightily uncomfortable, and said, "Aye. I want to hear what took place."

When we got back to my room, they refused to say more until I climbed back into bed. Fuckers.

I REMAINED QUIET and let the two of them tell the story in their own way, in their own time. It was painful to hear, but necessary.

My mind was grapplin' to take it all in, but my body was failin' me and I was losin' the fight with the sleepy medicine still in my system. Well, for all I knew, they were still pumpin' me performance reduction drugs through the IV. Medics can be sneaky little liars. But I processed the big picture and it was this.

The incident had stopped just a pubic hair short of my worst fear about Elora huntin' vampire. And it happened within just two weeks of her induction. The only thing keepin' it from bein' my terrifyin' scenario full blown was the fact that she was breathing, still hangin' onto life a couple doors down the hall. But from the sound of it, she'd had a pretty rough go and might need some psych recovery.

It had never occurred to me that something could happen to make me think about quittin' The Order, but right then, I was thinkin' that, if I could convince Elora, I'd take her, walk away, and no' look back.

What I said to my teammates was, "So the biggest monster turned out to be one of us. There must be some kind of lesson in that."

"Yeah," Storm said quietly. "I think it's time for you to catch a little nappy."

"She did no' contract the virus." I was no' sure if 'twas a statement or a question, more a request for confirmation really. "Even though she was bitten."

"No," Storm shook his head. "She didn't."

He started to move the wheelchair out. That woke me up. "Leave the chair," I said.

"You don't need to be galavanting about in a wheelchair. What was that the doc said?" He turned to Kay. "A concussion and a hundred and...?"

"Forty-three," Kay said.

"Forty-three stitches."

"If you want me to sleep, leave the chair," I gritted out.

"Of all the stubborn..."

"You better watch out, Storm," I said. "You're on the verge of surpassin' my reputation for cursin'."

He pressed his lips together, but left the chair by the bed so that I could reach out and touch it. "Fine. Here's your binky."

Kay reached over and pulled the covers up to my chin. I swatted at his hand. "Get away from me, arsewipe."

Kay chuckled and turned to Storm. "How can we tell if there was permanent brain damage? I mean, it's Ram."

I opened my mouth to say something else untoward, but Storm spoke first.

"Okay, Rammel, rest and take care of yourself," he said. "It's report time for us." Kay stepped out into the hall, but Storm turned at the door to voice one last thought. "Looks like you're a hero. Again. Your legend is starting to get out of hand, growing to epic proportions."

My eyelids were refusin' to stay all the way open, but I remembered to ask about Elora's dog. "Who's takin' care of Blackie?"

"He's with Sanction. You know," Storm hesitated before finishin' the sentence, "if it wasn't for that dog, we wouldn't have found her in time."

I think I said, "Good dog," but can no' be sure. I lost consciousness or went to sleep. I'm no' sure if there's a difference.

The next time I woke, 'twas to the smell of bacon. I cracked an eye open. Sunlight was streamin' through the window blinds and makin' a pattern across the floor. Somebody had moved the wheelchair and put a tray with breakfast in its place. I swore that the knife wound hurt more than it had the day before, if that was possible. All of a sudden I had a desire to see what it looked like.

Lookin' past the plate of eggs, bacon, biscuits, and hashbrowns with onions and green peppers – someone had made them the way I like, Storm was standin' there starin' at me.

"Wakey. Wakey, biscuits flakey," he said.

I stared at him, wonderin' if there was a part of him that was enjoyin' my pain and infirmity. I started to sit up, but the pain made me gasp and freeze in place.

Storm shoved the food tray aside and grabbed my arm to stabilize me and help me sit upright. "Almighty Woden. You look even paler than usual."

"Fuck. You," I managed.

He chuckled. "Good to know some things are still working."

"Elora," I said.

"Let's get you into a comfortable position so you can eat breakfast and I'll give you the rundown. I just got the full report from her doc."

"Tell me now."

"You're not in a position to be demanding."

"Is she okay?"

"*Okay* might be an assessment too far. I feel comfortable saying she's embracing recovery."

"Bathroom," I said.

He came to the side of the bed, crooked his arm, and made it stiff. "When did you get to be such a nursemaid?" I asked, then wanted to slap myself in the face when I realized what I'd just asked.

"Elora was in even worse shape when she was here before." That was all he said and I was glad he didn't elaborate on the months he'd spent helpin' her while I was actin' the fool.

Once my body absorbed the initial shock of standin' upright, I was able to get to the bathroom on my own, although any garden slug could have easily beat me there if he'd a mind to.

While I was in there, I took a look in the mirror. *Great Paddy.* My face was bad enough and swollen on the side with the knife wound. But 'twas no' so bad compared to the rest. I was no' goin' to be invited to do shirtless pin up posters any time soon. If ever. No' that I had been asked for such a thing in the past, but you never know. Just sayin'.

I hoped that there was more to me than my looks because I still had my mind set on makin' a certain red-and-pink-haired woman fall in love with me. I wondered if that stuff Monq gave Elora to make her skin heal without scarrin' would work on me.

It seemed like hours later when I was situated sittin' up and nibblin' at bacon. By that time, Kay had come in carryin' a big steamin' coffee from the Hub.

"...no internal damage or broken bones." Storm was givin' me the rundown. "Her red blood cells are restored to normal. Her white blood cell count's high and they're watching it. Some of the lacerations required stitches. Normally there would be scarring, but they already know Monq's regenerative skin salve works on her, so, based on her recovery pattern from before, they think she'll be good as new in a few weeks. Maybe sooner.

"They're giving her sedative to keep her sleeping for

another day. And that's about it."

"Has she said anything?"

Storm shook his head. "Nope. She's been out of it since we pulled her out of that cell."

I winced when he said it. I might no' have been there, but my mind filled in the spaces with imagery. I can no' say how accurate 'twas, whether 'twas more or less horrific than what had actually taken place, but what I saw in my head was more gruesome than I could stomach. I pushed the tray of food away.

"Kay," I said, "I'd be askin' you a favor if you please."

He did no' ask what. He just nodded as if to say the answer would always be o' course.

"Will ye go to Elora's apartment and hunt up her collection of..." 'Twas hard for me to say it, "...*fairy* tales. They're in a lace-up folder. She typed 'em from memory."

"I'll need to go to Operations and get somebody to let me in."

"The code is 'never'."

Storm cocked his head and gave me a strange look. I do no' know if that was because he was surprised I had the code or because he was curious why she chose 'never'. But he said nothin' about it either way. I do no' know if he also had the code. Judgin' from his expression, I'm guessin' no'. Paddy help me. In spite of his kindness, I was feelin' smug about that.

When Kay was gone, Storm said, "Why do you want the stories?"

"I have this theory that people show you what they need by the way they treat other people. When Touchstone was in recovery… you remember?" Storm nodded. "She used to come to his room after dinner and read him her stories."

"She did?"

"Aye. She did."

"You think they're goin' to let you do that?"

I looked at Storm. "You think they can stop me?"

"I think after last night they've ordered a stock of elephant darts just for you."

My gut pulled tight in a laugh which quickly turned to screamin'-out-loud pain. My hand reached for my middle, but just in time, I realized I couldn't put pressure on the stitches. Storm was laughin', enjoyin' the whole thing more than he should've.

"Do no' make me laugh or I will kick your arse when I'm out of here."

Storm could be odd at times and it seemed that was one of them. My declaration only served to make him laugh harder.

When Kay returned with the satchel of stories, I thanked him and he said, "Okay. Need anything else?"

"Well, I was wonderin' if Monq would share some of that miracle skin-fix with a humble knight."

Kay smiled. "What's the matter, pretty boy? Women like scars." When he did no' get a reaction from me, he said, "Yeah. I'll ask Monq about a special spa day for your beauty treatment."

They got up to leave. Storm said, "They're hoping you give them a reason to use the new elephant darts."

"Oh, aye. Very funny."

As soon as I was sure they had left the part of the buildin' designated as infirmary, I got myself into the wheelchair, put the stories in my lap and wheeled over to Elora's room. As luck would have it, no one was at the nurses' station or in the hall or in her room.

I rolled up next to the bed to get a good look. She looked pale, but I reveled in the comfort of hearin' the heart rate monitor. Steady as she goes. I unlaced the big folder and removed the first story, stapled together. I smiled at the small drops of cocoa near the bottom of the first page. And I began to read out loud.

She loved those stupid stories, but more importantly, I knew she might be aware on some level that there was someone here waitin' for her, hopin' she'd hear the sound of my voice and come back to me soon.

I was halfway through "Rapunzel", my throat feelin' parched and needin' a wettin', when a nurse came in to check Elora's IV and vital signs. When she saw me, her usual business-like rush faltered for a step, but 'twas no' long before the requisite bossy-nurse persona was back in place.

"Sir Hawking, does the doctor know you're in here instead of in your own bed? Where you're supposed to be?"

"I'm no' supposed to be in bed."

"You're not?"

"No. I'm supposed to be here readin' stories to the Lady Laiken."

"Hmmm," she grumbled. "I'm not sure you and your doctor are in agreement on that."

"Nevertheless, 'tis the case. And if 'twould no' trouble you overmuch, I would appreciate some water." She eyed me like she did no' quite know what to make of me. "And a bottle of Irish whiskey."

"Whiskey," she repeated.

"Aye. They have the kind I like in the bar on the top shelf. 'Tis called Redbreast. Just tell them 'tis for me and they'll give you no trouble."

"The idiots in the bar might offer no trouble, but I assure you that I would have a world of trouble with your doctor should I comply with such a ridiculous request."

After a few seconds of starin' at each other, her makin' as mean a face as has ever been seen on a woman, I said, "Just the water then."

Her chin came up as she was apparently finished with checkin' boxes on her little clickey tablet. "We'll see."

When she left, I wondered if she was goin' to get the doctor or the elephant gun, but I had no' long to wait to find out. Within a couple of minutes she was back with the doc. The same vaguely Asian-lookin' woman who'd tried to overpower me the night before.

"Sir Hawking," she said, "still causing trouble, I see."

"'Tis far from the truth. I'm sittin' here mindin' my own business, readin' stories to my partner. What's the harm in that?"

"The harm is not to your partner or the staff or The Order or Jefferson Unit or any other thing under the sun other than you. You are harming *you*. And as the extraordinarily valuable asset you apparently are, we simply cannot allow that to continue."

'Twas startin' to resemble the sorts of lectures I used to get from my father, who wrote the book on lectures. If I would no' stand for it from him, I certainly never saw the day when a slip of a medic would tell me where to be and what to do.

"I'm stayin' here."

"You are not."

"I am."

"I will simply have you carried out."

"To keep me from hurtin' myself? Just imagine how many stitches I could bust fightin' off orderlies. More important, imagine how much damage I'll do to the poor fellas you send for me."

The uncertainty was plain on her face as she looked me over. "I need you back in bed. What's it going to take?"

I looked at Elora's sleepin' form, then back at the doc. "Bring the bed in here. I'll get in it and stay."

She crossed her arms in front of her, pursed her lips, looked at Nurse Mean Face, and tapped her foot before sayin', "I have your word on that?"

I smiled before realizin' that smilin' hurt the stitches on my face. "Aye. You have my word. Now about the whiskey."

"No whiskey," she said flatly and I surmised that I should be content with the battle won. I could always ask Kay for it when next I saw him. For a berserker, and a big one at that, Kay was a softie at heart.

"Water."

"Water we can do. In fact we encourage it."

"See there. We agree. That was no' so hard."

She smiled and I realized that perhaps I could still be charmin' even with a jagged scar runnin' down my face. I nodded at her to convey my easy-goin' good naturedness.

When the bed was rolled in, I sat down on the side, drank half a pitcher of water, then with great care and a world of hurt, settled myself back to resume the tellin' of Elora's tales.

I can no' say when I went to sleep, but someone had taken the pages from my hands durin' the night. As soon as I remembered where I was and why I was there, I turned my head to make sure Elora was alright.

What I saw lookin' back at me dumped the chill of ice water into my veins, but I drew on every bit of discipline The Order had taught me to control my expression and no' show my true feelin's on my face. Elora's irises were so pale they were almost without color.

More than any person has ever wanted anything, I needed to believe the creature starin' at me was still Elora Laiken. Everything I knew to be true about vampire told me she was gone, replaced by a mindless creature with no trace of herself left. But the fact that she was lyin' quietly gave me enough hope to venture a test in the form of conversation. If she could have a dialogue, she was still in there.

"Hey," I said quietly.

She swallowed, then whispered, "Hey," in a ragged voice. "Are we alive?"

I was so relieved I wanted to sink to the floor, get on my knees, and thank Paddy, all the while sobbin' for joy. But that would no' be in the best interest of the crystalline-eyed beauty lyin' next to me.

So instead, I said, "Seems we are destined to die of old age, you and I."

"What fun would that be?"

I opened my mouth to speak, but felt a burnin' behind my eyes and my vocal chords did no' seem to care to respond. After several tries, I was finally able to get out a single syllable answer.

"Lots," was what I said. And I'd never meant anything more. A few weeks before I had no' especially cared how long I lived. Now I was findin' myself wantin' every minute I could get with my mate. Old age? Aye and aye again.

I swung my legs toward Elora, sat up and slid off the bed.

I heard her quick intake of breath and looked up. "Rammel. Oh, gods no, Ram! What's wrong with your face?"

"Well," I said, thinkin' that my face was the least of our problems, "I guess I'm no' so pretty anymore."

Something came over her face that was hard to read, but that was quickly followed by tears that ran from her eyes and fell on the pillow, breakin' my heart in their trail.

"Let me see," she said.

I was no' sure if 'twas the best thing, but I did no' have a good enough reason to say no. So I opened the blue cotton gown and let her see the jagged path of the knife, made even uglier by the 'cure' of stitches.

The way she looked at my body made me almost want to cry with her. I retied the gown and looked down, feelin' a little bit ashamed of the ugliness.

"Yes. You are, Ram – so pretty." Her beautiful bottom lip trembled as she battled catches in her breath that sounded like a series of little sobs. "Beautiful inside and out."

That made a whole new lump form in my throat, bigger than the last. I could no' stand her tears.

"Please do no' weep, Elora. Great Paddy, you will make me bawl as well."

I stepped closer so I could stand next to her bed, reached out and brushed tears away with my thumb. I hated seein' her cry and did no' want it to become a habit.

"I'll be right back." I shoved my feet into the hospital-issue slippers they'd left for me because the bare floor was cold and shuffled my way to the door. I looked back once just to make sure that I was no' imaginin' what I was seein'. So far as I knew, there had never been a case of someone bein' infected by the vampire virus and keepin' their wits about them. It seemed everything about Elora Laiken was new territory.

When I approached the nurses' station, they looked up surprised, and started to say something. I held up my hand to stop them, leaned over as far as possible without reinjurin' myself and said quietly, "Get the docs on duty here right now. Be quick about it and quiet as you can be."

One of the nurses jumped up, sendin' her wheeled office chair careenin' into a file cabinet, and hurried off to find the duty docs.

'Twas then I caught sight out of the corner of my eye of someone about to enter Elora's room. I gave myself a burst of speed without regard to consequences or pain, caught the nurse by the arm and jerked her back before she'd got the door open. She cried out, either in surprise or pain. I may have wrenched her hard enough to bruise, but I could no' let anyone in that room before they were prepared for what they'd see.

"No one goes into her room until I've talked to the doctors."

The nurse rubbed her arm with wide eyes and backed away just as the two on-duty doctors arrived.

The first said, "Sir Hawking, why are you out of bed? What is the emergency?"

The second, seein' the look on the nurse's face who'd been manhandled by me, said, "Now look here. You have simply got to stop terrorizing the staff."

I pulled them toward the wall, then lookin' at the nurse, I said, "I need to speak with the doctors privately."

The second doc raised an eyebrow, but nodded at the nurse which was, apparently code for, "You're dismissed."

"You need to keep your voices and your reactions quiet and controlled. Something is wrong with Lady Laiken. I want you to look at her, but I'm callin' Monq in and whatever he says goes." I hesitated to say the problem out loud, probably Irish superstition in my blood. "Her eyes have gone... pale.

"Be sure that you do no' show surprise when you see her. She does no' know anything is wrong and I do no' want her alarmed in any way." I nodded at the nurses' station. "And make sure that every person in this fuckin' place knows that no one else is to enter this room other

than her doctors, Monq, Sir Storm, Sir Caelian, or me. No'
unless I say so."

I called Storm from the nurses' phone. I do no' know
what they'd done with my phone. I did no' tell him what
had happened, only that he needed to show up on the
double and that he needed to bring Kay with him.

Then I called the Operations Office and, thank the
gods for small favors, got Farnsworth.

"I need the biggest bouquet of stargazer lilies, Mexican
red roses, and tree fern that can be reasonably accommo-
dated in a hospital room."

"Stargazers have a powerful aroma that isn't appreci-
ated by everyone. Are you sure?"

"Aye. 'Tis what I need. Cost is no' a consideration, but
time is. I need them delivered to the Lady Laiken's room
in the infirmary as fast as possible."

"Very well, Sir Hawking. And everyone is sorry to
hear about your partner."

"Thank you. Oh, and no baby's breath."

"Do you want a card included?"

My brain drew a blank for a few seconds and then it
came to me like it flashed across a marquee. My intention
to say it plain and true went awry when my voice cracked,
but I held it together long enough to get it out.

"Proud to be your partner," I said.

One of Monq's staff answered his phone. "This is Sir
Hawking. I need him on the phone right now."

When he answered, I said, "Come to the infirmary
right away. Whatever you're workin' on is no' as important as this. Hurry. Please."

The doctors had come from Elora's room lookin' both grim and perplexed. As I put down the phone, I had the curious sense that the room shifted.

I heard one of the docs said, "Elsbeth, get a wheelchair. Fast!"

I felt an arm go 'round my waist to keep me from fallin' and I could hear the man was strugglin' something fierce to hold me up. By the time I was seated in the chair, he was wheezin'. I tried no' to be judgmental about his lack of condition, since he was takin' himself to task to help me out and all. Right is right.

I was waitin' in the conference room across the hall from Elora's room where I could keep an eye on things when Monq rushed in.

"What's the matter?" he said, out of breath.

"Elora was bitten by vampire."

"I know," he said. "But she survived it."

"She did," I agreed. "But she woke this mornin' with pale irises."

"Oh," Monq said. He sat down lookin' from me to the two doctors. "What is your assessment?"

"So far as we can tell, everything is perfectly normal. I mean, given the extent of her injuries. Except for her eyes. She has a slightly elevated temperature, one degree off her baseline physiology. Other than that…"

"I see." Monq looked worried. He turned back to me. "Let me have a look."

"Do no' upset her," I warned.

"She hasn't been told."

"No. And I do no' want her to know. She needs time

to heal."

Monq stood, turned my wheelchair and pushed me toward Elora's room. When he wheeled me in, I said, "Look who I found outside."

"Good afternoon, Ms. Laiken."

"*Lady* Laiken." I corrected him. He waved me off like I was bein' pedantic, which I resented a bit. I mean Black Swan knights make a lot of sacrifices to do what we do. Aye. We have some nice perks, but we deserve every one of them, includin' the respect that goes along with the title.

Even though I knew what to expect, I was almost struck dumb all over again when Elora opened her eyes. I would have sold my soul into bondage for the remainder of eternity to see the beauty of turquoise residin' there instead.

"Hi," she replied with a little smile. "You gonna tell me what happened, Monq?"

"I think that can be arranged. Let me take a look around first." He reached for her face and she slapped his hand away. "My dear, in addition to the other bullet points outlined on my rather phenomenal resume, I am a medical doctor. My interest in you is purely clinical."

She looked at me with a question on her face. I nodded and said, "Aye, lass. Let him have a look 'round. 'Tis just a formality, but we need him to sign off."

Without waitin' for a response, I turned the chair around and headed for the door. Monq was no' the first guy I'd invite to a party, but he was the first guy I'd ask to save my matc from, well, whatever was wrong.

Ten minutes later, Monq stepped out into the hall.

"Every single one of my staff and I will stop what we're doing and put the entirety of our focus to bear on sorting this out.

"I'm sending a nurse in to draw blood and give her some pain medication. After that, well, I'll let you know as soon as there's something to tell. She needs to be kept as quiet as possible. Rest can only do her good, but she's probably not going to settle down until somebody fills in the blanks. I told her you would come back in and answer her questions."

"Aye. Alright. Would you ask the nurses to find my phone?"

"I will," he said as he held the door open for me to wheel myself back in.

I saw Storm and Kay comin' through the infirmary doors. I nodded toward them. "Take care of that, will you?"

Monq looked at my teammates and nodded.

When the door swished closed behind me, Elora said, "Come sit down and tell me what happened. I've waited long enough."

"They're comin' back in to pull some blood from ye. After that we'll have a nice long chat."

Elora's friend, Elsbeth, was the one who came through the door carryin' a tray of apparatus.

"What do you need blood for?" Elora wanted to know.

"Routine tests." Elsbeth was so nonchalant about Elora's eyes. I took that to mean that either she was a *very* good friend who cared about my girl or a passable actress. "You hungry?"

"No."

As she was pullin' blood into her little tubes, she said, "Your doctors say you can have anything you want. Hot chocolate? Brownies? Hot fudge sundae?" she taunted.

"No. Thank you though."

"Okay," Elsbeth smiled. "All done. If you change your mind about food, just use the call button." She patted Elora on the arm.

"Okay."

After Elsbeth pulled the door closed behind her there were no excuses left why Elora should no' hear what had happened. I pulled myself out of the wheelchair and sat on the side of my bed. Elsbeth had helped her roll onto her side so that her body was facin' toward me.

"Let's start with what you remember."

She blinked a few times. "After I was sure that Kay had you and there was nothin' more I could do, Baka and I started after the vamps. We were about ten minutes into the tunnel when I realized he wasn't with me anymore. I turned around. His face was frozen in the strangest expression... I started back to see what was wrong and then he fell to the ground. When he went down, I saw Ghost standing behind him holding a dart that was aimed at me. I thought maybe I could outrun it." She tried to lift a shoulder to shrug, but the movement was tiny. "There wasn't anything else to try. I knew he'd pin me before I could get a stake out of my boot. And the gel in the pistol wouldn't have any effect on him.

"I felt the hit pretty soon after I started sprinting away. I remember regretting going back for Baka because the last thing I thought was that I didn't want you to have to go through losing another partner, especially after the fuss I made about protecting you." She reached up to wipe a single tear away. "Stupid, wasn't it? That's all."

I could no' take hearin' her chastise herself. "None of us ever know how we'll behave in a given situation, but I suspect that any of us could have, would have, made the same choices."

She looked grateful, but said nothin' else. "Whatever I add is second hand because I was no' there. I'm repeatin' what was told me by Kay and Storm."

I covered Baka's plan to bury the nest and destroy the hidey holes in one stroke.

"O' course everybody's priority was you, gettin' you out alive. Baka insisted that there was no' enough time for standard search procedure. He remembered that you had asked for his shirt to train Blackie for trackin' vampire. Storm thought it might be a long shot, but he got Sanction to bring Blackie and a shirt from your hamper. The dog, Elora – your dog – was nothin' less than amazin'. They said they could no' have found you in time without him."

Big tears starting running down her face again. "Come now, darlin'. You know everything turned out right 'cause here you are. Alive to hear the tale. But you should give that dog steaks and kale for a month. Maybe a year." She smiled and nodded, again swipin' at tears.

"Anyway, Blackie led Storm, Kay, Sanction and Baka straight to you." I hesitated before goin' on, no' sure that tellin' her the whole story was the best thing, but unable to withhold at the same time. "Ghost left you shackled and locked away for two hungry vampire. You were bitten."

Elora stared at me for a full minute like she was waitin' for a shoe to drop. Suddenly her face contorted. She drew in a ragged gasp and looked at me with wild eyes. "Vampire…"

She choked and tried to sit up. I stood as fast as my body would allow, stepped to the bed and found the controls to the built in motor so I could raise the back of her bed to a sittin' position.

"They were touching me," she said with a shudderin' breath and a look of vulnerability that simply leveled me, "and…" For a few seconds her face froze into a silent cry of horror. "…biting." She looked down and began frantically shovin' the bed covers away. I realized what she was doin'. She wanted to see the evidence of what had been done to her.

"No!" My first instinct was to grab her wrists and restrain her, but then thought better of it and let go. No' that I would have been able to restrain her, even when at my best. And eventually she would have to see.

All modesty forgotten, she pulled the hospital gown up and away so that she could see her legs and abdomen. If seein' her terror acted out in front of me was no' enough, seein' her beautiful body torn and savaged was more than I could take. I wanted to scream, cry, and tear the infirmary apart. I wanted to hurt my teammates for killin' Nibelung before I had a chance at him myself.

Worst of all was Elora's reaction to seein' the red, swollen bites, gouges, and slashes. She looked at me with a vulnerability I shall never forget, pulled the gown down,

305

and wept.

I wanted so badly to do something to comfort her, but knew nothin' about what humans need at such times. Instinct led me to pull myself onto her bed, no' carin' if I damaged stitches. I took her in my arms and held tight while she sobbed.

AFTER A LONG time she quieted and let herself fall away from my chest and back on the pillow. Lookin' up at me with those eerie white eyes, puffy, and rimmed with red, she said, "I guess I'm the one who's not so pretty anymore."

I wished I could open her heart to mine so she would know that what I saw was the most precious thing in the universe. "You could no' be more beautiful, inside and out."

She sniffled and I knew she had no' *really* heard me.

"There was nothin' I could do, Ram." She took a tissue from me and held it to her nose for a minute. "It got so cold. I was shivering. The cold was worse than the pain."

"'Twas probably loss of blood." I ran my hand over her head as I had done the first night I saw her hair cut short. "But, 'tis over now, you know. Soon you're goin' to be good as new." I hoped to Paddy that was no' a lie.

"For a person who never cried until I came here, it seems like I've been doing it a lot."

"Aye. We're goin' to be changin' that."

Elsbeth came in to check on us 'round noon and tsked at me.

"Sir Hawking. Everyone on the floor is aware of the

agreement you made with Dr. Lao. There was no provision for sharing a bed. That's why your *own* bed was brought in here."

"You made a deal to share a room with me?"

"Aye." I gently moved away from Elora. "When you're right, you're right, nurse."

"Oh, now look at that." I followed her line of vision down to my gown. Sure enough there were bloodstains oozin' from the stitches I had stretched. "You've been a very bad boy."

"Do no' make me laugh, nurse."

"I'm not trying to make you laugh, Sir Hawking. I'm trying to make you behave. Lie back and let me have a look at what you've done."

She told on me to the doctor, who gave instructions on cleanin' the wounds and gave me a right proper lecture. My teammates arrived at the tail end of that and enjoyed hearin' me dressed down.

Kay brought the flowers in with him, set them down on the rollin' table at the end of Elora's bed, and handed her the card.

Without lookin' at the card, she turned to me and said, "Rammel, it's the most beautiful bouquet in the history of flowers." She read the card and then started cryin' all over again.

At that point I was too tired to pick my head up off the pillow. All I could manage was to say, "For Great Paddy's sake, woman, you can no' possibly have any more tears in there to shed. Will someone please have mercy on me and put a bit of chocolate in her pretty mouth?"

That made her laugh, which apparently hurt and made her laugh all the more, but her three teammates collectively breathed a sigh of relief. After all, there was no such thing as a vampire who laughed. And even as I said that to myself, I was rememberin' Baka's joyful laughter in that alley the night Elora had taken her first kill.

Storm and Kay came back at dinner time with food for the four of us. They thought we should eat together, as we usually did. 'Twas thoughtful, but Elora still wasn't hungry. That was worrisome, but I knew she was getting nourishment from the I.V. I never could have imagined a scenario in which I'd be thankful for damn needles.

We chatted quietly about the talk around J.U. Everyone was excited that the record number of disappearances was likely stemmed, if no' over altogether. Eventually Elora's mood turned somber and she got 'round to askin' what had happened to Ghost. They told her he died in the explosion and that, so far as E Team was concerned, he gave his life in the line of duty, a credit to The Order. She caught the glances they exchanged and read between the lines.

"And Baka?" she asked.

"No decision yet," Storm said. "I recommended some sort of new arrangement. Probation maybe."

"You recommended?" Her eyebrows were raised almost to her hairline in disbelief.

Storm shrugged. "I mean, he was singlehandedly responsible for bringing the crisis to an end and, in the process, he probably took out more vampire than anyone in the history of this organization. I guess I sort of vouched for him. I know it's hard to believe."

WHEN THE LATE night nurse came in for a round of chartin' vitals, we made a game of comparin' stats.

The nurse told Elora," Your temperature's half a degree higher than your normal."

I smiled at Elora. "Aye. To be sure she is perpetually hot and that is normal for her."

The nurse chuckled at my innuendo and told Elora, "You're a lucky girl." At the door, she stopped and said, "Okay kids. Lights out. This is not a slumber party. You both need sleep if you want to get well." She flipped the light switch, closed the door and left the room in darkness except for the LED lights from the machine read-outs.

"Ram?"

"Hmmm?"

"Thank you for telling me stories."

"You heard me."

"Yes."

"You're welcome."

"I especially liked it when the elf tied scissors to Rapunzel's hair and sent them up to the tower so she could cut her braid, tie it off and use it to climb down. I also liked it when the miller's daughter got Rumpelstiltskin in a choke hold and gave him the choice of either changing the offer or passing out in forty seconds. Your fairy tales were wonderful."

"Elf tales," was the last thing I said before sleep took mc.

THE NEXT MORNIN' we woke to Grand Central Station in our little hospital room. There were doctors, nurses, some of Monq's assistants and Monq lookin' like he had no' been to bed.

"Good morning, Ms. Laiken." He seemed lively for someone so bloodshot, rumpled and sportin' Einstein hair.

"*Lady* Laiken," I corrected. *Great Paddy. Get it right!*

"Whatever," Monq said, turnin' back to Elora, "You seem to be having a little reaction to the bites you sustained. We've determined that the inoculation you received wasn't up to the task of combating the concentrated levels of virus that were introduced to your body. Even though females have a hormone-based antitoxin that aids immunity, it wasn't enough to avoid infection altogether. We're going to give you a booster, and believe that it will reverse any side effects of the virus still in your system."

"Okay," she said. "Go ahead."

'Twas clear by her demeanor that my girl had no needle phobia. Monq produced a filled syringe and administered the injection himself.

"Are there side effects to look out for?" I asked.

He gave me a pointed look. "This won't take long enough to worry about that. The effect won't be instantaneous, but it's relatively fast acting." He turned his attention back to Elora who was lying quietly, but very alert. "By noon you'll be good as new. I'll be back in four hours to make sure of it."

The room had cleared except for Elsbeth. Elora said, "I need a shower," and started to move the covers away."

Instead of respondin' directly, Elsbeth looked at me. I knew Elora would want to know what that was about, but it could no' be helped. The situation was delicate.

I told Elsbeth, "Give us a minute, please?"

"Sure." She looked toward Elora. "Back in a few."

When she was gone, I said, "You heard what Monq said. By lunch time you'll be your perfect self."

"He said 'good as new'."

I felt a smile comin' on and shut it down. I'd learned my lesson about pullin' stitches and did no' want to look like Frankenstein for the rest of my life. "So he did. Will you trust me in this? Please. Just wait until after lunch to take your shower."

"Why?"

"I need you to trust me on this. As your partner."

She studied me for a few seconds, decidin' whether or no' I was worth her trust, I suppose.

"I feel grungy."

"And will you have whine with that?"

"Oh. And I'm not entitled to a little whine?" In truth, she was entitled to all the complainin' she might want to do. She was unique in the sense of bein' a woman who'd survived a vampire attack with personality intact. "What have you got to entertain me then?"

I looked around. "I could make my six pack dance. I know you like that one." I spoke before rememberin' that my six pack was in pieces, hastily put back together like Humpty Dumpty, and that there probably would be nothin' funny about such a performance.

She snorted, but did no' say, "Ew," even though I

knew she was thinkin' it.

I picked up the room phone and called Kay. They had still no' brought me my own phone.

When he answered, I said, "Could you grab Elora's laptop and stop by with it?" Pause. "Hmmm." Pause. "Yep."

I hung up the phone and said, "How about shoppin'? All that stuff you wanted at Bloomin'dale's that we could no' carry? You can buy it and have it delivered." She smiled brightly. "See? There's nothin' like spendin' money on shite you do no' need to change your outlook."

Kay brought me the computer and a decaf Americana from the Hub. He said the docs would have his hide if he'd brought real caffeine that would keep me from sleepin'. I got myself in the wheelchair and rolled out in the hall after him.

He looked down at me. "You've changed, Ram. You strike me as mated and mature."

"'Tis cruel of you to insult me so when I can no' defend myself."

He laughed, grabbed my shoulder, but froze before shakin' me, like he'd just remembered I was fragile as a china doll.

"Monq told us he thinks he has a fix for her."

"Aye. Stuck her with a horse-sized needle. I'm distractin' her with shoppin' to keep her from seein' what we see when we look at her."

Kay nodded, lookin' plaintive. "Yeah. I think that's best. All and all she seems to be handling this pretty well. I do think she acts like a dumb ass sometimes…"

"Hey!"

"…but I have to hand it to her. Coming to this dimension, which meant losing everybody who meant anything to her and everything she knew? I don't think many of us could have handled it as well. And adapted so quickly."

"Aye. She's special."

"That she is. Well, I'll let you get back in there. I know you'd rather be with her than out here talking to me."

"No worries, Kay. I'll always remember you were my first love."

"Fuck off."

I laughed, then winced and gritted my teeth for forgettin' again. He walked away, snickerin' at my pain. *Damn him.*

Elora was sittin' up with the laptop on her… lap, busily shoppin' her heart out. I crawled back in bed and was content to lie near her, listenin' to the keys click away. Everything was goin' to be okay. I felt it down to my bare feet.

We stayed like that through the mornin'. A couple of times nurses came in to do their busywork. A couple of times Elora turned and asked me questions about this or that. O' course I did no' care what she wore, but tried to seem interested enough to validate a choice or offer an opinion, for what 'twas worth. I was pleased and flattered that she cared what I thought and asked me.

I may have dozed from time to time, feelin' both tired and content. A little after eleven I roused, hearin' her say, "What do you think of the way these colors fall out? You like the gray or the black?"

I turned my head to the left to answer and came face to face with turquoise eyes shimmerin' like a kaleidoscope of golden and yellow flecks. I remembered a day in the Bahamas when I'd been struck by the beauty of sunlight shinin' on the shallows of a turquoise sea. I would have laughed with joy, but the sight had taken my breath away.

"What?" she asked, seemin' suddenly self-conscious about the way I was lookin' at her.

I simply reached for the call button. A female voice said, "Yes?"

"Get Monq up here now." Turnin' back to Elora I said, "Your eyes had temporarily lost their very fetchin' color. But, thank Paddy, you appear for all the world to be well. Take a shower when you wish."

Her lips parted and she blinked slowly. "I looked like a vampire?"

"Aye."

She processed that. "Wow. Everybody did a pretty good job of covering that up."

"'Tis proof of how much they care about you."

Elora insisted on walkin' to the shower without assistance, albeit slowly. The two of us would have probably been hilarious in a race at that point.

Monq arrived while she was groomin'.

"How long does she usually take?" he asked.

"First, I would no' know the answer to that question," I said. "Second, there's nothin' 'usual' about this circumstance."

He nodded and sat swingin' his foot until Elora emerged lookin' dazzlin' with a fresh scrubbed face, a mostly white gown with little printed blue things on it, and towel dried hair. I knew she did no' like wearin' patterned clothing because everything she chose was solid in color.

"Monq," she said.

"I am he." Sometimes I think Monq prides himself in bein' strange. "First, how do you feel? Are you hungry?"

She hesitated for a second, apparently decidin' to negotiate. "Can I get the I.V. out if I eat?"

"Yes," Monq said.

"Okay. Then I'll have pancakes with chocolate chips, two eggs over easy, and a cup of French onion soup. But I won't eat any of it until the I.V. is out of my life." With that, she sat down on the bed and pulled a blanket over her lap.

Monq nodded and disappeared from the room without another word. Two minutes later he returned, sayin', "Your order has been placed and I've instructed removal of the I.V."

"Thank you," Elora said.

"And I have more good news."

Monq waited for a response until Elora finally said, "Yes. Go on."

"As you may or may not know, The Order has been actively seeking a cure for the vampire virus since we had enough scientific understanding to know that it *is* a virus. It seems this incident made you an accidental catalyst. We believe your blood will serve as the basis for an antidote."

Elora stared at Monq, appearin' to process that revelation. When she spoke, what she had to say could no' have surprised me more. "You can cure Baka?"

"Definite possibility and we need a test subject."

"Let me ask him. I want to do it in person. Can you arrange for him to come here?"

"Given Sir Storm's surprisingly stellar recommendation, I don't think there will be a problem with that."

"Thank you. Will somebody bring me my phone?"

I was flummoxed with the implication of that request. "Please tell me you do no' have his bloody phone number!"

Elora looked sheepish. "He's so lonely, Ram. He's got no one."

I tried to come up out of the chair in a hurry, but the brakes were no' locked on the wheelchair and I ended up sittin' back down hard, which hurt like a demon beatin', but no' as bad as landin' on my arse would have been. I tried for as much indignation as I could manage while wearin' a little cotton gown and sittin' in a wheelchair.

"Great Paddy Shits in the Mornin', Elora! He's a vampire! No' a stray dog!"

"See? I knew that's how you would react, which is exactly why I didn't tell you." My mouth fell open at the blatant lack of repentance for her totally unacceptable behavior. Then she drove the nail into my heart by sayin', "Do not even think about hyperventilating."

I gave her a look that should have shamed her to the core, but instead of beggin' my forgiveness, she laughed!

"Ow," she said. And I know you will believe me when I say I took no pleasure in the consequence she paid for laughin' in my face.

"The death of me, Elora," I said, shakin' my head.

One of the duty nurses swept in, handed Elora her phone, and turned to rush away.

"Hey!" I protested. "Where's *my* phone? I asked first!"

Elora gave me a smug look followed by a wicked smile. "They like me better."

I sighed. Who could argue with that? I liked her better, too. But I wanted my phone.

Two hours later all four members of B Team were assembled in our hospital room awaitin' Baka's arrival. He knocked, then opened the door a few inches. Storm waved him in. He nodded at Storm, Kay, then me, but did no' move closer toward Elora.

"Hi," she said. The back of her bed was raised so that she was sittin' up.

"How are you feeling?" he asked, soundin' for all the world like he was actually concerned.

"Better. I want to thank you for your part in this. And I have a question."

"Ask," was all he said, no' takin' his attention away from Elora.

"What do you want more than anything?"

He was clearly surprised by the question. And why would he no' be? I'm certain that was the last thing he was expectin'.

He looked around the room for some clue as to where the line of questionin' might be headed, but since none of us knew, we wore blank expressions. Satisfied that he'd get nothin' by studyin' us, he turned back to Elora.

"That's a strange question. Certainly one I never expected to be asked. What is it you're after? Just speak it plain."

"It is a strange question. I know that, but humor me please. Just pretend for a minute that I have a magic wand and could make anything possible. Would you want to be CEO of a Fortune 500 company? A Broadway star? Professional athlete? Hugh Hefner?"

He smiled sadly and shook his head. He did no' take a lot of time to formulate an answer.

"Very well," he said like he was tired and givin' up. "You want soul baring. Sure. What difference does it make?" He glanced over my teammates and me once again, like the exercise was embarrasin' but he would do what she asked for the simple reason that she asked it.

"Nothing like any of those things. What I would want is just to have back what was taken from me: a wife, children, a trade I can be proud to work every day with a sense of purpose and accomplishment, a bowl of stew at night, a warm bed with a soft and willing woman who believes she loves me, a chance at old age, and people to mourn me when I'm gone."

Elora nodded and smiled. "Baka. You don't disappoint me. I think you deserve to have that wish come true. Monq thinks something good may have come from this." She gestured toward her body. "He thinks he has a cure for the virus and needs a test subject. We suggested you."

Baka stared for a full minute without shiftin' his stance or changin' his expression. A couple of times he opened his mouth, but then closed it as if he'd either lost the thought or was searchin' for a more perfect response.

What he finally settled on was, "Thank you." His voice

broke. Kay and Storm both looked away, apparently moved by the vampire's desire to be nothin' more than a simple man with a simple life. Once again. And I wondered if they had bonded in that unique way that occurs when people have experienced a battle or a crisis together.

Elora looked between Storm and Kay. "Will you show him the way to Monq's lab?" To Baka, she said, "I hope you get what you want, Istvan."

He smiled, said, "My Lady," and gave her an old world sort of combination between a nod and a bow.

WHEN THEY'D GONE, I said, "How did that feel, Gepetto?" She looked at me like she did no' get the reference. "You turned the vampire into a real boy, did you no'?"

"Why, Ram, have you become an aficionado of fairy tales?"

I dropped my chin in mock exasperation. "Elf tales."

CHAPTER 26

Ram

TWO WEEKS LATER Elora and I had both had the external stitches removed. We were given clearance to leave for the holidays. We'd had a lot of time off that year, between Lan's death and sheet time, but it was our year for Yule and our names stayed on the roster.

We had ten days between December 20th and New Years.

I was waitin' in the hallway outside Elora's apartment, knowin' her habits and that she'd be back from walkin' Blackie at any minute. I could no' wait to show her the New Forest and spend time with her at the huntin' cabin.

She smiled brightly when she got close. "Hey."

"Hey, yourself."

"What's up?"

"Can I come in?"

"Sure. You want some cocoa?" she asked as she was punchin' her code into the pad.

I followed her inside. "No. I'm here to ask you a question."

"Oh?"

"Just found out we've got leave to go home for Yule."

"I know. I heard." She took Blackie's leash off, gave him a pet, and stood up to look at me. "I'm going to California with Storm. What are you doing?"

I took a step toward her, wantin' to take her by the shoulders and make her understand that we were mates. She looked alarmed at the change in my expression, but I needed her to be payin' attention. 'Twas no' goin' to be a casual conversation after all.

"No. Elora, you can no' do this." In hindsight I admit that statement was no' as well thought out as it could have been. Tellin' someone like Elora that she can no' do a thing is throwin' down the gauntlet.

"Of course I can."

"You love him?"

"Ram, where is this coming from?"

"Just answer. Do you love him?"

"Like a brother."

"'Tis no' enough, Elora."

"Well, it will have to be."

I could tell she was both determined and re-signed. 'Twas playin' out just as Kay had predicted in Romania. I was in a panic knowin' I had to find a way to interrupt the course in progress. I could no' think of anything to do except tell her the truth. She had to understand.

"No. You do no' understand. You're mine. My mate." I took her by the shoulders and willed her to look in my cyes. I nccded her to see my sincerity and know the truth of what I was sayin'. "The only one I will ever have."

"Ram." She pulled away, laughin'. "Don't be ridiculous. I made up my mind a long time ago that I'm not going to end up like one of your toss-aways."

"My what?"

"I know all about your man whore reputation. Elsbeth told me."

So that was the root cause of her resistance. So many things fell into place. If this did no' go well, I would burn Elsbeth alive in the middle of the Courtpark and sell tickets.

"Els…!" I was confounded. "Elora. You've got this wrong. I have no' so much as looked at another female since layin' eyes on you. Other women – 'twas practically the same as masturbation. I was just markin' time while waitin' for you."

For a moment her resolve faltered. I could see it, but she recovered and laughed again, like it was nothin' more than elf mischief. "Rammel." She shook her head.

I was feelin' desperate and probably lookin' wild-eyed. Then I remembered the book. I turned and started rummagin' through the piles of stuff on her dinin' desk.

"Ram, what are you doing?"

I found it and held it up. *Everything You Ever Wanted to Know About Elves But Were Afraid To Ask.*

"Lookin' for this. Did you read it?"

"Sort of."

"Sort of?" I started through the pages.

"Ram. What is it that you…?"

"Just a minute," I said. I found the passage, grabbed one of her yellow markers, colored over the lines and handed her the open book. "Read this!" She hesitated, looking serious. Finally. Then reached out and took it. "Out loud."

She looked at me like she did no' appreciate me givin' her orders, but let it go and started to read. "As a species, elves have a strong sex drive. Male elves, in particular, are highly promiscuous until they recognize their mates. Afterward they are singularly devoted and strictly monogamous."

Every trace of amusement had faded from her face and I was sure she was comin' to an understandin' of the fact that I was no' lookin' for a fuck buddy. "And you believe that I'm your mate?"

"'Tis no' a matter of belief. 'Tis an instinct unerrin'. One that can no' be either changed or denied. That day in New York when you asked me what I want more than anything, the reason I could no' say was no' because I did no' know. Of course I know. 'Tis you, Elora. *Only* you. And it always will be. Only you."

She turned away from me, shakin' her head, and quietly said, "I hope that's not so, Ram."

Gods in heaven and hel, I thought, *this could no' be happenin'.*

I moved closer. "Elora. Please. Do no' do this thing. If I recognize you as my mate, there must be a part of you that knows we fit together. We're right for each other because we were made to be together. You must know it. Come home with me. Marry me."

She shook her head and pulled back. "You know what you mean to me, Ram. I'd do anything for you. Anything but this. Storm saved my life." I opened my mouth to respond, but she added. "Twice," and I felt myself flinch at that.

"That's a reason to be grateful. 'Tis no' a reason to give yourself to someone you do no' love." I took hold of her again and searched her eyes hopin' to find recognition that we were a pair. "I know you're tryin' to do the right thing. 'Tis part of who you are and I love you for it. O' course I get that. But, if you choose Storm, you'll be sentencin' all three of us to a life of unhappiness."

She shook her head, lookin' miserable, but resolute.

"Elora, you can no' say no to me. This can no' be right."

I pulled her close enough to put my forehead against hers and said, "Kiss me." There was no question in my mind that she had to come to me. I knew it like an age old ritual playin' out by intuition. It had to be her choice, though I was dyin' inside at the hands of a very profound fear that she would cling to her decision.

She did no' pull away, but did no' move to close the short distance between us.

"Kiss me," I repeated, hearin' that my voice had gone gruff, the words ragged with my anguish and desperation.

"I can't, Ram. Please. Stop. My mind is made up."

It was over. As much as I did no' want to give it up, as much as I knew walkin' away would be a death sentence, I'd given it my best shot and there was nothin' left to say. I took a step back, looked her over and saw that she would hold firm. She would no' be moved. I felt a kind of numbness wash over me, inside and out. 'Tis difficult to explain. 'Twas like one minute I was seein' the world clear and true, and the next I was strugglin' to make out colors. Like tryin' to look through a distorted screen or filter.

I think I heard Blackie whine and bump my leg with his nose. My eyes were open, but nothin' was in focus. It took a lot of will to make my body move toward the door. I left without another word. I'd used all the words I could think of to make her understand and words had failed me. I closed the door.

I can no' say how long I stood in the hallway outside. I know that I was no' motivated to move at first.

I went through the motions of packin' my things, knowin' in my heart of hearts that I would no' be back and also knowin' that I would no' be needin' what I left behind.

When Farnsworth called to say my plane was landin', I shrugged on my pea coat, slung my duffle over my shoulder and took one last look 'round. The last thing I picked up was a package wrapped by Bloomin'dales.

I knocked on her door. When she answered, I drunk her in, knowin' 'twould be the last time I saw her.

"I'm goin'," was what I said, while my mind was re-peatin', "Please do no' let me. Please stop me and tell me there's been a mistake."

All she said was, "Now?"

I handed over the cheerful-lookin' package. "Happy Yule," I said. "If you change your mind, or if you need me, this is how to find me." I pulled a note from my pocket and put it in her hand. I'd written out the directions to New Forest, no' believin' she would ever look at them.

Still, I had to do it.

With brows drawn together, she took the note in her hand, hesitated for half a second lookin' like she might be blinkin' back tears. She threw her arms around me and I knew it was goodbye.

I shut my eyes tight, wantin' to memorize the feel of her, the smell of her. I hugged her back and indulged in turnin' my head into her hair for one last breath of wild jasmine.

She put her lips next to my ear and whispered, "Don't be mad."

"I'm no' mad, Elora," I said into her hair. "Can no' be mad at you. You're my darlin' girl."

I pulled away fast, hidin' my face from view. Prolongin' the inevitable was only goin' to make things more painful. Although I was no' altogether certain that was possible. I did no' look back. I do no' know if she watched me leave or no'. What difference would it make? Things would be the same either way.

I made my way to the landin' strip and boarded the jet for Edinburgh, never before in my life feelin' so low or so alone. Jefferson Unit receded from view seconds after take off.

"Well, that's that," I thought to myself.

CHAPTER 27

Storm

I WAS FEELING pretty good about things. Elora was well on her way to a full recovery. Same with Rammel.

For a while there, I thought she wasn't going to choose me. But she did. I pulled our bags off the jeep onto the tarmac and couldn't help a grin. I turned to her and said, "We're going to have a wonderful life".

I figured it was time to call an end to the farce Sol was calling an office romance policy. The woman was going to be my wife. She knew it. I knew it. And I'd never even kissed her. It was high time to put a stop to the hands-off nonsense.

She returned my smile and tilted her face up when I leaned in for a kiss. To say that didn't go the way I'd planned in my imagination? Well, that would be the understatement of the century.

Elora jerked back like she'd just been tasered by my mouth, leaving me wondering, what the devil? She was looking around like she was seeing things I couldn't see. It was alarming and, well, weird.

"What's wrong? Please tell me my kissing isn't that

bad."

When she looked up at me, her eyes were full of tears that hadn't yet spilled over. I felt my shoulders slump because I knew what was coming next.

"I'm so sorry, Storm. I don't expect you to forgive me so I won't ask."

Feeling suddenly self-conscious about my hands, I put them in my pockets. "Ram," was all I could think to say.

"I owe you my life – two times over. And I do love you. But not this way. If it was just the two of us…" she trailed off and paused to wipe tears away with the back of her hand. "I wanted it to be you. Please believe that."

I looked over at the plane taxiing and gave a slight nod, already feeling miles away. In just a few more minutes we would have been on that plane together.

I cleared my throat. "I do believe you, Elora. It'd be dishonest if I said I was completely surprised. I guess you'd have to be blind not to see that the two of you are in love."

My hand went to my breast pocket where I'd stowed the photo of the vineyard. I was going to tell her about it on the plane ride, maybe drive her over there while we were home in the valley for the holiday. That wasn't going to happen. "Sometimes hope and denial go hand in hand." I said it looking out at the plane, but I forced myself to turn and face her.

"I'd like to hate him. But I can't. I loved him first. I'd like to blame him for wanting you, but I can't really do that either, can I?" I reached out and ran my fingers down her wet cheek. "You sure this is what you want? I've known Ram a long time. He's a mixed bag."

"It's not a choice, Storm. I thought it was, but it's not." She put her arms around my waist and squeezed tight. "I won't forget how much I owe you. I swear it."

I pulled away and ducked down so we were eye to eye. "You don't owe me a thing, Princess. I did what I did and I wouldn't change it."

If Sol had taught me anything, it was that a person's reaction to trying times is what defines them. I wanted to be worthy of my vocation. So I decided to take the high road. I pulled her to me and pressed a lingering kiss to her forehead, gave my best impression of a smile, picked up my bag, and started walking toward the plane. One foot in front of the other.

I wanted to turn around, but forced myself to keep facing forward.

I won't lie. It wasn't a pleasant event, but those of you who know my story also know that it was the best thing. Not just for Ram and Elora. For me, too. All these years later, I have no regrets.

I wouldn't change a thing.

CHAPTER 28

Liam O'Torvall

IT HAD BEEN snowin' for about an hour. Moira and I had just sat down to enjoy a supper of shepherd's pie, when we heard a knock at the door. We looked at each other as if to ask if either of us was expectin' anyone, as we did no' often have callers after dark.

"I'll get it," she said.

I nodded. That was fine with me. I was in no hurry to separate myself from my wife's shepherd's pie which was perfection and served at the exact right moment, temperature wise. When I heard her laugh, my spoon full of goodness stopped midway to my mouth. The old woman rarely laughed with the abandon I was hearin'.

I rose to go see what was the matter and felt my heart grow lighter when I saw Rammel Hawking on the threshold given my wife a right and proper huggin'.

"What's this?" I said. "A wayward prince come callin' on a dark Yuletide night?"

"'Tis." The boy looked up and smiled at me, but I could see something was no' right. I had known him since he was waist high and, because I paid attention, I knew him well.

"Come in out of the cold. So happens we're enjoyin' your favorite dish and there's plenty."

"Shepherd's Pie?" he asked.

"Indeed," I said. "Take off your coat. Put your bundle down. And come share supper with two old people glad to see ye."

My wife fetched another bowl from the cupboard and dished the boy a generous portion, as she knew the extent of his appetite.

"You stoppin' off here on your way home for Yule?" I asked.

"No," he said. "I'm stayin' at the cabin this season."

I frowned, knowin' that was no' like him. He held no lost love for his father, the king, but he made a point of bein' home for Yule to please his mum when he could.

"Well," I said. "You can't start that way tonight. You'll stay with us. Sleep in your old bed until the morn."

He nodded absently, lookin' like he was concentratin' on the food before him, even though he was no' eatin'.

"Something wrong with the pie?" asked Moira.

He looked up at her, down at the bowl, and back at her again. "No, Moira. 'Tis wonderful as always. I must be tired is all."

Rammel. Too tired to eat? No' in a haymaker's week. I exchanged a worried look with my wife.

"Your mare is in good stead. The Abernathy boy has been ridin' her every day, keepin' her in good condition for ye."

That got a half smile out of him. "That's nice, Liam.

I'm lookin' forward to seein' her." Just as quickly as the smile had come, 'twas gone again.

"O'Bannon and his sons put a new roof on the cabin in September."

"Oh?" he said. "That's good. Means I'll be sleepin' in a nice dry bed."

"Aye. Sent your father the bill." I laughed, but Ram didn't respond. "Do no' feel like ye must keep us company, lad. Our bond is too long and too old for formalities. Go on off and get yourself a good night's rest then."

Ram looked between the two of us. "Thank you," he said. "For everything you've done for me."

He rose and started away.

"Is there anything at all you'd like to tell us? We're good listeners with great affection for ye. We're also good at keepin' secrets, as you well know."

"No' tonight. But thanks for askin'. Means the world."

With that he disappeared 'round the corner, leavin' me with a fitful night's rest and a heaviness settlin' in the spirit of the house.

The next mornin' gave me even more concern. Ram took the little stock of supplies that Moira put together and tied it to the saddle. As he ran his hand over the mare's neck, he said, "You're right, Liam. She looks wonderful to be sure. The Abernathy boy has done a good job carin' for her in my absence."

He paused and I waited with a strong sense that Rammel had more to say.

"Will ye check on me from time to time? As ye did when I was young?"

"When ye were young?" I laughed. "Rammel Hawking. Ye're young now!"

"When I was younger, I mean."

"Is something in particular worryin' ye?"

He shook his head. "Nothin' in particular. 'Tis just that, I plan to do some bow huntin' and things happen in the woods. I'll leave the horse in the stable at such times and, should difficulty befall me, I want to know that she will be taken care of."

I studied his face, which I would call beleaguered if I had to put a name to it. I decided to tell the truth, plain and simple. "Rammel. You are worryin' me."

"No need," he answered quickly. "'Tis just that, the older I get, the more I understand that things do no' always turn out the way we hope or expect."

"'Tis true," I agreed, wantin' to press him further, but wantin' more to give him the respect that his age and station deserved. "Someone will check in on you every couple of days. We'll bring ye some chicken, cheese, wine, and maybe some applesauce put away for such an occasion."

He tried to smile, but did no' quite succeed. "Liam. You should have been everybody's father," he said. And I blinked, no' knowin' how to respond to such a great compliment as that. He looked down at the bridle reins in his hands and said, "There is a very small chance, no' really worth mentionin'. But just in case, if a human, a most uncommon lass, comes to the gate, bring her to me. Her name is Lady Elora Laiken."

Just like that everything became clear. The boy was

actin' like an elf who'd lost his mate.

Swingin' himself up in the saddle, as only young men in the bloom of strength can do, he nodded at me and trotted off into the woods. The snow had stopped soon after it had started so that there was a good dustin' on the ground, but 'twas no' too deep. I looked at the sky and determined that he would have no trouble arrivin' safely before more weather came in.

TWO DAYS LATER, I was thinkin' about my promise to look in on Ram. I was gettin' old to be traipsin' back and forth into the forest, but certainly he was on my mind. If I was right about him havin' found a mate and lost her, I needed to keep a close eye on him. We'd all heard stories of elves simply pinin' away from grief over bein' separated from mates.

I answered the door. O'Craig was standin' there practically jumpin' up and down.

"What are you doin' there, Colin? Stop that at once."

"There's a lady at the gate, sir. Askin' for ye."

O'Craig looked at me like I was daft when I responded with a big grin. "'Tis good news, Colin."

"'Tis?"

"Aye. The best. Did she say her name was, um, Laiken?"

"Laiken. Aye. I believe so."

"'Tis a fine day," I said to O'Craig as I hurried along toward the gate with as much speed as a man of my age and girth can muster.

"Aye, sir. 'Tis."

"Tarnation, man! Open this gate!"

"Aye, sir."

Standin' there as the hefty gate swung open was as lovely a young lady as anyone ever set eyes on. I knew in an instant that she was right for our boy. An old man has a sense about such things.

I smiled. "Lady Laiken, welcome to Black-On-Tarry. I'm Liam O'Torvall. Please to call me Liam." She'd brought two suitcases, which I hefted up and began carryin' toward the cart I'd planned to take to the cabin. "If we start right away, we shall be there by midday."

"How do you do, um, Liam. Is this not my destination?"

She kept up with me with the effortlessness of youth.

"Oh no. We'll be takin' a cart. I'd been plannin' to go so 'tis already laden. 'Tis some distance to the huntin' cottage."

"A cart?"

"Aye. This way then."

The girl was lookin' 'round as if she'd ne'er seen elves before. Likewise, the townspeople were stoppin' to stare as if they'd never seen a stranger. Well, to be fair, strangers were a very rare occurrence. 'Twas hard to gain access to the Preserve.

"Travel by cart is the only way to get to the huntin' cottage besides walkin' or ridin' and either of those would be tricky with your very fine bags with the little wheels. If you were walkin', you would also need to be wearin' your wellies on a day such as today. If you were ridin' you would need a different sort of cloak, would you no'?"

"I suppose all of that is true."

"If you be peckish, we may find a repast to your likin' before we start away. My wife might possibly be the world's best cook."

She smiled in a most engagin' way and said, "No. I'm not hungry. Just eager."

That made me chuckle and, suddenly, I could hardly wait to get to the cabin. I suspected my passenger carried the cure to all that was ailin' our lad. Yellow Horse was hitched to the cart just outside the stable. I set her bags in the cart and helped her to her seat.

I was about to pull myself up beside her when I had an idea.

"I'll be back in just a minute." I went into the stable and put a halter on the young bay geldin', led him out, and tied the lead to the rear of the cart. She watched with interest, but said nothin' at all.

I tried to keep up my end of the conversation, knowin' that I could accidentally learn a lot by encouragin' her to talk.

After a few minutes she said, "Why, may I ask, are we leading the pretty gelding?"

That told me that she was a horse lover, like Ram, or at least that she knew enough to know he was "pretty". Indeed he was one of the finest horses ever bred in the Preserve, although no' as fast or strong as Ram's mare.

"Oh. I would no' leave ye in the forest with just one horse! This three-year-old belongs to your host. Sleek and strong, but good-natured and *very* gentle. He'll be givin' you no trouble at all." I saw her smirk out of the corner of my eye, which told me that she probably did no' require a good-natured, gentle horse as many humans do. "And a very fine horseman he is, too."

"Ram?"

"The same."

"So there are no cars here?"

"No cars, electronics, or anything powered by something other than human or beast. Rammel's great-grandfather was responsible. He was a visionary who saw the future of the world and caused these lands to be set aside to preserve the old ways. Those of us who live here have chosen to forego the excitement and convenience of electricity for the serenity of peace and the beauty of nature. Life is good and we have him to thank."

She looked around, clearly curious about the environs. "I see. You sound like a philosopher."

"Oh, no. Truly. A simpler man may no' be found on the green earth. The young prince has always preferred the woods to palace life. Wild child he was." I chuckled, rememberin' how near feral he'd been.

"Wild child. Ram once called *himself* that."

"Aye. The young prince may have been only ten the first time he ran away and came here. After three times his father settled a charge on me to watch after the boy when he showed up at the cottage. 'Tis why my wife and I have such a deep and abidin' fondness for the lad."

"But that's not the same hunting cottage we're going to. Is it?"

I was confused. Where had the conversation taken a strange turn? "Aye, the very same."

"So Ram has the prince's permission to use his hunting cottage?"

I realized in an instant that I had divulged information that was no' mine to share. I was afraid that, in my eagerness to learn about the young lady, I'd overstepped my station and made a serious error.

"Em. I hope I have no' spoke out of turn."

"What do you mean?"

There was no turnin' back. The cat was out of the bag and the lass was clearly too intelligent to fool.

"I mean His Highness," I glanced sideways and spoke deliberately, "Rammel Hawking, speaks very highly of you. Calls you a most uncommon lass. And here we are."

We were a few yards away from the cottage, when I pulled the horse to a stop. I started to get down, but the lass grabbed me by the forearm with the strength of a man.

"You're saying that Ram is this young prince."

I thought I'd been clear. "That he is. And the finest ever born should you ask me." It could no' hurt to put in a good word for him.

I came 'round to her side and offered my hand, sayin', "Come down. I will help you." She took my hand but did no' place weight on it, jumpin' to the ground with the grace of a deer. "If he is no' here, I'll build you a nice fire before I go."

I knocked on the door and called out, but there was no answer. So I let myself in. The place was neat and tidy as always. We'd insisted that, at the very least, he no' live like an animal and it seemed the trainin' had stuck. The room was clean as if a woman was in residence.

"Make yourself at home," I told her. "The fire has

died, but I'll have it rekindled in no time."

I stopped by the stable and saw that the mare was in her stall. Judgin' from the water in her trough and the clean condition of the hay, Rammel had seen to her that very day.

Next I carried an armload of firewood inside and got a nice cracklin' blaze goin'. The cottage was well-built with a tall chimney to draw smoke. 'Twould be cozy in no time at all. On the chance that Rammel would be a while, I replenished the stack of firewood by the hearth. I knew he'd no' want me to leave the girl cold and without resources.

I then unloaded the stores Moira had packed, which would last for several days.

"'Twas a pleasure to meet you, Lady Laiken. Rammel would want ye to help yerself to whatever ye can find. I shall be seein' ye again on yer way back to the world from which ye came."

She smiled. "Yes, you will. The pleasure has been mine, Liam. And please call me Elora."

"Very well. Give my regards to your... friend."

"Yes. I shall."

I closed the door behind me, put the geldin' in the stall next to Ram's mare, gave him water, fresh hay and a handful of oats. He whinnied when he saw I was leavin' as if he did no' want to stay in a strange place.

"Do no' worry, lad," I said to him. "Horses dream of havin' the prince for their master."

Turnin' the cart for home, I could no' help whistlin' as I went, believin' that all would be right with the world.

CHAPTER 29

Ram

T HERE HAS BEEN one and only one constant in my life and that has been the cabin in the New Forest. More than any place, that is what I think of as home. 'Tis the place that gives me comfort and solace, my fortress against all the world's evils and disappointments.

It has never failed to restore my soul. Until now.

'Tis no' the fault of the cottage. It has done no' wrong. 'Tis simply that there is no help for me. I have had the misfortune to have a human mate who does no' recognize me as her other half. Fate does no' take the difference in species into account however. My heart grieves as if she'd died.

The first thing I did upon returnin', even before re-movin' my coat, was to put the photo of the two of us in New York on the mantel where I could see it from every corner. You may say I was a glutton for punishment, but havin' a photo of her was better than no'. 'Twas as simple minded as that.

I was no' able to eat for three days. Nor could I sleep. I knew 'twas the beginnin' of the end and I welcomed it, hopin' 'twas sooner rather than later. There's no point in prologin' misery to no end. All that was left for me was to write letters to my mother, my sister, my teammates, Liam and Moira, tellin' each the true feelin's that would never be expressed otherwise or again. I planned to light candles that very evenin' and see to the task as the light faded.

I went out into the forest with my bow. I pulled my hair back behind my ears because there was no reason to disguise who and what I was in my grandfather's own Preserve. I wandered the woods that I had learned and loved as a boy, half seein' what was in front of me, and asked myself if I would change things if I could.

If I had known ahead of time that it would end this way, would I choose never to know Elora Laiken? The answer was a resoundin' no. No matter what the cost, I would choose to see her turquoise eyes sparkle in the sun. I'd want to watch her runnin' and playin' with the big black dog she saved from a life of torture. I'd die a dozen times over just to see her smile at me the way she did when she was tryin' on hats on our day in New York. For those and a hundred other reasons that flashed across my mind, I could no' imagine no' havin' known her. I supposed that was love.

I realized my feet had taken me back to the stream that ran in front of the cottage. Big puffy flakes of snow were beginnin' to fall. The Forest was beautiful and I was grateful that I'd had such a unique opportunity to know it like an old friend. I had no' been payin' attention to where I was goin', but when I looked up I stopped dead still.

Something was wrong. There was a spiral of smoke

curlin' from the chimney. I was certain the fire had been out when I left hours before.

I jumped across the stream and strode toward the door. When I reached the threshold, the door opened on its own. Standin' there was a hallucination come to taunt me. 'Twas so like Elora it made my heart break anew. I wondered what 'twould say and do to torture me more, that cruel illusion.

I set my bow leanin' against the casement, pulled the quiver over my head and set it next to the bow. I would no' give the thing the satisfaction of speakin' first. 'Twas an indication of madness for certain, bein' alone in the Forest talkin' to myself.

Unbelievably, the thing my mind conjured said, "Hi," then gave a little chest high wave, the very replica of Elora's quirky little greetin'. My head turned toward the gloved hand that waved and I realized that the colors 'round me were comin' back to life. I was feelin' my body as I had no' for, I did no' know exactly how long, days I supposed.

I looked up into the doppelganger's face and saw concern. 'Twas then I decided she was no' the creation of madness. 'Twas the one thing, in the flesh, that could make me live. Elora Laiken.

My mind leapt to the next logical conclusion. She'd no' gone home with Storm, but traveled halfway 'round the world to find me. That could mean only one thing. She was mine.

I stepped toward her so that she had no choice but to back into the cabin. I could see that she had on her clothes for travelin' and, perhaps, had been thinkin' about leavin'. That was no' gonna happen.

I could no' take my eyes away from her beautiful face.

"Um, nice place." She sounded nervous and began talkin' faster than usual. "I just dropped by to say Happy Holidays and was on my way out. Liam brought me. Very nice man. Talks a lot. We came in a cart drawn by the biggest horse I ever saw. He built the fire and brought in more wood." She gestured toward the hearth. "I had some of your ale to help warm up after the ride through the woods. I hope you don't mind. It was very good."

While she was talkin', I pulled the knit hat away from her hair, the same one we'd bought together in New York, then ran my hand slowly over her head. I was grateful for the return of color so that I could savor each and every gorgeous unusual strand of hair. The feel of it between my fingers was so marvelous I wanted to close my eyes in ecstasy, but did no' dare take my eyes away from her. Just in case she did turn out to be an illusion, I did no' want it to end.

"Where are you goin' in such a hurry?" I said smilin' with all the joy I felt in my heart and perhaps a bit of a leer as well.

"I, ah, want to be back in the village before dark. Great to see you. Gotta go."

I was choosin' to ignore her, slowly unwindin' the scarf from 'round her neck, bein' sure that I was blockin' her path to the door. I let her go once. 'Twas no' gonna happen again. "There's plenty of time," I said, "and you've come such a very long way." My words were remindin' even myself of the wolf in the story about the red-hooded lass, but I was no' about to be deterred by that comparison. "Why do you no' stay for tea? And tell me the true reason for your visit? After that I will take you to the village if you still want to go."

'Twas a lie. I was never willin'ly lettin' her out of sight again.

I began undoin' the buttons on her coat, indulgin' in a brush with the close proximity of her cleavage beneath. She shivered in response to my touch and, naturally that delighted me no end.

"And did I mention how very glad I am to see you?" I asked.

I pushed her coat back from her shoulders and draped it over a bare limb of the sculptured tree coat rack by my door.

She wore a prim little sweater with a neckline that began just under her clavicle. It was white and appeared to be cashmere. The sweater thrilled me in odd ways. I knew she'd worn white because I'd told her I liked seein' her in it. She wanted to please me. And, gods knew, I wanted to spend the rest of eternity pleasin' her.

I took the little collar of the sweater between my fingers and said, "Soft." Raisin' my eyes to meet hers I could see that she had heard the unmistakable innuendo. Her breath was becomin' shallow.

She shook her head a little and said, "I can't stay for tea unless you make tea, Rammel."

I dropped my hand, but smiled like a man who had won no' just the battle, but the war. There was no hurry.

We would take things at her pace. I began to remove my outerwear, notin' her interest with great satisfaction. I took off the scarf, coat and tartan leavin' me in boots, my sileathers and a long-sleeved tee. She was watchin' me as closely as if I was an unpredictable predator.

I poked the fire, makin' room for another log, and went to the kitchen to start tea. Elora was still standin' exactly where I'd left her by the door. The nervous chatter had turned to uncharacteristic quiet and I wondered if she was afraid of bein' alone with me.

I turned my attention to puttin' her at ease. "Sit down. Please. Tea standin' up is no' nearly as good." She looked at the couch like it was some kind of elaborate trap, but made no move to sit. So I continued. "How long have you been here?"

"I don't know. Couple of hours?" she said absently, still studyin' the couch like it was a trick question.

I pumped water into the tea kettle, brought it to the hearth, and hung it on the hinge. "How was the trip?"

"It was... liberating, the first time I've traveled without people I know. It made me feel... free. Independent. Even though the details were skillfully worked out by Ms. Farnsworth."

I saw that Elora was still tryin' to decide where to sit. "Are ye cold?"

She shook her head no and smiled. I took that as a good sign. I mean a smile is never a bad thing. Right?

I left her to go back to the kitchen and assemble a tea service, realizin' that, for the first time in days, I was hungry. I had my back to her, but was gratified when she initiated conversation.

"So, partner, in all the time we spent together, you never got around to telling me you're a royal? A prince even? Liam was worried about having 'spoke out of turn'."

My head came up in reflex and I stopped for a moment before resumin' the work of assemblin' a tea tray.

I did no' turn 'round, but began answerin' her question while still puttin' together the tray.

"As far as I'm concerned, I'm Sir Hawking, no' Prince Hawking. I've earned my knighthood a dozen times over. I did nothin' to become a prince except have the dubious fortune to be born royal. I never wanted people I work with to think of me as different, probably for the same reason you do no' like it when Storm calls you Princess."

"How did you know I don't like it? I never said."

I looked over my shoulder and had to smile at that. "'Tis my job to pay attention to you, Elora."

"Do Storm and Kay know? About your, uh, family?"

"Aye. We've spent a lot of time together. 'Tis little we do no' know about one another." After a short pause I added, "Probably."

I carried the wood tray in and set it on the tree stump table near the fire. Elora had settled at the far end of the sofa nearest the door. I pulled the leather ottoman over and sat facin' her, close enough that my knees were almost touchin' hers. Close enough to make her heartbeat quicken if she was feelin' what I was feelin'.

"The water will be hot in a minute or so."

She looked at the fire, at the snow out the window, at the spot where our knees almost touched, and got lost in thought as she often did. I could tell by the way her eyes were unfocused. She went away on private, inner journeys where she sorted things out. I hoped that someday she would trust me enough to tell me about them. While she was busy on a flight of fancy, I took the opportunity to move just a little closer and rest my hands on her knees.

I was absently tracin' small circles on the leggin's coverin' her thigh when the tea kettle began to whistle. She jumped and I laughed. The sound seemed to rumble in my chest like I was tryin' to shake off rust.

"Welcome back." I could no' resist teasin' her. To be fair, the kettle was loud. I'd always liked it that way and was used to it. "I've got Irish Breakfast, Earl Grey, Orange Pekoe, Black, and some very fine hot chocolate I brought just in case you might be here one day."

"Yes, indeed," she smiled. "I would like some of your very fine hot chocolate, Sir Hawking. 'Twould be grand in fact."

"Your wish is my pleasure, Lady Laiken," I said, carefully pourin' steamin' water over her chocolate and stirrin' thoroughly before handin' her the cup. "I also have biscuits." I held up a plate of baked goodness.

She looked at them and dropped her chin. "Those are cookies, Ram."

"No' here. Here, they are biscuits."

I began to steep some Irish Breakfast for myself while sayin', "And now you will tell me the details of how fortune has blessed me with the privilege of servin' you chocolate on this fine winter day."

She closed her eyes when she took a sip, then returned

her cup and saucer to the tray.

"I was actually on the tarmac, ready to leave with Storm. The jet had landed and was taxiing." I nodded, wantin' her to continue. "He kissed me. For the first time."

That was no' what I'd wanted to hear. Every muscle in my body went taut at that revelation, but I worked hard to keep my features passive. Scarin' her off was no' on my agenda.

She stopped and ran her eyes over me, noticin' a change in my posture, but continued. "And what happened was strange. I have no explanation and probably never will. It gave me a jolt – like an electrical shock – that felt real and physically painful. In the space of a couple of seconds I saw this parade of images, all memories of you, including the night we, um, found out that aphrodisiacs are not a myth."

She remembered. I held my breath, eager to hear the rest.

After a big sigh, she said, "I couldn't go with Storm. You were right. It wouldn't be fair to him because I don't know how to be happy without you." She looked at me with expectation. I did no' want to disappoint her with my reaction. So I searched her eyes tryin' to glean what she needed from me. "And it wouldn't be fair to you because…"

That was all I needed to hear. In one motion I rose to my feet, pullin' her with me. I took her in my arms and clung to her like the salvation she was. She arched her body into mine just as I leaned forward to crush a kiss onto her tremblin' mouth. If I lived to be a thousand, I assure you nothin' would ever feel so perfect as that moment. 'Twas as if we had been cast in a mold as a pair, then separated, and reunited. I was gloryin' in the feel of her and thinkin' about the next step when, suddenly, she broke the kiss and pulled away.

"There's a reason why I was leaving, Ram, why I was going to be gone before you got back." *Wait. What?* "Because I can't do palace life. No matter how I feel about you, I can never go back to that. It swallows me up. It smothers me. And it's possible you could be king someday."

"Elora," I gently pulled her back to me where she belonged, "you must have faith that we're well matched. I'll no' ask you to do anything you do no' want. Ever. If you never want to set foot in my brother's house, then we will no'. If circumstances put kingship in my path and you ask me to pass on the crown, I'd be glad for it because, truly, 'tis the last thing I want."

Elora tilted her head to the side. "You have that choice?" She studied my face. "Liam told me you used to run away."

"Aye. Understand this. The only person who can *force* me to do anything is you."

"Really?"

I was thinkin' perhaps she sounded a bit too intrigued by the possibilities. But no matter. There was nothin' I would deny her.

She stepped back into close contact with my body as I enveloped her in my arms. Buryin' her face in my neck I heard her drag in a sniff of my smell and I laughed softly, knowin' she was utterly and completely *mine*. Her body moved closer to mine, meltin' against me in the perfect fit of a true mate.

"So you will no' be needin' a ride to the town then."

I knew the answer o' course, but could no' resist the pleasure of feelin' smug. She raised her chin and opened her mouth to reply, but whatever she intended to say was muffled by a consumin' kiss ever so much more potent than memory.

I growled in approval when she responded by tanglin' her tongue with mine, her breath comin' ever faster. My hand found its way beneath her sweater, straight to a nipple standin' at attention just beggin' to be touched.

I scowled when she pulled away sayin', "Just a minute."

I saw the flush on her face, the shine in her eyes, and knew she was ready for me. So 'twas most confusin' when she left the business of love makin' to go fishin' 'round in her backpack.

In less than a minute, she said, "Here they are!" and waved three strips of neon-bright condoms in the air. "Heart Throbs. Guaranteed feminine satisfaction."

My ego was reelin' as I tried to imagine why she thought I would no' take care of her needs. "And you do no' think I can guarantee feminine satisfaction?"

She laughed. "I know you can, but we need protection. I mean, I guess we got lucky last time, but…"

'Twas excitin' that she had come prepared and 'twas further evidence that she had already reached a conclusion of the inevitability of us, before she'd arrived. 'Tis also flatterin' to any male when his lover chooses extra large, even when it is the only possible option.

I was elated by the fact that she'd thought about us in an intimate way and I hated to bring her excitement to a sober end, but 'twas clear she did no' understand we did no' need protection from pregnancy. There would be no pregnancy in our future.

That thought must have been reflected on my face because she looked both serious and deflated. "What is it, Ram?" she asked.

It has been my experience that there's no' really a way to soften hard truths. Like pullin' off a bandaid, 'tis best to simply be out with it. So I said, "Elora, my darlin', elves and humans are rarely matched by the Fates. When it does occur, there is no procreation."

"We won't have children?"

I shook my head no.

She sunk down onto the couch behind her. I realized that I had come to terms with no' havin' elflings, but had no' considered that it might be a hard thing for her as well. I pulled the ottoman in front of her and sat down, once again puttin' my hands on her knees. I found it impossible to no' be touchin' her now that I had carte blanche to do so.

She searched my eyes. "So that's why you said having children wasn't important."

At first I did no' recall havin' said that, but it did come back to me. "Our day in Manhattan. Aye. I said 'tis no' important. And I meant it."

"You're not disappointed?"

"Disappointed! My darlin' girl, I'm the farthest thing from that. I consider myself to be the luckiest elf in the world." I hoped she heard it for the truth 'twas. I took her hand, kissed her knuckles without takin' my eyes from hers, and said, "Besides, there are little ones who are left alone in the world through no fault of their own. We could be their mum and da. Make them ours."

I saw her eyes mist over just before she reached over to trace the scar that ran down my face. No one would be callin' me 'pretty boy' again anytime soon.

She smiled and said, "Adopt."

"Aye. Adopt."

"There's really nothing about you that isn't wonderful, is there?"

I tried to think of a way to answer that question with humility, but decided that 'twas more important that my mate be pleased with her male. So I smiled and said, "No. There's no'." I pulled her to her feet again, pressed her close, and grew serious. What I wanted most in that moment was to impress upon her that we had a future to look forward to. "We'll be happy, Elora. I swear it."

I believed she'd know I do no' take swearin' lightly. I would let nothin' stand in the way of givin' her what she needed to be happy.

"And there's another benefit to bein' elf and human."

"What is it?"

"I do no' think I could remain erect while wearin' the tart pink or the fiery orange."

"But lime yellow works for you?" She laughed. "Well, I guess that gives us some time to get to know each other, just the two of us."

"All the better to have my way with you, my dear." I deliberately referenced that story about the wolf and nuzzled her neck, feelin' the shivers go down her body. I hoped we were done with conversation for the time bein', but no' quite.

"The night I was drugged you said you wanted the first time to be... not like that."

"Aye. I did say that." I was twirlin' the pearl buttons on her sweater.

"So show me what you had in mind."

"Can no'."

"Why no'?" She teased mimickin' my accent.

"Because, all those nights I was lyin' in my bed alone thinkin' about bein' with you, what I pictured was a slow burn savorin' of every inch of this heavenly body. But these past days, I thought you were lost to me... seemed more like years in hel than days. I do no' think I'm good for anything right now but hard and fast." I pulled her close, walkin' her backwards. "I need you to wrap yourself around me and hold on tight while I pound into you, balls flyin', both of us knowin' beyond question that you *are* mine."

Her lips parted as her eyes moved from my eyes to my mouth and back again. "That," she swallowed, "sounds good, too."

It took little time to divest ourselves of clothing and be as we were meant to be, gloriously naked and fallin' onto my bed together. Feelin' her bare skin, next to mine... Knowin' she was in complete control of her faculties and choosin' me was by far the most erotic thing that had ever happened to me.

I was desperate for every touch, every one of her little gasps and sexy sounds. The more intense was my desire for her, the more she responded.

She did no' beg, but I could see the word 'please' in her eyes. I plunged into her and ravished her with a ferocity that I did no' know I had in me.

The short winter day was givin' way to darkness. I raised myself up to look into her eyes in the dim light. Never saw anything as beautiful as the woman lyin' with me, lookin' like 'twas where she belonged.

I knew the answer, but asked just to hear her put the words in the air to forever float around the world. "Are ye mine then?"

"Completely."

I could no' have fantasized a more perfect answer nor a more perfect mate.

Feelin' the night chill begin to set in, I rose and closed the shutters before settin' about rekindlin' the fire and startin' a second smaller fire in the kitchen. 'Twas my secret hope that she would like the cottage and want to return there with me from time to time, so I wanted to be sure she was comfortable.

As I was makin' adjustments to the way the fire was banked, I had the idea of havin' dinner there on the floor, near the hearth. I'd seen something similar in romantic movies I'd watched as "homework".

I pulled cushions from the sofa to make a soft place to sit and assembled roast chicken, bread, cheese, and ale on a tray. Since I had no' eaten anything Moira had sent for me, there was plenty.

"What are we doing?" she said.

"Havin' dinner by the fire. Come."

She pulled the fur throw around her as she rose and walked on bare feet to join me, smilin', her hair a glorious mess of color and tousle.

As she sat, I pulled a bit of chicken away and held it toward her lips. She latched on with her teeth, takin' it from my hand, and I found that feedin' her in that way satisfied me to the marrow. It also seemed to interest my cock, no' that most things she did were no' interestin' to the fucker.

When I was sure she'd had her fill of our hand to mouth repast, I began to pull the sable throw away from her body. Her hands jerked up to cover the still-red marks where deep wounds were healed over, but no' faded.

Knowin' that she was self-conscious because of marks received in the line of duty, specifically huntin' down the vampire that had scarred me and left me for dead, my heart clenched in my chest like a vice grip. I could no' stand the thought of her feelin' shame about her body. No' with me.

I made no issue of it then, but filed it away in my heart as a sort of to do list of how I would find ways, at the right time and in the right place, to assure her that she was worshipped exactly as she was, that I would no' change a hair on her head.

I laid the fur over the cushions so that it made a small bed for one person or two people *very* close to one another.

"Now let's see about the savorin'," I smiled as I urged her to lie with me.

I had determined that I would be painstakin' in showin' my mate that she was adored in every way. I took my time learnin' her body and mind, explorin' what touches would ignite her passion, how hard, how soft, how fast, how slow. All the tiny catches of breath, the low murmurs and moans, the pressure she applied when she clutched at me in reponse, I catalogued in my mind so that I might become the perfect mate for her. I learned what every squeal, giggle, gasp, cry, shout, growl, moan, murmur, and purr meant and I reveled in every sound elicited. But none was as good to the ears as her mantra. "Ah, Ram. You feel so good."

Education had never been so good and she made it easy, bein' exceptionally expressive physically and emotionally, and no' shy about lettin' me know the difference between good and ecstasy. I spent extra time where the evidence of her wounds remained. I bathed those places in little kisses, licks, and nuzzles until there could be no doubt in her mind that I loved all of her.

She returned the favor by ministerin' to my own scars in seriously sensual ways and found out that an elf's ears are sensitive to the ministrations of a mate. When she licked her way 'round my ears, she delighted in my shivers, sayin'. "I've been wanting to do that ever since the night I discovered that elves are real in your world."

"Our world," I corrected.

"I guess so," she replied as if she had no' completely

committed to the idea.

When the fire needed tendin', I urged her to climb back in bed and warm herself beneath the covers. I put a green log on the coals with a smatterin' of kindlin' wood and threw myself onto the bed next to Elora.

She was quiet, but that was okay because I had the sense about me that she was content. I lay on top of the covers starin' at the ceilin' and, for some reason, blurted out, "I've no' had a woman in my bed before. Ever. Just wanted you to know."

In light of the fact that I'd never shared the cottage with anyone, 'twas surprisin' that it felt so natural. Comfortable.

"You mean this bed?"

I turned to look at her so that we were mere inches apart. "I mean any bed designated as mine whether permanent or temporary. No' hotel or tent or Romanian fortress."

She leaned up on one elbow so that she was lookin' down on me.

"Was there someone in a Romanian fortress who wanted to crawl in bed with you?"

I ran my hand slowly down her bare arm. "You tell me."

"You'll never know," she said playfully as she reached down and lightly drug her fingers up my thigh until she held my balls in her hand. Literally and figuratively.

She apparently got the reaction she wanted, because she began to massage in earnest in ways that would be sophisticated for a sex worker.

"And just where did you learn that, Little Miss Innocence?"

"On the plane to Edinburgh," she said with a casual toss of her head. "*Vogue Magazine.* "'The Lost Art of the Handjob'." She smiled wickedly. "Like it?"

"Astoundin'." She had my rapt attention right up until my dick spurted like the Epcot Fountain of Nations.

Elora was lookin' at my male bits with a wide-eyed fascination that as much as said she'd never seen an ejaculation before. It occurred to me that she probably had no'. Her reaction was a little comical, but also special. I found I liked bein' her first 'handjob'.

"Let's do it again," she gushed with an excitement that would have been contagious at a later time.

I laughed, pullin' her hand away from my cock, a thing I could never have pictured a few hours earlier.

"I'll be happy to oblige with a repeat performance, but my balls need a little break to manufacture more juice for your viewin' pleasure."

"Well, hurry up then! Consider it a Command Performance."

I thought back to the day when I told Kay in my suite in Drac Unit that I had no choice but to love everything about her. 'Twas true, o' course, but those were just words I'd been taught since childhood. The reality of matin' went far beyond the mundane limits of description. It was perfection. Pure joie de vivre.

I loved that she was so responsive to my touch, so demandin' when excited, so greedy for my cock, and receptive to new experiences. Last, but no' least, she was affectionate to a fault. And I was contented as an elf can be.

I rose durin' the night to put more logs on the fire and poke at it. While I was up, I shoved bites of cheese, chicken, crackers, and apple into my mouth like I'd been a starvin' man. And I suppose that was true because I had no' eaten for a couple of days. When I was full, I climbed back into bed, the same bed that had been cold all my life, but 'twas now toasty warm with Elora's elevated temperature. My eyelids grew instantly heavy listenin' to the sweet, rhythmic lullaby of her breathing. I turned into her, gently spoonin' so as no' to wake her, and fell right away into the sleep of the enchanted.

The next time I roused I knew without openin' my eyes that 'twas light outside. Runnin' my hand across the sheet next to me, eyes still closed, I found the bed was missin' an extra warm body. My first reaction was an unreasonin' fear that I had imagined that the Lady Laiken had found her way across the sea and into my bed in my grandfather's New Forest huntin' cottage.

Hearin' something from behind in the kitchen, I rolled over. What to my wonderin' eyes then appeared was Elora's behind as she bent over peerin' into a lower cabinet. The word JUICY was proudly displayed across her exquisite derriere and I indulged in a silent laugh of delight. The day before had begun in a pit of despair, with plans to write final letters, but it had ended in rapture.

Without gettin' up, I said, "I knew those very fine pants would look amazin' on your gorgeous arse."

She turned her head. "You said 'very fetchin' britches'.

And I said you don't have permission to talk about my gorgeous ass. But thank you for the present. And the compliment. Happy Yule."

I grinned for the pure joy of havin' my beautiful mate sassin' me proper first thing in the mornin'.

"What are you lookin' for?"

She stood and turned around. With the JUICY pants, she was wearin' a white, long sleeve tee with no bra and fuzzy brown slippers with moose heads. I was certain 'twould no' be possible for a person to be cuter.

"Breakfast. I found peanut butter. Which looks and smells really good right now, but it has to be an import. I'm sure they used fuel-powered machinery to make it so it must be contraband." She narrowed her eyes. "Have you been bad?"

"I have been bad, but no' with peanut butter. 'Tis legal. Will there be enough left for me?"

"I can't say. We'll have to wait and see."

At that I got up and strode toward the kitchen allowin' her to look her fill on the grand sight of a healthy, young elf first thing in the mornin'. When she realized that I and my erection were headed straight toward her, she laughed and moved to the other side of the butcher block island, puttin' it squarely between the two of us.

"Oh. No sir," she said. "I'm hungry. Keep that very fine penis away from me unless it's covered in peanut butter."

Well, no' bein' one to dodge a challenge, I was thinkin' that sounded like a fine idea. And, I might add, one I would no' have thought of on my own. Probably.

Seein' the look on my face, I knew she could tell where my mind had headed. She did no' have to wait long for confirmation. I reached for the peanut butter jar, pulled a huge dollop away with two fingers and began dressin' my, *what was it she'd said?*, very fine penis. Felt surprisin'ly good goin' on and my cock was distendin' just thinkin' there was a possibility of havin' peanut butter removed by Elora's tongue. Preferably painstakin'ly slowly.

I watched her lips part in the most attractive way as I covered every centimeter with peanut goodness. When her tongue peeked out to wet her lips, I swear I felt a drop of precum rise to the tip.

Suckin' the excess from my fingers, I held out my arms and said, "Well?"

"Diabolical," she replied, but there was a generous hint of interest underneath the straight face she showed me.

I wiggled my eyebrows. "Love spelled backward is evol."

She moved in front of me and lowered herself like a debutante at a comin' out party, never takin' her eyes away from the peanut butter treat attached to my body. When her tongue emerged from her lips, my cock jumped of its own accord.

I grabbed onto the base with one hand to hold the fucker still for her, but she replaced my hand with hers and set to work givin' me the most amazin' blowin' in the history of sex. By the time she'd cleaned off the gooey mixture, I was aroused past reason.

I took her from behind, bent over the butcher block island and, judgin' from the sounds she made, she liked it every bit as much as I did. I leaned over her so that she could feel my breath on her ear when I said, "This was my fantasy when I gave you these lovely britches."

As I looked over Elora's head at the front door, I had the unwelcome thought that it might no' be locked. Since I'd asked Liam to look in on me, as a ruse to make sure the horse was no' abandoned, I began to fear havin' someone walk in and see my mate in a compromised position. I could no' abide the sort of interruption that would steal the moment, so I reasoned that the best option was to hurry things along. I found her nub with my fingers and massaged so that we might come at the same time.

Without statin' my reasons for doin' so, I hurriedly pulled up the JUICY pants.

Elora smirked at me. "So this was really a Yule present for yourself. That means you owe me a present."

"Anything you want." And I never meant anything more.

After pullin' on pants and a Henley, I poured some hot mulled wine into the kettle and set it on the edge of the hearth. While I was slicin' the loaf of bread Moira sent, I explained how the plumbin' worked.

"If you want, I can fill the tub with water from the hot spring."

The radiant smile on her face told me she thought that was a brilliant idea, so I pumped water until the kitchen was filled with steam.

Makin' sure the door was locked, I climbed into the tub first and, restin' against the curved back, gestured for Elora to lie back against me.

Even though I'd had the best night's sleep of my life, I was gettin' drowsy in the quiet calmin' closeness of Elora, skin to skin.

I roused when she said, "So you were huntin' yesterday?"

"Oh, no. The creatures in the New Forest are under the protection of the king. My brother owns everything here."

"You were carrying a bow."

"For self defense. Some of the creatures in the wood have no' got the memo that this is a more civilized time."

She rearranged the linen square that was coverin' her abdomen from view. "I've decided you're officially an enigma; an elf who shreds metal, worships Metallica, and chooses to retreat to a society that bans electricity."

"An enigma, hmmm? Well, I'm hopin' that will keep you interested for a long, long time."

I felt her muscles tense. "What do you mean? I thought mates are forever."

"Aye, in elfdom 'tis true. But I've observed that humans are no' always so...committed. Seems that, for humans, 'ever after' is hard to come by."

She was silent for a bit before sayin', "My people don't divorce. We choose. Then marry and stay together. I'll never leave you, Ram. No matter what."

At those words, I felt all worry give way. "My darlin' girl, you ease the fear in my heart."

"Please don't let there be uncertainty between us," she said. "You're my charming prince."

The idea of that made me chuckle, knowin' that there

was often such a figure in her beloved stories and that he was an idealized fantasy. I knew that I would like very much to be that for her.

"Agreed," I said, thinkin' 'twould be a good time to press the point about her self-consciousness. "Please do no' let there be shame between us either."

"Shame?"

"Elora…" I stopped to gather my thoughts, knowin' that words can no' be recovered once spoken, "…first, I love that my woman is the first female knight in the history of Black Swan. It honors me more than I can say. I hate that you went into that tunnel without your team, but I love and admire you for it, too. Please do no' hide from me. The sight of your body, as it is this very hour, could no' excite me more. If you bear these marks forever, you will still be the most beautiful female in the world to me. What can I do to convince you 'tis so?"

For some time she gave no response. I did no' push further, but let her digest my opinion, for better or worse. At length she set the cloth away, wrung it out and hung it over the side of the tub.

I pulled her head back onto my shoulder and kissed her temple, bein' greatly honored that she believed and trusted me.

At length she said, "What will we do about Black Swan?"

No' really wantin' to think about anything outside the copper tub in which we sat, I sighed. "How did you leave things with Storm?"

"He said he wasn't surprised, that anyone could see we

were in love, and that he doesn't have regrets about anything."

In a way that was the sort of thing I'd expect from Storm. In another way his admission that he knew we were meant for each other was shockin'. 'Twas cruel of the Fates to throw my mate in his path. After all, who would no' fall in love with her given half a chance?

"When we get back we'll go to Sol and explain that we'll marry." When she said nothin' in reply, I added, with a little anxiety, "You do plan to marry me?"

Her hesitation worried me.

"As proposals go…" She pulled the cloth back into the water and began to bathe with it, runnin' it over her face and arms, dippin', squeezin', repeatin'.

At a loss for patience, finally I said, "Aye? As proposals go…"

"That may not be the worst one *ever*, but I think you can do better."

I relaxed and sat back, knowin' it was merely a matter of findin' the words that would please her. "How's this then? Tell me your dreams so I can make them come true."

She did no' turn around, but I could tell she smiled. "Much better. And, yes, if you promise to make my dreams come true, I will marry you." She chuckled. "What do you think Black Swan's policy will be regardin' married knights?"

Truthfully, I found nothin' amusin' about that prospect. When I came to my cottage, I did no' expect to return to Black Swan. I expected to expire of grief. Since

Elora's arrival, I had no' confronted the notion of her bein' a knight in the field again.

"So…" I began slowly. "You're thinkin' you will return to active duty?"

At that, she did turn around, sloshin' water everywhere, to face me.

"Of course." I watched her gaze flick to the scar on my face and travel down the path the vampire's knife had taken before comin' back to my eyes. A new clarity settled on her expression. "Oh. You thought that, because of the incident, I wouldn't go back to B Team." I remained still without a flinch or shrug or blink. "Are you giving it up? Because of what happened to you?"

I took in a deep breath and really considered the idea of movin' on to something else, while we still could. While I was runnin' scenarios in my head, tryin' to imagine doin' something other than huntin' vampire, she interrupted my thoughts.

"What are you thinking?"

"I'd think 'tis too big a decision to make in haste."

She nodded. "I see that."

"Would you like to get out?"

"Okay. Sure." She looked 'round and started to rise from the tub.

I took hold of her wrist. "No. I meant would you like to get out of the cottage? See some of the New Forest? Maybe go for a ride?"

She grinned. "Would love it."

An hour later we stepped inside the stable. She walked around like the queen while I hauled tack and began dressin' the beasts for an outin'.

"This is nice, Ram. South facing. Tight against the wind. I'll take that one."

When she pointed to my mare, I was almost speechless. "Ah…" I said, like a dullard. "I've already put *my* saddle on her."

"Well, here," she said, smiling brightly. "Let me help you make the switch."

"I, em, I'm no' sure this is the right mount for you. She can be temperamental at times and she's used to me."

"Oh, don't worry. She'll get used to me."

Don't worry?

I frowned, no' wantin' to insult her, but no' wantin to have this outin' end badly either. "I really think you'd be more comfortable on the geldin'. He'll be inclinded to do as ye ask whereas my mare has a mind of her own and spends her time thinkin' up deviltry to give me a challenge."

She laughed. "Now I know you're exaggerating. Look at it this way. If I fall, it won't hurt me."

She had me there. Under my breath, I said, "Paddy bless mischievous mares and stubborn women."

"What was that?" asked Elora.

"Oh, nothin'." I pulled *my* saddle off *my* mare with a huff. The horse pricked her ears forward and looked at me as if wonderin' what was up. I did no' say more, but went about dressin' the horses for a ride.

"Come let me help you up," I said. I bent and cupped my hands for her left foot. "Put your left boot right here in my hand and I'll give you a boost. She's tall, as you see.

Almost fifteen hands."

When Elora was mounted, I handed her the reins. "Nudge her *gently* with your heels to 'go'. Hold the reins in your hands like this, no' too much pressure, no' too much slack. If she moves to go somewhere you are no' directin', pull back, but no' hard enough to hurt her."

Elora nodded as if she was understandin' me, but I was no' too sure and hoped I was makin' the right decision, lettin' her try ridin' on a horse like that.

I swung my body up onto the geldin', turned to Elora, and said, "Ready?"

She said, "Um hum," then laughed out loud and kicked my mare hard in the ribs. She shot out of the stable, in front of the cottage, and jumped the stream in a fluid motion that told me in a flash I'd made a fool's assumption that she was no' already a rider. The geldin' was eyein' me over his shoulder. "What are you lookin' at?"

She led me on a chase for twenty minutes before pullin' up to let the geldin' catch up.

"Very funny," I said.

Her laugh was made exponentially gorgeous by the color in her cheeks and the surroundin' woods. "Like your horse, lover."

"Aye. Me, too. Want to trade?"

She chuckled. "Maybe tomorrow." I shook my head. "So give me a tour of this very magical place."

"Magical," I repeated, lookin' around. "Aye. 'Tis magical," I agreed. We walked the horses through the east part of the woods for another hour.

"This is wonderful, Ram. Can we do it again tomorrow?"

"O' course," I said, overjoyed that she was at home both on a horse and in my woods. "Are ye hungry?"

"Yes. The peanut butter was *very* good…"

I interrupted with a wicked smile. "I concur."

"…but I need more than love to sustain me."

I nodded and turned the horse 'round. "You ride as well as an elf. In case you do no' know it, 'tis a high compliment indeed."

"Thank you, then. I rode all my life at… home. I was competing in equestrian events by the time I was ten."

I realized then that there was still so much about my mate that I did no' know and I looked forward to uncoverin' each story includin' the secrets buried within.

I made a stew of the remainin' chicken, root vegetables, and a glass jar of green beans. Elora could no' wait so I sliced the rest of the bread loaf and handed her a skewer.

"Here," I said. "Take this to the hearth and toast it to your likin' over the fire."

She took both, lookin' pleased and said, "How very cottagey."

"You know you just sounded like a brat."

"Even if I did, you can't say so. You're supposed to adore me."

"I do adore you, faults and all."

"Ugh!" she replied. "You're not supposed to see my faults."

I chuckled. "Sorry."

"Okay, then, what are they?"

"Oh, no."

Stepped in it, idjit.

I shook my head vigorously, gettin' very busy with stew stirrin'. "No' a road I'm goin' down."

"You started it."

"A fact for which I could kick my own arse."

"Tell me."

"No' a chance."

"I will withhold sex."

I barked a laugh at that. "Elora. I believe I could easier make that threat than you."

Her brows drew together as she thought that over, seemin' to come to the same conclusion.

"Okay. Tell me what I want to know and tomorrow I'll let you ride your own horse."

"Very generous of ye."

"I thought so."

When I did no' say more, she finally pressed. "Well?" She took a bite of the toast at the end of her skewer. "This is good. I think it's somehow better when you do it yourself over a fire."

I nodded. "You want jam?"

"No. You're changing the subject."

"Imagine that."

"Just one."

"One what?"

"You're being deliberately exasperating."

"Somehow that seems better than bein' accidentally exasperatin'."

"Gods on fire, Ram. Tell me what I want to know!"

"Just one?"

"Yes."

"And then you'll leave it be?"

She narrowed her eyes and took another bite of toast. "Maybe." She said it so slowly 'twas almost like an elf song, intended to enchant me into doin' her will.

"No maybes. If you promise to leave the subject behind, I will name one fault."

"Okay, I agree. On the condition that the one you name is the thing about me that you like the least."

"Done. The thing I like least about you is that you want to be a vampire hunter. I knew 'twas goin' to be near impossible to go in the field with ye, worried out of my mind that something might happen. But now that it has happened, I'm no' sure how to do it and remain sane."

Elora set the skewer and the remainin' toast down next to where I was workin', put her arms 'round my neck and kissed me into believin' I could die happy at that moment because nothin' could ever be better.

"We have six days left to talk it through."

THE REMAININ' DAYS flew away like sparks in a wind. 'Twas a whirl of elemental and sensual pleasures, accompanied by mulled wine and laughter. She was more beautiful with every day that passed and my hunger for her seemed to grow rather than recede. The more I got of her, the more I wanted and I knew I would never get enough if I lived to be two hundred.

I greeted Liam and his cart in front of the cottage on the day we were to leave and returned to fetch Elora's things. She was standin' in the middle of the room in her travelin' clothes, lookin' like leavin' was the last thing she wanted.

I thought about tellin' her we did no' *have* to go, but we'd hashed it every which way and made our decision. And I knew she'd hold firm to it and no' be moved.

So I came up behind, encircled her in my arms, and said, "We'll be back."

"Promise?"

"Oh, aye." I nuzzled her neck feelin' pleased that she loved the New Forest as she did. "'Tis one of the best parts of happily ever after."

CHAPTER 30

SOL WAS SURPRISED that we were back a day early, but we wanted to get things straightened out before Storm and Kay were due to report.

He steepled his hands as he always did when makin' decisions.

"Suitable for a married couple? Has to be the oddest request I've ever received. I guess you just can't keep a good office romance down, huh?" Elora and I exchanged a quick glance. "Matter of fact," he said, "I'd already agreed to loan B Team to Edinburgh temporarily. Things are pretty quiet around here since so many vampire have met their end. So I'd ask you to stay on for one more assignment before we talk about permanent change."

I knew my mouth was standin' open. "Fairyland! You did *no'* agree to send us there, temporary or otherwise."

"Don't worry, Hawking. Your teammates will watch your back." I could no' believe he was dismissin' my concerns like they were irrelevant. "Lady Laiken, you're unusually quiet. Do you have similar concerns about Scotia?"

She shook her head. "No. I don't care about the assignment as long as he's there." I could no' help but grin at that, even in the face of bein' assigned to the land of fairies. "It's Blackie. I understand that, technically, he belongs to Jefferson Unit, but I think he'd be happier with me."

Sol smiled. "Consider him a wedding present from Jefferson Unit. We'll make sure the usual quarantines are lifted. Be ready to leave in four days."

I had been at Jefferson Unit long enough to know when I'd been dismissed by the Sovereign. I was turnin' to leave when I realized Elora was no' with me. I turned to see she'd run 'round the desk to give Sol a big kiss on the cheek.

Storm and Kay were back in time for dinner in The Mess. 'Twas awkward with Storm and I hoped 'twould be less so in time. I described Sol's reaction to Elora's kiss. "He turned pink as a Tequila Sunrise." I laughed. "She rendered him speechless, which set a record so far as I know."

Kay laughed with me, but Storm did no' find it amusin'. Can no' say I blamed him. When I thought I'd lost her, I did no' take it well either.

Next morn I took Blackie out for a walk and stopped on the way back for a to go hot chocolate for my girl. But instead of greetin' me, grabbin' for the cocoa, I found her barfin' in the toilet, lookin' more green than pink.

I knelt beside her and pulled her hair back from her face, tryin' my best to ignore the smell. "What in Paddy's name, Elora?"

Lookin' more like an impression of Linda Blair than herself, she snarled at me. "I'm sick! Duh!"

Well, 'tis true that was obvious, and ill said, but she

had made a point of tellin' me she'd never been sick. "You said you never get sick."

"I don't!" she shouted and barely turned her head back to the toilet in time before throwin' up again. I was glad it went in the can because she looked like she'd have been okay with spewin' on me instead.

I wet a wash cloth with cold water. I'd seen that in a movie, I think, and gave it to her to put on her face and neck. Seemed to help a little, but no' as much as I would've liked. When twenty minutes had passed, I thought her stomach had to be empty.

"Come on. We're goin' to the infirmary."

"I have to brush my teeth. I won't try to describe what my mouth feels like."

I waited while she brushed her teeth.

"If you do no' feel like walkin', I can get them to come here or take you in a wheelchair."

She looked tired and worn down as she raised her eyes to me. "I can walk. Let's get this over with."

'Twas the same doctor I'd negotiated with to get my bed moved to Elora's room. She told me to wait outside.

I paced 'round the waitin' area, no' doin' much of anything but, well, waitin'. My fear was that it had something to do with the introduction of the vampire virus into her system. I mean, who knew how an alien might react to such a thing? Those worries grew louder in my head with every minute that passed. 'Twas near half an hour before a nurse came to tell me I could go in.

Elora was sittin' on the side of the bed clearly no' happy to see me. In fact, she was glarin' at me. For the life of me, I could no' imagine what I could have done to draw her anger.

"You said humans and elves don't procreate." 'Twas said like an accusation and I must say, of all the things I was prepared to hear, that was no' among them.

"They do no'," I said defensively.

"Yes. They. Do. I'm pregnant!"

Well, obviously 'twas no' impossible for Elora to be pregnant. But 'twas impossible for me to be the father. I will no' go into the images that came into my head. Let it suffice to say that I was no' pleased.

Still, the woman was mine. My mate. I was keepin' her and her baby no matter what.

As if she could hear my thoughts, she said, ""Ram! Of course you are the father. This is bad enough without you thinking otherwise."

"I… Well, makes no difference. You're mine. You always will be. No matter what."

Instead of bein' relieved and grateful for my magnanimity and grace, she went from mad to irate in under two seconds. "Get. Me. Monq."

I swear the woman was capable of bein' scary when mad. Still I was brave enough to venture a question. "Why?"

"Because. Rammel. There is a perfectly logical explanation for this, and when it comes to solving mysteries, Monq is our go-to guy. Right?"

No' wantin' to antagonize her further in her delicate state, I thought it best to play along and humor her. So I took out my phone, which had eventually been found and given back to me, and called Monq.

"We need you in the infirmary to take a look at Elora and we'd appreciate you bein' quick about it."

"Again?" he said.

"Aye. Again."

I put the phone back in my pocket and sat in the chair to wait for Monq. Elora used the time and her imagination to come up with inventive ways to torture me. I could tell by the way she looked at me.

Monq arrived ten minutes later. "Ms. Laiken."

I opened my mouth to correct his use of improper salutation, but Elora spoke first. "Shut the door," she ordered without greetin' or any semblance of her usual pleasantries.

He did.

"I'm pregnant. Ram's the father. He doesn't believe it."

Monq looked at me, then between the two of us, sayin', "Well, first, congratulations. And, second," he turned to me, "you don't believe she's pregnant or you don't believe you're the father?"

"Don't be an arse. And I did no' say that. Exactly."

"He doesn't believe he's the father," she huffed, makin' me sound like a cad.

Monq said, "Why not?"

"Why no' what?"

"Why do you not believe you're the father?"

"Because elves and humans can no' procreate." As an afterthought, in the interest of precision, I added: "With each other. 'Tis a biological fact no' up to interpretation. The chromosomes do no' line up. I did no' just make this up. Everyone knows it."

I was offended by the derisive bark of a laugh he let out in reaction to my pronouncement, and frowned at him. I was no' crazy. I studied biology, courtesy of The Order, as a teenager.

"And what could you be findin' amusin' about this... situation?"

"She's an elf, you idiot! Her DNA is 99.90% the same as yours. The .10% difference is that her ears are not pointed."

I stared for a few seconds, my brain no' seemin' to respond to new information. Elora, on the other hand, was no' slow on the uptake. She turned her malice on Monq, which was alright with me. I was glad to have her turn the ire in a different direction so I could catch a breather.

"And you didn't think this was information you should pass along?" She challenged him to defend his thoughtlessness.

"First, is it my job to keep up on gossip and know that the two of you are an item? No. Second, aren't elves supposed to recognize each other as mates? That didn't happen in your case?"

I felt the frown recede from my face as a grin took its place. Certainly there had been clues. The way she sang. The way she rode. And just like that the revelation washed over me like the miracle 'twas.

"Aye," I said, feelin' a deep seated wonder as magical as any of the 'tales' Elora loved so much. "'Tis exactly what *did* happen. Great Paddy! We're havin' a baby." I rushed at Elora and tried to kiss her, but she swatted me away like I was an annoyance. I was too elated to let that bother me. An image of my mum came to mind and I could see her doin' a jig all over the palace at Derry, possibly creatin' a national holiday. "I need to call my mother."

I like my mother, but 'twas probably the first time I was ever truly excited about the prospect of givin' the old dame a call.

Lookin' back at Elora, thinkin' she would share this moment with me, I did no' see the joy and elation that should have been there. What I saw instead was hurt and betrayal doin' battle with royally pissed. 'Twas when I knew I was in a shit hole of my own diggin'.

"Elora," I started, "I'm sorry I reacted badly. I…"

She stopped me cold with a look that said I'd be better off no' utterin' another word. She slid off the bed, and walked out without turnin' back.

Monq shrugged and said, "You're on your own."

I thought it best to give her a little time to get used to the idea of bein' pregnant and havin' a mate who did no' believe her when she was tellin' Paddy's own truth. I knew I'd be welcome in the bar. So I headed there to seek out my old friend, Irish whiskey.

Several shots later I opened the door to her apartment with a speech I'd composed in collaboration with my friend, Irish whiskey. I never got the chance to deliver a word of it.

"Get out," she said, before slammin' the bedroom door closed.

I took that to mean that she needed more time to come to grips with the fact that she'd been claimed by a numbskull. So I drug myself to my own apartment next door and spent a very restless night there. It held the familiarity of a place where I'd spent time, but seemed to have lost all sign of life. I supposed that was because my entire life was next door alone with hurt feelin's and me unable to console her because I was the culprit who did the hurtin' though I'd sworn that would never happen.

I did no' sleep well. My emotions were all over the place. I wanted to do penance for the crime I'd commited in denyin' the truth of our good fortune. On the other hand, I was thrilled beyond measure with the very shockin' news that I was goin' to be Da to some little pink-haired elfling. After makin' my peace with bein' childless, 'twas a big adjustment thrust on me all at once. No' that I was feeln' sorry for myself. After all, I was no' the one makin' an adjustment to bein' pregnant.

The next mornin' I tried again to enter the apartment next door only to find she'd changed the code. I banged on the door until my hand hurt and then started callin', but she would no' pick up her phone.

I went down to the Courtpark to see if she was out with Blackie.

Blackie was out, but no' with his mistress.

"Where is she?" I said to Glendennon Catch as he threw an orange Frisbee.

"She's not feeling well. Asked me to take him for the day."

"Oh," I said. "'Twas nice of ye."

Walkin' back toward the solarium, I pulled out my phone and called Kay.

"I need you," I said.

"Where are you?"

"Solarium."

"Okay. Ten minutes."

"You want something?"

"Breakfast burrito and a spiced pumpkin latte."

That almost made me sick to my stomach, but I said okay and went to the bistro to place an order.

I was sittin' at a table in the far corner watchin' Glen play with Elora's dog when Kay pulled out the chair across from me. I shoved his mess of food and drink in front of him and told him what had happened.

"She'll listen to you. She always has. Even when nobody else has sway. 'Tis like she thinks you're some wise old sage or some such."

Kay laughed. "Maybe she's the discerning one. After all, who'd you call when your baby mama won't talk to you? Kay. That's who."

I nodded. How could he be in such a good mood when I was so miserable? "Just tell me what to do."

He took a big bite of burrito and chewed thoughtfully occasionally glancin' at what was inside the tortilla wrapped concoction. I watched his mouth work and his occasional fastidious dabs with the napkin I'd thoughtfully included with the stash of disgustin' food and drink. After a time I began to wonder if he'd forgotten why we were here.

"Kay. You with me?"

He raised his eyes. "I'm thinkin' it over."

I let my hands fall. "Aye. Well, we're no' gettin' any

younger and I have a little one growin' in the belly of a mate who will no' speak to me!"

"Yeah. It's a problem."

"You think?"

I let out an annoyed chuff. "Look. Could you just go tell her that I swear I will never again doubt anything she says no matter how unlikely or improbable it might seem to the casual observer. If she says the Earth will reverse the direction in which it rotates on Tuesday, I will ask, 'What should we do to prepare?' I am wholly, truly, desperately sorry for bein' an arse."

"You know Rammel, getting to hear you say that has almost made putting up with you worthwhile."

"Kay." I was losin' patience.

He held up his hand. "Yes. I will go talk to her, but you have to swear to me right here, right now, that if I convince her to talk to you, you will, as you said, not doubt her again."

"I swear. Great Paddy. I swear it on my life and the life of our son. Or daughter." 'Twas the first time it had occurred to me that we might have made a lass and I experienced a momentary panic, wonderin' if I was clever enough to father a female.

"That's a pretty serious oath."

"'Tis. And I mean every word."

"Alright. You may find this hard to believe, but I've been in the doghouse with Katrina a time or two and I know that nothing is right with reality until the crack gets fixed. I'll head up there. Just in case she decides to hear you out, I'd suggest you lay off the whiskey."

"'Tis nine o'clock in the mornin'. What do you take me for?"

"A lunatic elf who could become a drunk elf without much provocation."

What could I say to that? He had a point.

"Coffee only." I took my phone out and put it on the table in front of me.

"If you get a call from me, you better know what you're going to say and it better be good."

I nodded, but the speech that sounded so good last night felt like it had gone sour since mornin'. I had no idea how to mend such a monumental fuck up.

Two hours later I saw a flash of light. I looked down hopin' to see Kay's number, but 'twas Elora.

"Elora…" I began.

"Come up," she said and ended the call.

I shoved people out of the elevator. "This one's taken," I said. I could apologize later. When I got to our floor, I practically ran down the hall. It felt like it'd been weeks since I'd last seen her, months since I'd last touched her.

I knocked on the door and it opened within seconds. Elora grabbed my collar and pulled me in.

"Rammel," she sniffed tearfully. "I'm pregnant."

"I know, love. We did no' plan it, but I'm *so* very glad of it."

"You are?" She wanted confirmation that we were in it together and I wanted nothin' more than to reassure her of exactly that.

"I've never been so happy about anything in my life. Well, except for findin' you at the cottage, ready and willin' to claim me as your mate."

She put her arms around me and squeezed, no' too tight. Just right. I must tell you that nothin' had ever felt so good. Relief flooded me like a sedative.

"You promise you'll never call me a liar again."

"I, uh, did no' exactly call you a liar…"

"Ram!"

"Aye," I said quickly. "I promise. Elf's honor."

"Okay. Get me some jamocha almond fudge ice cream."

I grinned. "Only if you give me the new code to *our* apartment."

"Elftale."

I wanted to run her errand and get her way-too-chocolate concoction, but once I started kissin' her, I could no' stop.

"Can the sweet treat wait?"

She smiled, pullin' me toward the bedroom. "Can you deliver in twenty minutes or less?"

I barked out a laugh. "Aye, if that's the order you're placin'."

"I'd like an option on more," she said, reachin' for my waistband.

"Goes without sayin'." I pulled her hand away from my crotch so she'd know I was serious, and halted our progress toward the bedroom. With my arms 'round her, I said, "We could stop off at Derry on the way to fairyland and let my mum throw us a right proper Irish weddin'."

Elora went still and blinked slowly. When she focused on my eyes, her beauty took my breath away. I suspected it always would.

"That's very practical."

My face fell. "I did no' mean it to sound like a chore."

She smiled. "I'm just kidding. It's a wonderful idea. What are you going to tell your family about me?"

Cripes. How was I goin' to explain marryin' someone appearin' to be human and carryin' my elfling?

As I mulled that over, Elora's hand found her way to the buttons on my jeans again. At the time I assumed that would always make me smile. I have no' been right about everything, but I was right about that.

"We'll figure it out later," I said.

THE ORDER OF THE BLACK SWAN
Winner BEST PARANORMAL ROMANCE SERIES
two years in a row!

Knights of Black Swan 1. My Familiar Stranger

Knights of Black Swan 2, The Witch's Dream

Knights of Black Swan 3, A Summoner's Tale

Knights of Black Swan 4, Moonlight

Knights of Black Swan 5, Gathering Storm

Knights of Black Swan 6, A Tale of Two Kingdoms

Knights of Black Swan 7, Solomon's Sieve

An Order of the Black Swan Novel Prince of Demons

Knights of Black Swan 8, **Journey Man** (March 2016)

THE HYBRIDS

Exiled 1. **CARNAL, The Beast Who Loved Me**
(February 2016)

Exiled 2. CRAVE (2016)

THE WEREWOLVES

New Scotia Pack 1, Shield Wolf: Liulf

New Scotia Pack 2, Wolf Lover: Konochur

CONTEMPORARY ROMANCE

Sons of Sanctuary MC, Book 1. Two Princes

I'm an Indie author, which means
nobody pays me to write.

You can help me stay in business and write more books
by leaving a review.

Thank you again for choosing to read the first installment of Ram's story. I hope you enjoyed it. At some point in the future, I will write the second book of Ram, as told to his granddaughter, Garine'en, the first female knight of Black Swan who is a native of Loti Dimension.

I invite you to keep up with this and other series. By subscribing to my mail list. I'll make you aware of free stuff, news, and announcements and never share your addy. Unsubscribe whenever you like.

Also browse more from my library at the end of this book.

Victoria Danann

SUBSCRIBE TO MY MAIL LIST

Website

Black Swan Fan Page

Facebook Author Page

Twitter

Pinterest

AUTHOR FAN GROUP

New York Times and USA Today Bestselling Romance Author

Winner BEST PARANORMAL ROMANCE SERIES
–Knights of Black Swan
two years in a row!

And when you've read my books, check out my friends.

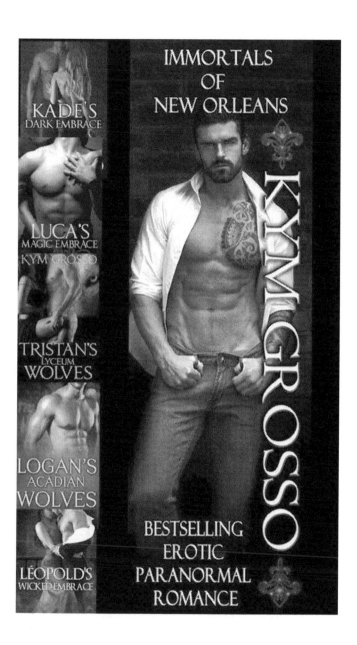

KADE'S
DARK EMBRACE

LUCA'S
MAGIC EMBRACE
KYM GROSSO

TRISTAN'S
LYCEUM
WOLVES

LOGAN'S
ACADIAN
WOLVES

LÉOPOLD'S
WICKED EMBRACE

IMMORTALS
OF
NEW ORLEANS

KYM GROSSO

BESTSELLING
EROTIC
PARANORMAL
ROMANCE

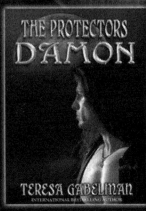

Made in the USA
Middletown, DE
22 May 2016